POKÉMON™
ADVENTURES
RUBY & SAPPHIRE

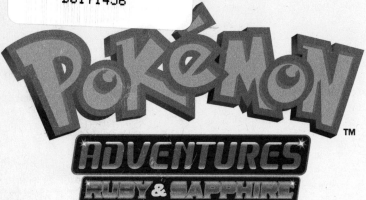

**Pokémon ADVENTURES
Ruby and Sapphire**
Volume 20
Perfect Square Edition

Story by **HIDENORI KUSAKA**
Art by **SATOSHI YAMAMOTO**

© 2014 The Pokémon Company International.
© 1995–2014 Nintendo/Creatures Inc./GAME FREAK inc.
TM, ®, and character names are trademarks of Nintendo.
POCKET MONSTERS SPECIAL Vol. 20
by Hidenori KUSAKA, Satoshi YAMAMOTO
© 1997 Hidenori KUSAKA, Satoshi YAMAMOTO
All rights reserved.
Original Japanese edition published by SHOGAKUKAN.
English translation rights in the United States of America,
Canada, the United Kingdom, Ireland, Australia, New Zealand
and India arranged with SHOGAKUKAN.

English Adaptation/Bryant Turnage
Translation/Tetsuichiro Miyaki
Touch-up & Lettering/Annaliese Christman
Design/Shawn Carrico
Editor/Annette Roman

Printed in the U.S.A.

Published by VIZ Media, LLC
P.O. Box 77010
San Francisco, CA 94107

10 9 8 7 6 5
First printing, January 2014
Fifth printing, May 2017

www.perfectsquare.com   www.viz.com

Pokémon™ Adventures Ruby & Sapphire

20
VOLUME TWENTY

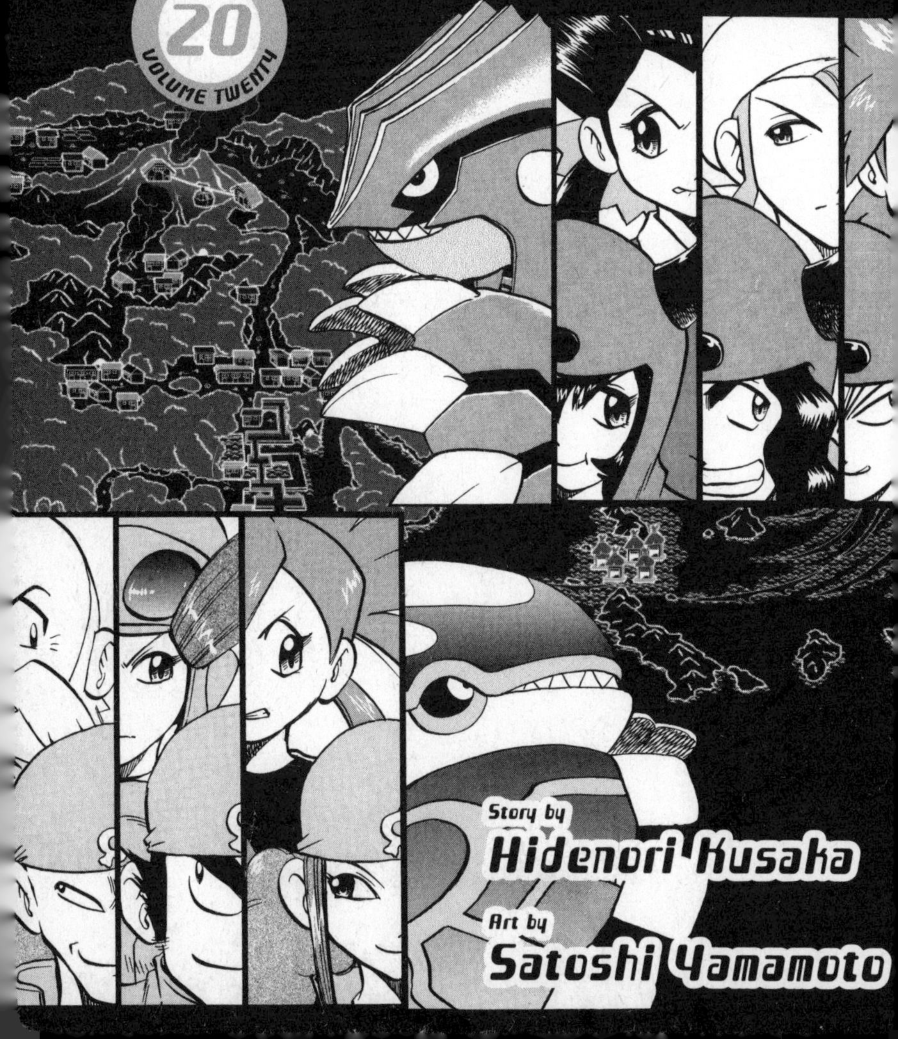

Story by
Hidenori Kusaka

Art by
Satoshi Yamamoto

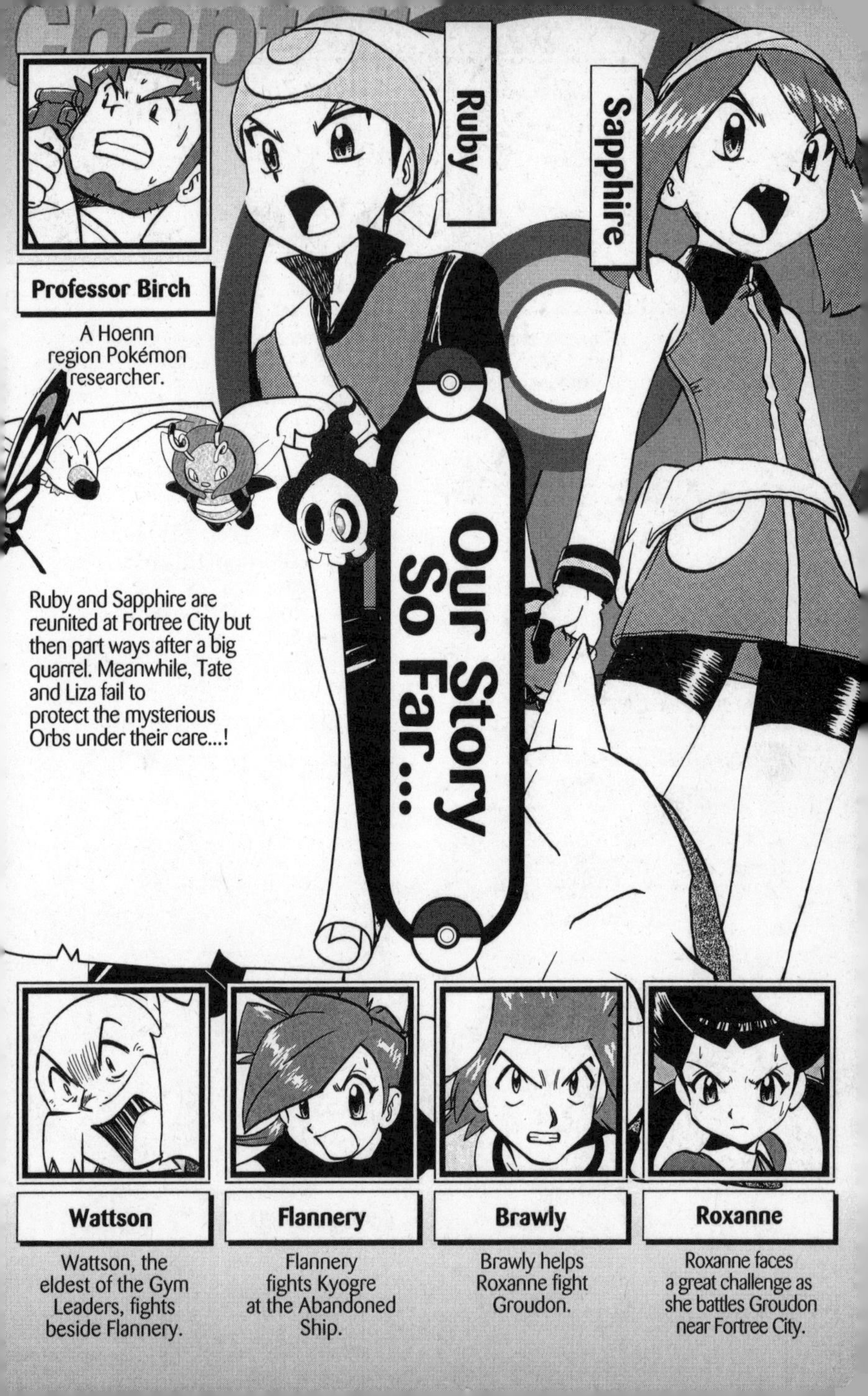

Our Story So Far...
Sapphire
Ruby
Professor Birch
A Hoenn region Pokémon researcher.
Ruby and Sapphire are reunited at Fortree City but then part ways after a big quarrel. Meanwhile, Tate and Liza fail to protect the mysterious Orbs under their care...!
Roxanne
Roxanne faces a great challenge as she battles Groudon near Fortree City.
Brawly
Brawly helps Roxanne fight Groudon.
Flannery
Flannery fights Kyogre at the Abandoned Ship.
Wattson
Wattson, the eldest of the Gym Leaders, fights beside Flannery.

Story of The Four

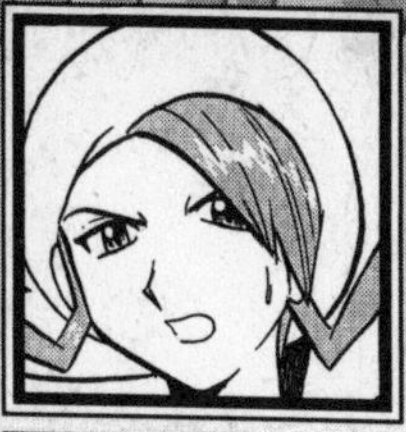

Wallace

The trainer who helped Ruby put things in perspective and clarify his priorities.

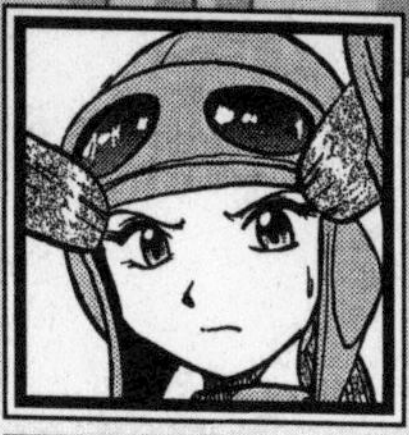

Winona

The leader of the Gym Leaders, who is trying to keep everything under control.

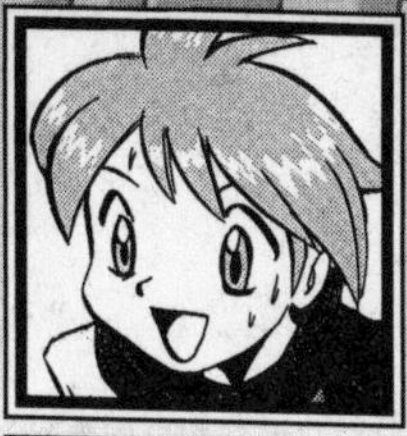

Wally

Ruby's young friend, who is currently receiving medical treatment for some health issues.

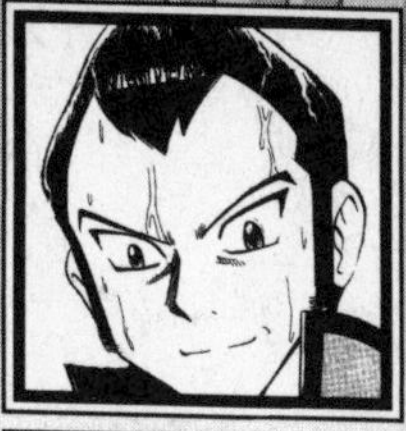

Norman

Ruby's father, the Gym Leader of Petalburg City.

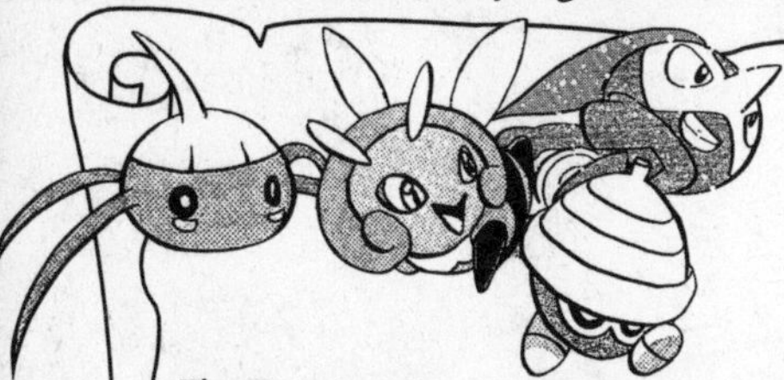

The Gym Leaders band together in an attempt to bring the rampage of the legendary Pokémon to a halt and to protect the citizenry from the resulting natural catastrophes in the Hoenn region. But in order to succeed, they must first defeat the people who are controlling these Legendary Pokémon. Then Ruby and Sapphire patch up their differences and, with the aid of Relicanth, head for the Seafloor Cavern to target the root of the problem...

The Gym Leaders of Mossdeep City Gym are defeated by Team Magma. The legendary Blue Orb and Red Orb, which once saved the world from destruction, have been stolen. Team Magma and Team Aqua, having temporarily joined forces, head to the Seafloor Cavern where they awaken Kyogre and Groudon.

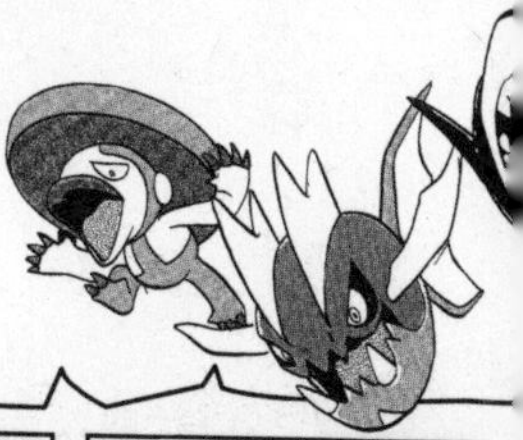

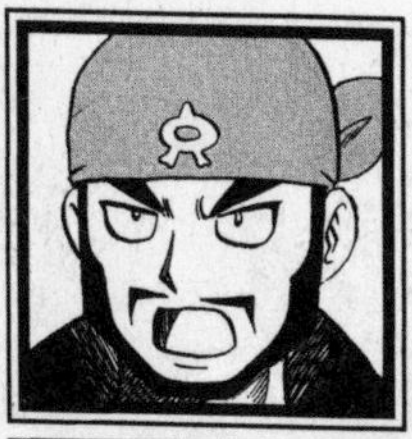

Archie

The leader of Team Aqua, who is convinced that his team has won. Have they?

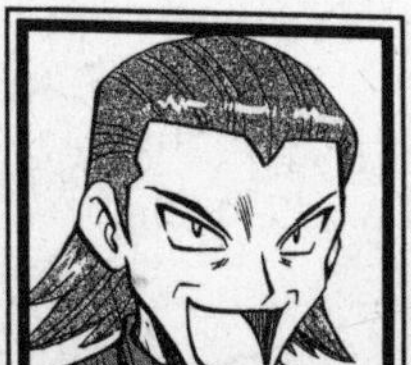

Maxie

The leader of Team Magma, who has obtained both the Red Orb and the Blue Orb.

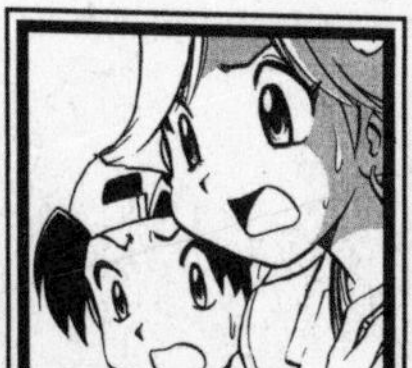

Gabby and Ty

These two journalists are in hot pursuit of the truth behind the news.

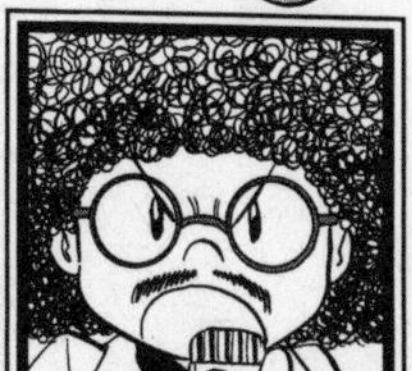

Pokémon Association President

The Executive Leader of the Hoenn Disaster Countermeasure Team

TRAINERS OF THE FOURTH CHAPTER

SAPPHIRE
RUBY

SAPPHIRE ● AGE 10

A wild trainer whose dream is to challenge and defeat every single Gym Leader in the Hoenn region!!

CHIC (BLAZIKEN ♀)

Introverted. Uses fire-type moves.

RONO (LAIRON ♂)

Mischievous. Proud of its toughness. Its favorite move is Take Down.

LORRY (WAILORD ♂)

Bold. Sapphire rides the waves on Lorry's back.

PHADO (DONPHAN ♂)

Befriended by Sapphire at Mauville City. Hasty nature.

TROPPY (TROPIUS ♂)

Sapphire flies through the air on Troppy's back. This calm Pokémon usually stays outside its Poké Ball.

RELLY (RELICANTH ♂)

Has the power to take people with it to the very depths of the ocean. Hardy natured.

RUBY ● AGE 11

A trainer who wants to be the champion of all the Pokémon Contests. Visual beauty is a priority for Ruby. He has zero interest in Pokémon Battling. But does he secretly have a talent for it...?

MUMU (SWAMPERT ♂)

A Pokémon given to Ruby by Professor Birch. Easygoing. Represents Toughness.

NANA (MIGHTYENA ♀)

Intense. Represents Coolness.

KIKI (DELCATTY ♀)

Naive. Represents Cuteness.

FOFO (CASTFORM ♀)

Changes form in response to weather changes. Cautious.

Pokémon™ Adventures
Ruby & Sapphire

20
VOLUME TWENTY

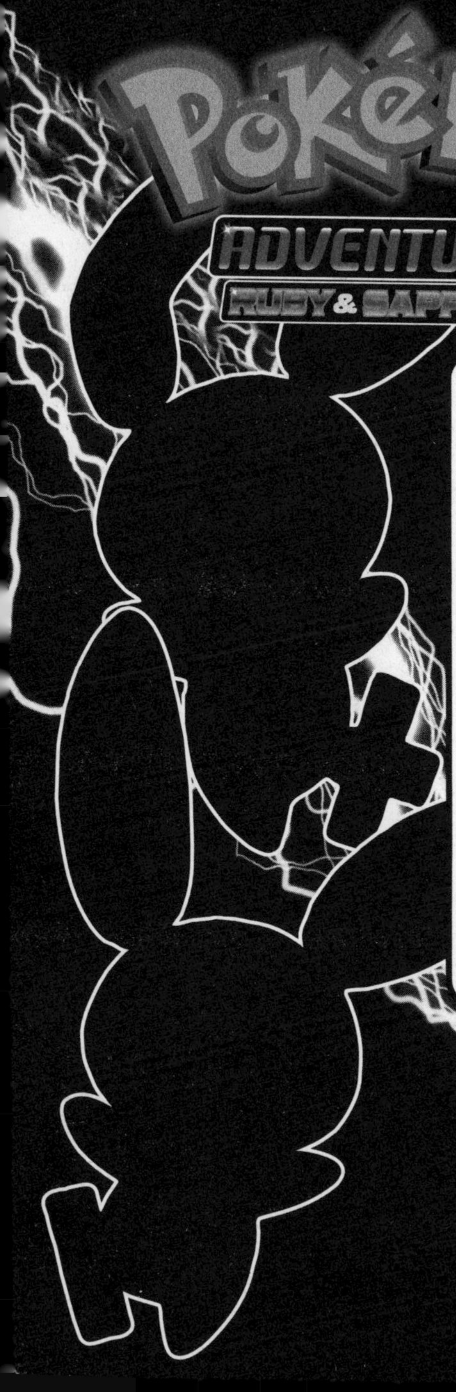

CONTENTS

● Chapter 239 ●

The Beginning of the End with Kyogre & Groudon VII

Pokémon Adventures Ruby & Sapphire

The Fourth Chapter

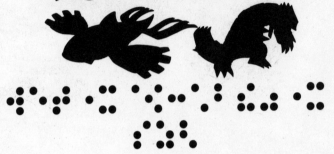

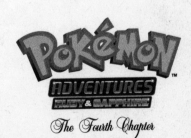

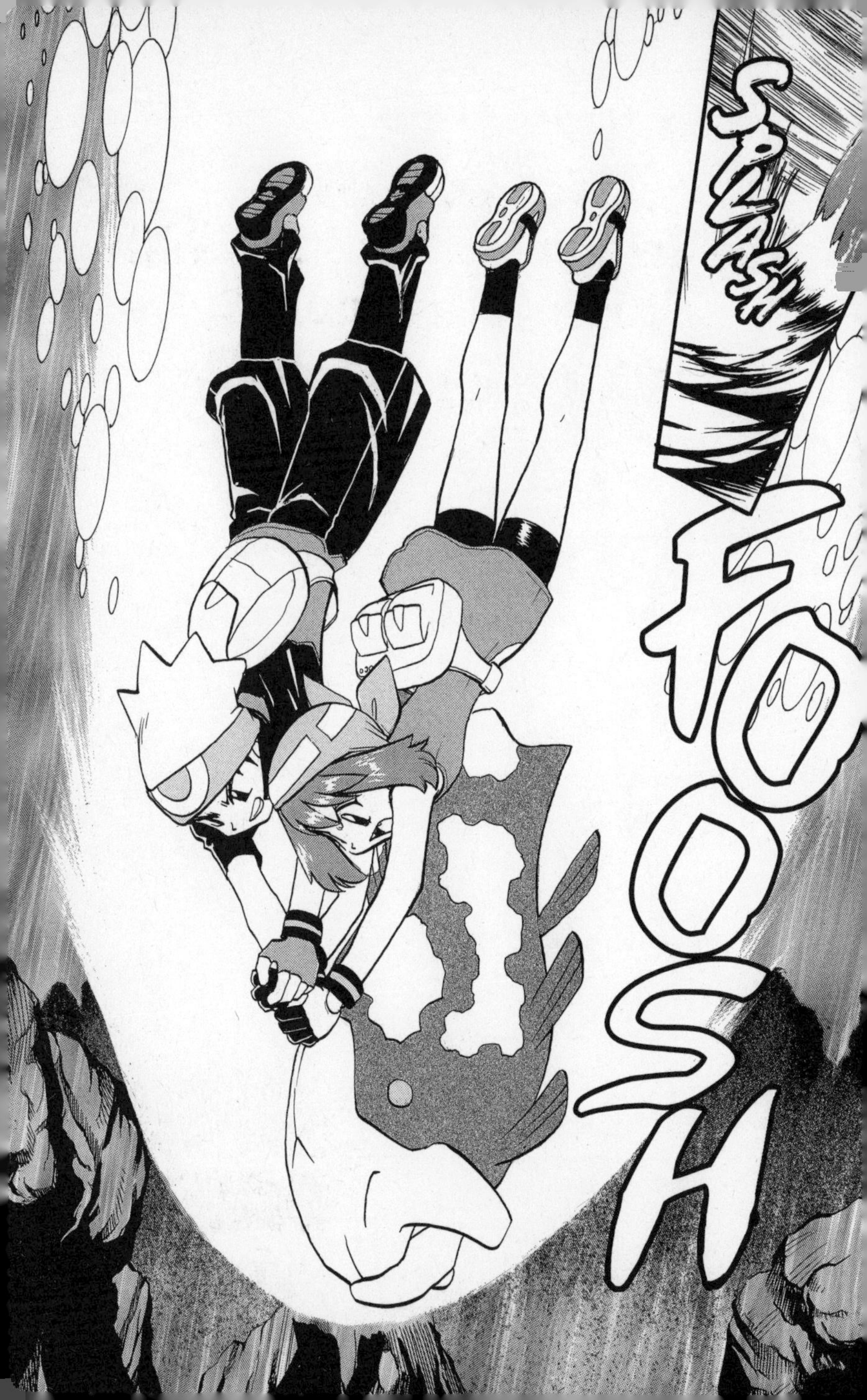
SPLASH
FOOSH

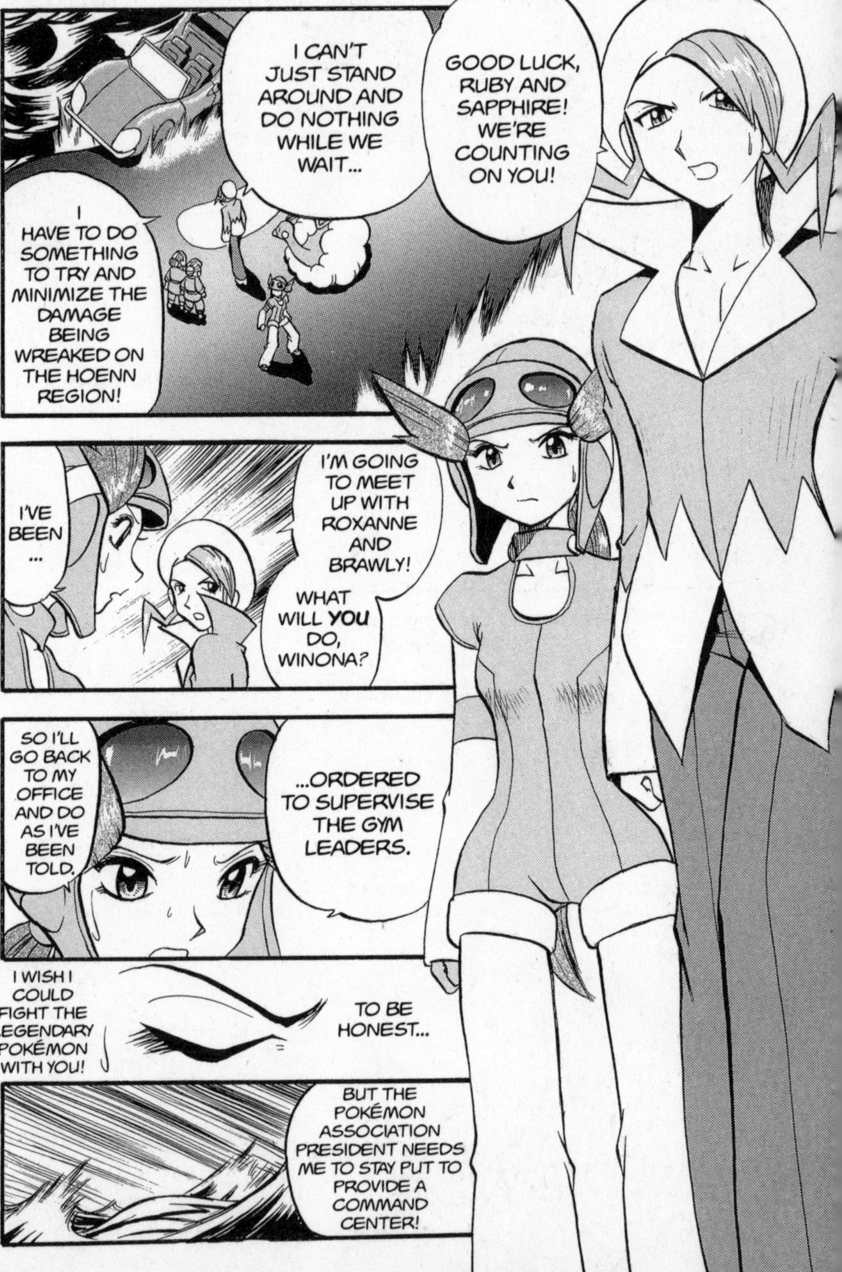
GOOD LUCK, RUBY AND SAPPHIRE! WE'RE COUNTING ON YOU!
I CAN'T JUST STAND AROUND AND DO NOTHING WHILE WE WAIT...
I HAVE TO DO SOMETHING TO TRY AND MINIMIZE THE DAMAGE BEING WREAKED ON THE HOENN REGION!
I'M GOING TO MEET UP WITH ROXANNE AND BRAWLY!
WHAT WILL **YOU** DO, WINONA?
I'VE BEEN ...
...ORDERED TO SUPERVISE THE GYM LEADERS.
SO I'LL GO BACK TO MY OFFICE AND DO AS I'VE BEEN TOLD.
TO BE HONEST...
I WISH I COULD FIGHT THE LEGENDARY POKÉMON WITH YOU!
BUT THE POKÉMON ASSOCIATION PRESIDENT NEEDS ME TO STAY PUT TO PROVIDE A COMMAND CENTER!

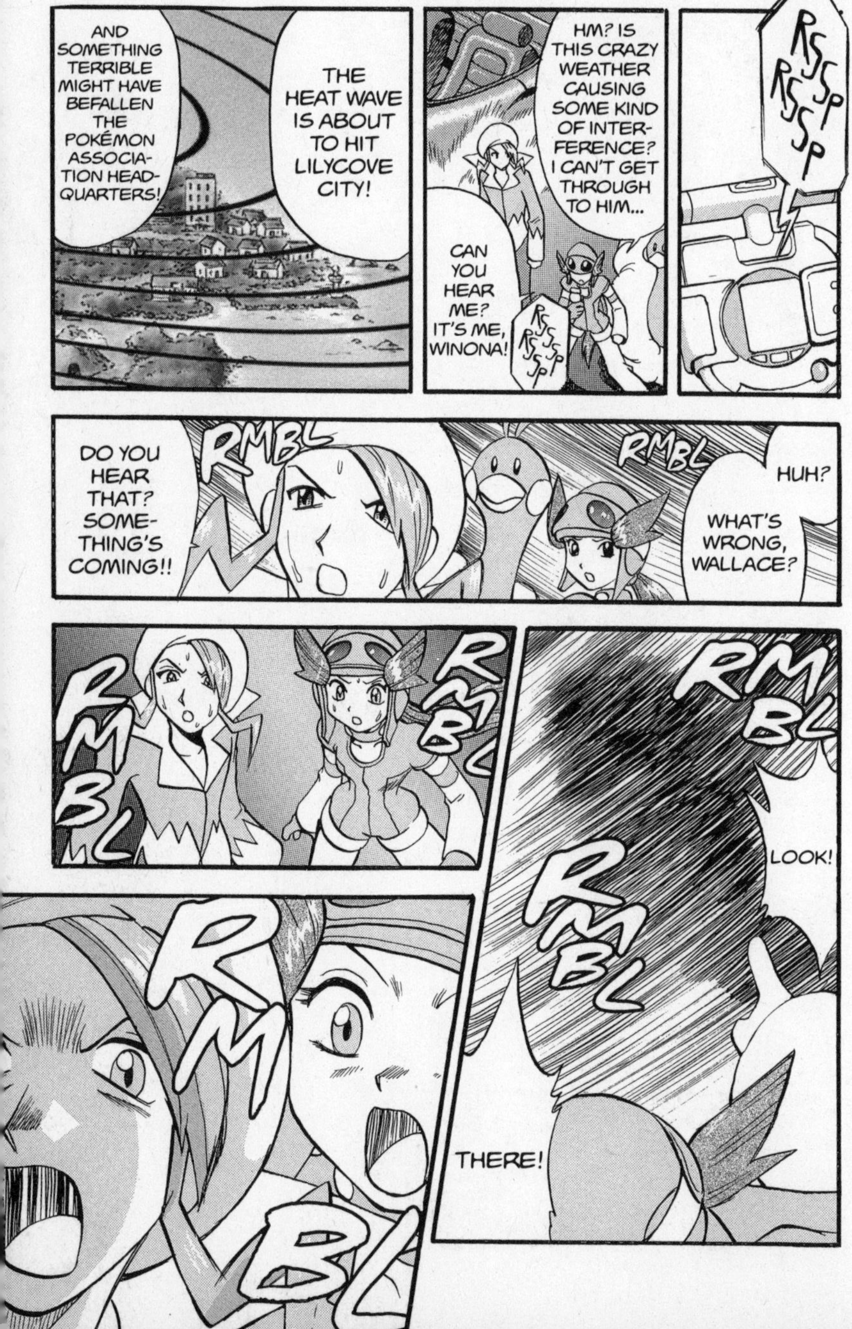
RSSP RSSP
HM? IS THIS CRAZY WEATHER CAUSING SOME KIND OF INTER-FERENCE? I CAN'T GET THROUGH TO HIM...
CAN YOU HEAR ME? IT'S ME, WINONA!
RSSP RSSP
THE HEAT WAVE IS ABOUT TO HIT LILYCOVE CITY!
AND SOMETHING TERRIBLE MIGHT HAVE BEFALLEN THE POKÉMON ASSOCIA-TION HEAD-QUARTERS!
HUH?
WHAT'S WRONG, WALLACE?
RMBL
RMBL
DO YOU HEAR THAT? SOME-THING'S COMING!!
RMBL
LOOK!
RMBL
THERE!
RMBL
RMBL
RMBL

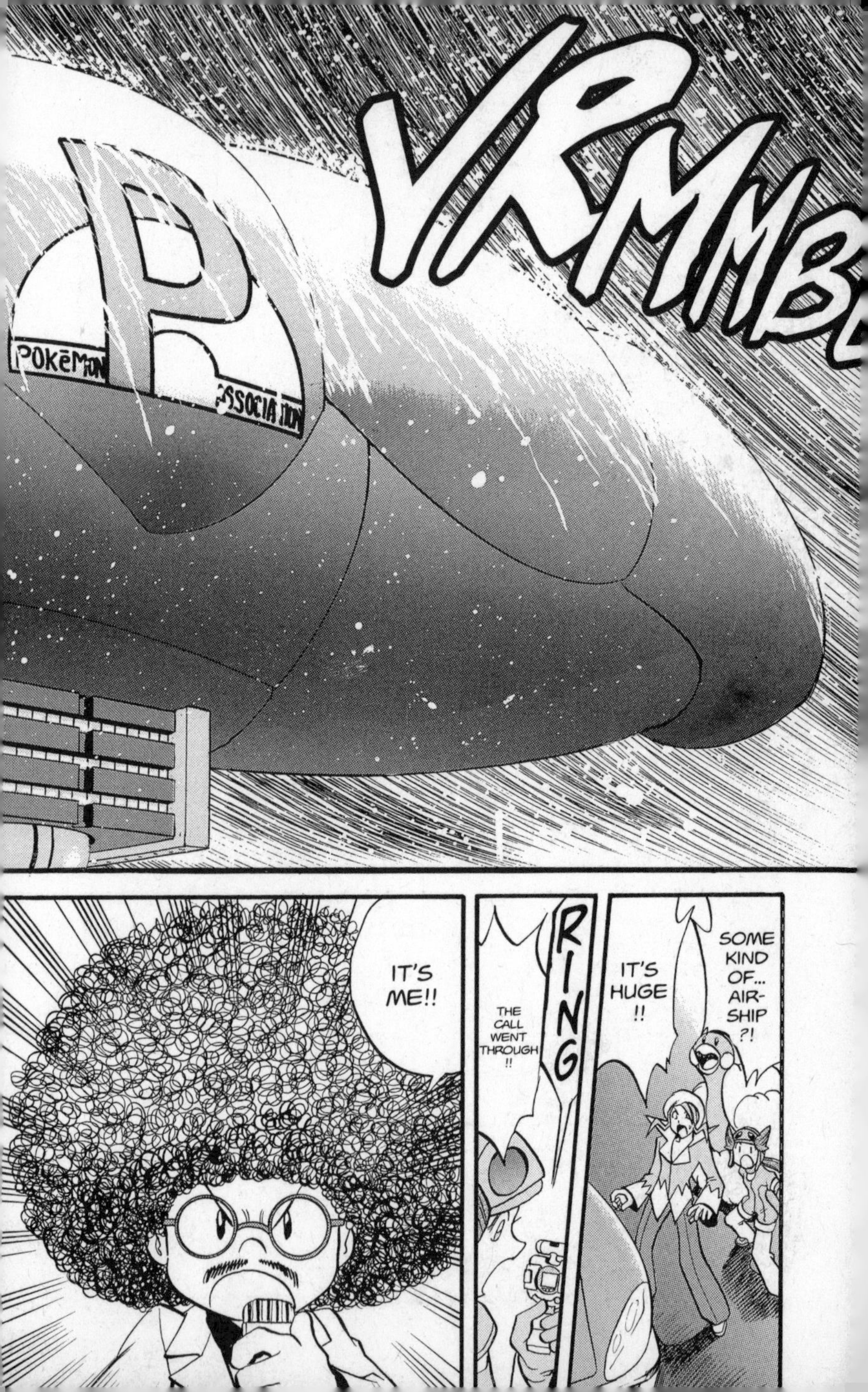
VRMMB
POKéMON
ASSOCIATION
SOME KIND OF... AIR-SHIP ?!
IT'S HUGE !!
RING
THE CALL WENT THROUGH !!
IT'S ME!!

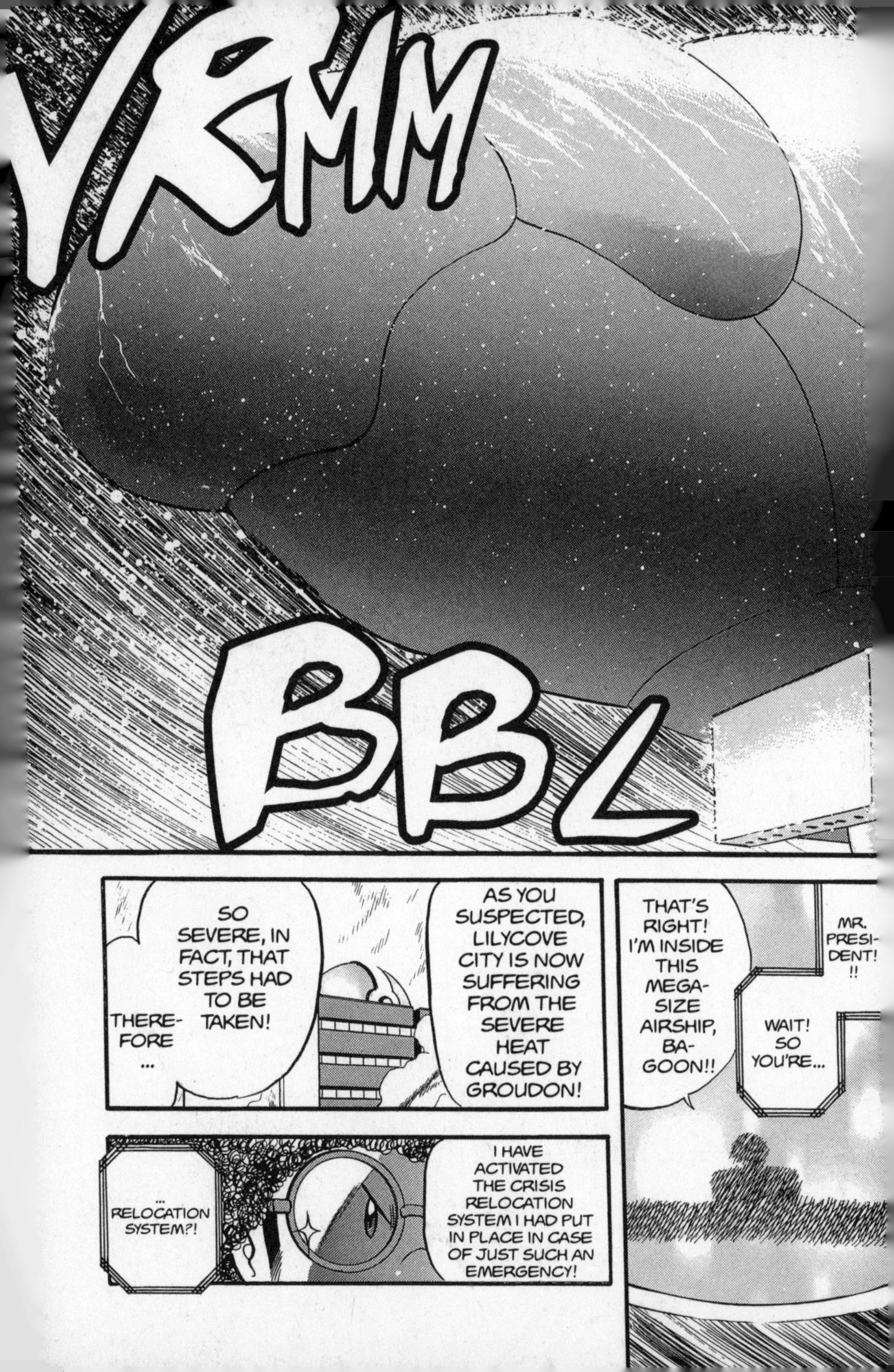
VRMM
BBL
MR. PRESIDENT!!
WAIT! SO YOU'RE...
THAT'S RIGHT! I'M INSIDE THIS MEGA-SIZE AIRSHIP, BAGOON!!
AS YOU SUSPECTED, LILYCOVE CITY IS NOW SUFFERING FROM THE SEVERE HEAT CAUSED BY GROUDON!
SO SEVERE, IN FACT, THAT STEPS HAD TO BE TAKEN!
THEREFORE ...
I HAVE ACTIVATED THE CRISIS RELOCATION SYSTEM I HAD PUT IN PLACE IN CASE OF JUST SUCH AN EMERGENCY!
... RELOCATION SYSTEM?!

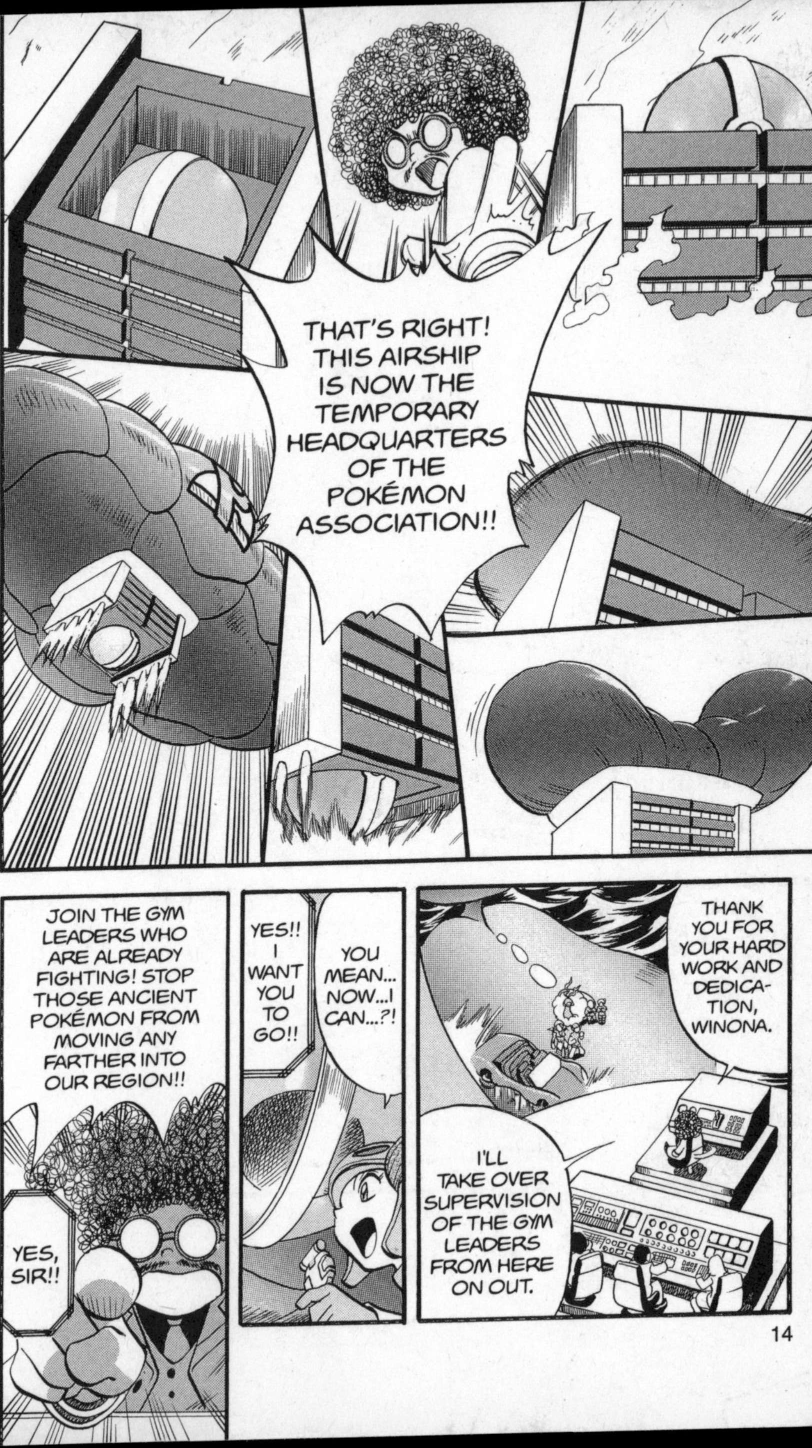
THAT'S RIGHT! THIS AIRSHIP IS NOW THE TEMPORARY HEADQUARTERS OF THE POKÉMON ASSOCIATION!!
THANK YOU FOR YOUR HARD WORK AND DEDICA-TION, WINONA.
I'LL TAKE OVER SUPERVISION OF THE GYM LEADERS FROM HERE ON OUT.
YOU MEAN... NOW...I CAN...?!
YES!! I WANT YOU TO GO!!
JOIN THE GYM LEADERS WHO ARE ALREADY FIGHTING! STOP THOSE ANCIENT POKÉMON FROM MOVING ANY FARTHER INTO OUR REGION!!
YES, SIR!!

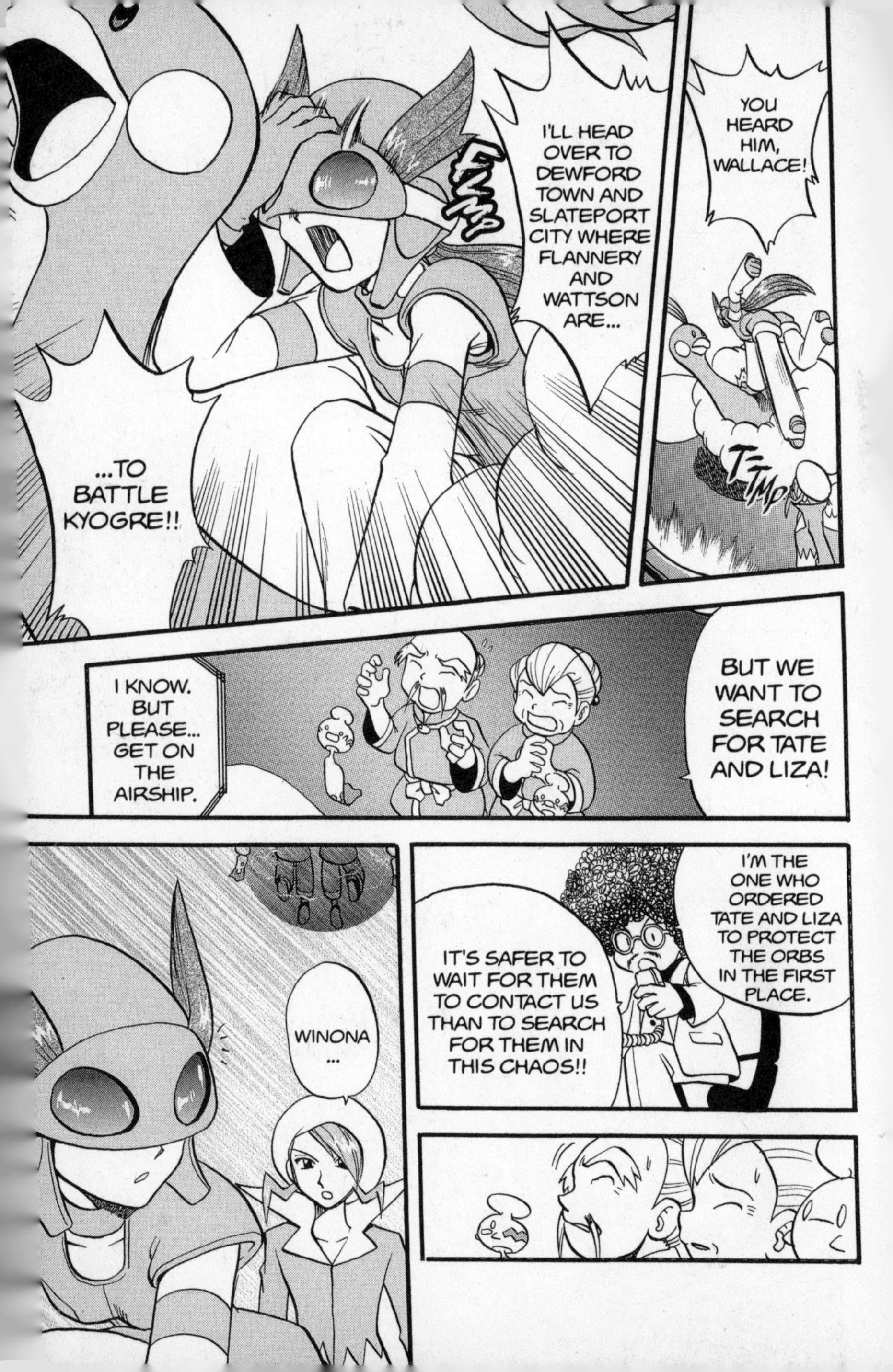

YOU HEARD HIM, WALLACE!
I'LL HEAD OVER TO DEWFORD TOWN AND SLATEPORT CITY WHERE FLANNERY AND WATTSON ARE...
...TO BATTLE KYOGRE!!
BUT WE WANT TO SEARCH FOR TATE AND LIZA!
I KNOW. BUT PLEASE... GET ON THE AIRSHIP.
I'M THE ONE WHO ORDERED TATE AND LIZA TO PROTECT THE ORBS IN THE FIRST PLACE.
IT'S SAFER TO WAIT FOR THEM TO CONTACT US THAN TO SEARCH FOR THEM IN THIS CHAOS!!
WINONA ...

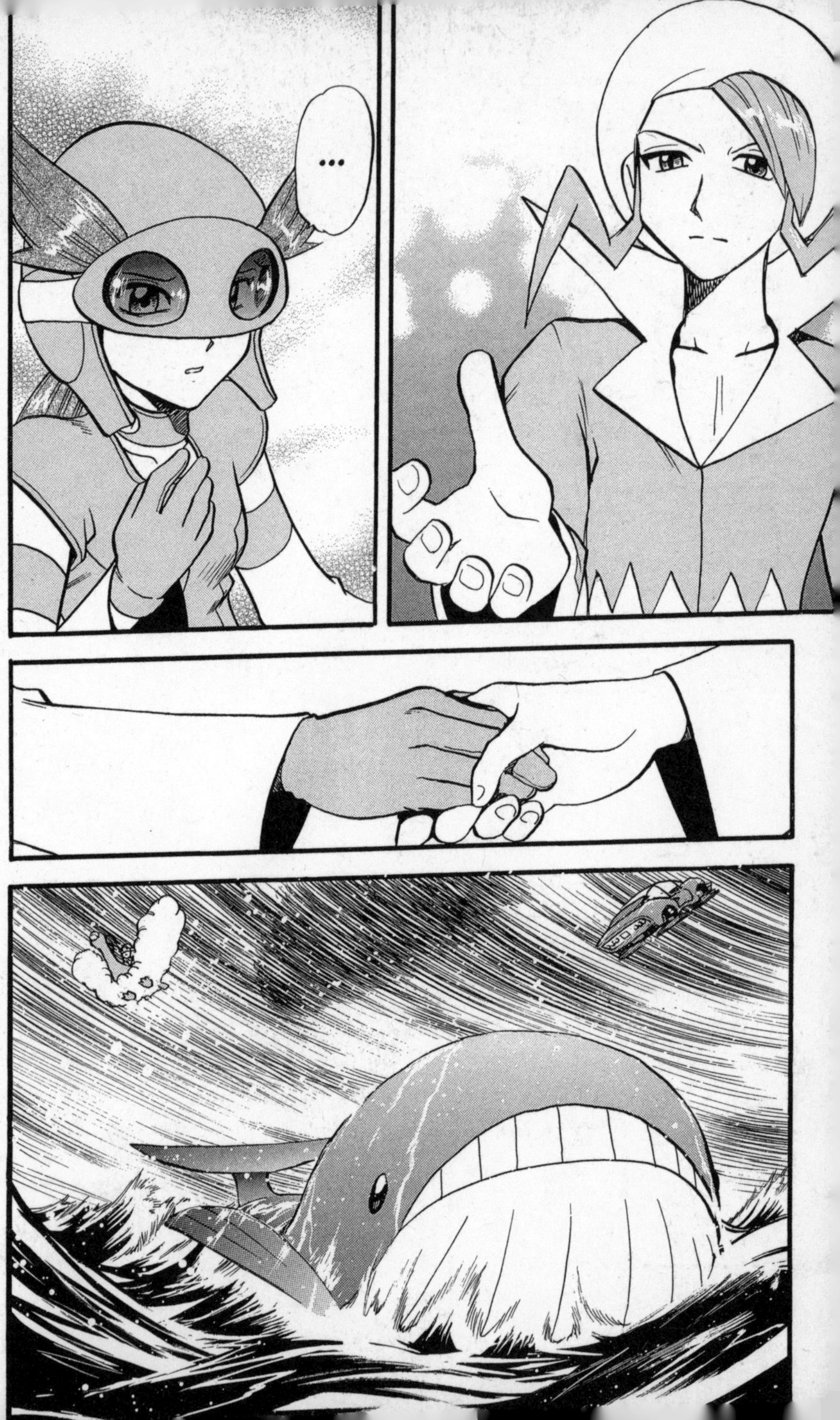
...

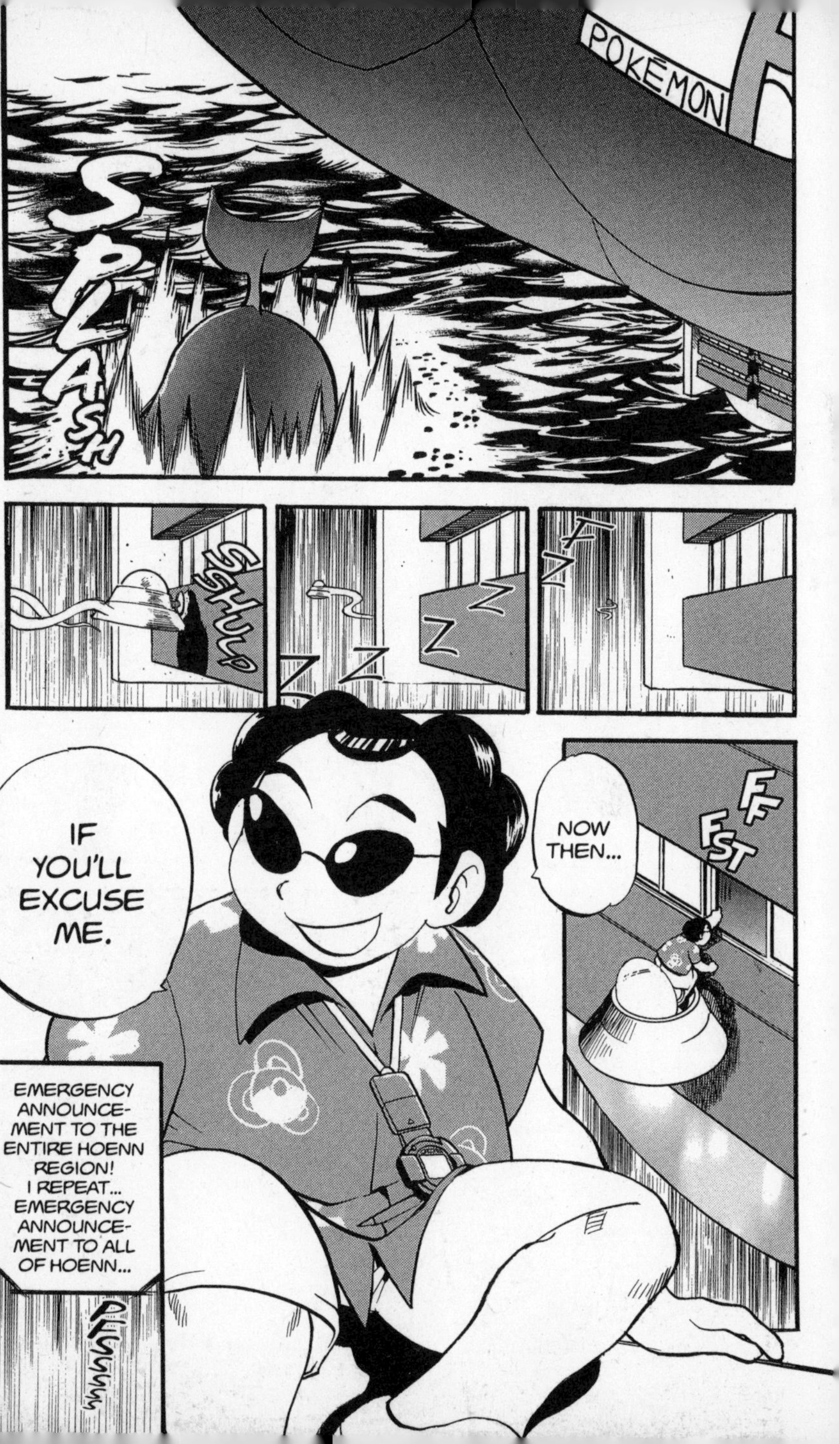
POKÉMON
SPLASH
FZZ
ZZZZ
SSHULP
NOW THEN...
FFFST
IF YOU'LL EXCUSE ME.
EMERGENCY ANNOUNCEMENT TO THE ENTIRE HOENN REGION! I REPEAT... EMERGENCY ANNOUNCEMENT TO ALL OF HOENN...
PFSSSSS

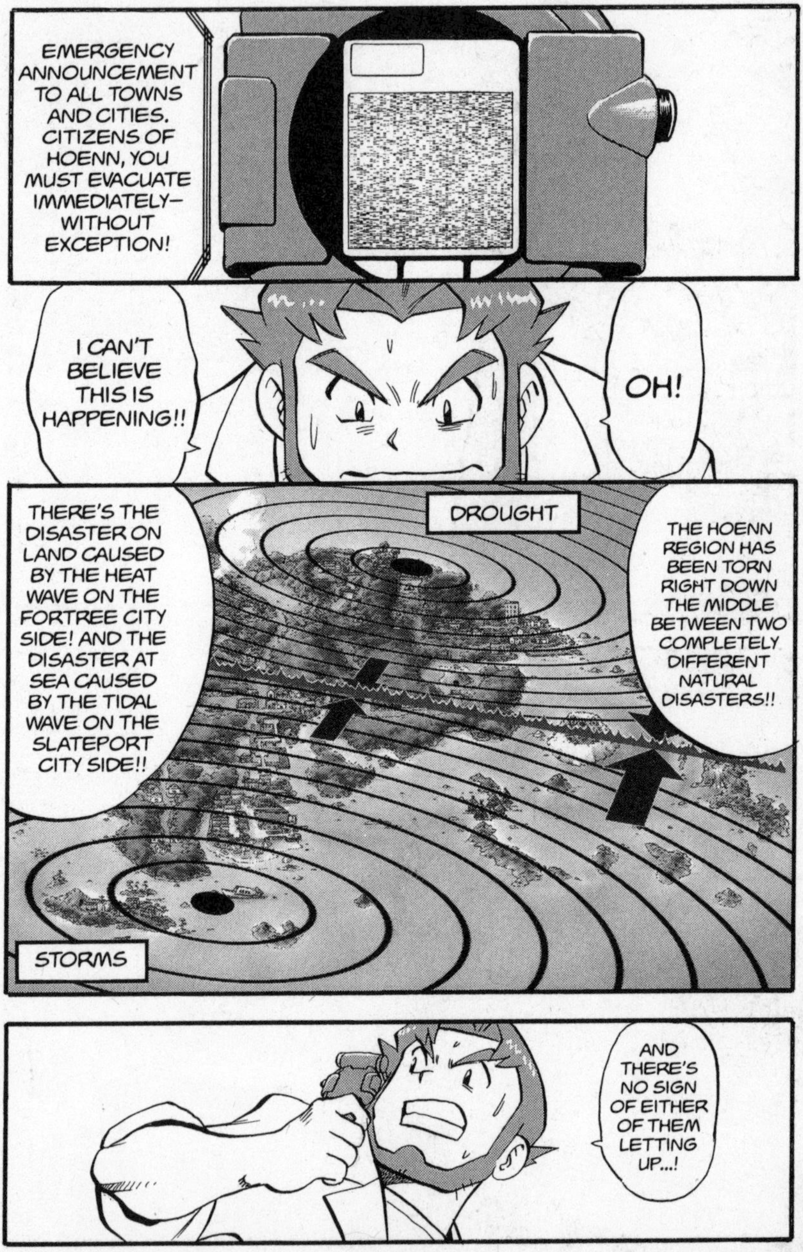
EMERGENCY ANNOUNCEMENT TO ALL TOWNS AND CITIES. CITIZENS OF HOENN, YOU MUST EVACUATE IMMEDIATELY—WITHOUT EXCEPTION!
OH!
I CAN'T BELIEVE THIS IS HAPPENING!!
THE HOENN REGION HAS BEEN TORN RIGHT DOWN THE MIDDLE BETWEEN TWO COMPLETELY DIFFERENT NATURAL DISASTERS!!
DROUGHT
THERE'S THE DISASTER ON LAND CAUSED BY THE HEAT WAVE ON THE FORTREE CITY SIDE! AND THE DISASTER AT SEA CAUSED BY THE TIDAL WAVE ON THE SLATEPORT CITY SIDE!!
STORMS
AND THERE'S NO SIGN OF EITHER OF THEM LETTING UP...!

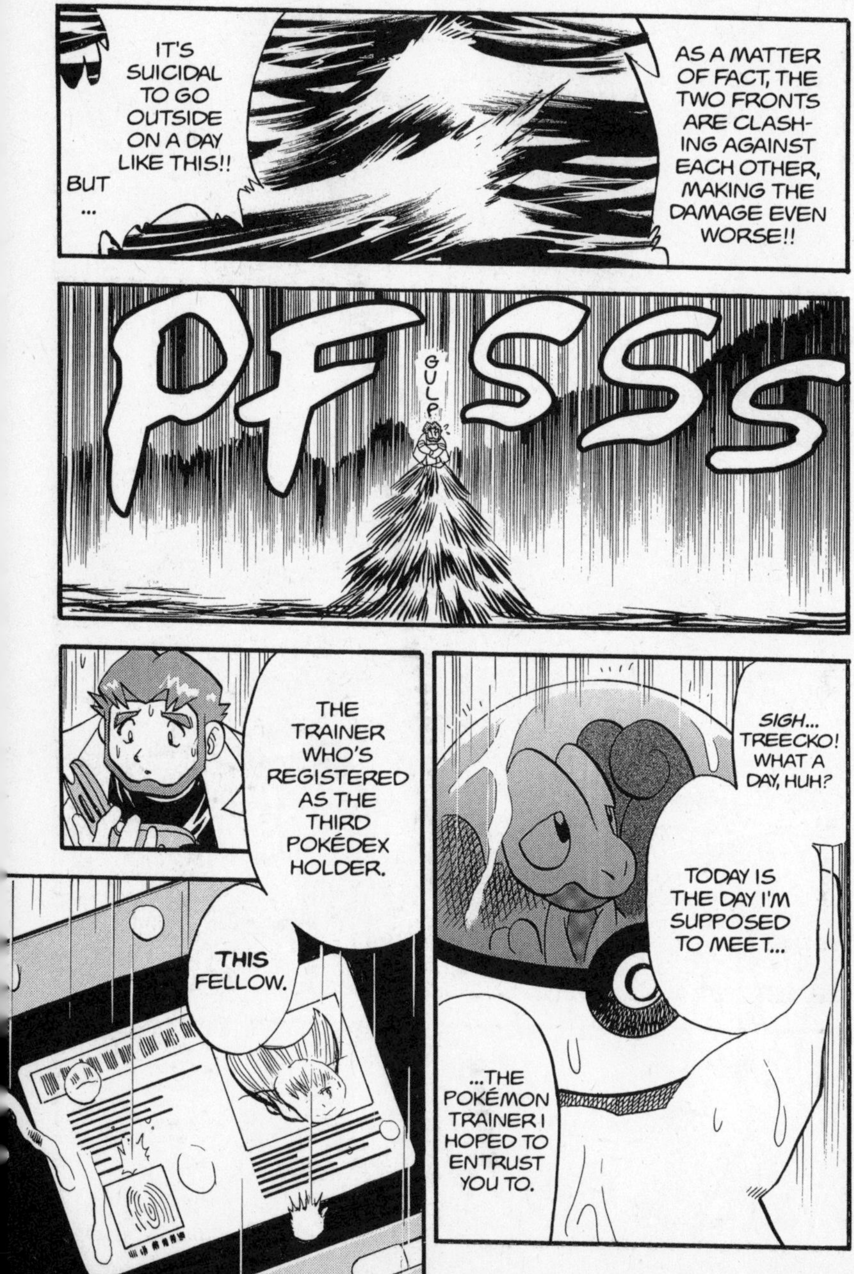
AS A MATTER OF FACT, THE TWO FRONTS ARE CLASHING AGAINST EACH OTHER, MAKING THE DAMAGE EVEN WORSE!!
IT'S SUICIDAL TO GO OUTSIDE ON A DAY LIKE THIS!!
BUT ...
PFSSS
GULP
SIGH... TREECKO! WHAT A DAY, HUH?
TODAY IS THE DAY I'M SUPPOSED TO MEET...
...THE POKÉMON TRAINER I HOPED TO ENTRUST YOU TO.
THE TRAINER WHO'S REGISTERED AS THE THIRD POKÉDEX HOLDER.
THIS FELLOW.

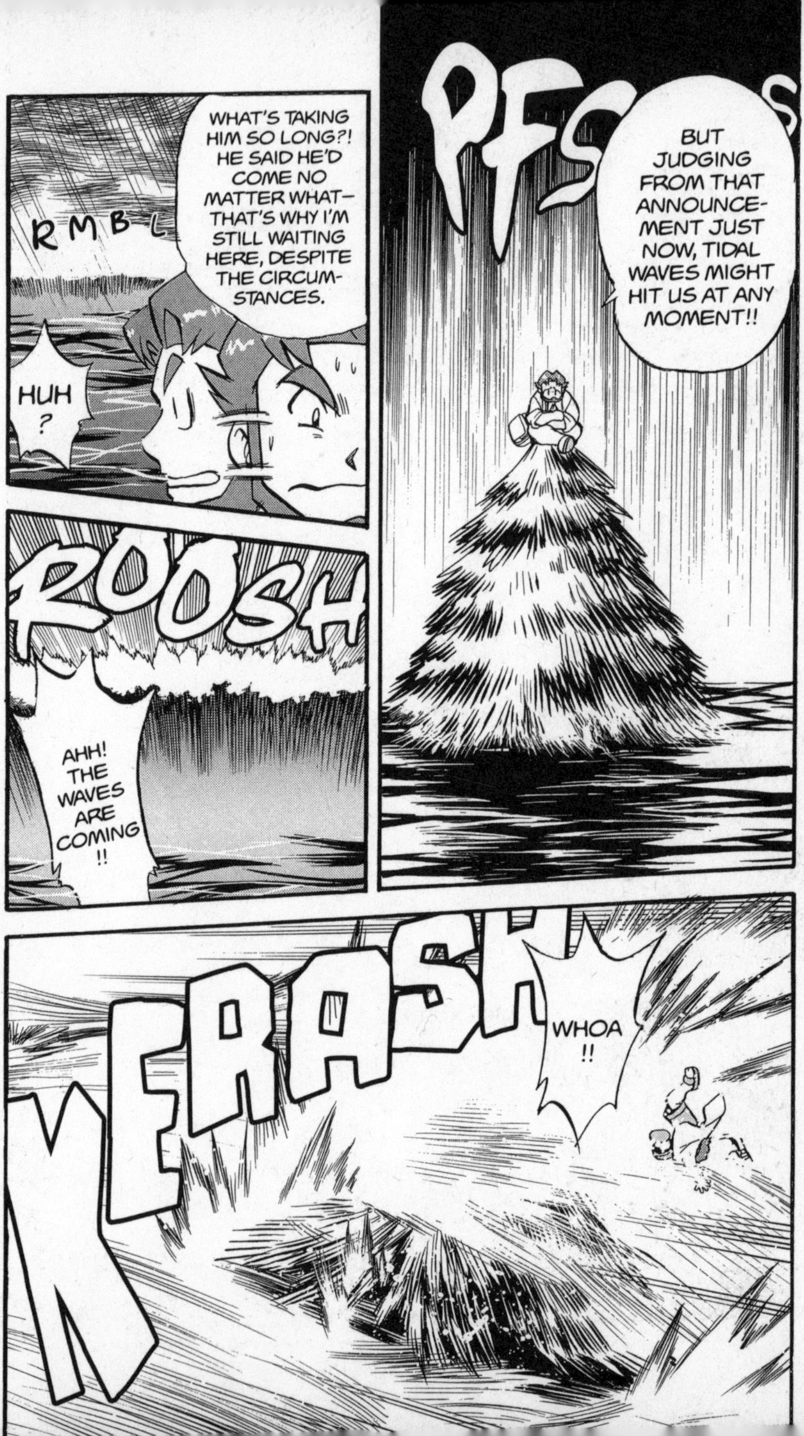
PFSS
BUT JUDGING FROM THAT ANNOUNCEMENT JUST NOW, TIDAL WAVES MIGHT HIT US AT ANY MOMENT!!
RMBL
WHAT'S TAKING HIM SO LONG?! HE SAID HE'D COME NO MATTER WHAT—THAT'S WHY I'M STILL WAITING HERE, DESPITE THE CIRCUMSTANCES.
HUH?
ROOSH
AHH! THE WAVES ARE COMING!!
KFRASH
WHOA!!

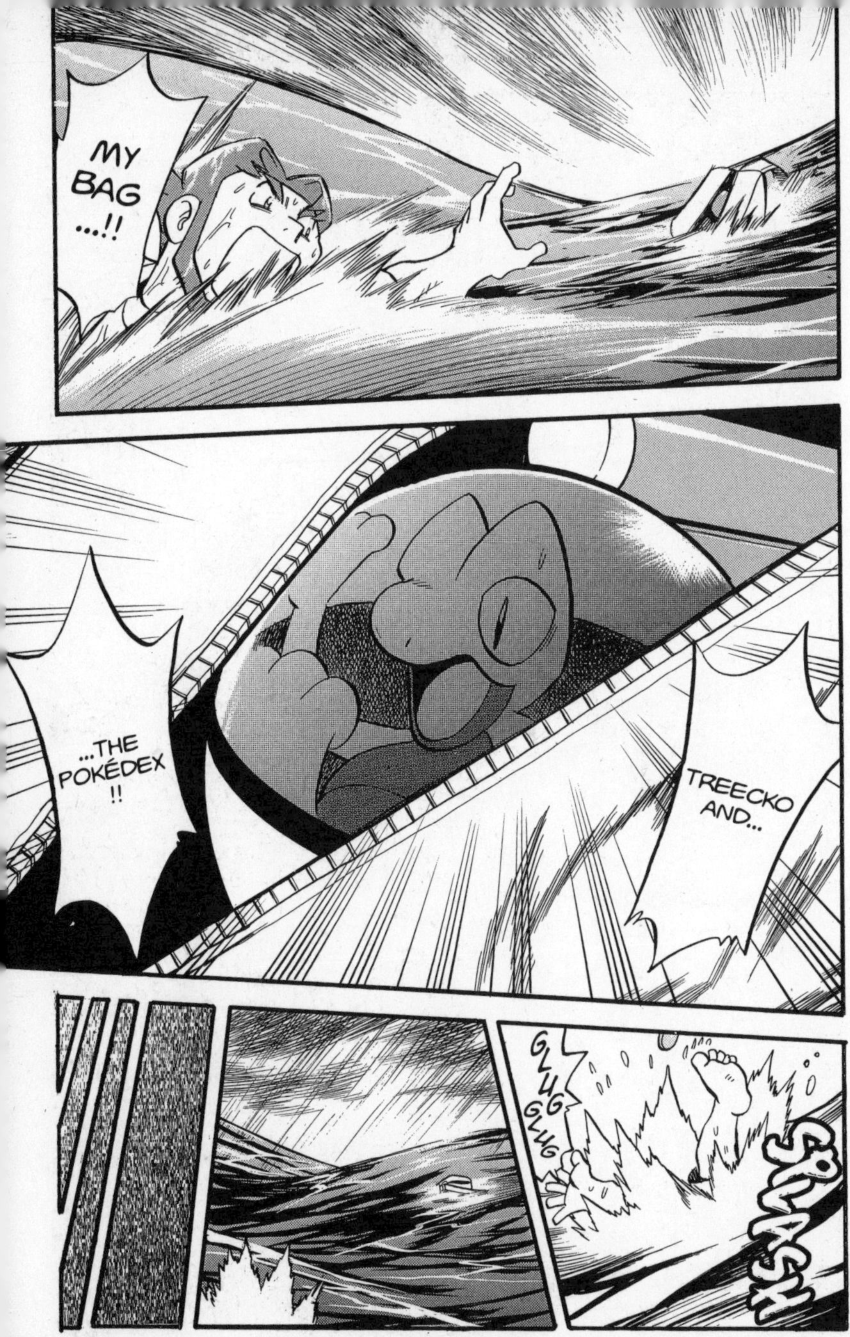
MY BAG ...!!
TREECKO AND...
...THE POKÉDEX !!
SPLASH
GLUG GLUG GLUG

ADVENTURE MAP

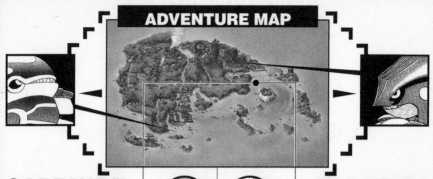

SAPPHIRE

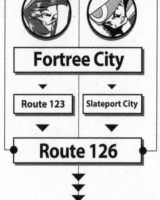

Name	Pokémon	Level
CHIC	Blaziken ♀	Lv40
RONO	Lairon ♂	Lv41
RELLY	Relicanth ♂	Lv47
PHADO	Donphan ♂	Lv48
TROPPY	Tropius ♂	Lv46
LORRY	Wailord ♂	Lv48

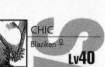

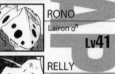

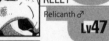

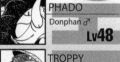

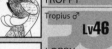

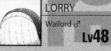

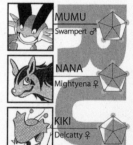

RUBY

Name	Pokémon
MUMU	Swampert ♂
NANA	Mightyena ♀
KIKI	Delcatty ♀
FOFO	Castform ♀

Fortree City

Sapphire: Route 123 → Route 126

Ruby: Slateport City → Route 126

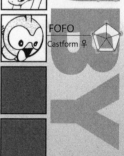

Stone Badge	Knuckle Badge	Dynamo Badge	Heat Badge
Balance Badge	**Feather Badge**	**Mind Badge**	**Rain Badge**

	Cool	Beauty	Cute	Smart	Tough
Normal					
Super					
Hyper					
Master					

● Chapter 240 ●

Talk About Timing, Treecko

Pokémon™ Adventures Ruby & Sapphire

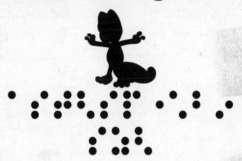

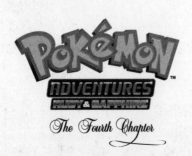

The Fourth Chapter

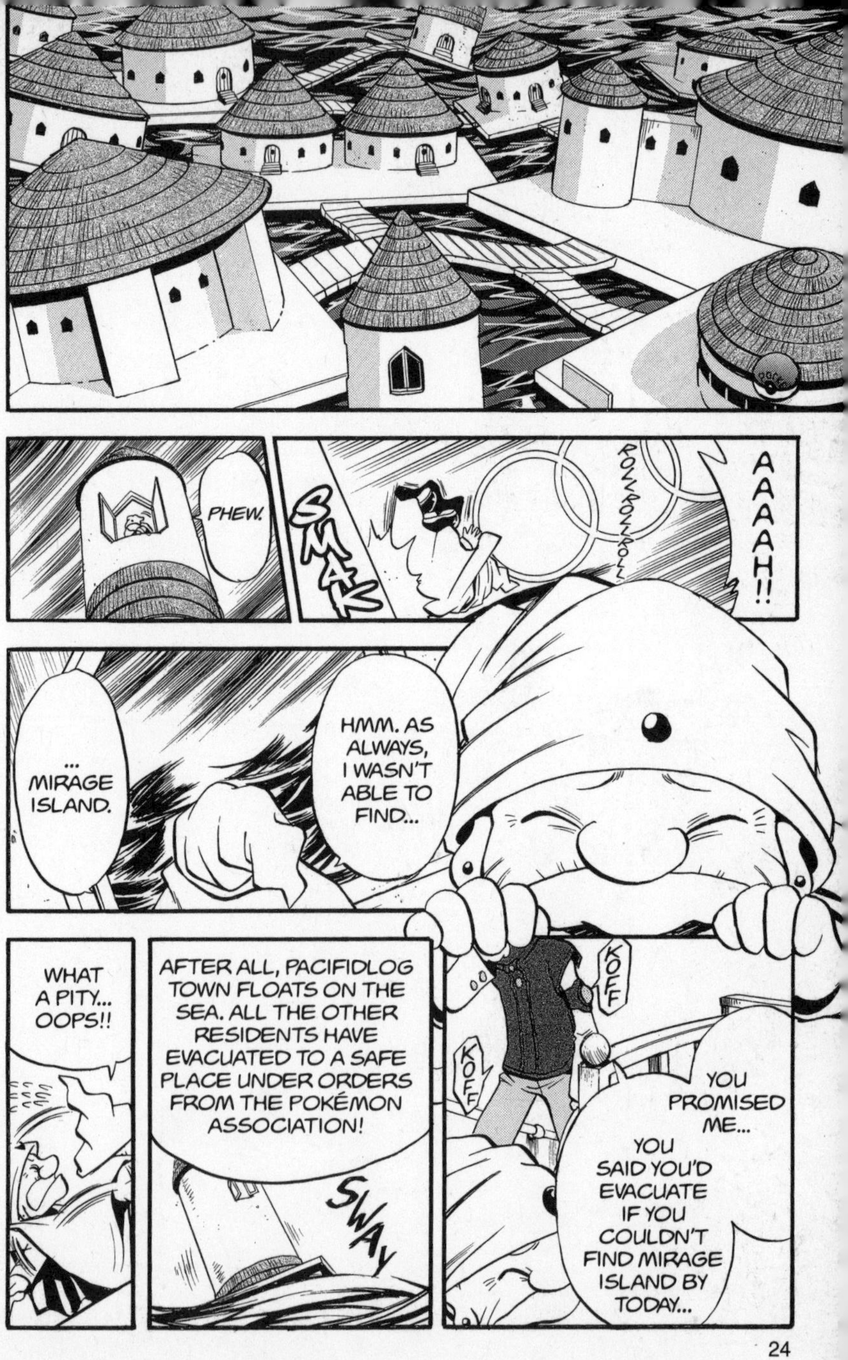
AAAAH!!
ROLLROLLROLL
SMAK
PHEW.
HMM. AS ALWAYS, I WASN'T ABLE TO FIND...
... MIRAGE ISLAND.
KOFF
KOFF
YOU PROMISED ME...
YOU SAID YOU'D EVACUATE IF YOU COULDN'T FIND MIRAGE ISLAND BY TODAY...
AFTER ALL, PACIFIDLOG TOWN FLOATS ON THE SEA. ALL THE OTHER RESIDENTS HAVE EVACUATED TO A SAFE PLACE UNDER ORDERS FROM THE POKÉMON ASSOCIATION!
SWAY
WHAT A PITY... OOPS!!

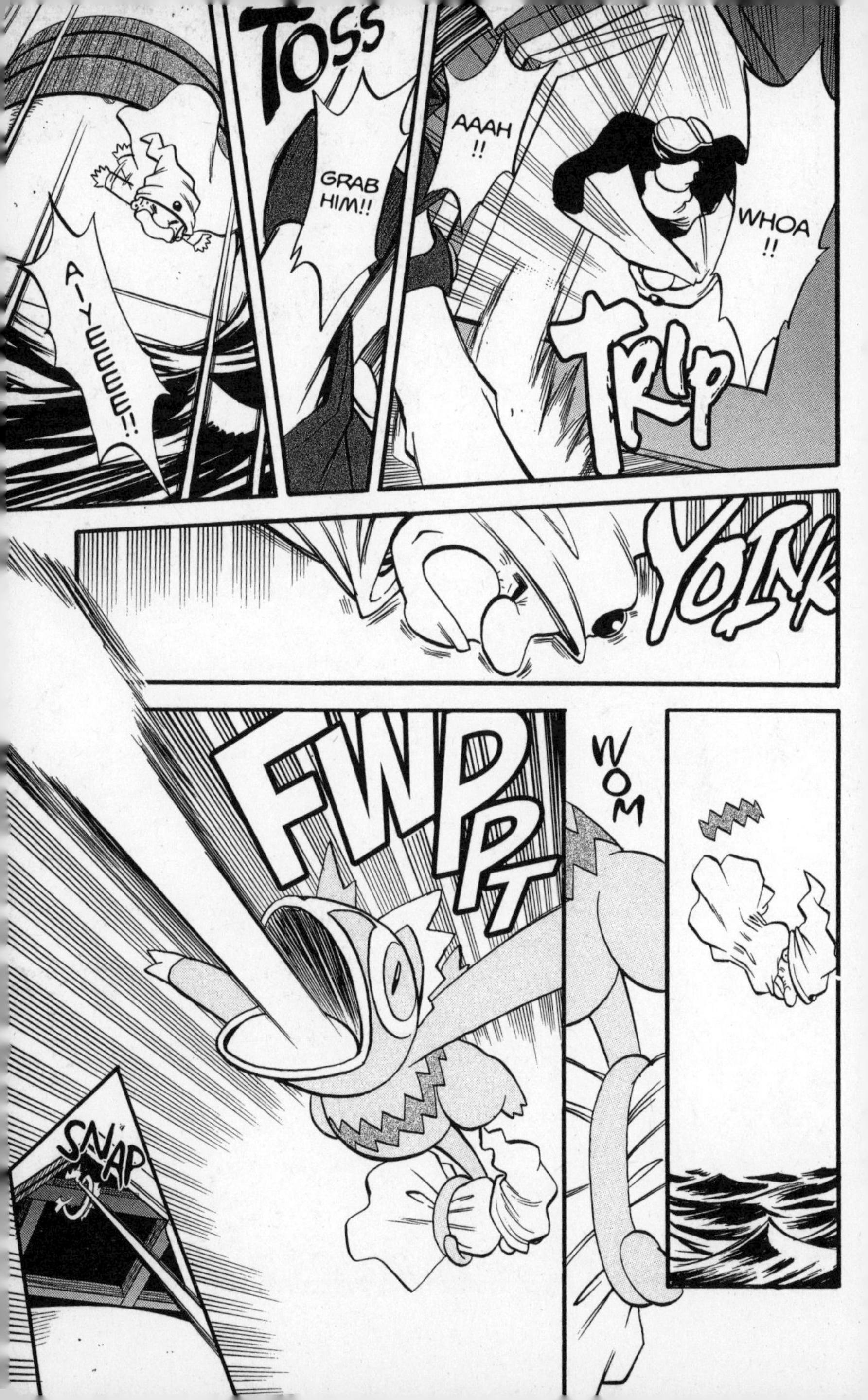
WHOA!!
AAAH!!
TRIP
TOSS
GRAB HIM!!
AIYEEEEE!!
YOINK
WOM
FWPPT
SNAP

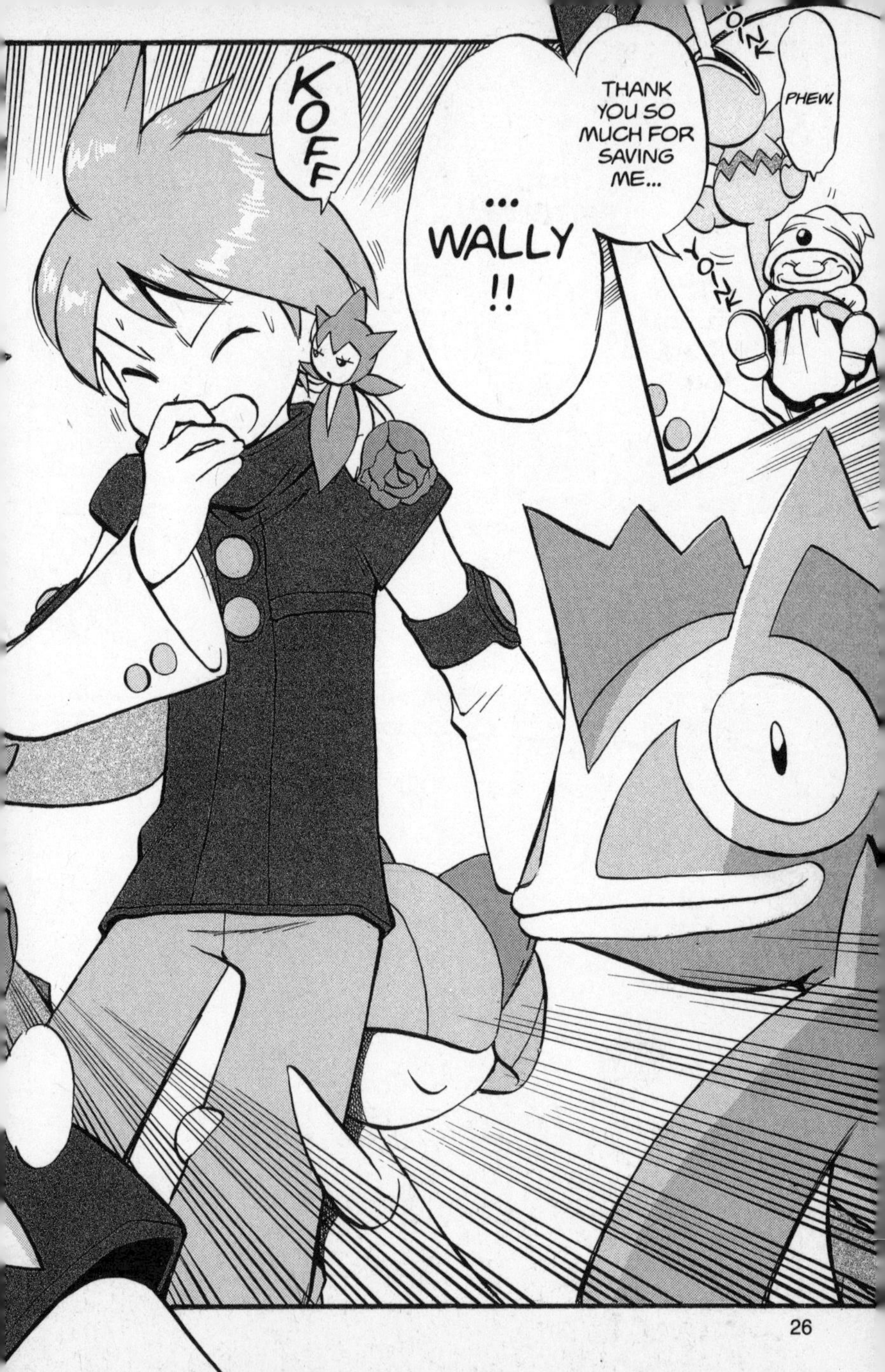
OINK
PHEW.
THANK YOU SO MUCH FOR SAVING ME...
YO-INK
...WALLY!!
KOFF

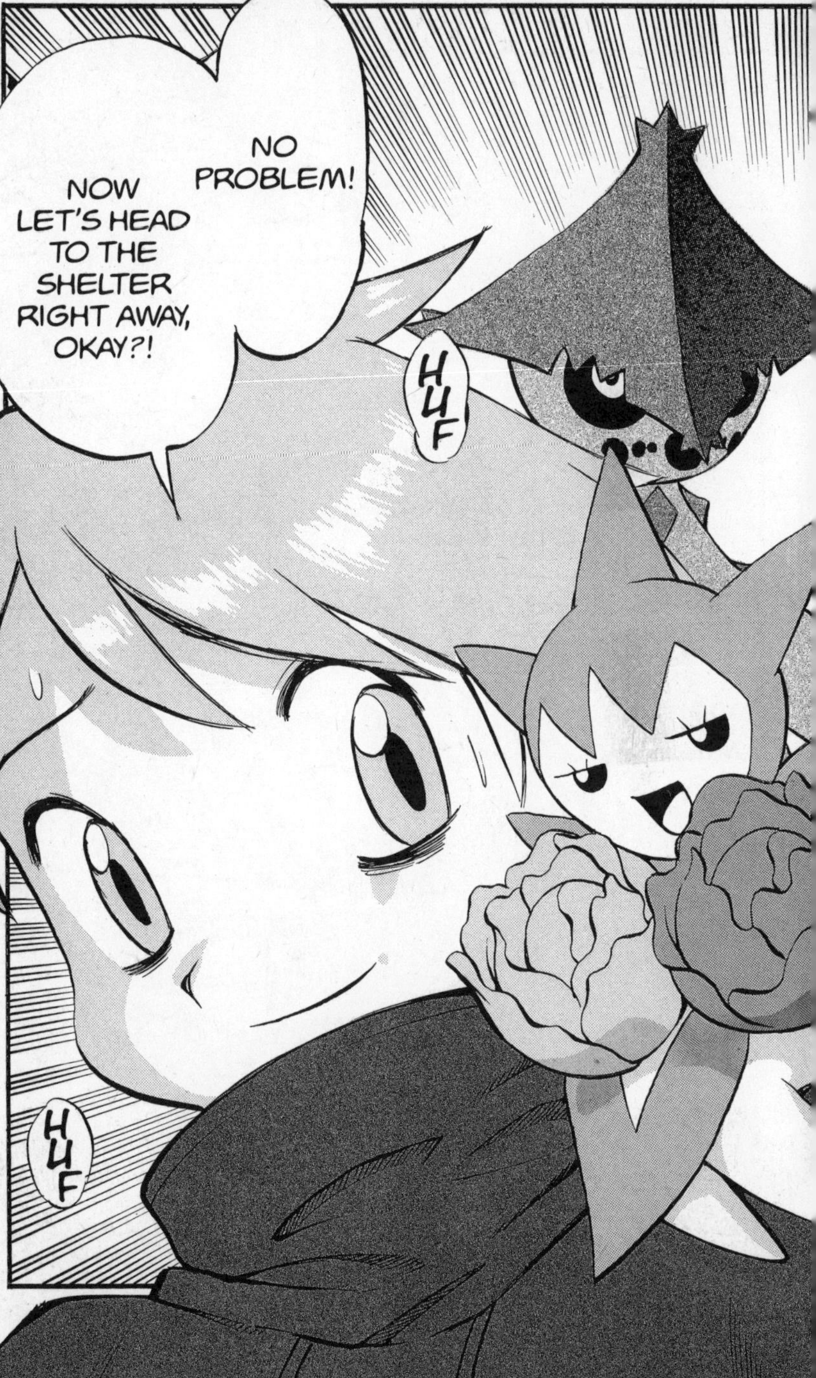
NO PROBLEM!
NOW LET'S HEAD TO THE SHELTER RIGHT AWAY, OKAY?!
HUF
HUF

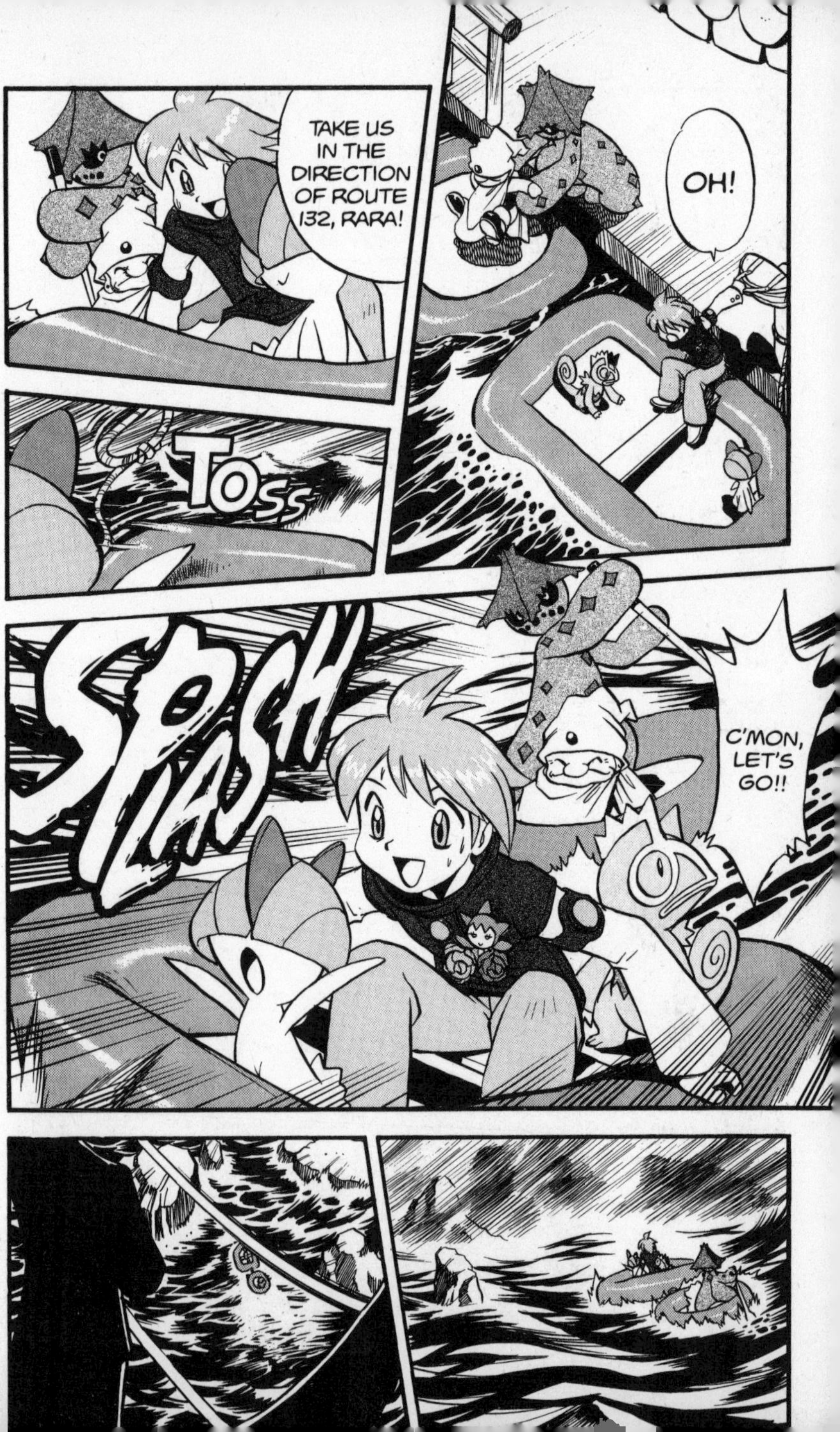
OH!
TAKE US IN THE DIRECTION OF ROUTE 132, RARA!
TOSS
C'MON, LET'S GO!!
SPLASH

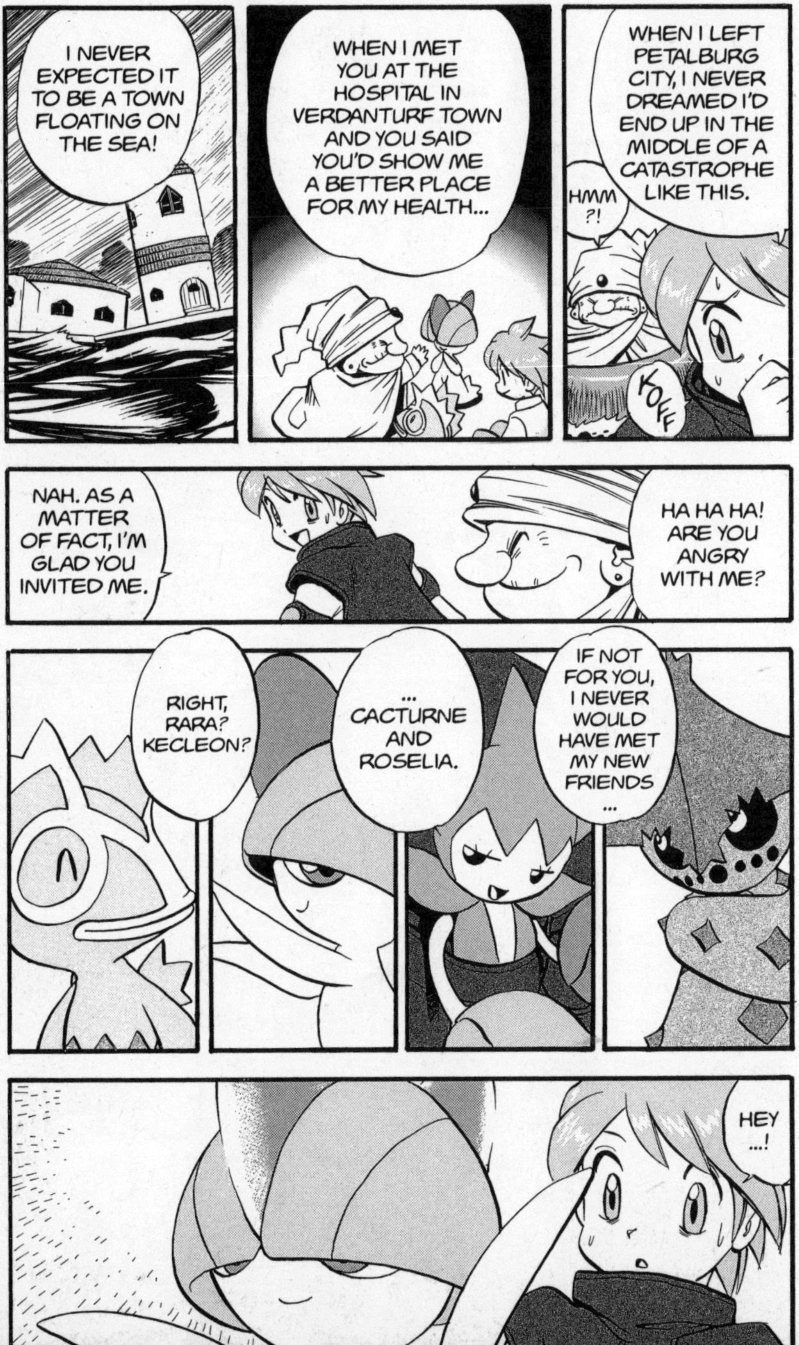
WHEN I LEFT PETALBURG CITY, I NEVER DREAMED I'D END UP IN THE MIDDLE OF A CATASTROPHE LIKE THIS.
HMM ?!
KOFF
WHEN I MET YOU AT THE HOSPITAL IN VERDANTURF TOWN AND YOU SAID YOU'D SHOW ME A BETTER PLACE FOR MY HEALTH...
I NEVER EXPECTED IT TO BE A TOWN FLOATING ON THE SEA!
HA HA HA! ARE YOU ANGRY WITH ME?
NAH. AS A MATTER OF FACT, I'M GLAD YOU INVITED ME.
IF NOT FOR YOU, I NEVER WOULD HAVE MET MY NEW FRIENDS ...
... CACTURNE AND ROSELIA.
RIGHT, RARA? KECLEON?
HEY ...!

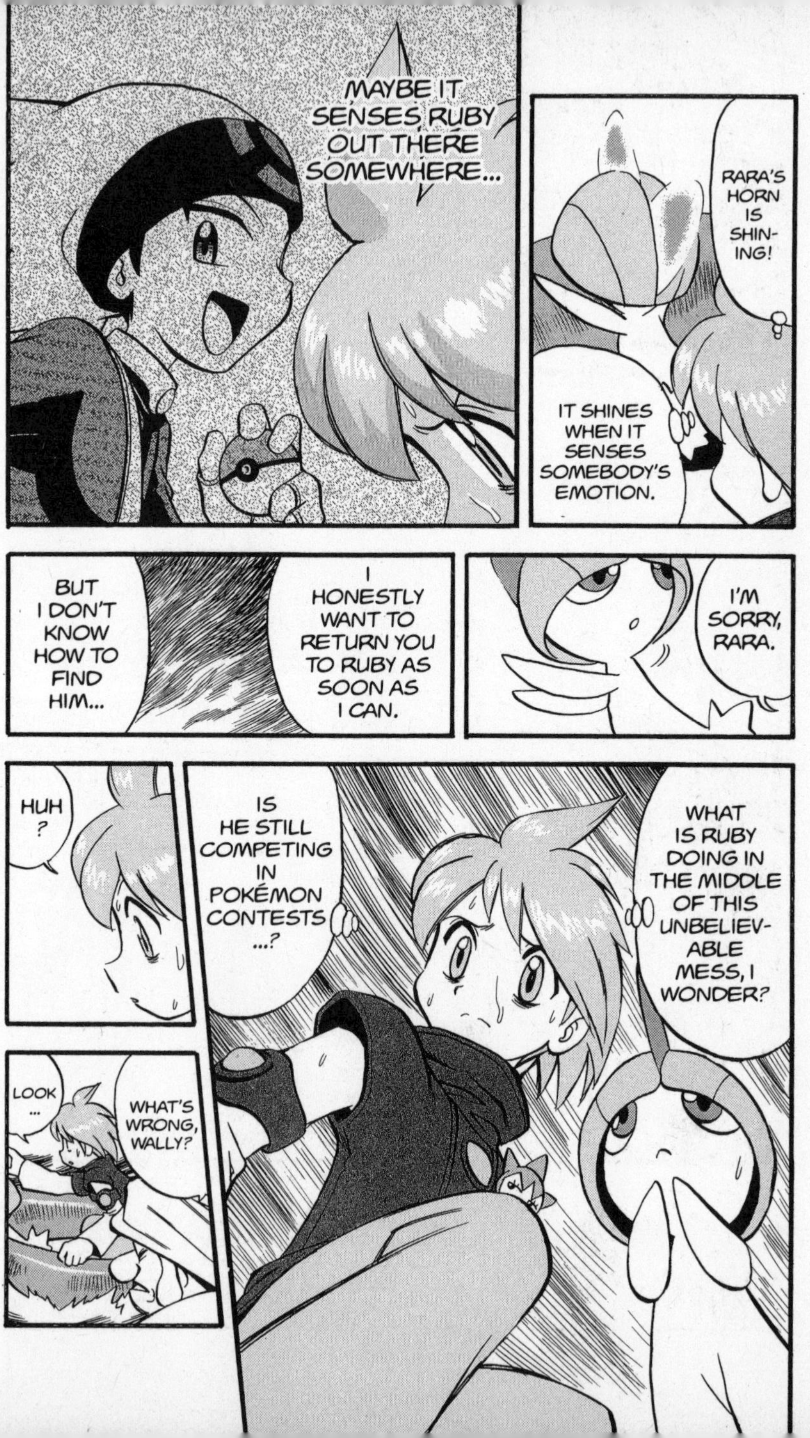
RARA'S HORN IS SHIN-ING!
IT SHINES WHEN IT SENSES SOMEBODY'S EMOTION.
MAYBE IT SENSES RUBY OUT THERE SOMEWHERE...
I'M SORRY, RARA.
I HONESTLY WANT TO RETURN YOU TO RUBY AS SOON AS I CAN.
BUT I DON'T KNOW HOW TO FIND HIM...
WHAT IS RUBY DOING IN THE MIDDLE OF THIS UNBELIEV-ABLE MESS, I WONDER?
IS HE STILL COMPETING IN POKÉMON CONTESTS ...?
HUH?
WHAT'S WRONG, WALLY?
LOOK ...

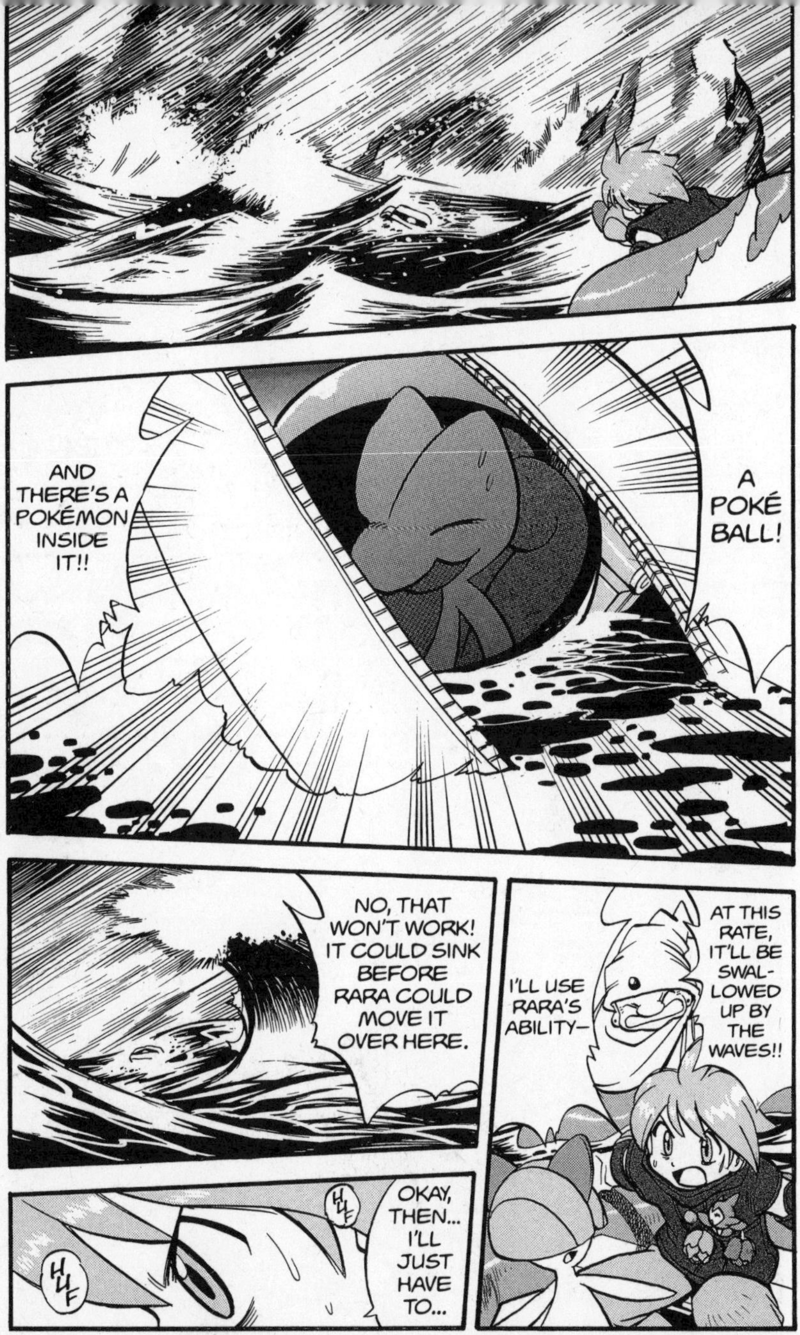
A POKÉ BALL!
AND THERE'S A POKÉMON INSIDE IT!!
AT THIS RATE, IT'LL BE SWAL-LOWED UP BY THE WAVES!!
I'LL USE RARA'S ABILITY—
NO, THAT WON'T WORK! IT COULD SINK BEFORE RARA COULD MOVE IT OVER HERE.
OKAY, THEN... I'LL JUST HAVE TO...
HUF
HUF

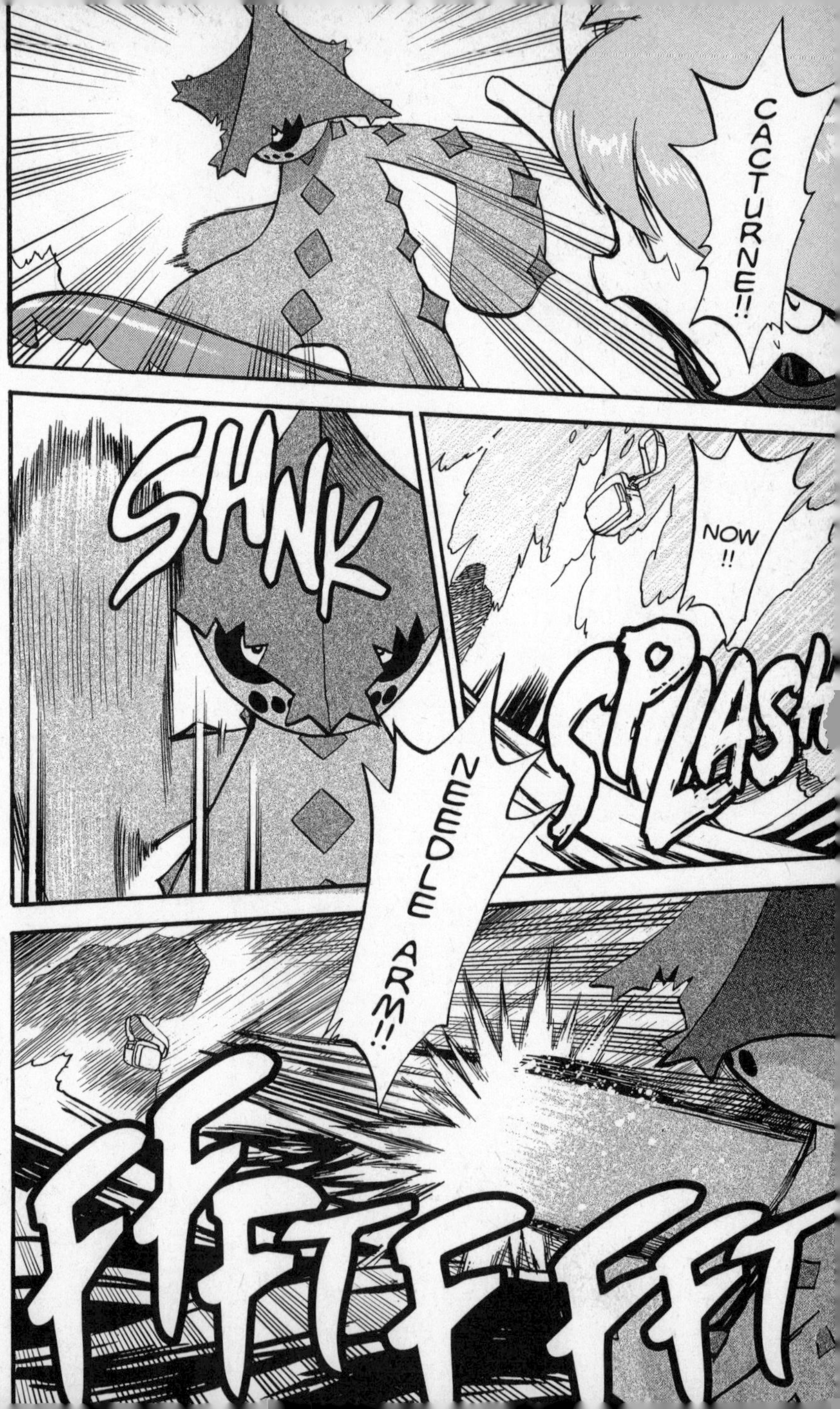
CACTURNE!!
NOW!!
SPLASH
SHNK
NEEDLE ARM!!
FFFT FFFT

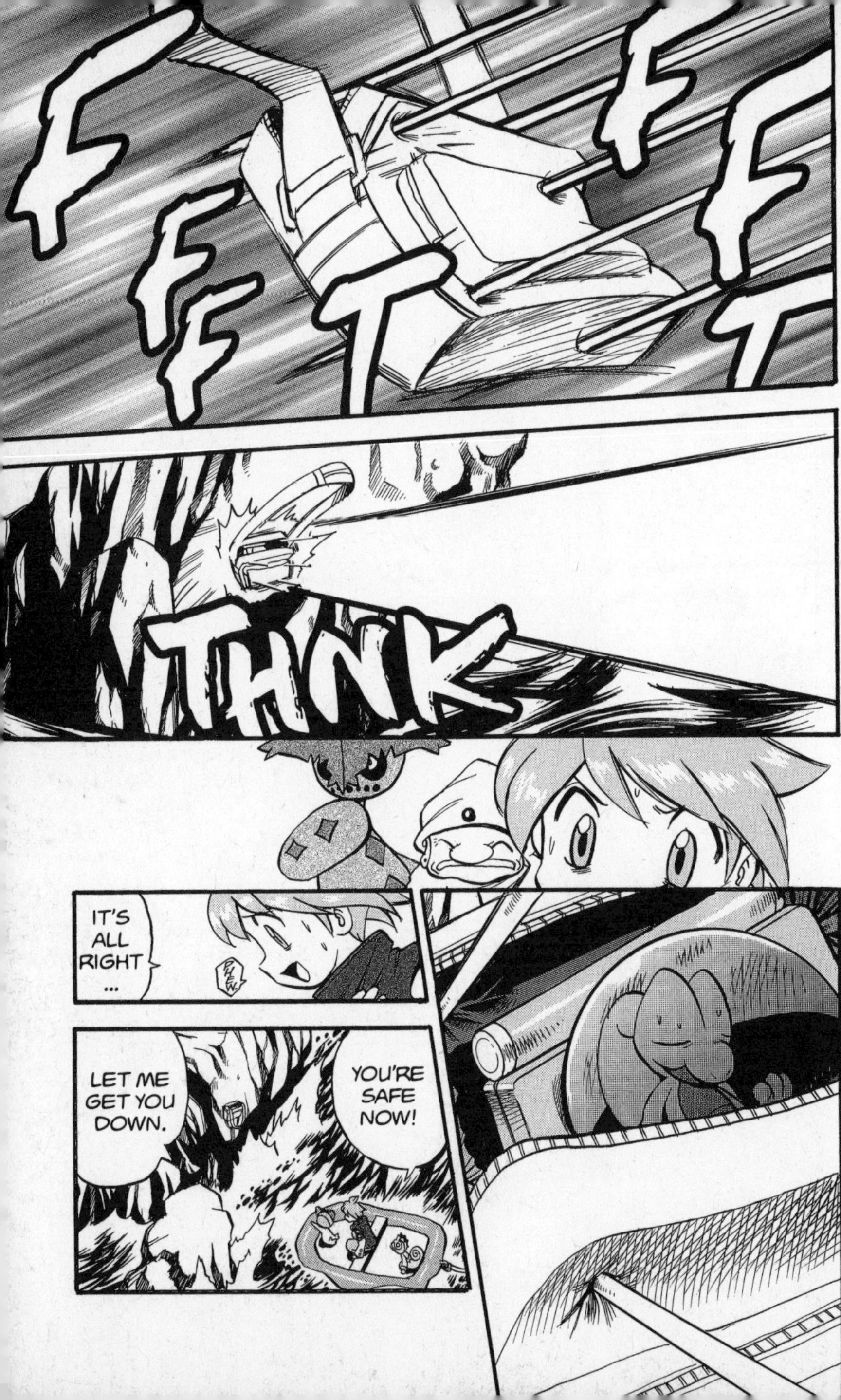
FFFT
FFFT
THNK
IT'S ALL RIGHT...
PHEW
YOU'RE SAFE NOW!
LET ME GET YOU DOWN.

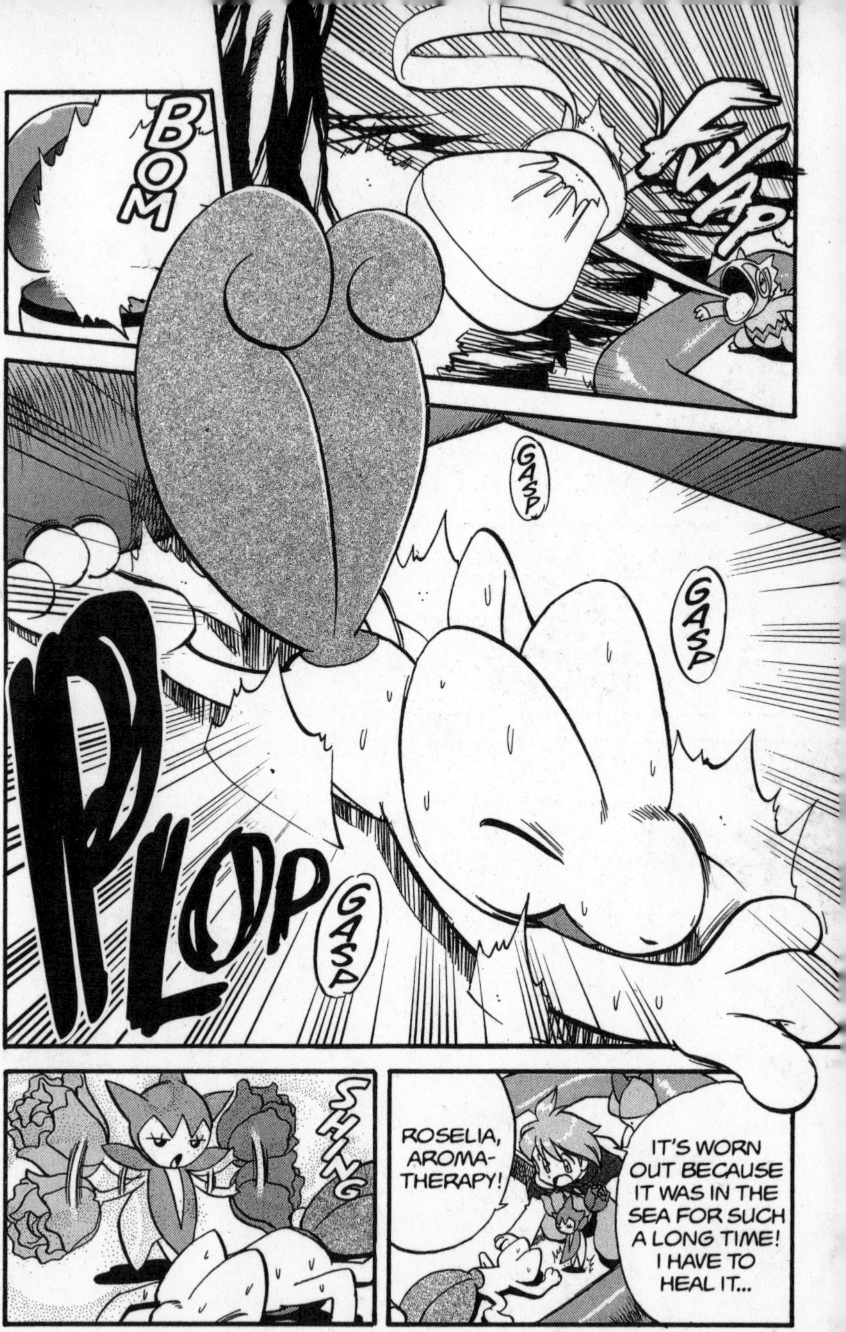
FWAP
BOM
GASP
GASP
PLOP
GASP
IT'S WORN OUT BECAUSE IT WAS IN THE SEA FOR SUCH A LONG TIME! I HAVE TO HEAL IT...
ROSELIA, AROMA-THERAPY!
SHING

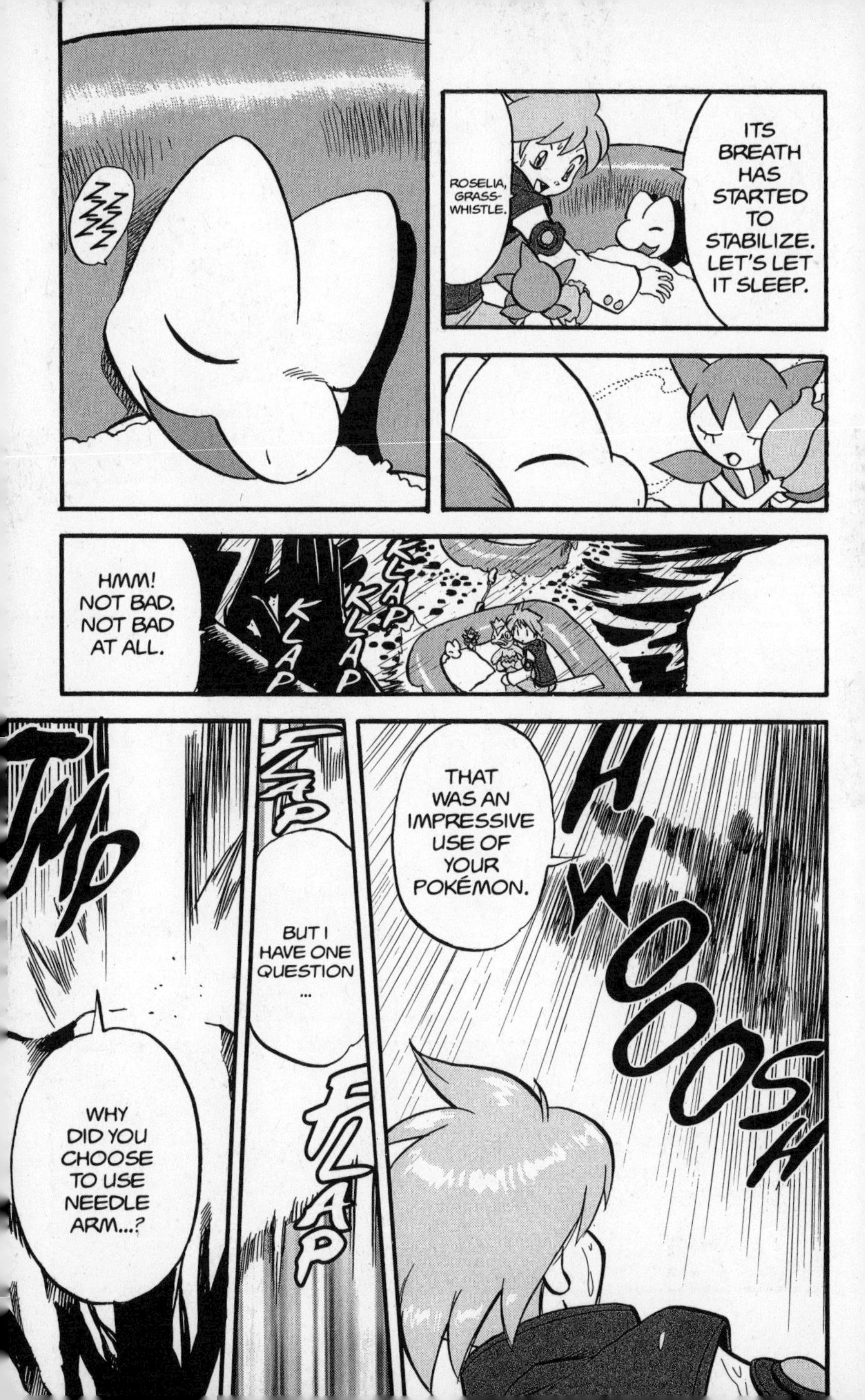

ITS BREATH HAS STARTED TO STABILIZE. LET'S LET IT SLEEP.
ROSELIA, GRASS-WHISTLE.
ZZZZZ
KLAP
KLAP
KLAP
HMM! NOT BAD. NOT BAD AT ALL.
WHOOOSH
THAT WAS AN IMPRESSIVE USE OF YOUR POKÉMON.
FLAP
BUT I HAVE ONE QUESTION ...
FLAP
TMP
WHY DID YOU CHOOSE TO USE NEEDLE ARM...?

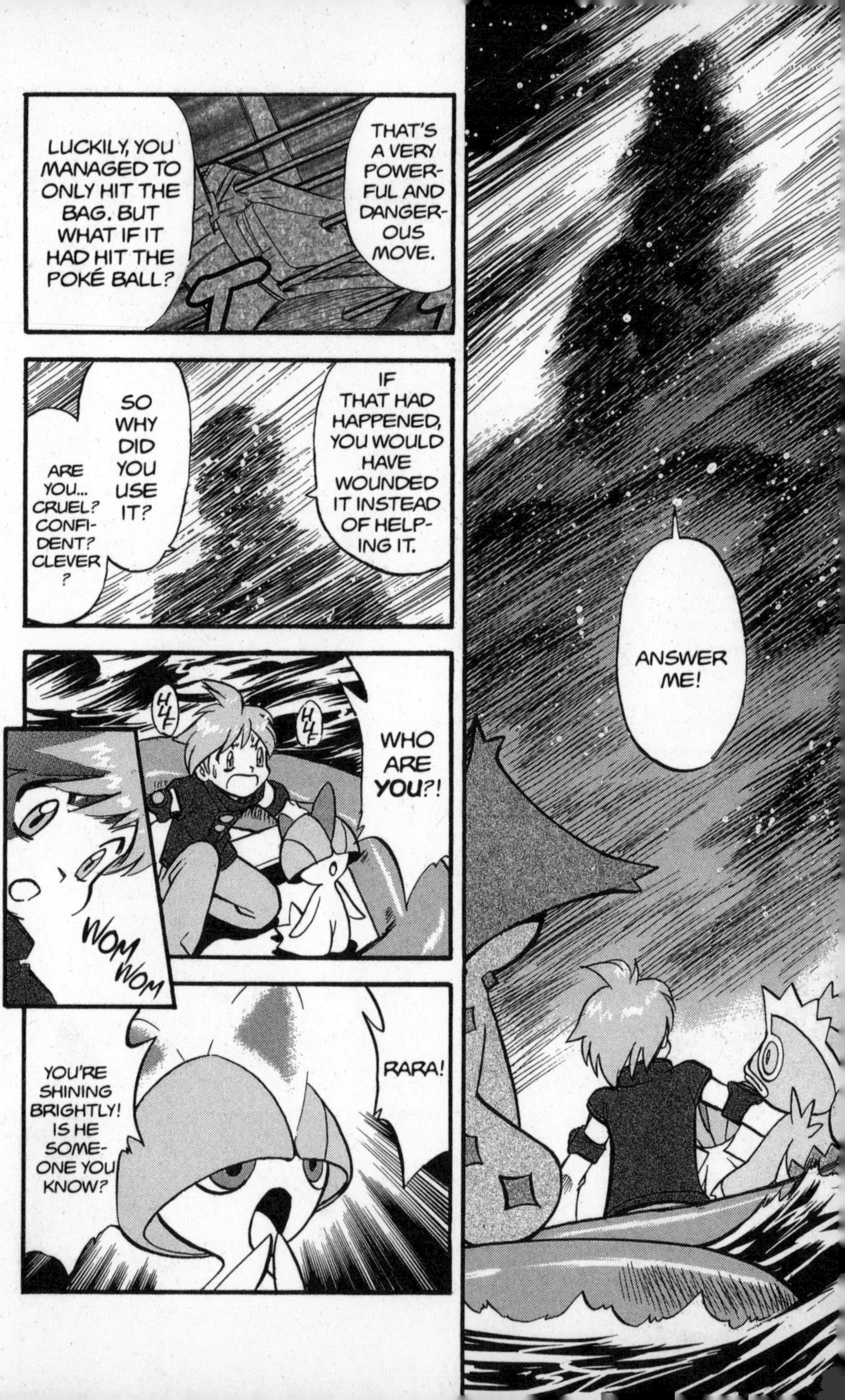

ANSWER ME!
THAT'S A VERY POWERFUL AND DANGEROUS MOVE.
LUCKILY, YOU MANAGED TO ONLY HIT THE BAG. BUT WHAT IF IT HAD HIT THE POKÉ BALL?
IF THAT HAD HAPPENED, YOU WOULD HAVE WOUNDED IT INSTEAD OF HELPING IT.
SO WHY DID YOU USE IT?
ARE YOU... CRUEL? CONFIDENT? CLEVER?
HUF
HUF
WHO ARE YOU?!
WOM WOM
RARA!
YOU'RE SHINING BRIGHTLY! IS HE SOMEONE YOU KNOW?

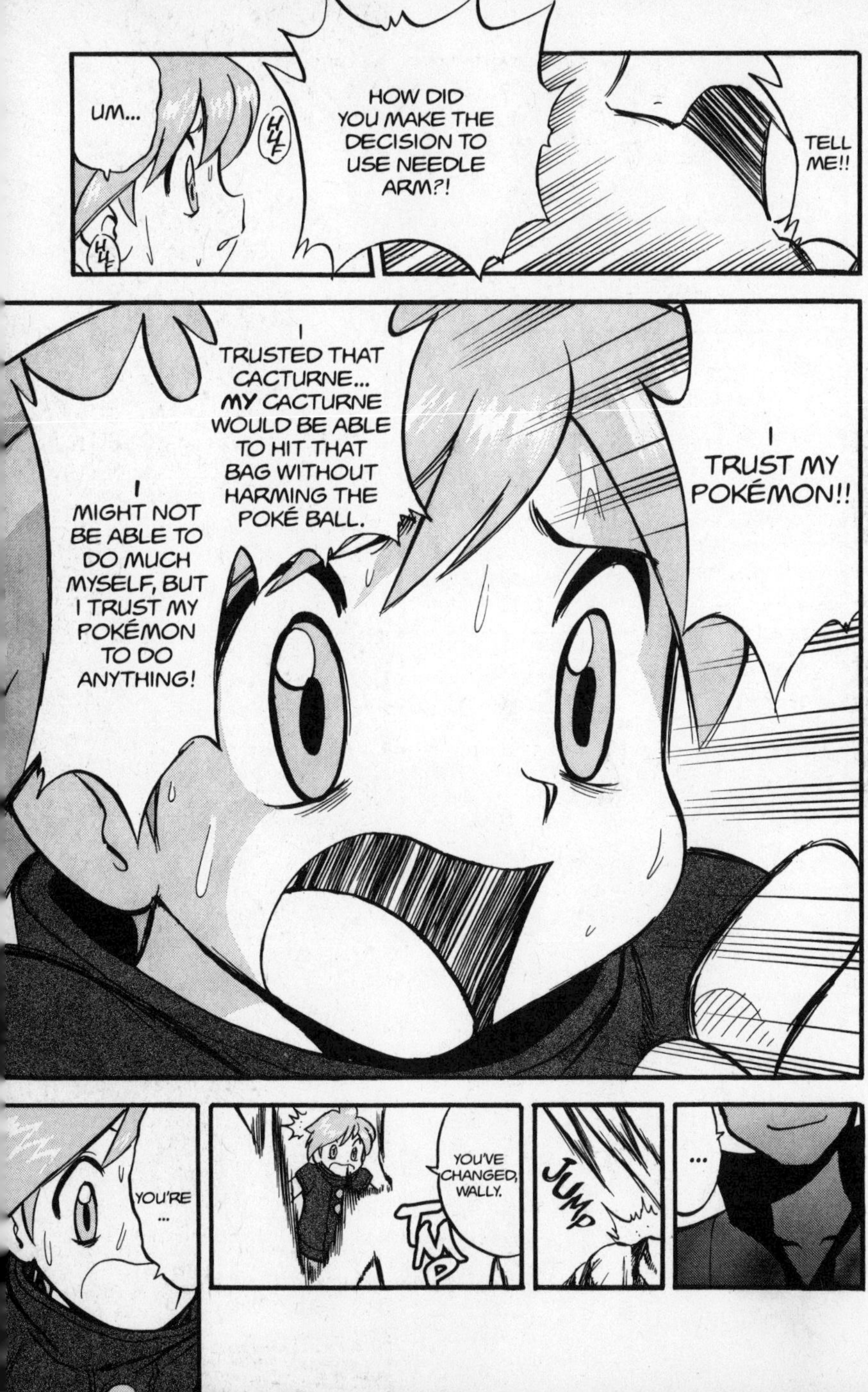
HOW DID YOU MAKE THE DECISION TO USE NEEDLE ARM?!
TELL ME!!
HUF
UM...
HUF
I TRUST MY POKÉMON!!
I TRUSTED THAT CACTURNE... MY CACTURNE WOULD BE ABLE TO HIT THAT BAG WITHOUT HARMING THE POKÉ BALL.
I MIGHT NOT BE ABLE TO DO MUCH MYSELF, BUT I TRUST MY POKÉMON TO DO ANYTHING!
...
JUMP
YOU'VE CHANGED, WALLY.
TMP
YOU'RE ...

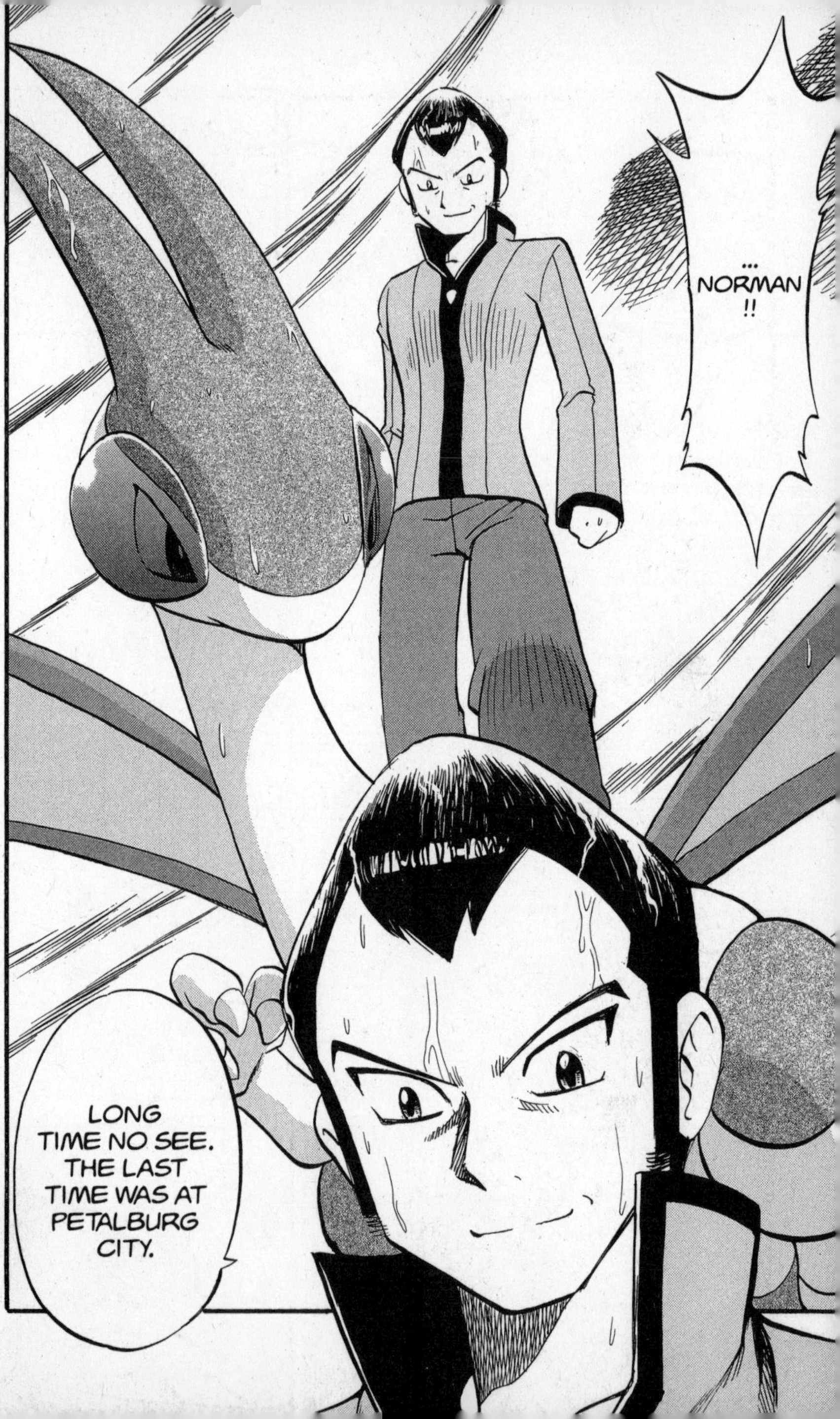
...NORMAN!!
LONG TIME NO SEE. THE LAST TIME WAS AT PETALBURG CITY.

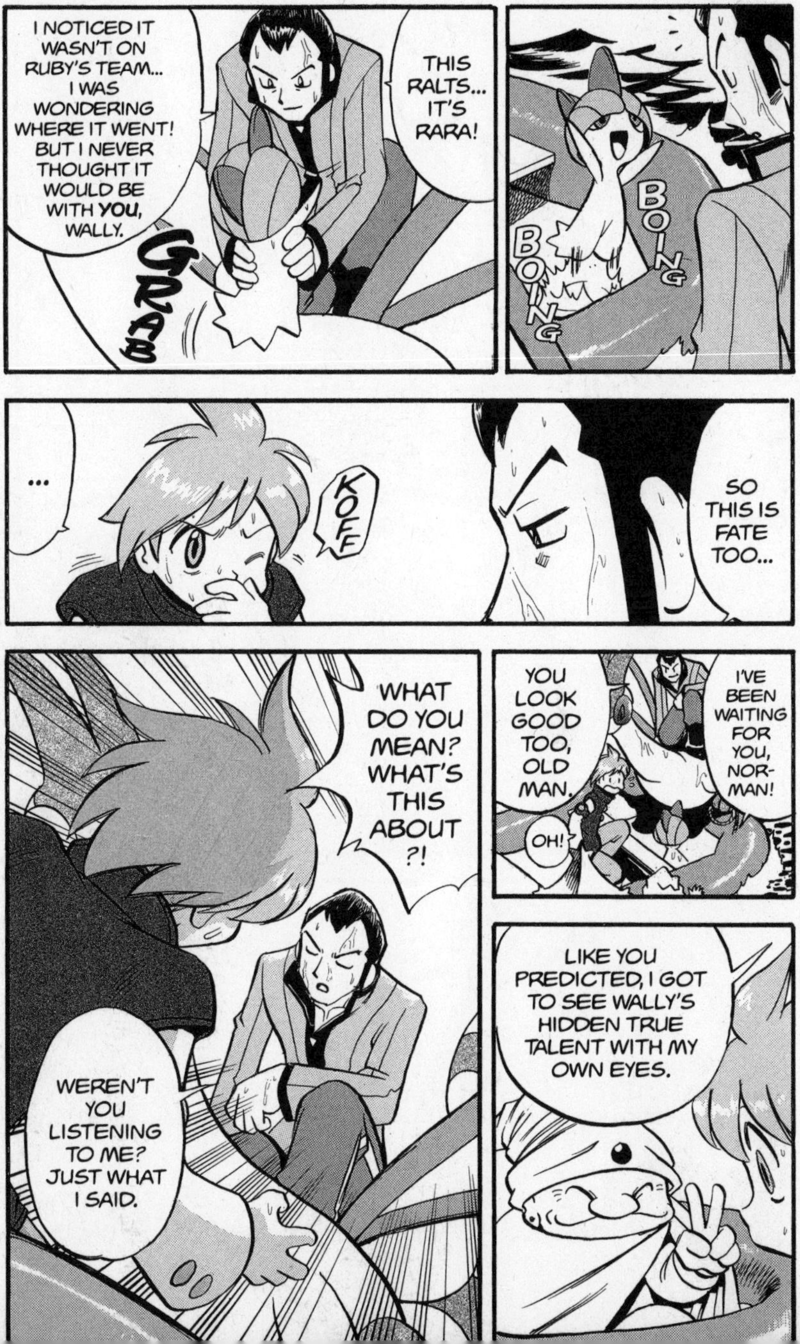
BOING
BOING
THIS RALTS... IT'S RARA!
I NOTICED IT WASN'T ON RUBY'S TEAM... I WAS WONDERING WHERE IT WENT! BUT I NEVER THOUGHT IT WOULD BE WITH **YOU**, WALLY.
GRAB
SO THIS IS FATE TOO...
KOFF
...
I'VE BEEN WAITING FOR YOU, NORMAN!
YOU LOOK GOOD TOO, OLD MAN.
OH!
LIKE YOU PREDICTED, I GOT TO SEE WALLY'S HIDDEN TRUE TALENT WITH MY OWN EYES.
WHAT DO YOU MEAN? WHAT'S THIS ABOUT?!
WEREN'T YOU LISTENING TO ME? JUST WHAT I SAID.

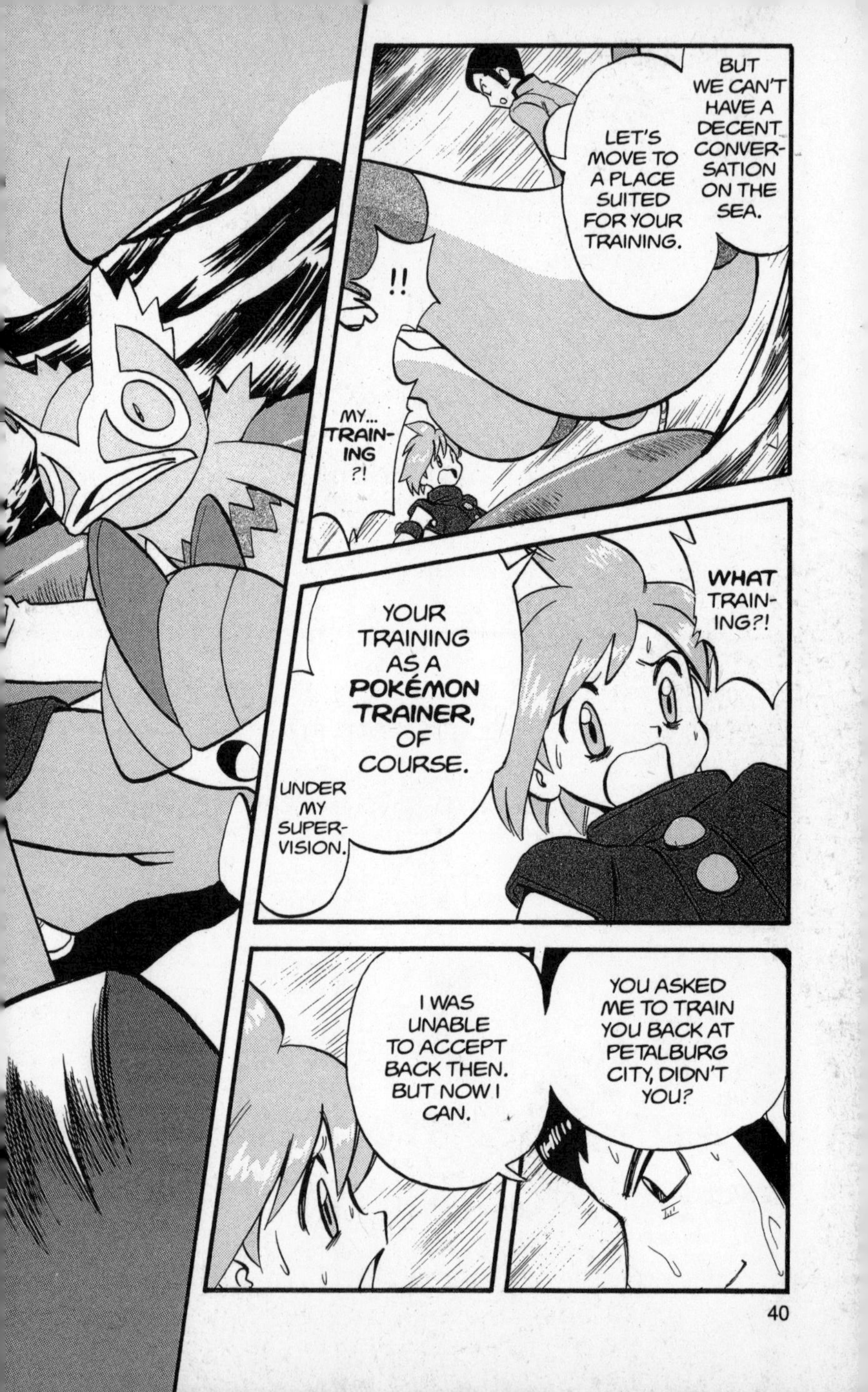
BUT WE CAN'T HAVE A DECENT CONVERSATION ON THE SEA.
LET'S MOVE TO A PLACE SUITED FOR YOUR TRAINING.
!!
MY... TRAINING?!
WHAT TRAINING?!
YOUR TRAINING AS A POKÉMON TRAINER, OF COURSE.
UNDER MY SUPERVISION.
YOU ASKED ME TO TRAIN YOU BACK AT PETALBURG CITY, DIDN'T YOU?
I WAS UNABLE TO ACCEPT BACK THEN. BUT NOW I CAN.

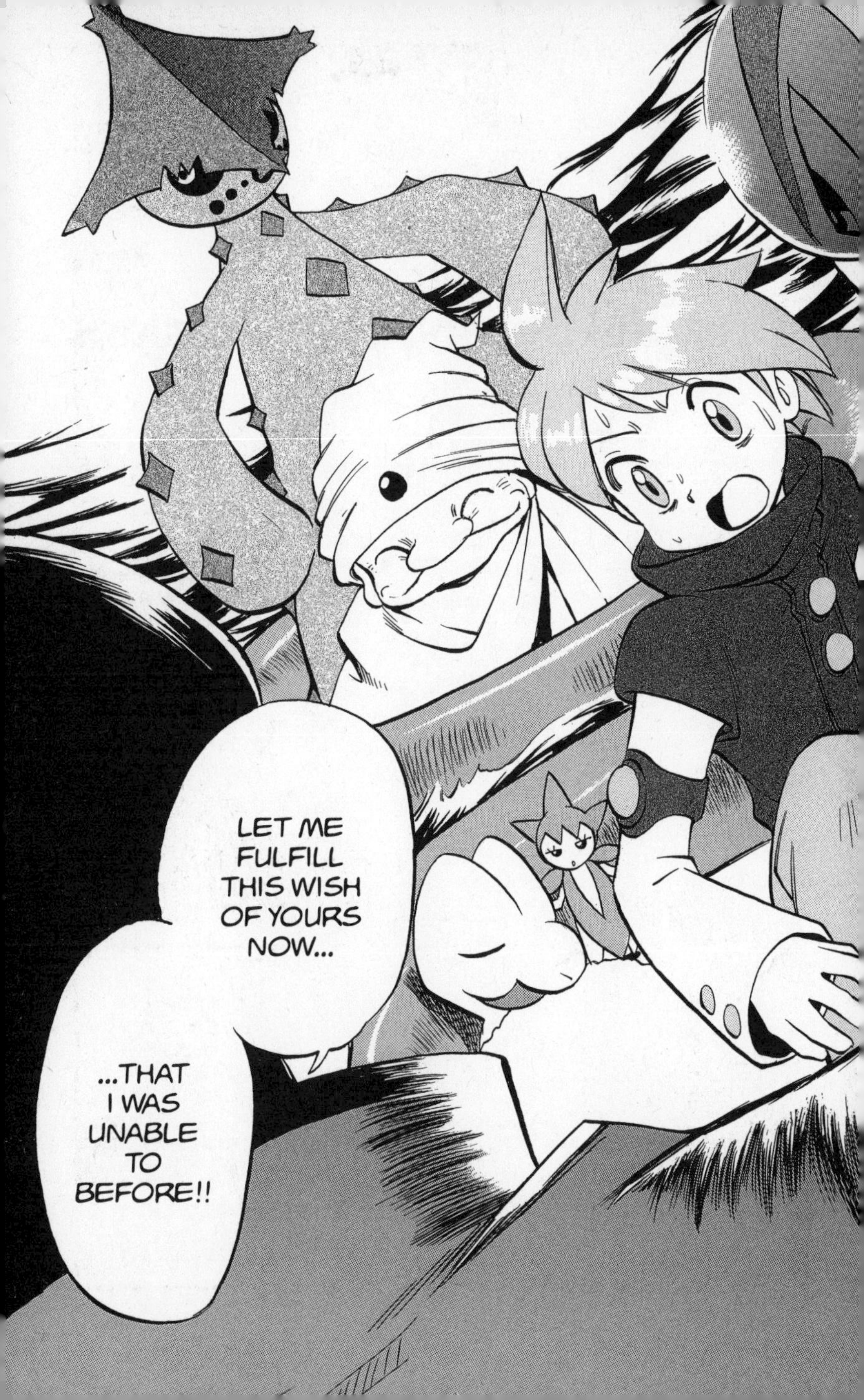
LET ME FULFILL THIS WISH OF YOURS NOW...
...THAT I WAS UNABLE TO BEFORE!!

● Chapter 241 ●
Dreadful Dealing with Dusclops

Pokémon Adventures Ruby & Sapphire ™

The Fourth Chapter

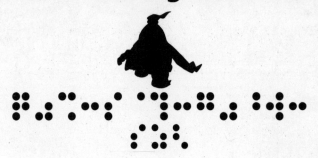

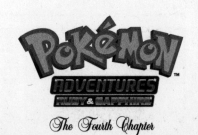

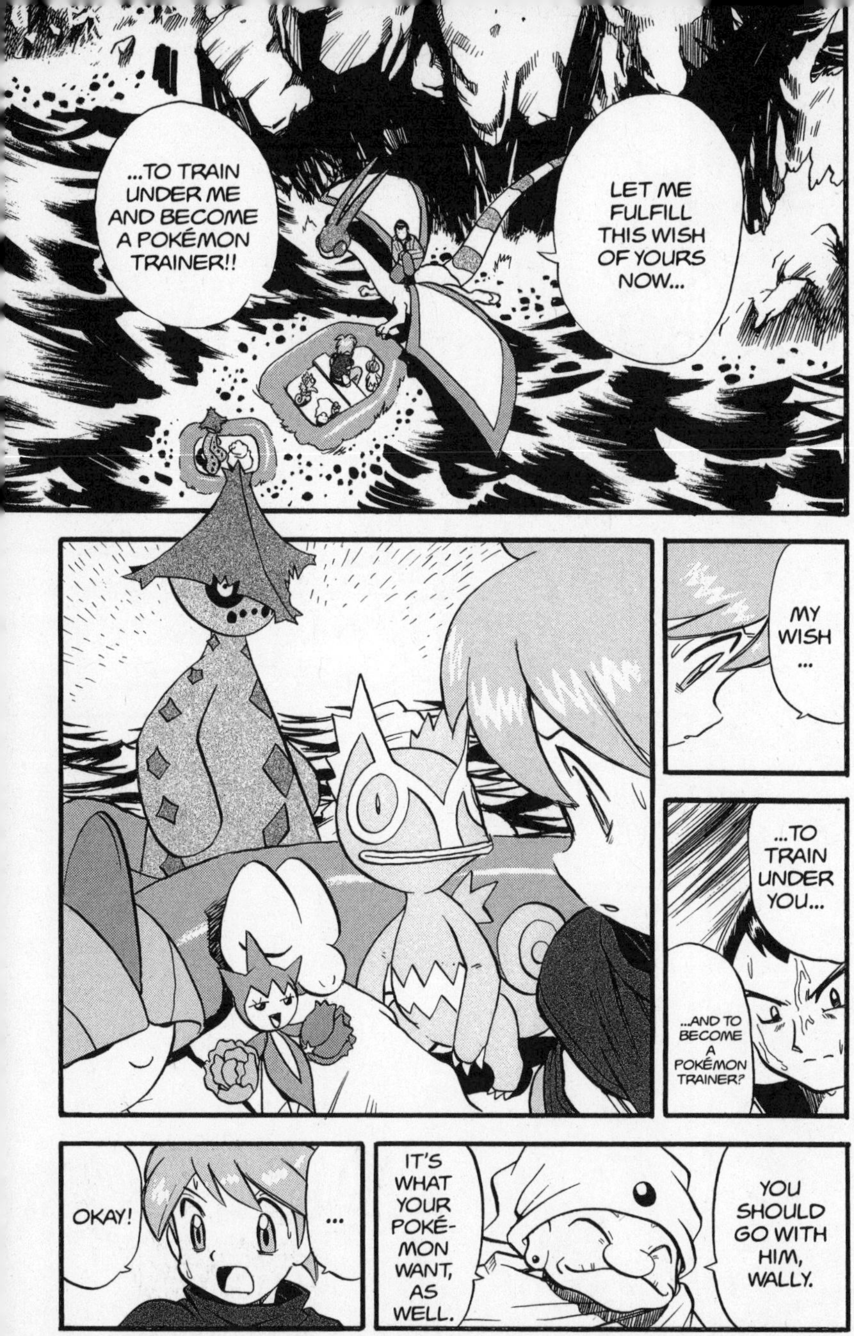
LET ME FULFILL THIS WISH OF YOURS NOW...
...TO TRAIN UNDER ME AND BECOME A POKÉMON TRAINER!!
MY WISH ...
...TO TRAIN UNDER YOU...
...AND TO BECOME A POKÉMON TRAINER?
YOU SHOULD GO WITH HIM, WALLY.
IT'S WHAT YOUR POKÉ-MON WANT, AS WELL.
...
OKAY!

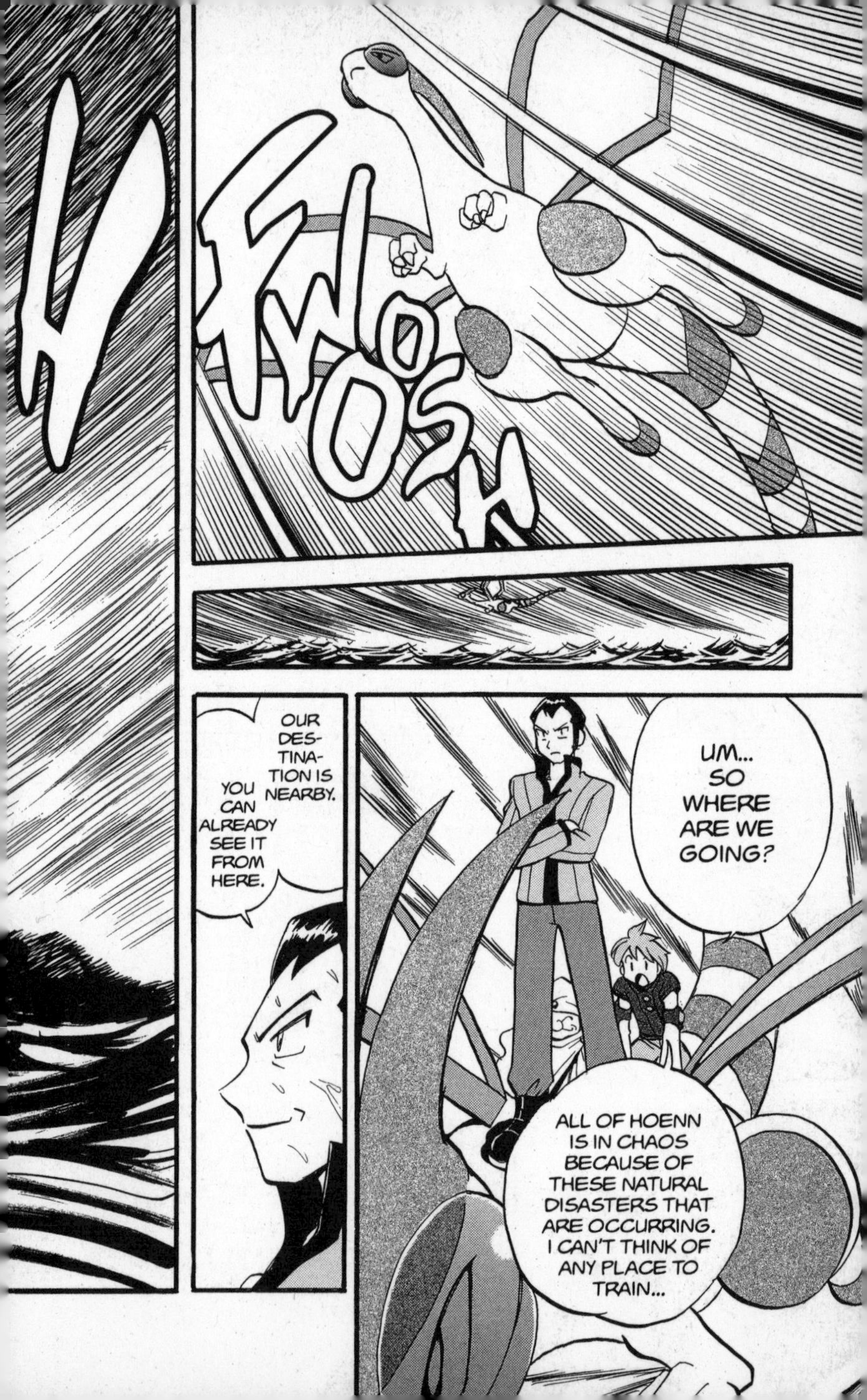
FWOOSH
UM... SO WHERE ARE WE GOING?
ALL OF HOENN IS IN CHAOS BECAUSE OF THESE NATURAL DISASTERS THAT ARE OCCURRING. I CAN'T THINK OF ANY PLACE TO TRAIN...
OUR DESTINATION IS NEARBY.
YOU CAN ALREADY SEE IT FROM HERE.

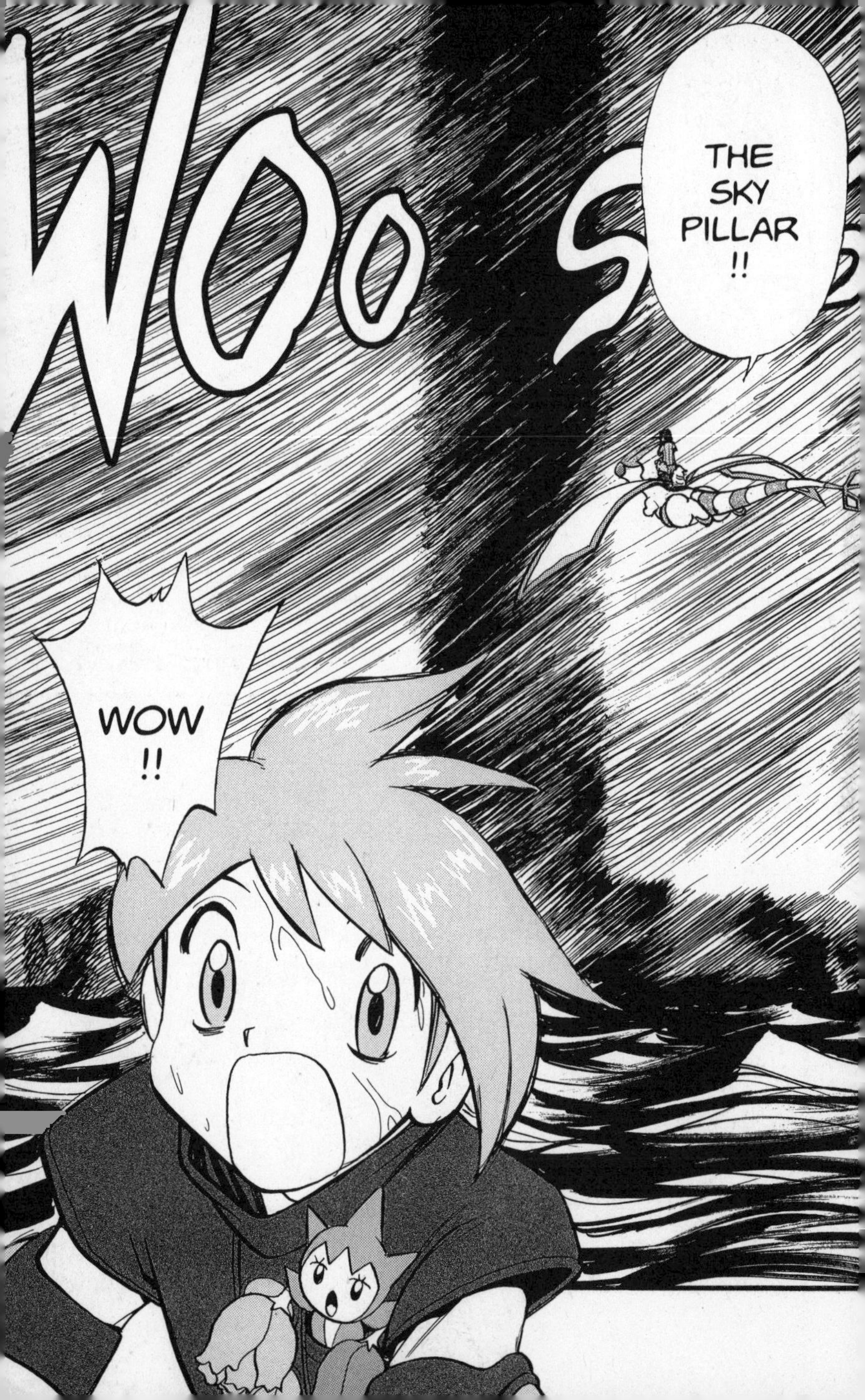
WOOO
THE SKY PILLAR !!
WOW !!

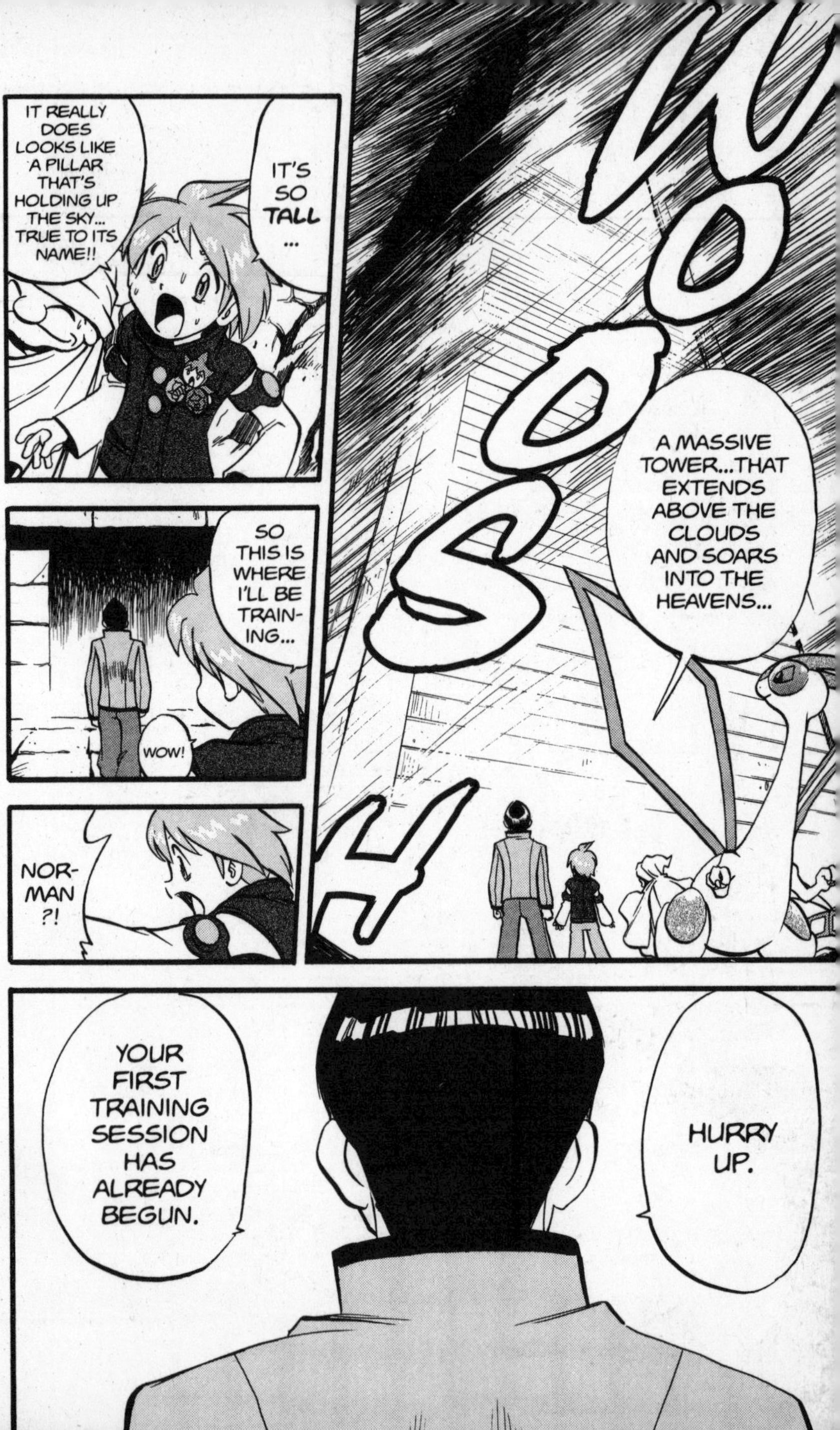
WOOSH
A MASSIVE TOWER...THAT EXTENDS ABOVE THE CLOUDS AND SOARS INTO THE HEAVENS...
IT'S SO **TALL** ...
IT REALLY DOES LOOKS LIKE A PILLAR THAT'S HOLDING UP THE SKY... TRUE TO ITS NAME!!
SO THIS IS WHERE I'LL BE TRAIN-ING...
WOW!
NOR-MAN ?!
HURRY UP.
YOUR FIRST TRAINING SESSION HAS ALREADY BEGUN.

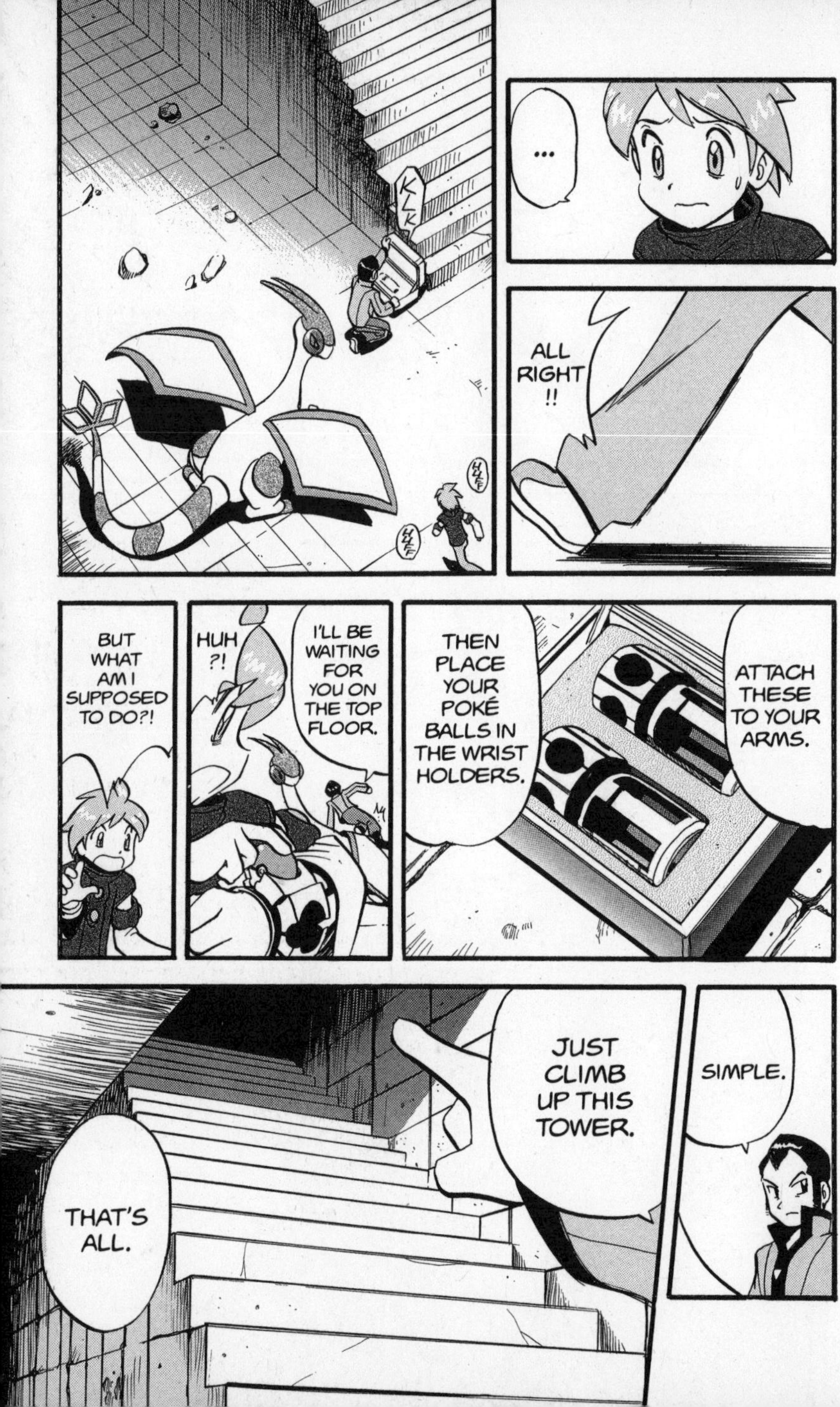
...
ALL RIGHT !!
KLK
HUFF
HUFF
ATTACH THESE TO YOUR ARMS.
THEN PLACE YOUR POKÉ BALLS IN THE WRIST HOLDERS.
I'LL BE WAITING FOR YOU ON THE TOP FLOOR.
HUH ?!
BUT WHAT AM I SUPPOSED TO DO?!
SIMPLE.
JUST CLIMB UP THIS TOWER.
THAT'S ALL.

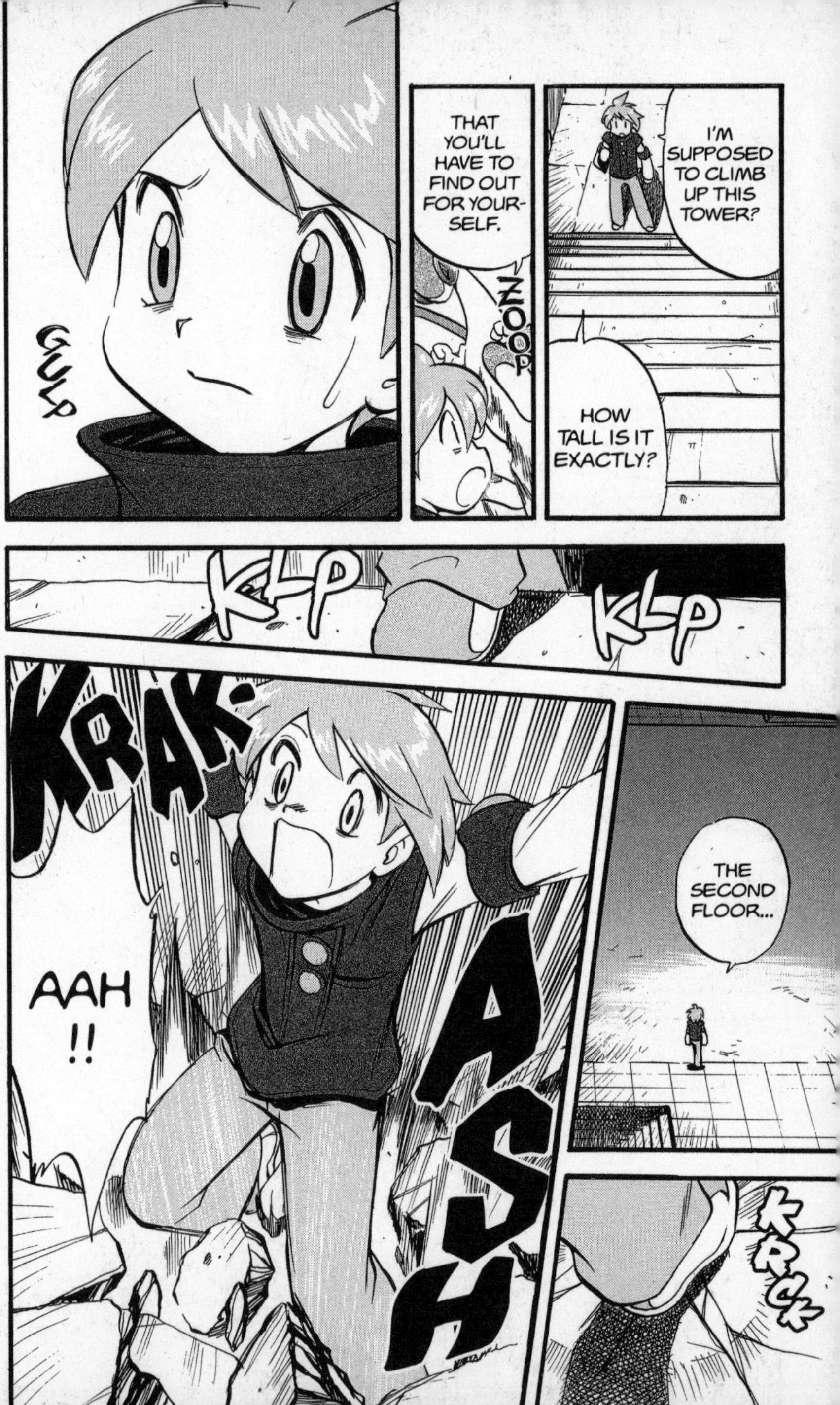
I'M SUPPOSED TO CLIMB UP THIS TOWER?
HOW TALL IS IT EXACTLY?
THAT YOU'LL HAVE TO FIND OUT FOR YOUR-SELF.
ZOOOP
GULP
KLP
KLP
THE SECOND FLOOR...
KRCK
KRAK-
ASH
AAH!!

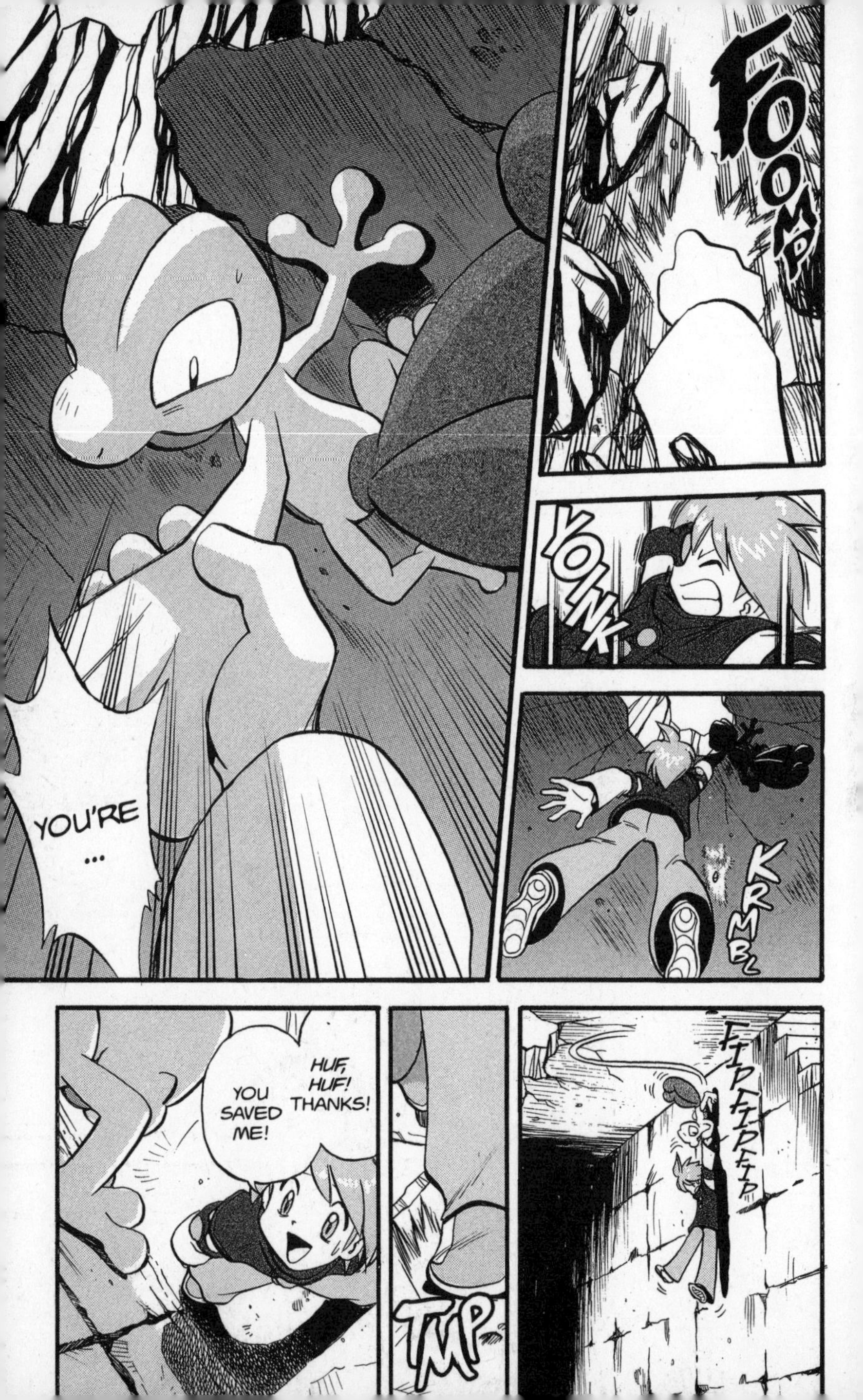
FOOMP
YOINK
KRMBL
YOU'RE ...
FIPFIPFIP
TMP
HUF, HUF! THANKS!
YOU SAVED ME!

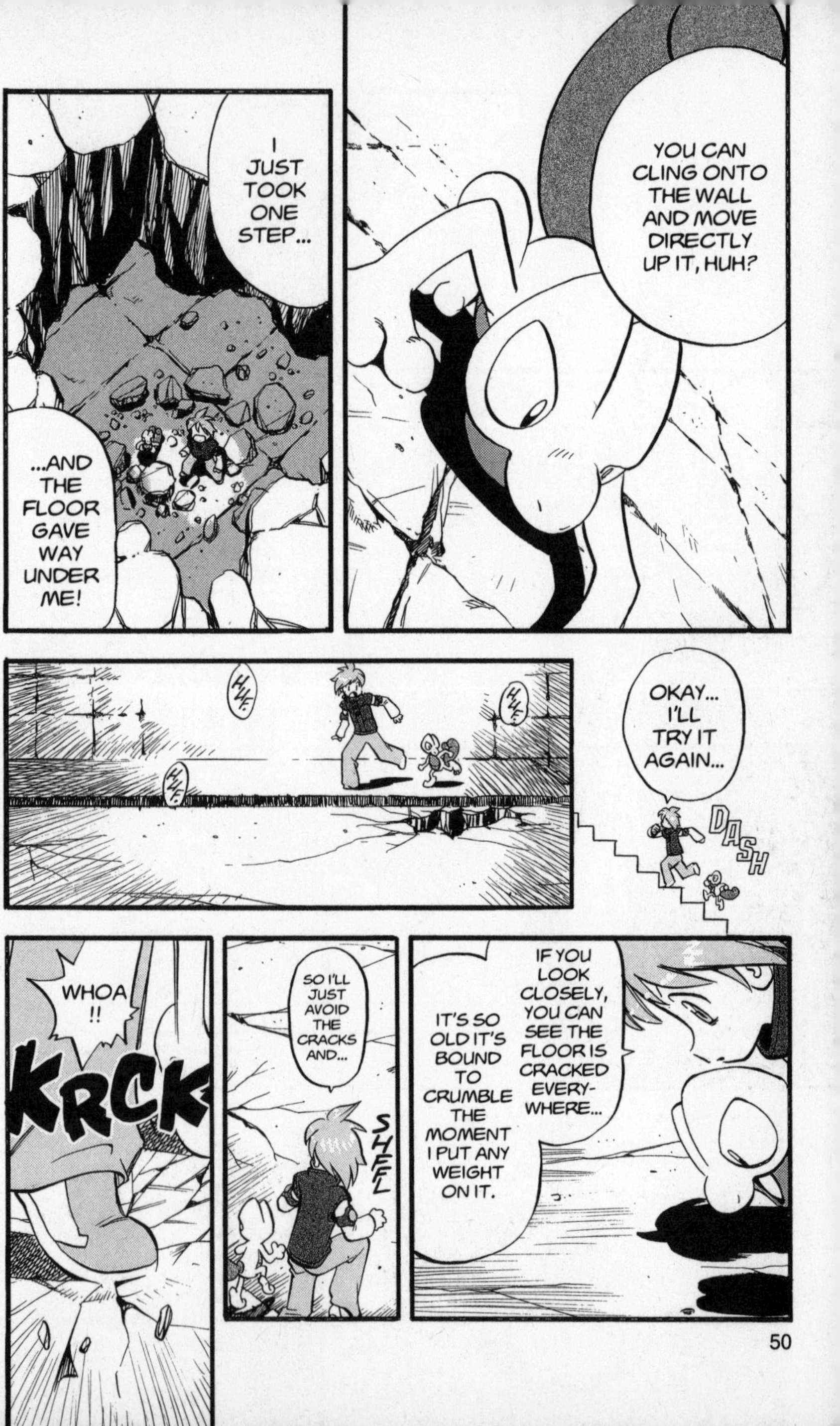
YOU CAN CLING ONTO THE WALL AND MOVE DIRECTLY UP IT, HUH?
I JUST TOOK ONE STEP...
...AND THE FLOOR GAVE WAY UNDER ME!
OKAY... I'LL TRY IT AGAIN...
DASH
HUF
HUF
HUF
IF YOU LOOK CLOSELY, YOU CAN SEE THE FLOOR IS CRACKED EVERY-WHERE...
IT'S SO OLD IT'S BOUND TO CRUMBLE THE MOMENT I PUT ANY WEIGHT ON IT.
SO I'LL JUST AVOID THE CRACKS AND...
SHFFL
WHOA !!
KRCK

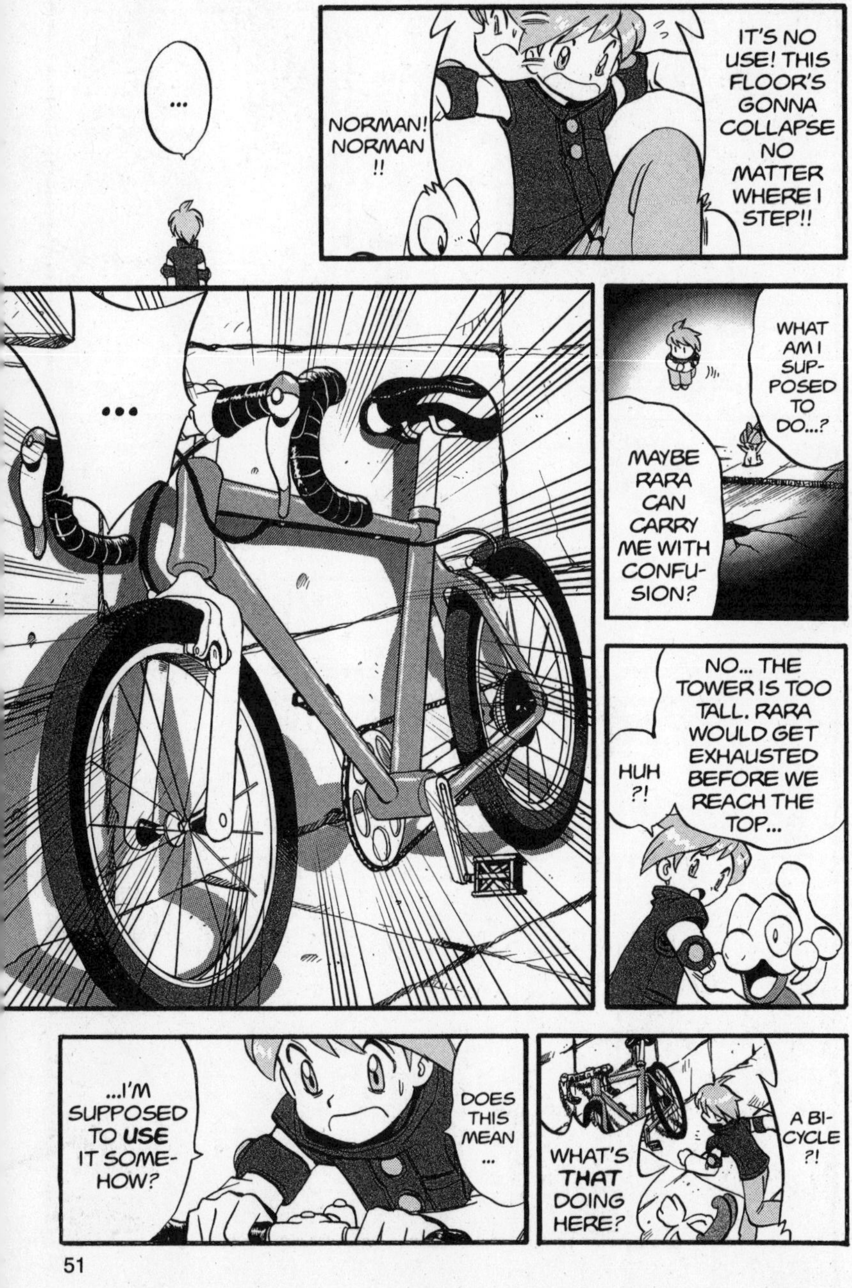
IT'S NO USE! THIS FLOOR'S GONNA COLLAPSE NO MATTER WHERE I STEP!!
NORMAN! NORMAN!!
...
WHAT AM I SUP-POSED TO DO...?
MAYBE RARA CAN CARRY ME WITH CONFU-SION?
NO... THE TOWER IS TOO TALL. RARA WOULD GET EXHAUSTED BEFORE WE REACH THE TOP...
HUH ?!
...
A BI-CYCLE ?!
WHAT'S THAT DOING HERE?
DOES THIS MEAN ...
...I'M SUPPOSED TO USE IT SOME-HOW?

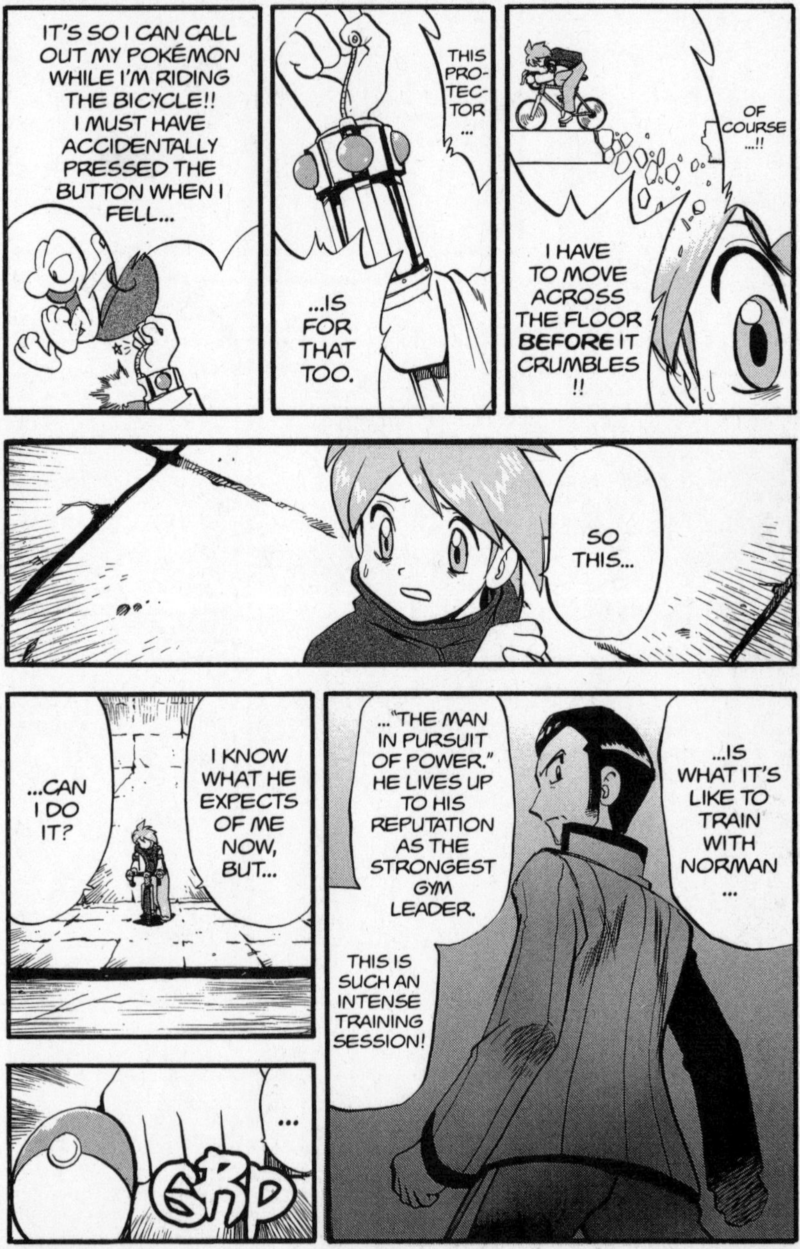
OF COURSE ...!!
I HAVE TO MOVE ACROSS THE FLOOR BEFORE IT CRUMBLES !!
THIS PROTECTOR ...
...IS FOR THAT TOO.
IT'S SO I CAN CALL OUT MY POKÉMON WHILE I'M RIDING THE BICYCLE!! I MUST HAVE ACCIDENTALLY PRESSED THE BUTTON WHEN I FELL...
SO THIS...
...IS WHAT IT'S LIKE TO TRAIN WITH NORMAN ...
..."THE MAN IN PURSUIT OF POWER." HE LIVES UP TO HIS REPUTATION AS THE STRONGEST GYM LEADER.
THIS IS SUCH AN INTENSE TRAINING SESSION!
I KNOW WHAT HE EXPECTS OF ME NOW, BUT...
...CAN I DO IT?
...
GRP

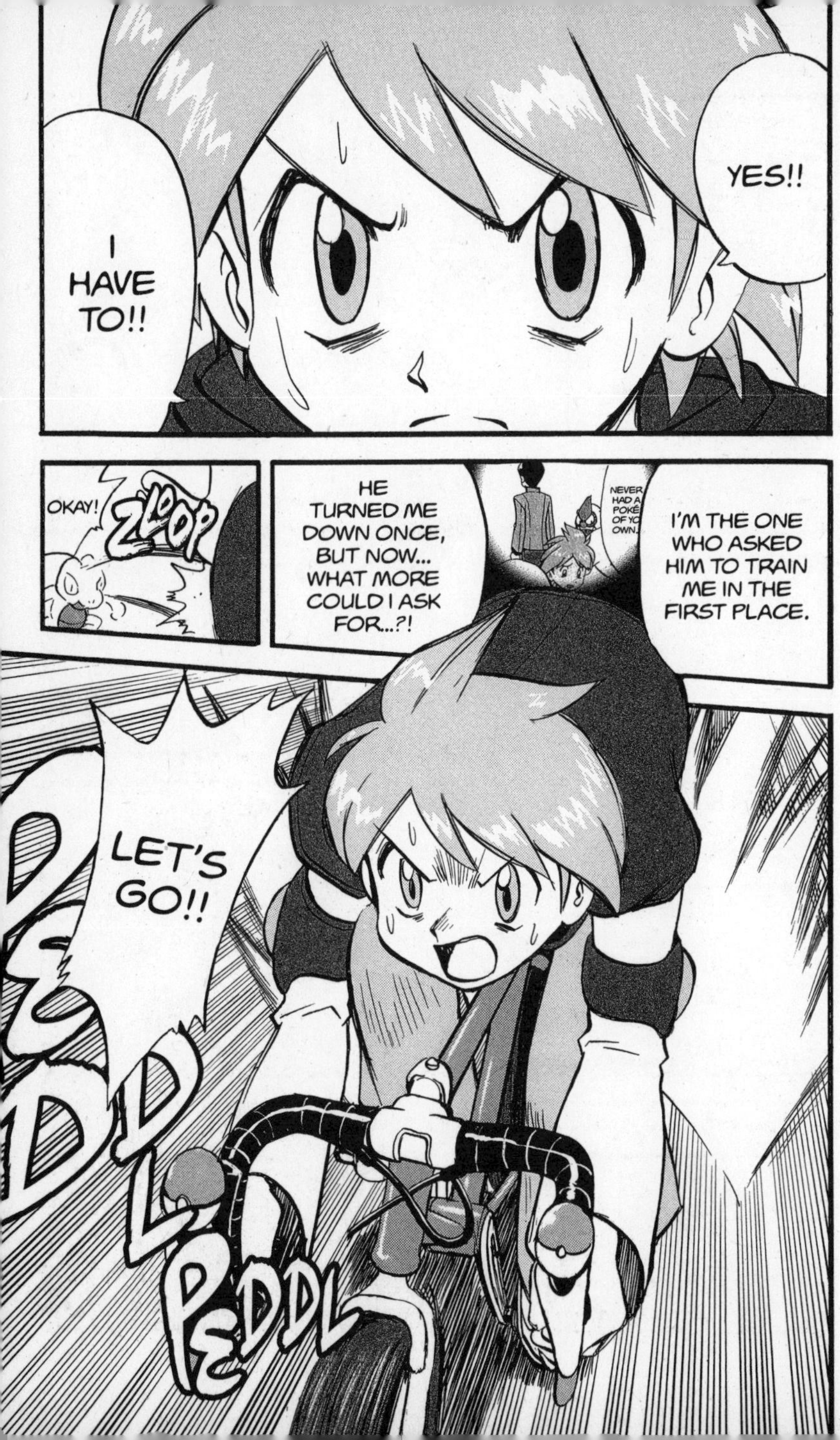
YES!!
I HAVE TO!!
I'M THE ONE WHO ASKED HIM TO TRAIN ME IN THE FIRST PLACE.
HE TURNED ME DOWN ONCE, BUT NOW... WHAT MORE COULD I ASK FOR...?!
OKAY!
ZLOOP
LET'S GO!!
PEDDL

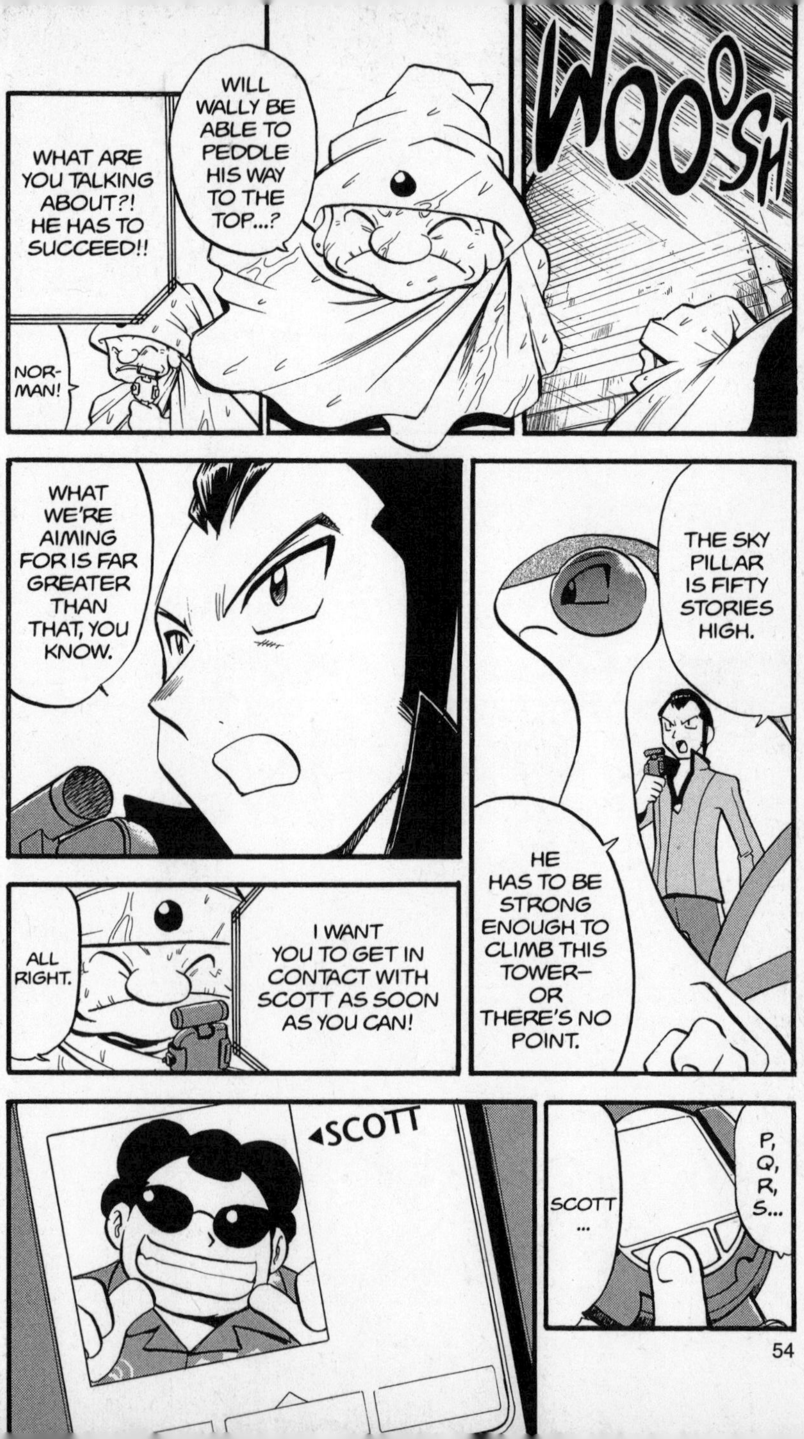
WOOOSH
WILL WALLY BE ABLE TO PEDDLE HIS WAY TO THE TOP...?
WHAT ARE YOU TALKING ABOUT?! HE HAS TO SUCCEED!!
NOR-MAN!
THE SKY PILLAR IS FIFTY STORIES HIGH.
HE HAS TO BE STRONG ENOUGH TO CLIMB THIS TOWER—OR THERE'S NO POINT.
WHAT WE'RE AIMING FOR IS FAR GREATER THAN THAT, YOU KNOW.
I WANT YOU TO GET IN CONTACT WITH SCOTT AS SOON AS YOU CAN!
ALL RIGHT.
P, Q, R, S...
SCOTT ...
◂SCOTT

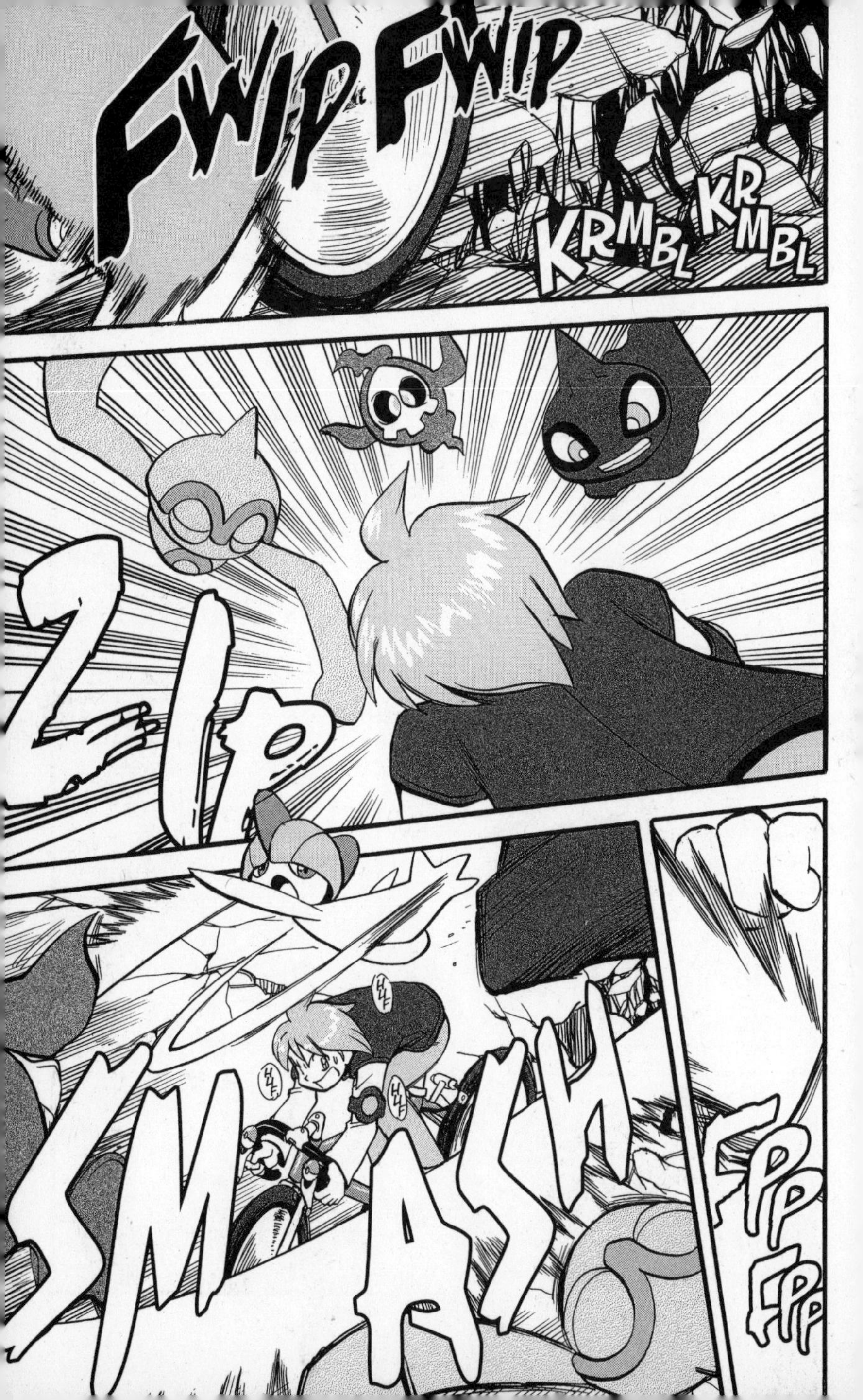
FWIP FWIP
KRMBL KRMBL
ZIP
FPP FPP
HUF
HUF
HUF
SMASH

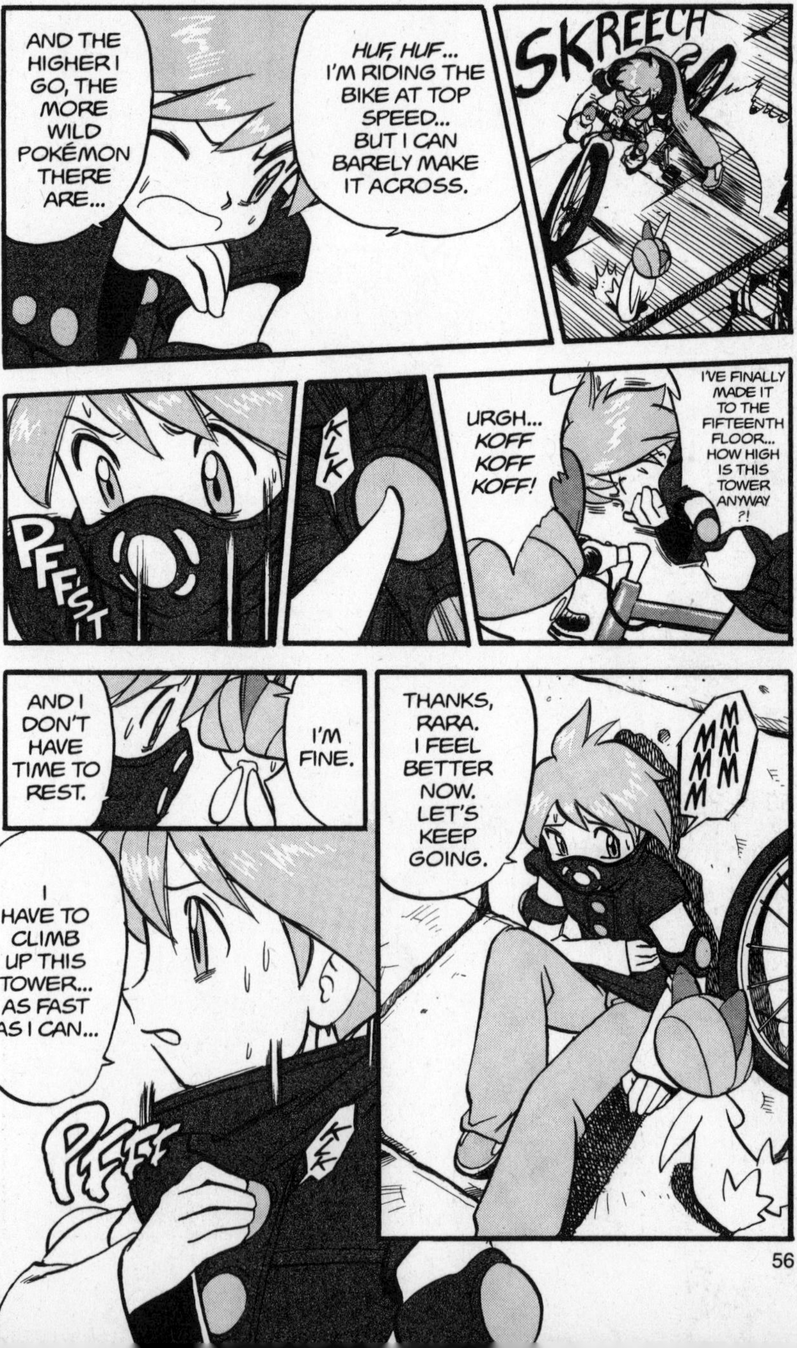
SKREECH
HUF, HUF... I'M RIDING THE BIKE AT TOP SPEED... BUT I CAN BARELY MAKE IT ACROSS.
AND THE HIGHER I GO, THE MORE WILD POKÉMON THERE ARE...
I'VE FINALLY MADE IT TO THE FIFTEENTH FLOOR... HOW HIGH IS THIS TOWER ANYWAY?!
URGH... KOFF KOFF KOFF!
KLK
PFFST
THANKS, RARA. I FEEL BETTER NOW. LET'S KEEP GOING.
MMMMMMMMM
I'M FINE.
AND I DON'T HAVE TIME TO REST.
I HAVE TO CLIMB UP THIS TOWER... AS FAST AS I CAN...
KLK
PFFFF

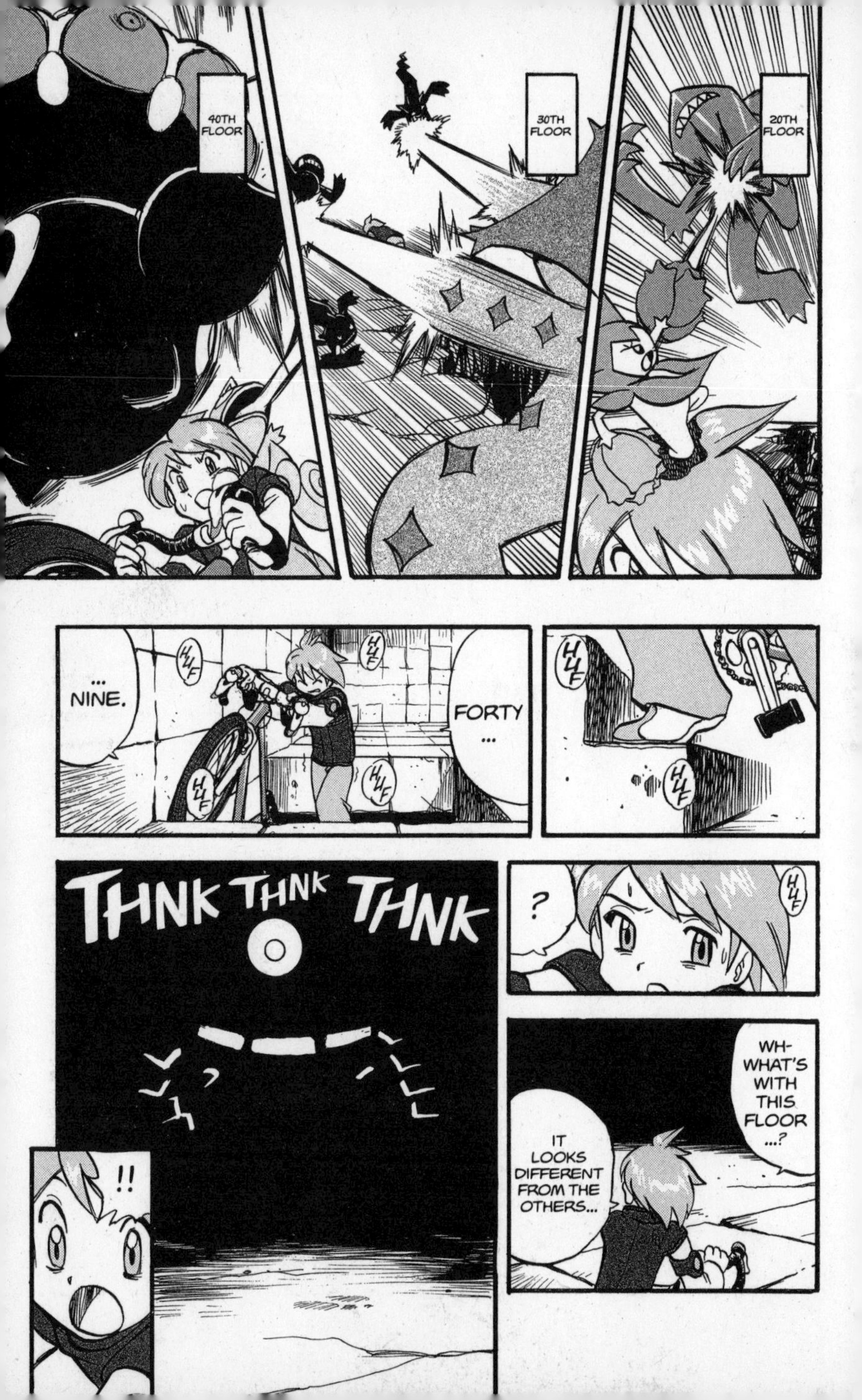
20TH FLOOR
30TH FLOOR
40TH FLOOR
HUF
HUF
HUF
FORTY ...
HUF
... NINE.
HUF
HUF
?
WH-WHAT'S WITH THIS FLOOR ...?
IT LOOKS DIFFERENT FROM THE OTHERS...
THNK THNK THNK
!!

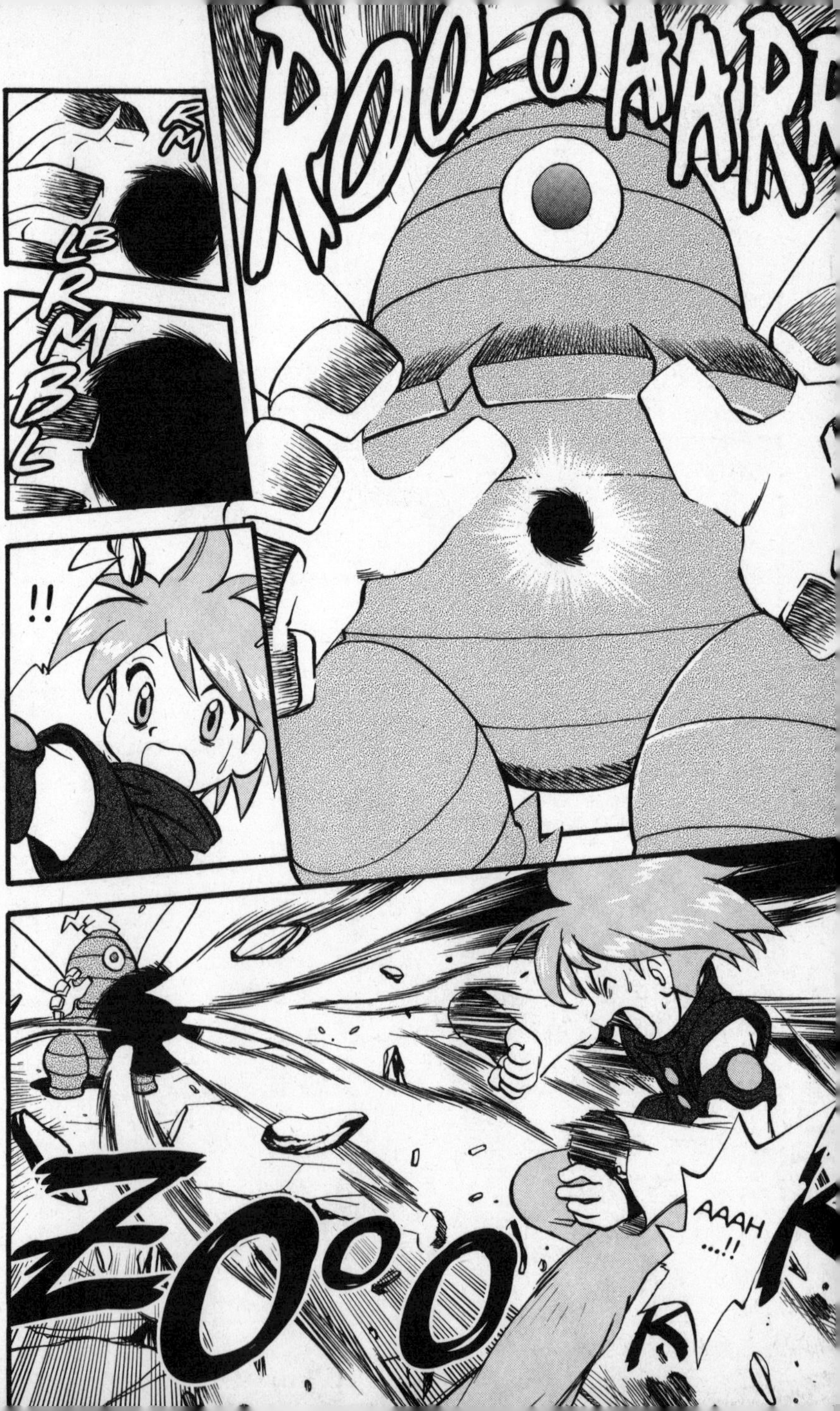
ROO-OAARR
BLRMBL
!!
AAAH ...!!
ZOOO

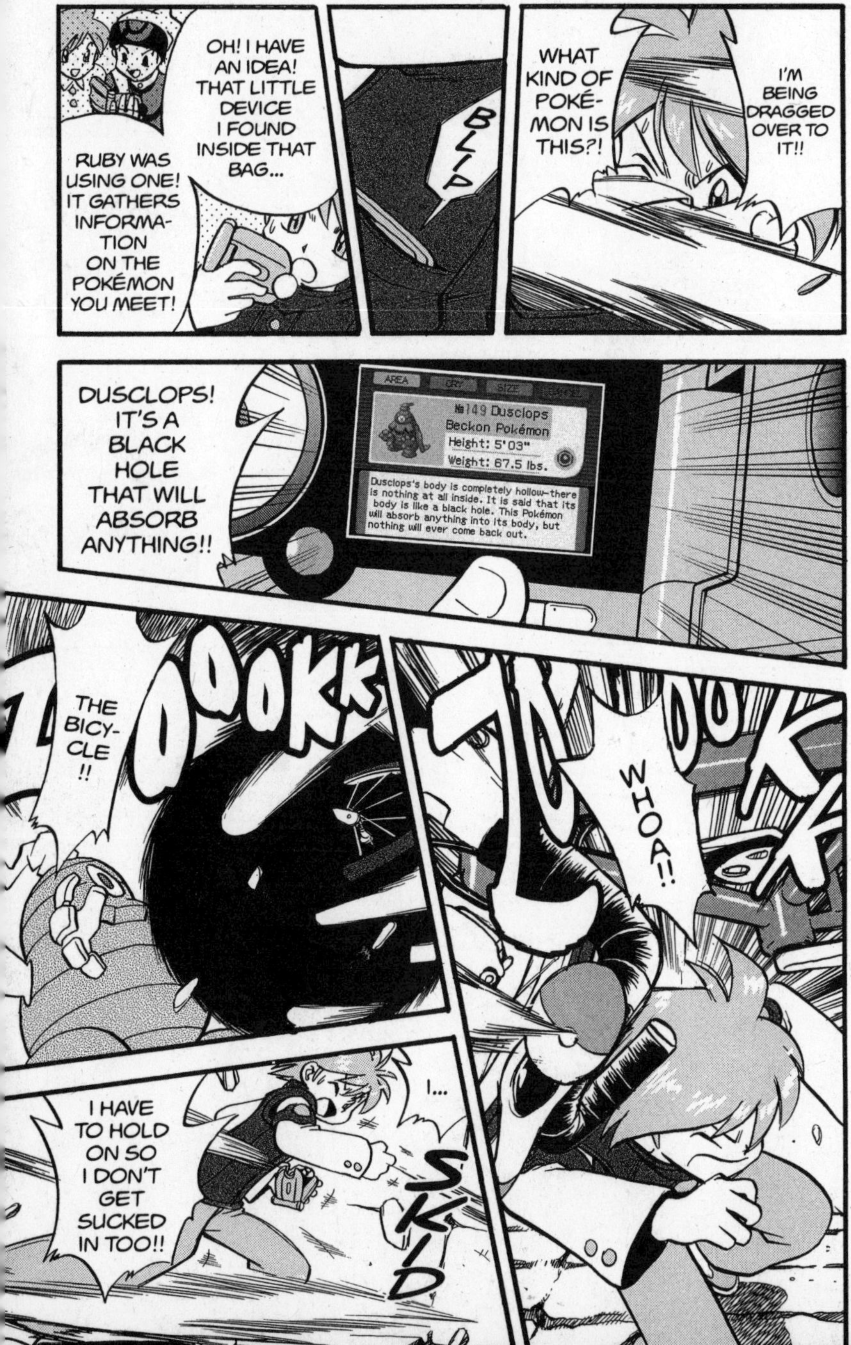
I'M BEING DRAGGED OVER TO IT!!
WHAT KIND OF POKÉ-MON IS THIS?!
BLIP
OH! I HAVE AN IDEA! THAT LITTLE DEVICE I FOUND INSIDE THAT BAG...
RUBY WAS USING ONE! IT GATHERS INFORMA-TION ON THE POKÉMON YOU MEET!
AREA
CRY
SIZE
№149 Dusclops
Beckon Pokémon
Height: 5'03"
Weight: 67.5 lbs.
Dusclops's body is completely hollow—there is nothing at all inside. It is said that its body is like a black hole. This Pokémon will absorb anything into its body, but nothing will ever come back out.
DUSCLOPS! IT'S A BLACK HOLE THAT WILL ABSORB ANYTHING!!
DOOKK
WHOA!!
DOOKK
THE BICY-CLE!!
I...
SKID
I HAVE TO HOLD ON SO I DON'T GET SUCKED IN TOO!!

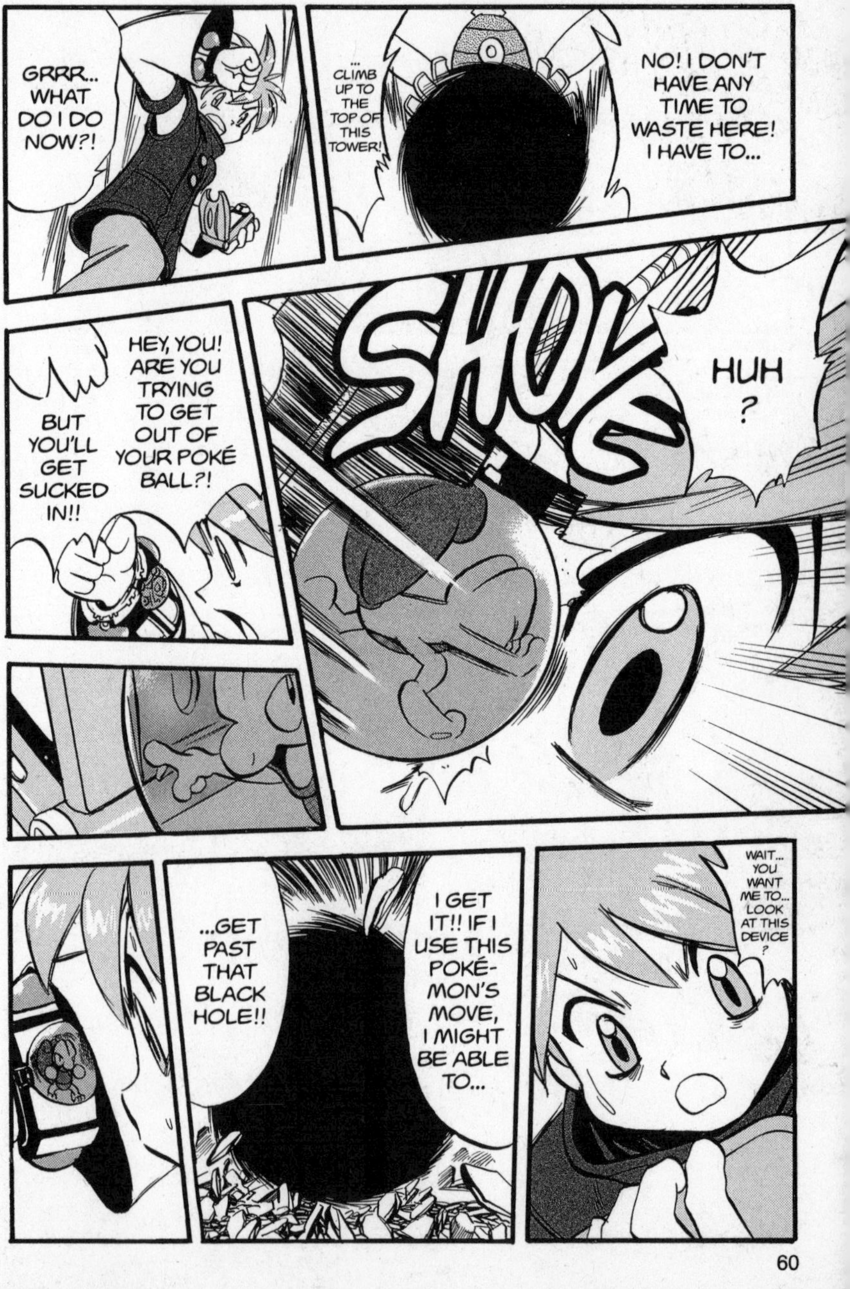
NO! I DON'T HAVE ANY TIME TO WASTE HERE! I HAVE TO...
...CLIMB UP TO THE TOP OF THIS TOWER!
GRRR... WHAT DO I DO NOW?!
HUH?
SHOO
HEY, YOU! ARE YOU TRYING TO GET OUT OF YOUR POKÉ BALL?!
BUT YOU'LL GET SUCKED IN!!
WAIT... YOU WANT ME TO... LOOK AT THIS DEVICE?
I GET IT!! IF I USE THIS POKÉMON'S MOVE, I MIGHT BE ABLE TO...
...GET PAST THAT BLACK HOLE!!

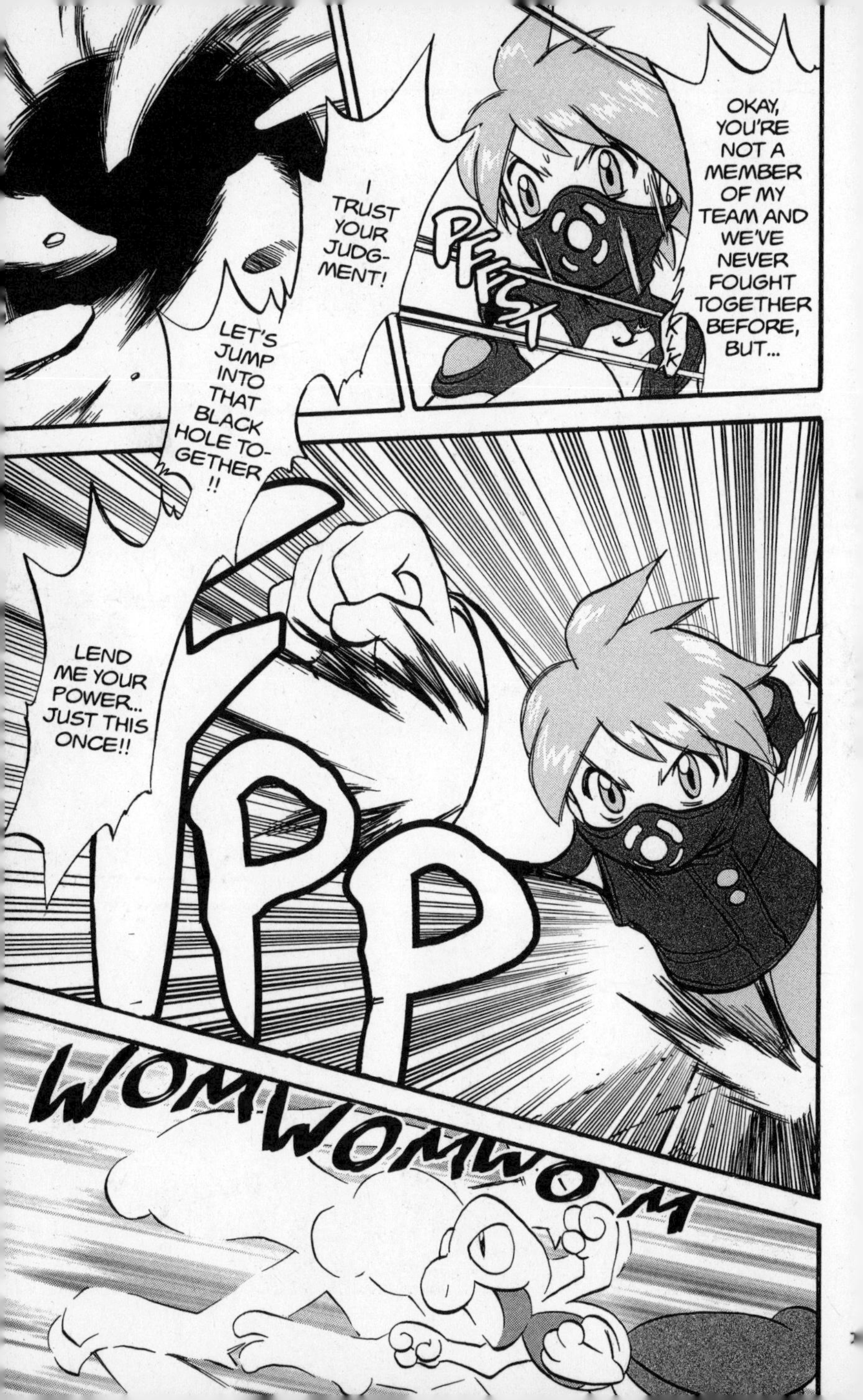
OKAY, YOU'RE NOT A MEMBER OF MY TEAM AND WE'VE NEVER FOUGHT TOGETHER BEFORE, BUT...
PFFST
KLK
I TRUST YOUR JUDG-MENT!
LET'S JUMP INTO THAT BLACK HOLE TO-GETHER!!
LEND ME YOUR POWER... JUST THIS ONCE!!
WOMWOMWOM

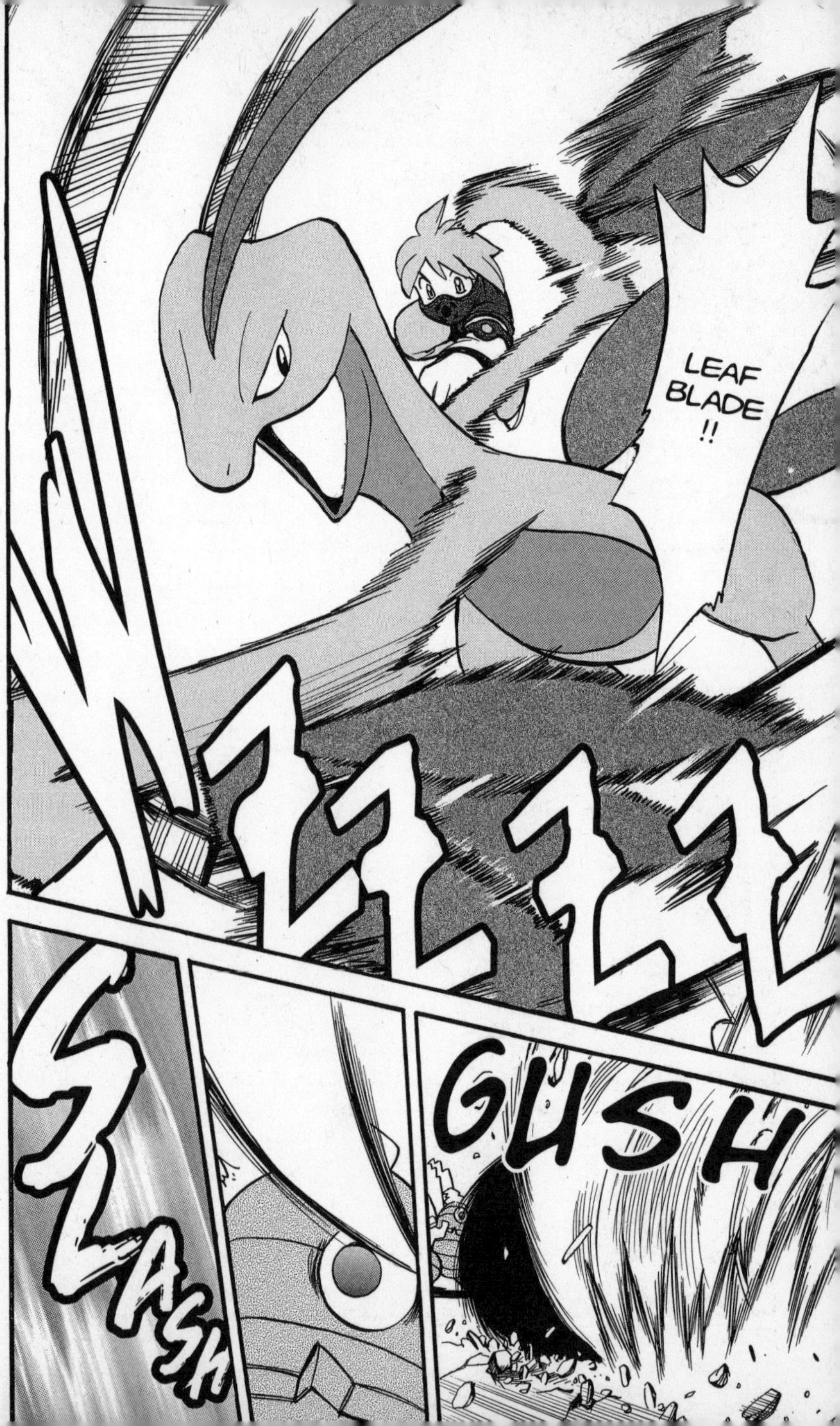
LEAF BLADE !!
GUSH
SLASH

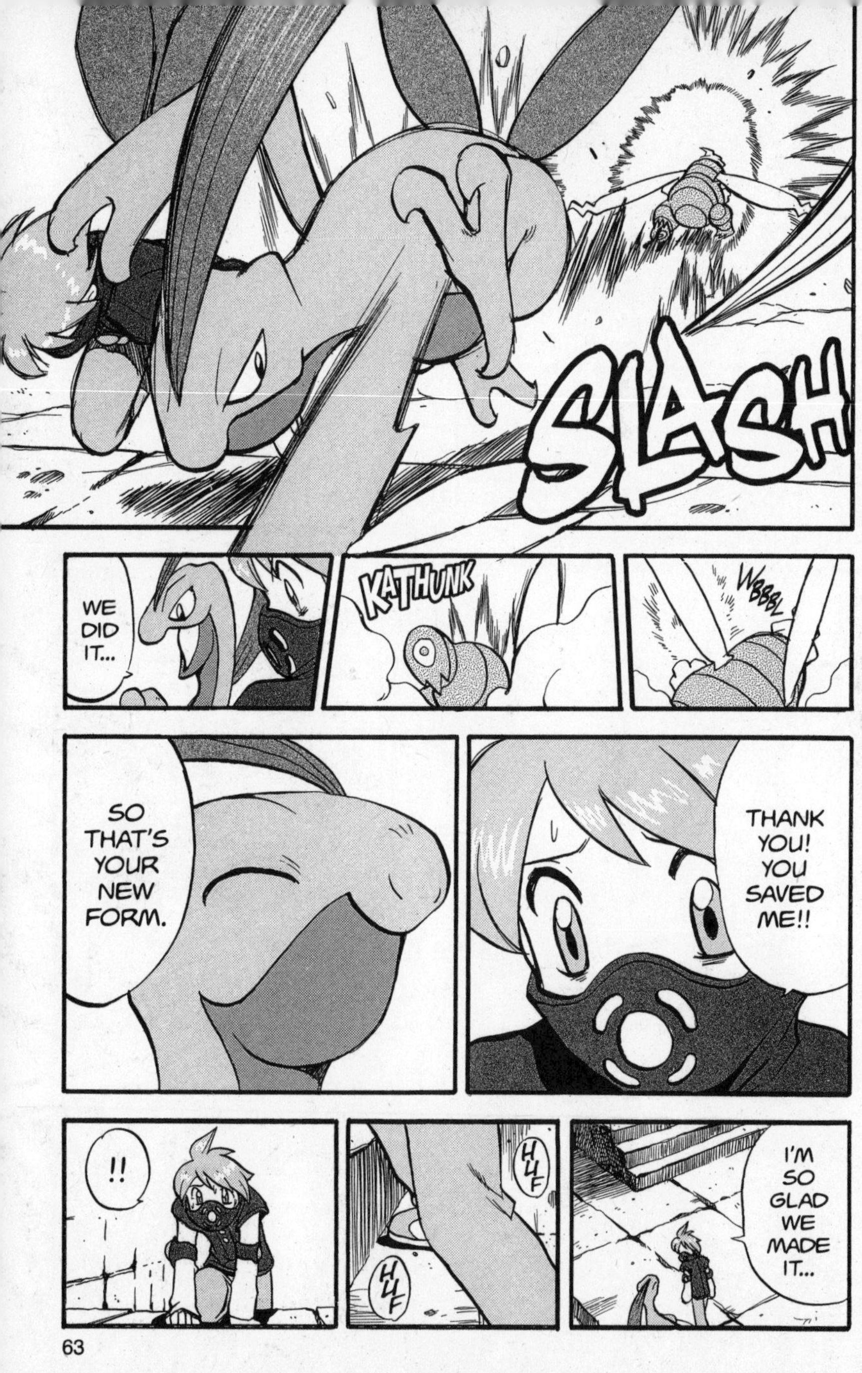
SLASH
WBBBL
KATHUNK
WE DID IT...
THANK YOU! YOU SAVED ME!!
SO THAT'S YOUR NEW FORM.
I'M SO GLAD WE MADE IT...
HUF
HUF
!!

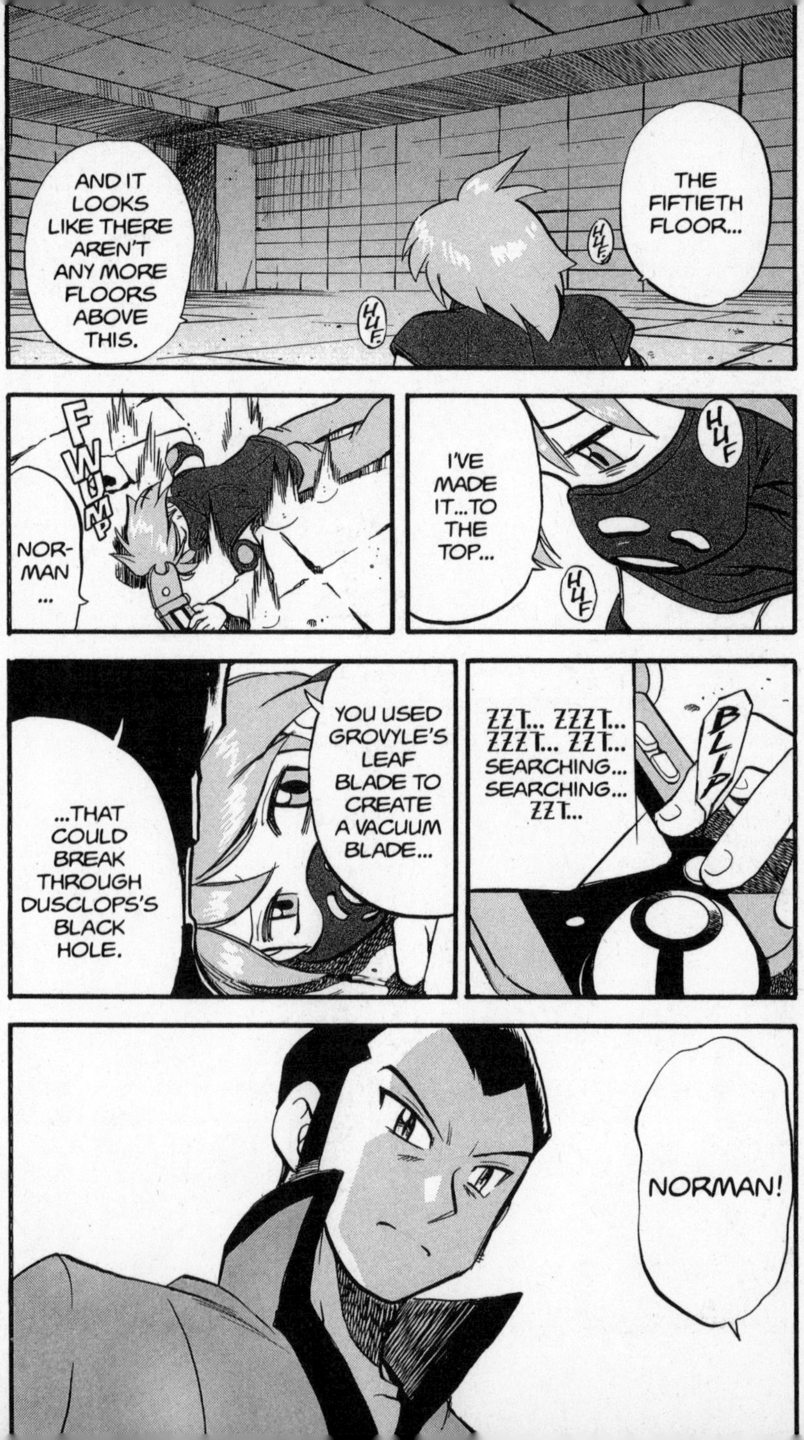
THE FIFTIETH FLOOR...
HUF
HUF
AND IT LOOKS LIKE THERE AREN'T ANY MORE FLOORS ABOVE THIS.
HUF
I'VE MADE IT...TO THE TOP...
HUF
FWUMP
NOR-MAN ...
BLIP
ZZT... ZZZT... ZZZT... ZZT... SEARCHING... SEARCHING... ZZT...
YOU USED GROVYLE'S LEAF BLADE TO CREATE A VACUUM BLADE...
...THAT COULD BREAK THROUGH DUSCLOPS'S BLACK HOLE.
NORMAN!

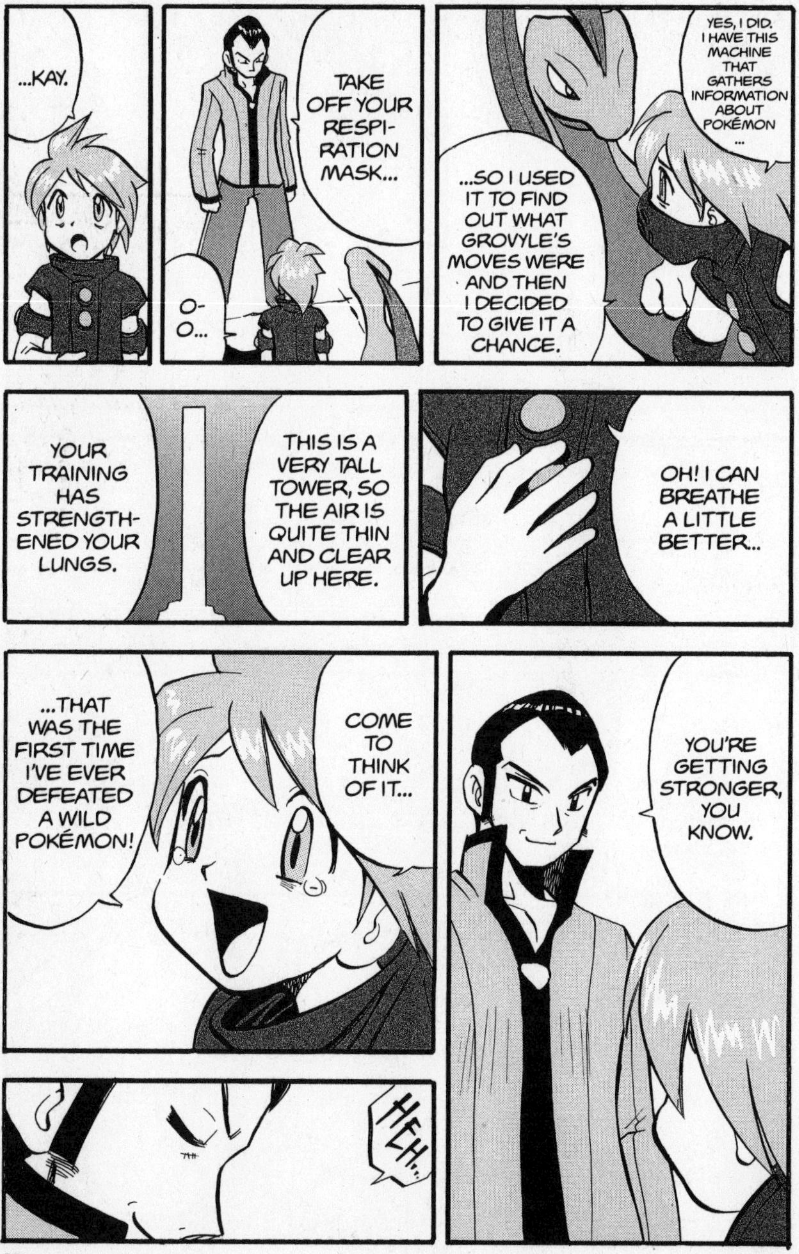
YES, I DID. I HAVE THIS MACHINE THAT GATHERS INFORMATION ABOUT POKÉMON ...
...SO I USED IT TO FIND OUT WHAT GROVYLE'S MOVES WERE AND THEN I DECIDED TO GIVE IT A CHANCE.
TAKE OFF YOUR RESPI-RATION MASK...
O-O...
...KAY.
OH! I CAN BREATHE A LITTLE BETTER...
THIS IS A VERY TALL TOWER, SO THE AIR IS QUITE THIN AND CLEAR UP HERE.
YOUR TRAINING HAS STRENGTH-ENED YOUR LUNGS.
YOU'RE GETTING STRONGER, YOU KNOW.
COME TO THINK OF IT...
...THAT WAS THE FIRST TIME I'VE EVER DEFEATED A WILD POKÉMON!
HEH...

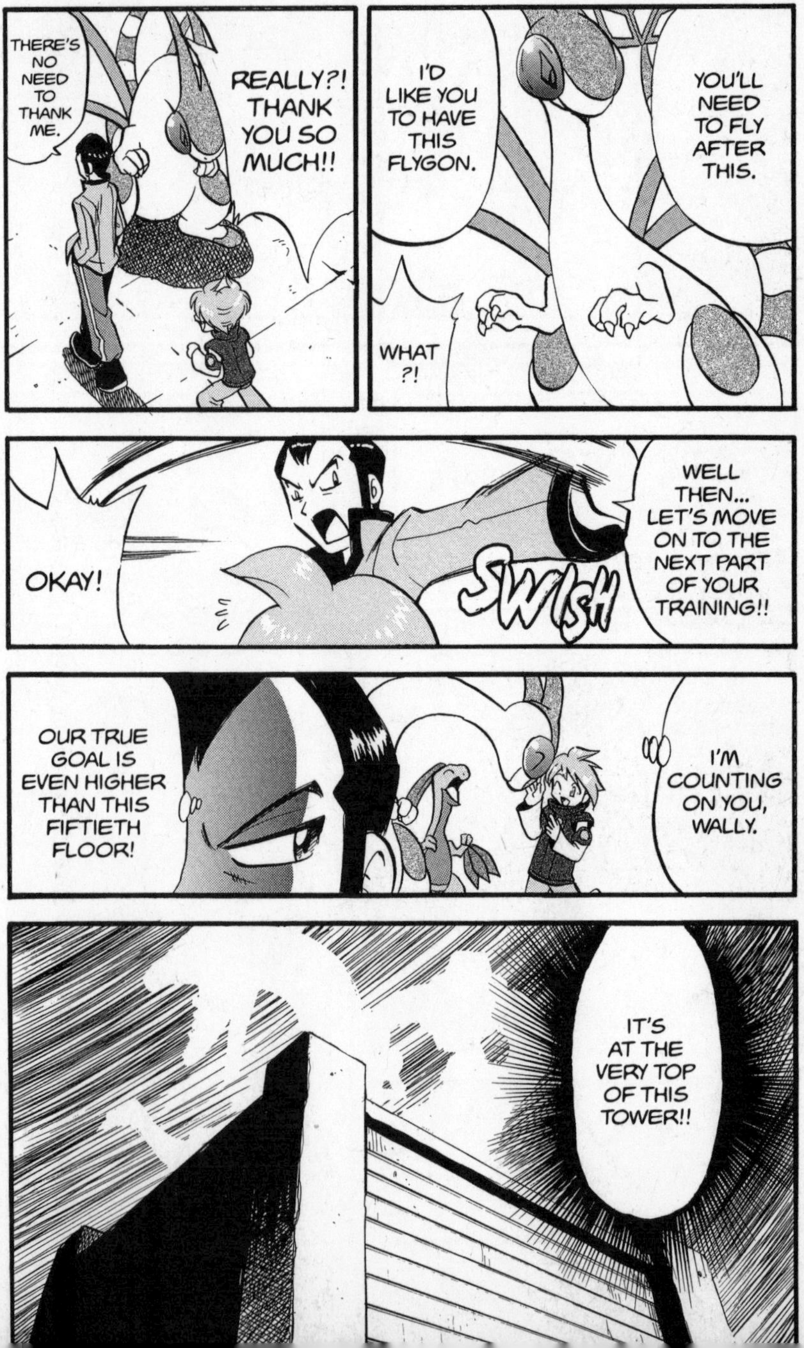
YOU'LL NEED TO FLY AFTER THIS.
I'D LIKE YOU TO HAVE THIS FLYGON.
WHAT?!
REALLY?! THANK YOU SO MUCH!!
THERE'S NO NEED TO THANK ME.
WELL THEN... LET'S MOVE ON TO THE NEXT PART OF YOUR TRAINING!!
SWISH
OKAY!
I'M COUNTING ON YOU, WALLY.
OUR TRUE GOAL IS EVEN HIGHER THAN THIS FIFTIETH FLOOR!
IT'S AT THE VERY TOP OF THIS TOWER!!

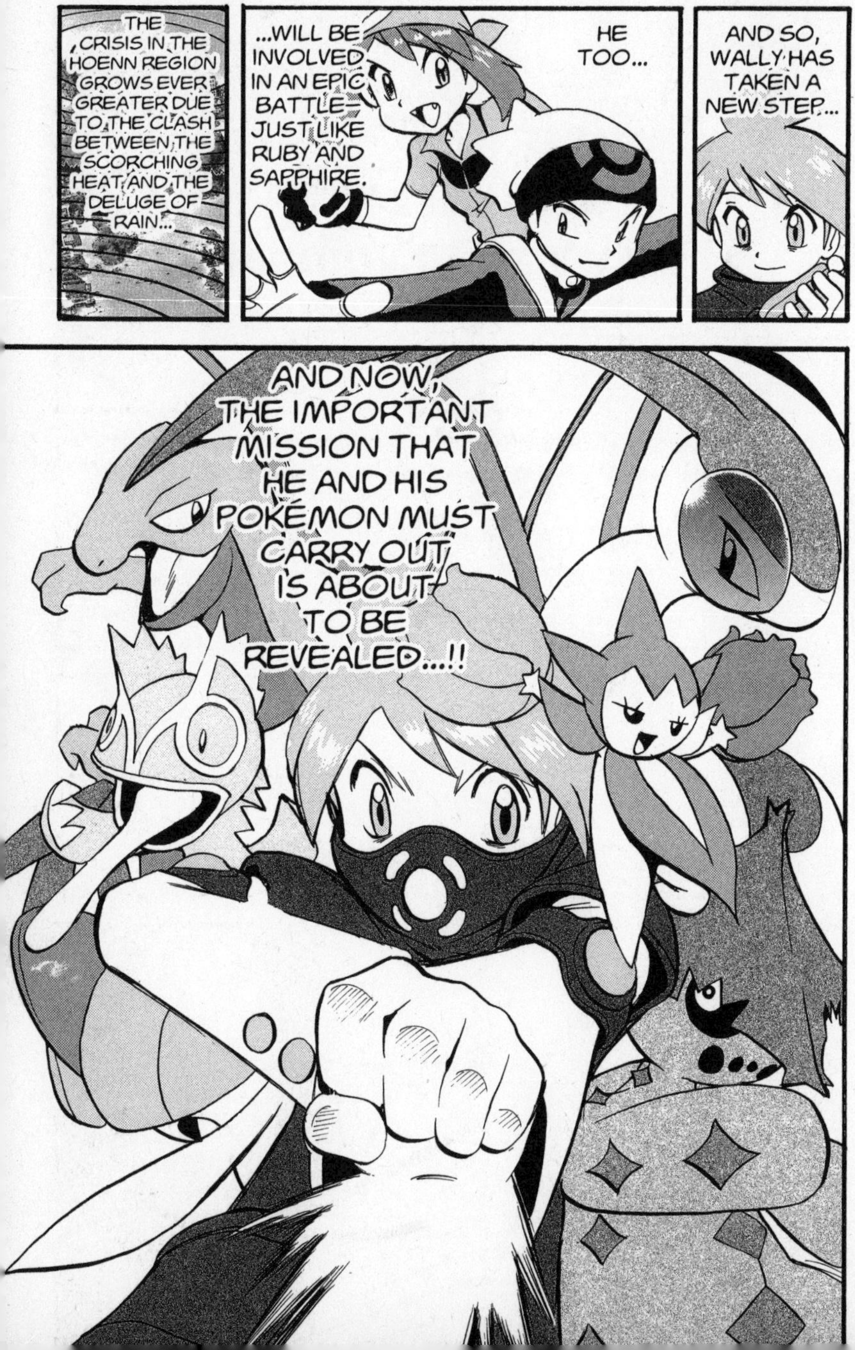
AND SO, WALLY HAS TAKEN A NEW STEP...
HE TOO...
...WILL BE INVOLVED IN AN EPIC BATTLE—JUST LIKE RUBY AND SAPPHIRE.
THE CRISIS IN THE HOENN REGION GROWS EVER GREATER DUE TO THE CLASH BETWEEN THE SCORCHING HEAT AND THE DELUGE OF RAIN...
AND NOW, THE IMPORTANT MISSION THAT HE AND HIS POKÉMON MUST CARRY OUT IS ABOUT TO BE REVEALED...!!

● Chapter 242 ●
Very Vexing Volbeat

Pokémon™ Adventures Ruby & Sapphire
The Fourth Chapter

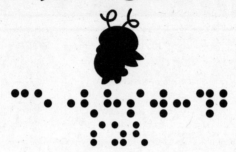

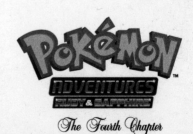

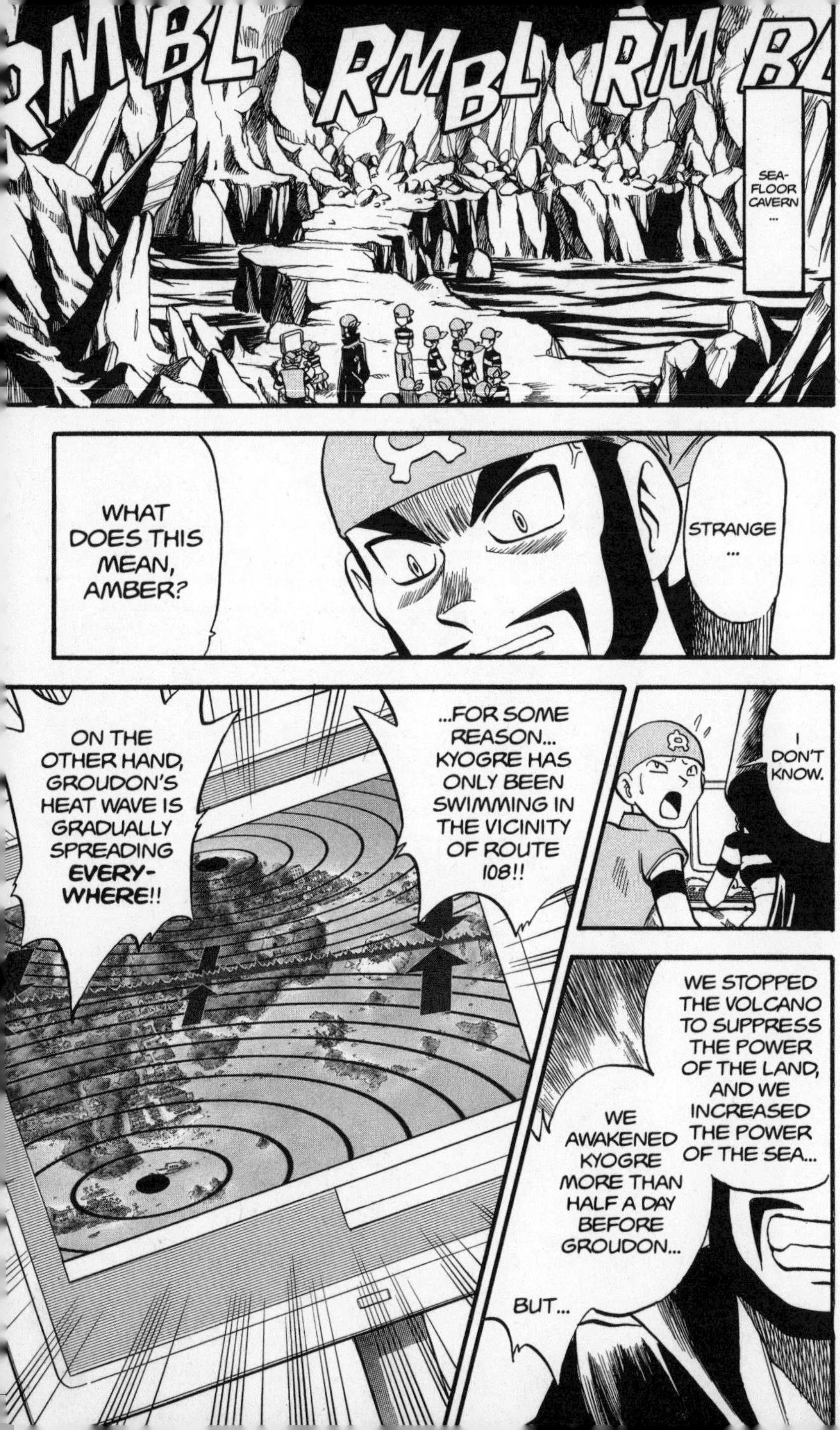

SEA-FLOOR CAVERN ...
RMBL
RMBL
RMBL
STRANGE ...
WHAT DOES THIS MEAN, AMBER?
I DON'T KNOW.
WE STOPPED THE VOLCANO TO SUPPRESS THE POWER OF THE LAND, AND WE INCREASED THE POWER OF THE SEA...
WE AWAKENED KYOGRE MORE THAN HALF A DAY BEFORE GROUDON...
BUT...
...FOR SOME REASON... KYOGRE HAS ONLY BEEN SWIMMING IN THE VICINITY OF ROUTE 108!!
ON THE OTHER HAND, GROUDON'S HEAT WAVE IS GRADUALLY SPREADING **EVERY-WHERE!!**

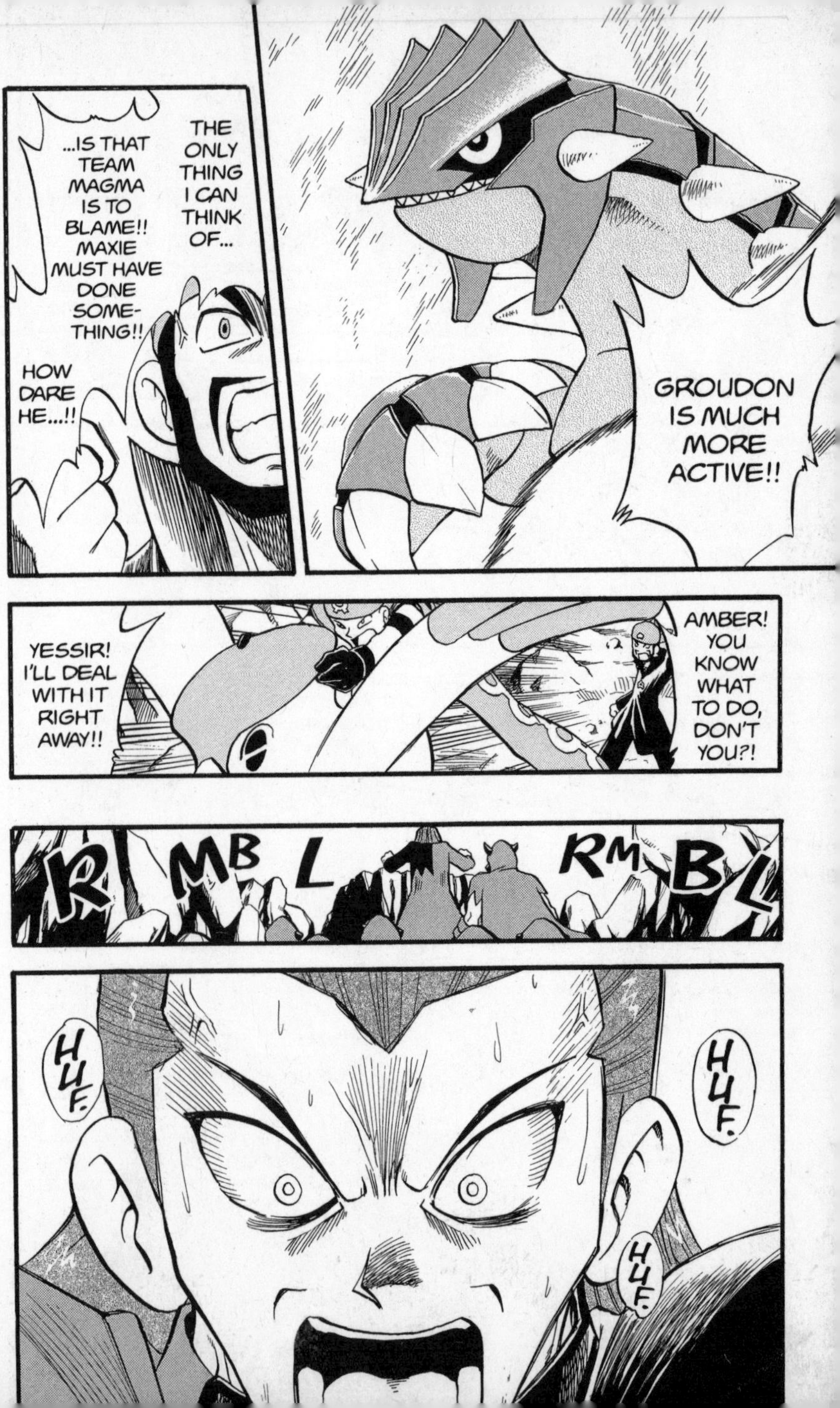
GROUDON IS MUCH MORE ACTIVE!!
THE ONLY THING I CAN THINK OF...
...IS THAT TEAM MAGMA IS TO BLAME!! MAXIE MUST HAVE DONE SOME-THING!!
HOW DARE HE...!!
AMBER! YOU KNOW WHAT TO DO, DON'T YOU?!
YESSIR! I'LL DEAL WITH IT RIGHT AWAY!!
RMBL
RMBL
HUF.
HUF.
HUF.

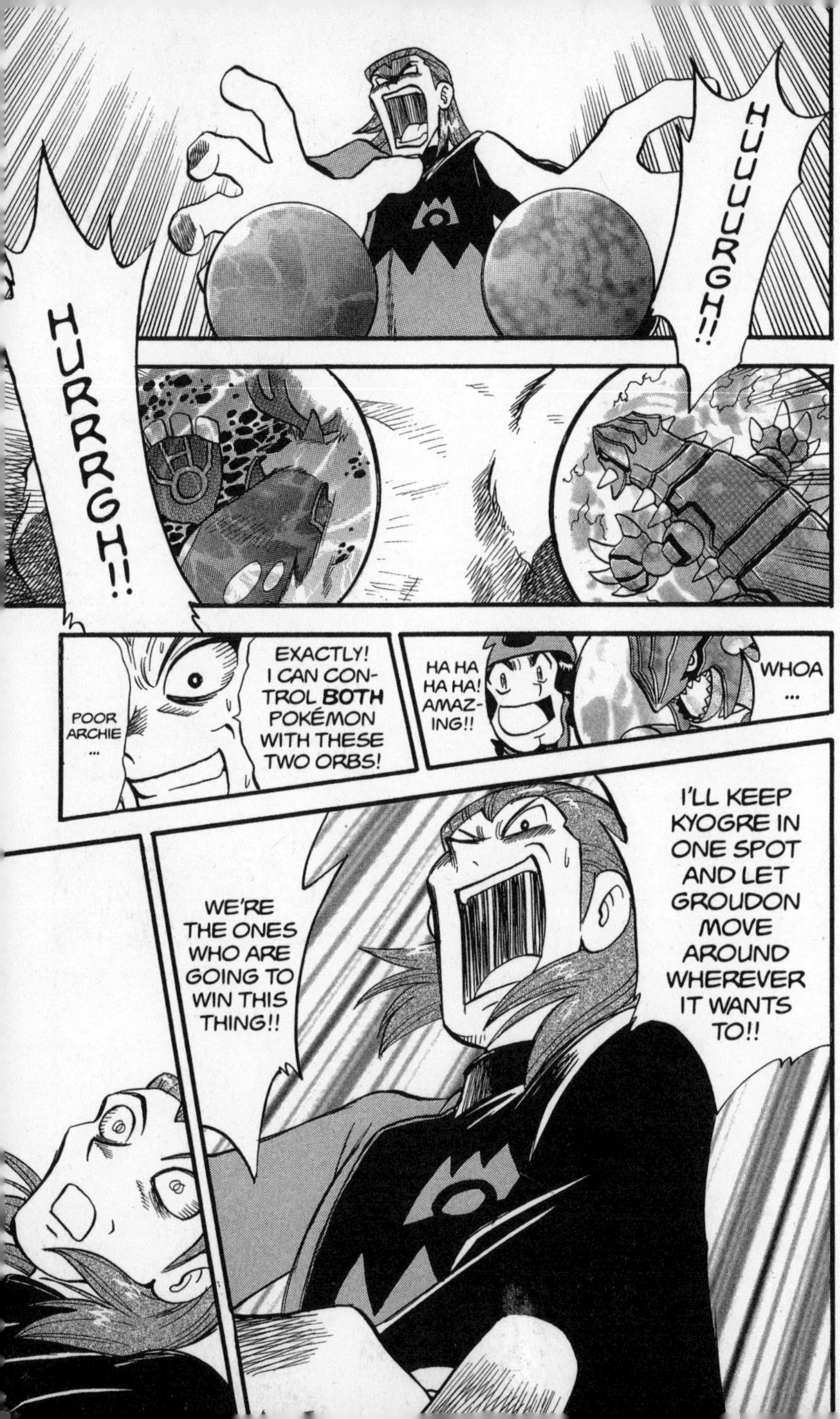
HUUUURGH!!
HURRRGH!!
WHOA ...
HA HA HA HA! AMAZ-ING!!
EXACTLY! I CAN CON-TROL **BOTH** POKÉMON WITH THESE TWO ORBS!
POOR ARCHIE ...
I'LL KEEP KYOGRE IN ONE SPOT AND LET GROUDON MOVE AROUND WHEREVER IT WANTS TO!!
WE'RE THE ONES WHO ARE GOING TO WIN THIS THING!!

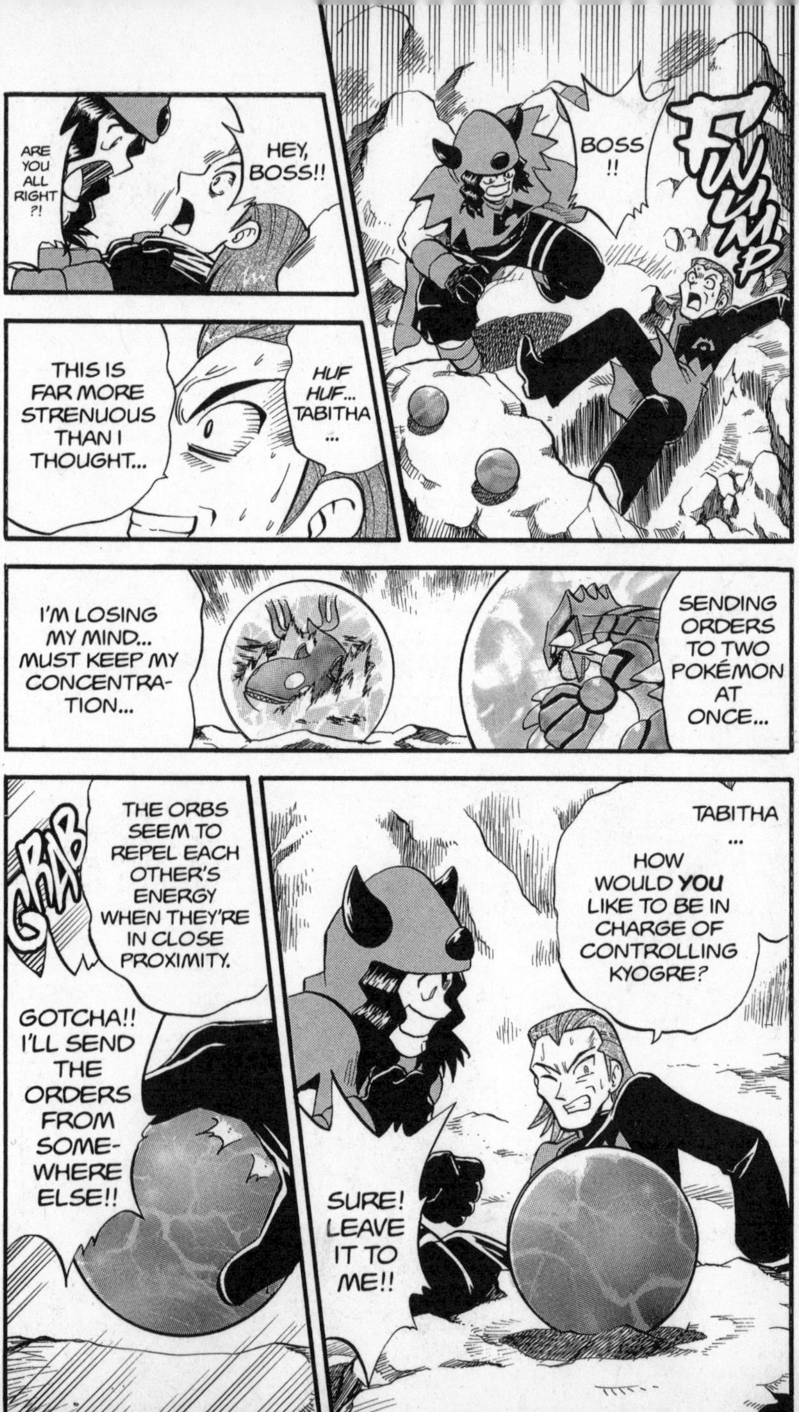

BOSS!!
FWUMP
HEY, BOSS!!
ARE YOU ALL RIGHT?!
HUF HUF... TABITHA...
THIS IS FAR MORE STRENUOUS THAN I THOUGHT...
SENDING ORDERS TO TWO POKÉMON AT ONCE...
I'M LOSING MY MIND... MUST KEEP MY CONCENTRATION...
TABITHA...
HOW WOULD **YOU** LIKE TO BE IN CHARGE OF CONTROLLING KYOGRE?
SURE! LEAVE IT TO ME!!
GRAB
THE ORBS SEEM TO REPEL EACH OTHER'S ENERGY WHEN THEY'RE IN CLOSE PROXIMITY.
GOTCHA!! I'LL SEND THE ORDERS FROM SOME-WHERE ELSE!!

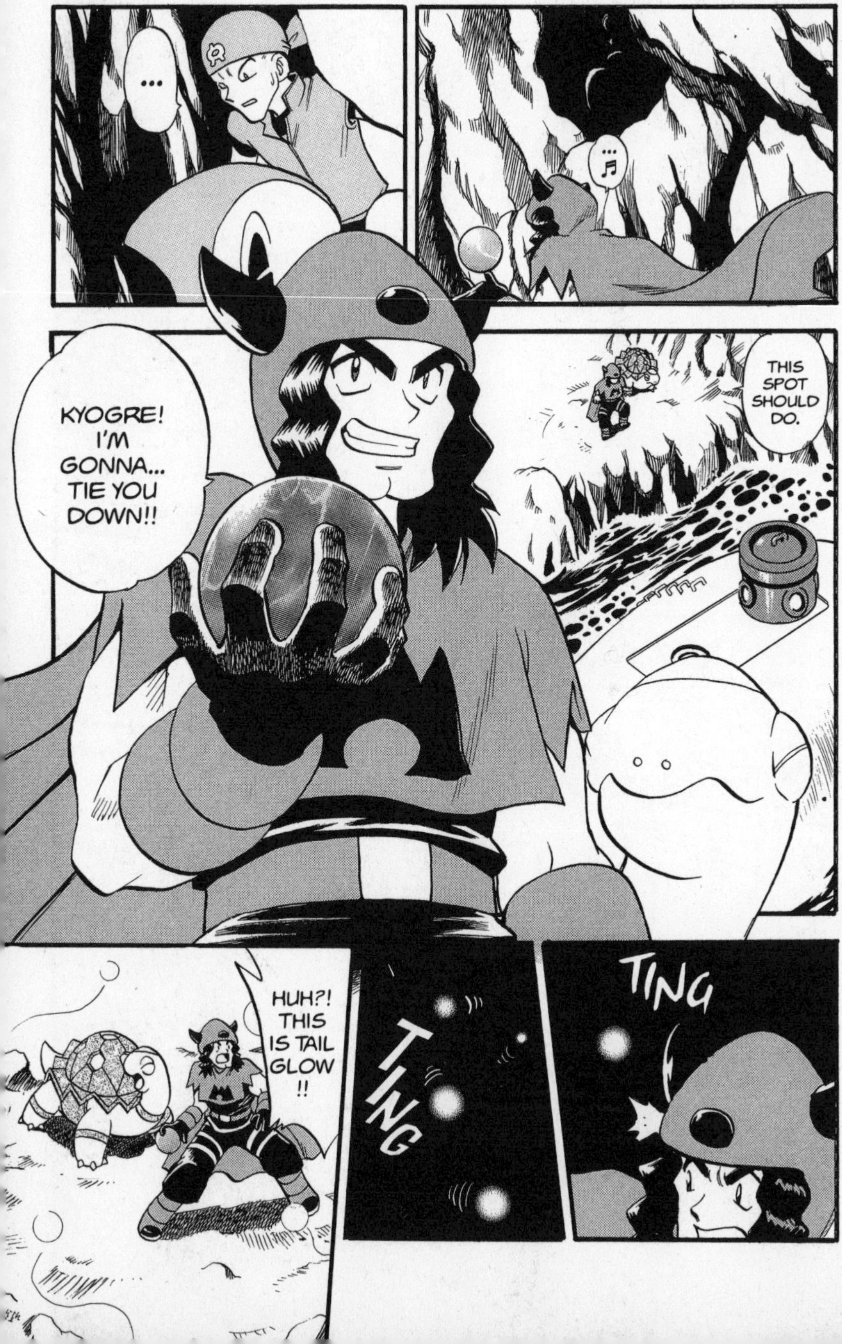
...♪
...
THIS SPOT SHOULD DO.
KYOGRE! I'M GONNA... TIE YOU DOWN!!
TING
TING
HUH?! THIS IS TAIL GLOW!!

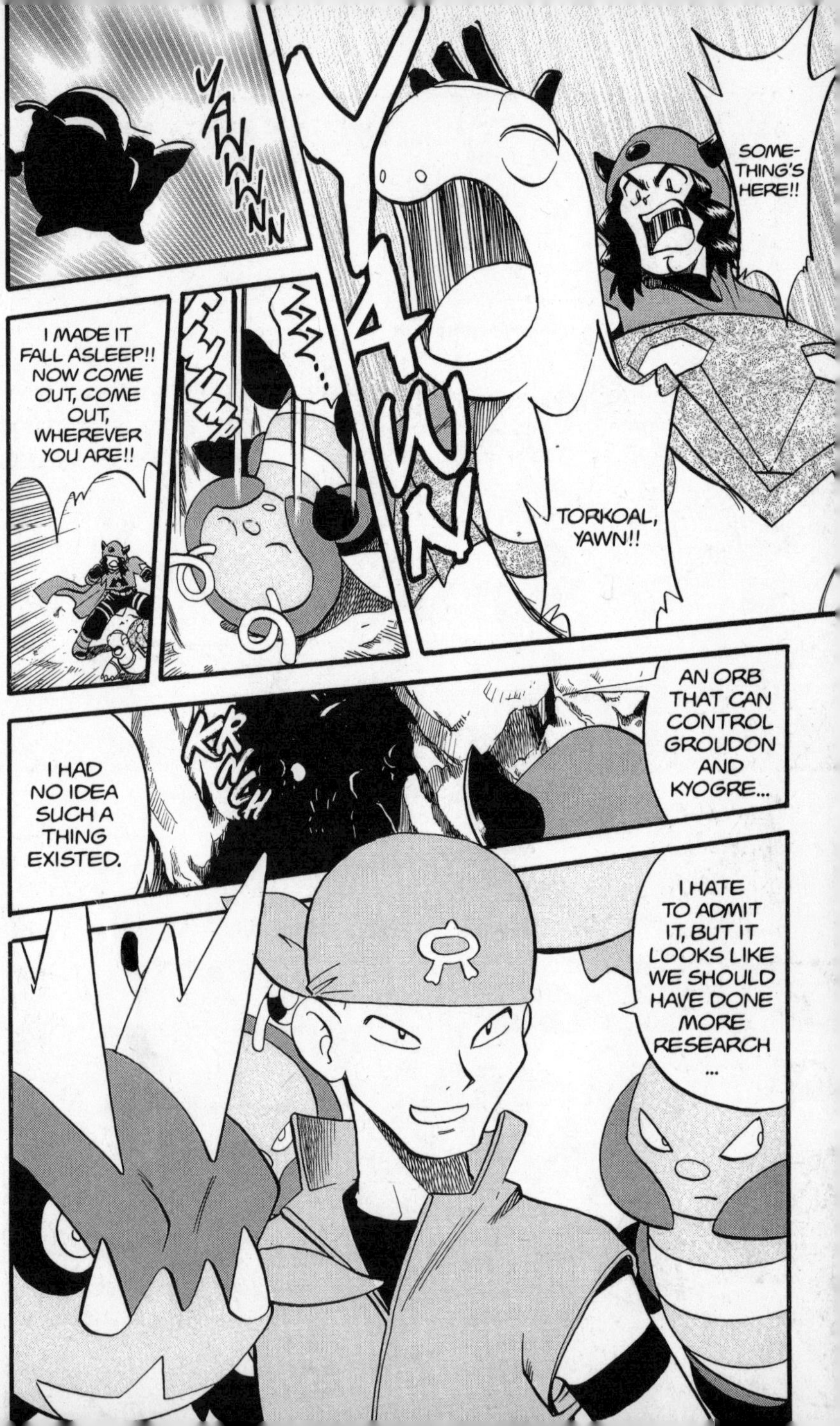
SOME-THING'S HERE!!
YAWN
TORKOAL, YAWN!!
YAWWWNNN
ZZZ...
FWUMP
I MADE IT FALL ASLEEP!! NOW COME OUT, COME OUT, WHEREVER YOU ARE!!
AN ORB THAT CAN CONTROL GROUDON AND KYOGRE...
KRNCH
I HAD NO IDEA SUCH A THING EXISTED.
I HATE TO ADMIT IT, BUT IT LOOKS LIKE WE SHOULD HAVE DONE MORE RESEARCH ...

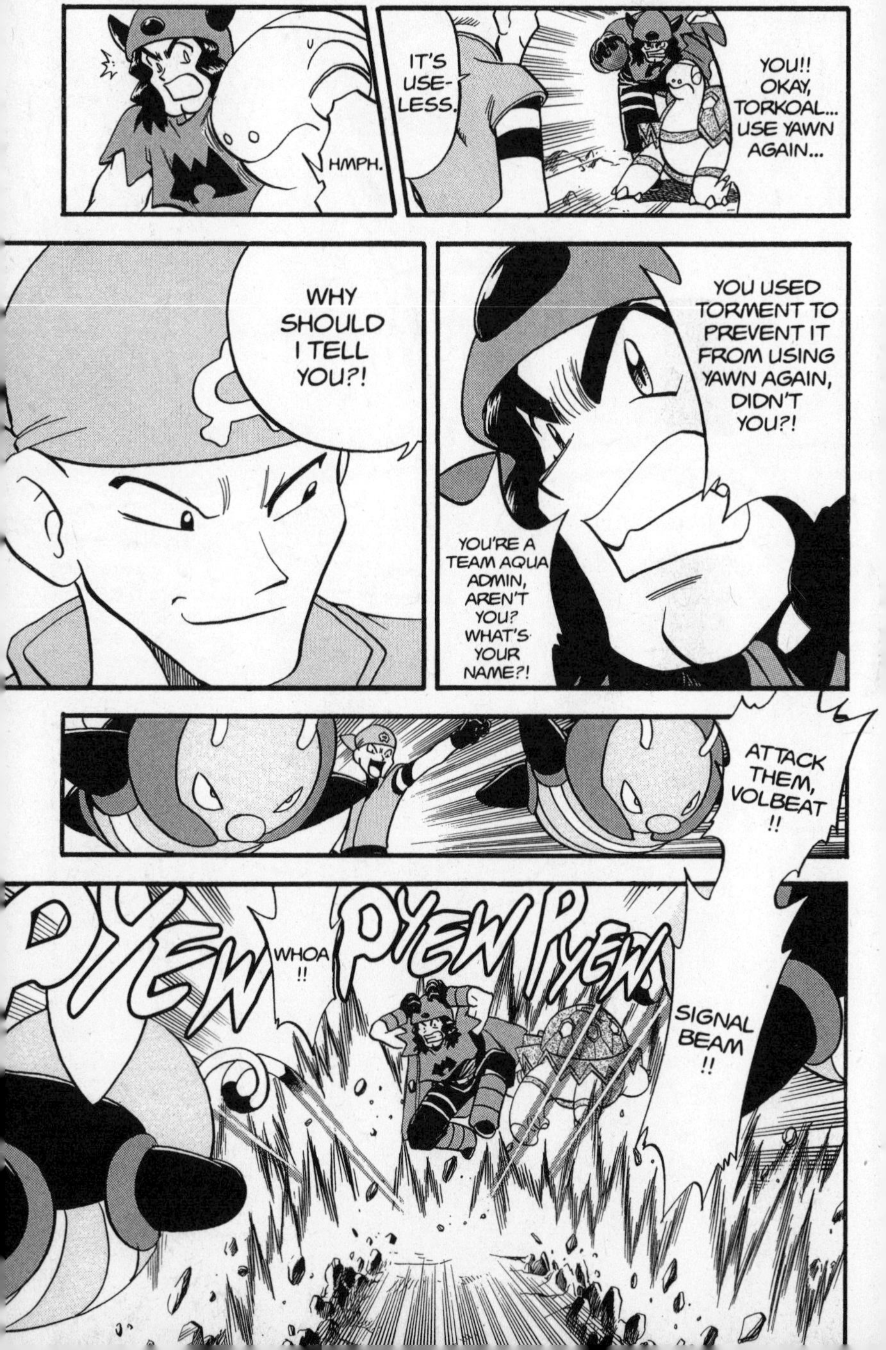
YOU!! OKAY, TORKOAL... USE YAWN AGAIN...
IT'S USE-LESS.
HMPH.
YOU USED TORMENT TO PREVENT IT FROM USING YAWN AGAIN, DIDN'T YOU?!
YOU'RE A TEAM AQUA ADMIN, AREN'T YOU? WHAT'S YOUR NAME?!
WHY SHOULD I TELL YOU?!
ATTACK THEM, VOLBEAT!!
PYEW
SIGNAL BEAM!!
PYEW
WHOA!!
PYEW

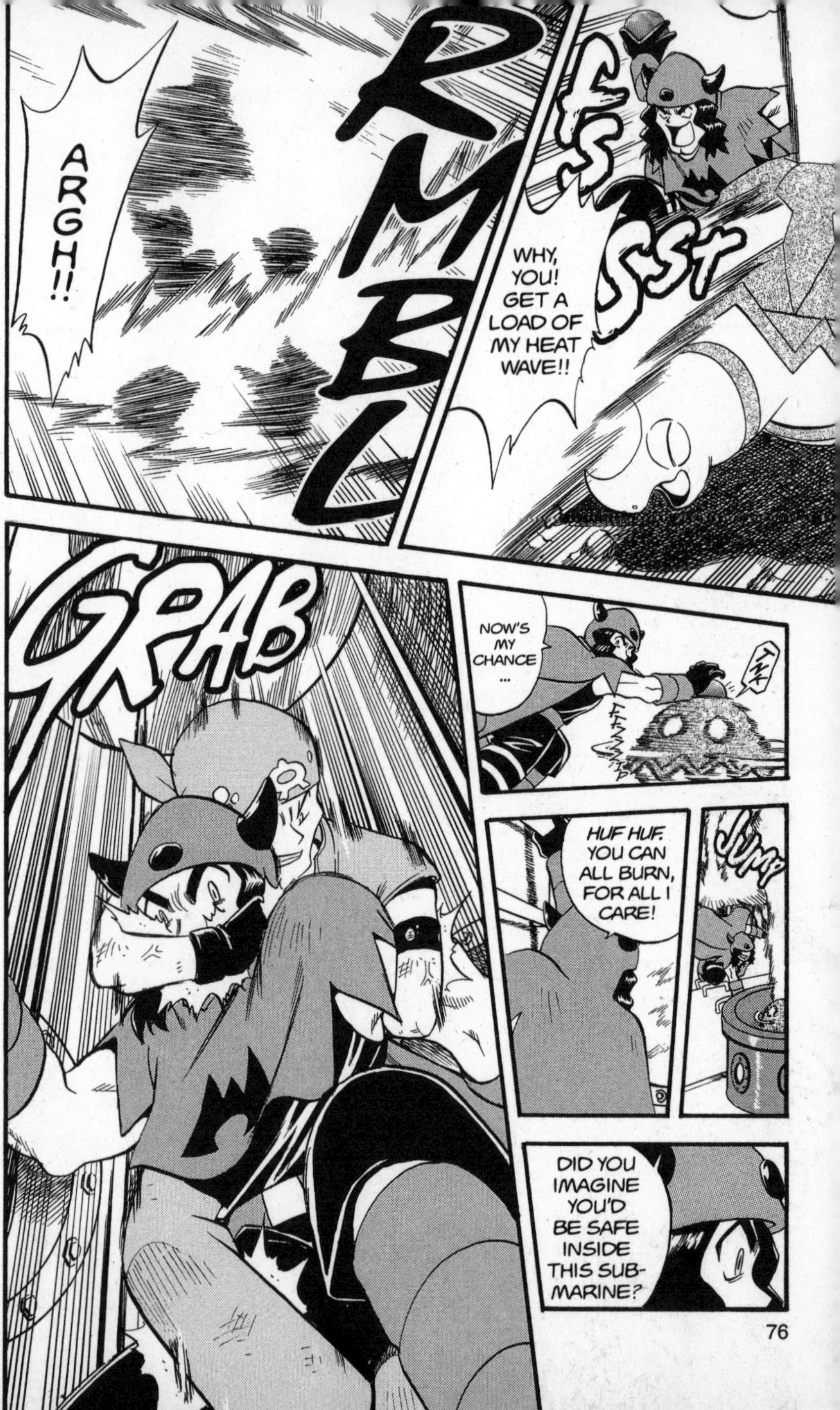
WHY, YOU! GET A LOAD OF MY HEAT WAVE!!
RMBL
ARGH!!
NOW'S MY CHANCE ...
TNK
JUMP
HUF HUF. YOU CAN ALL BURN, FOR ALL I CARE!
DID YOU IMAGINE YOU'D BE SAFE INSIDE THIS SUB-MARINE?
GRAB

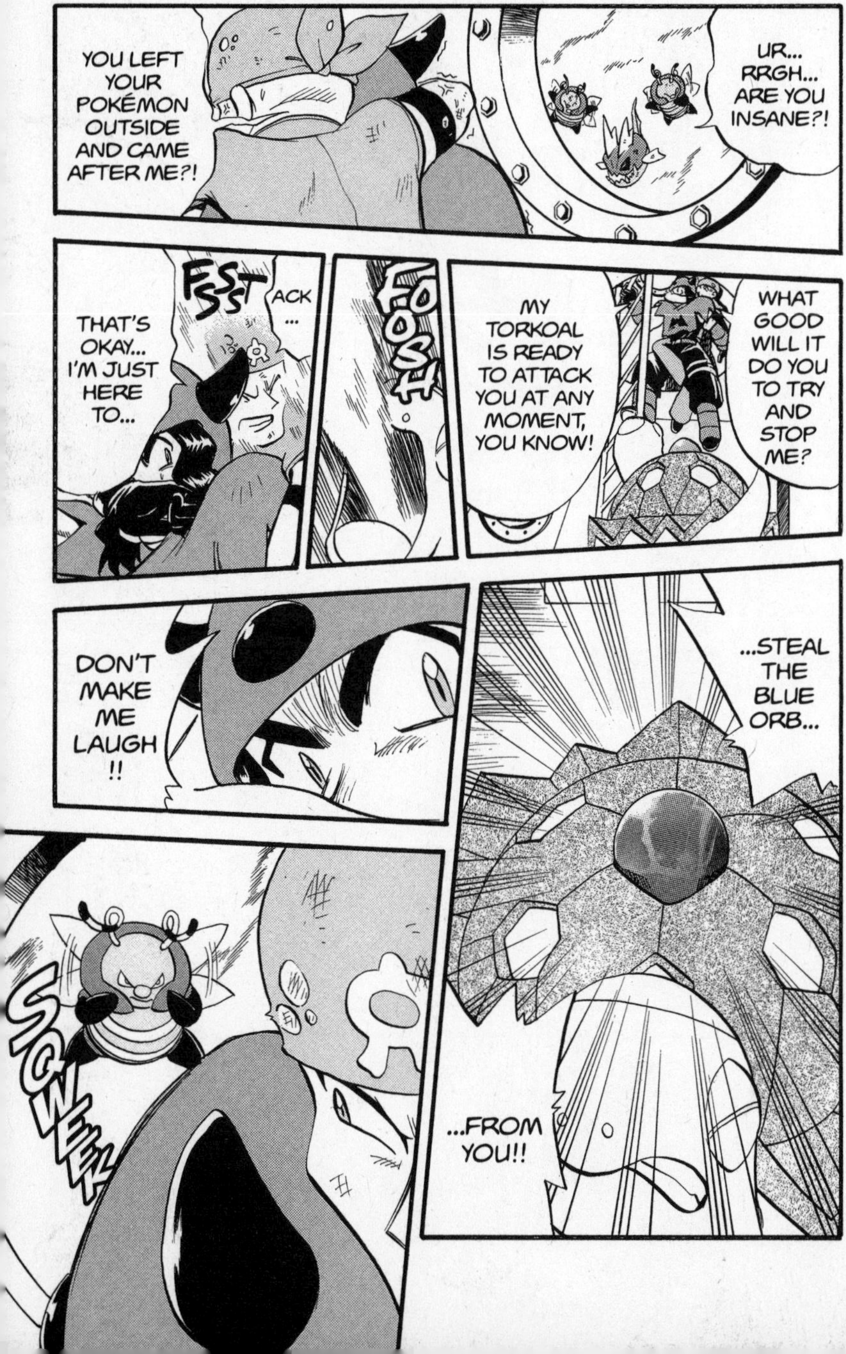
UR... RRGH... ARE YOU INSANE?!
YOU LEFT YOUR POKÉMON OUTSIDE AND CAME AFTER ME?!
WHAT GOOD WILL IT DO YOU TO TRY AND STOP ME?
MY TORKOAL IS READY TO ATTACK YOU AT ANY MOMENT, YOU KNOW!
FOOSH
FSST
ACK...
THAT'S OKAY... I'M JUST HERE TO...
...STEAL THE BLUE ORB...
...FROM YOU!!
DON'T MAKE ME LAUGH!!
SQWEEK

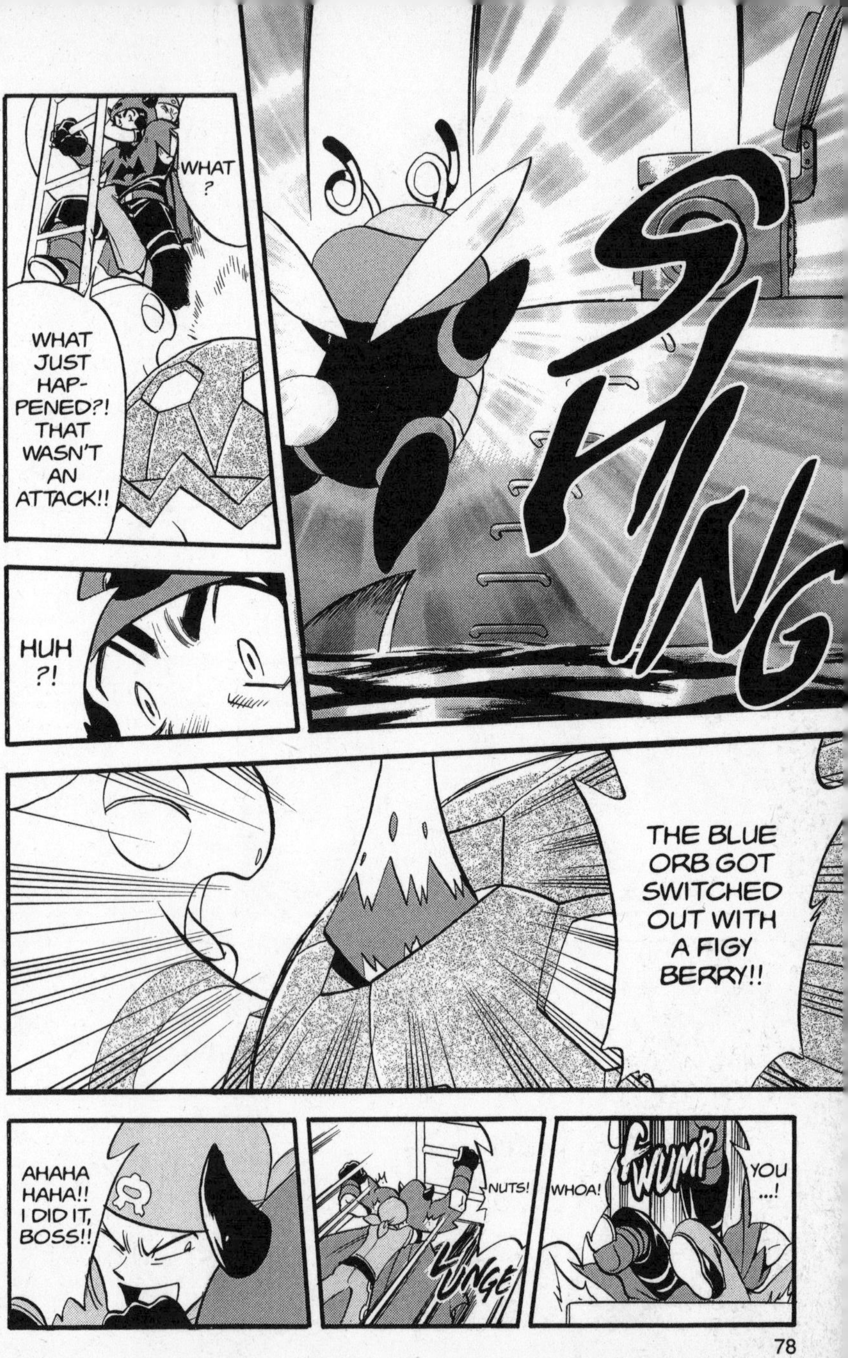
SHING
WHAT ?
WHAT JUST HAP-PENED?! THAT WASN'T AN ATTACK!!
HUH ?!
THE BLUE ORB GOT SWITCHED OUT WITH A FIGY BERRY!!
YOU ...!
FWUMP
WHOA!
NUTS!
LUNGE
AHAHA HAHA!! I DID IT, BOSS!!

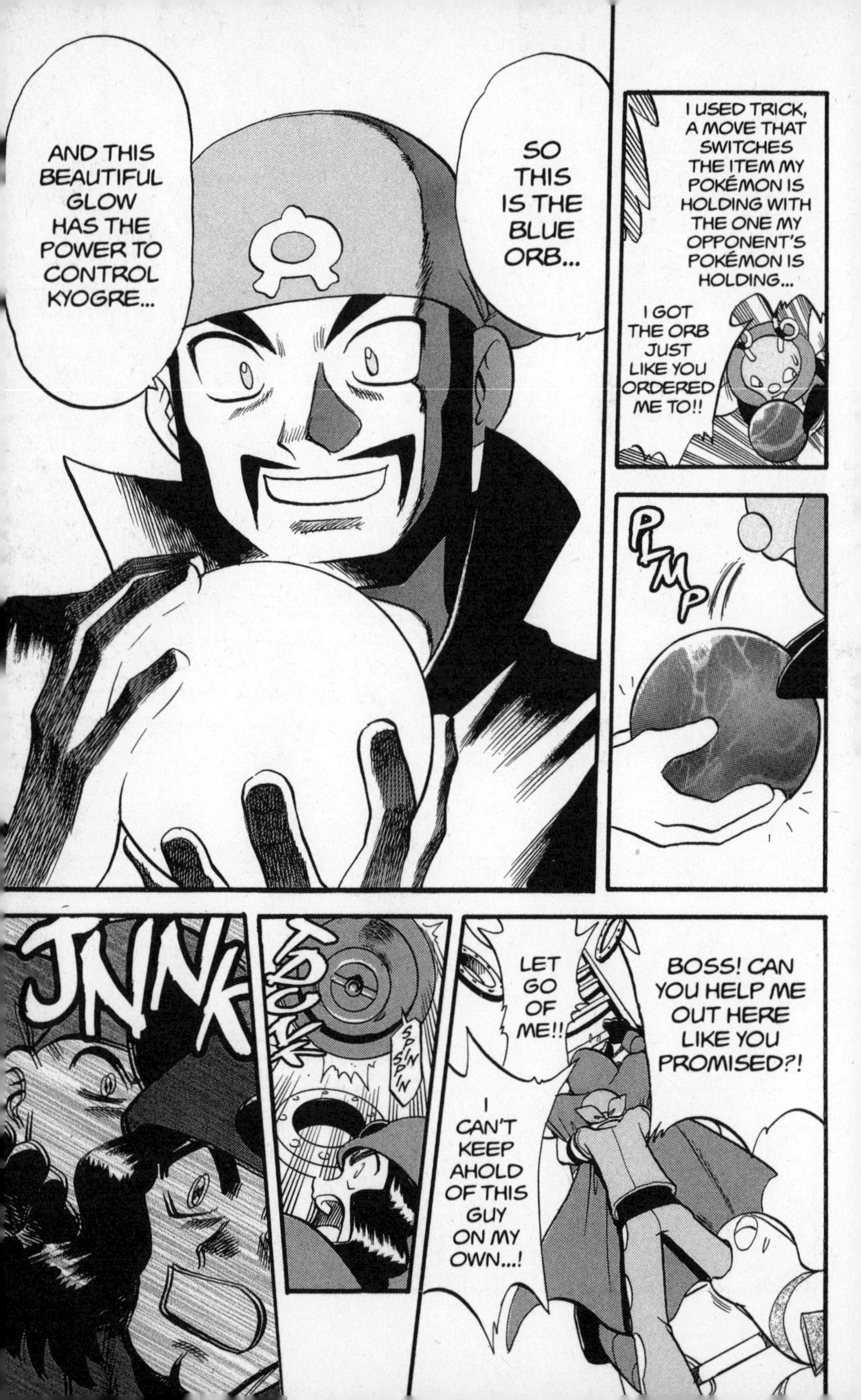
I USED TRICK, A MOVE THAT SWITCHES THE ITEM MY POKÉMON IS HOLDING WITH THE ONE MY OPPONENT'S POKÉMON IS HOLDING...
I GOT THE ORB JUST LIKE YOU ORDERED ME TO!!
PLMP
SO THIS IS THE BLUE ORB...
AND THIS BEAUTIFUL GLOW HAS THE POWER TO CONTROL KYOGRE...
BOSS! CAN YOU HELP ME OUT HERE LIKE YOU PROMISED?!
LET GO OF ME!!
I CAN'T KEEP AHOLD OF THIS GUY ON MY OWN...!
SPIN SPIN
JNNK

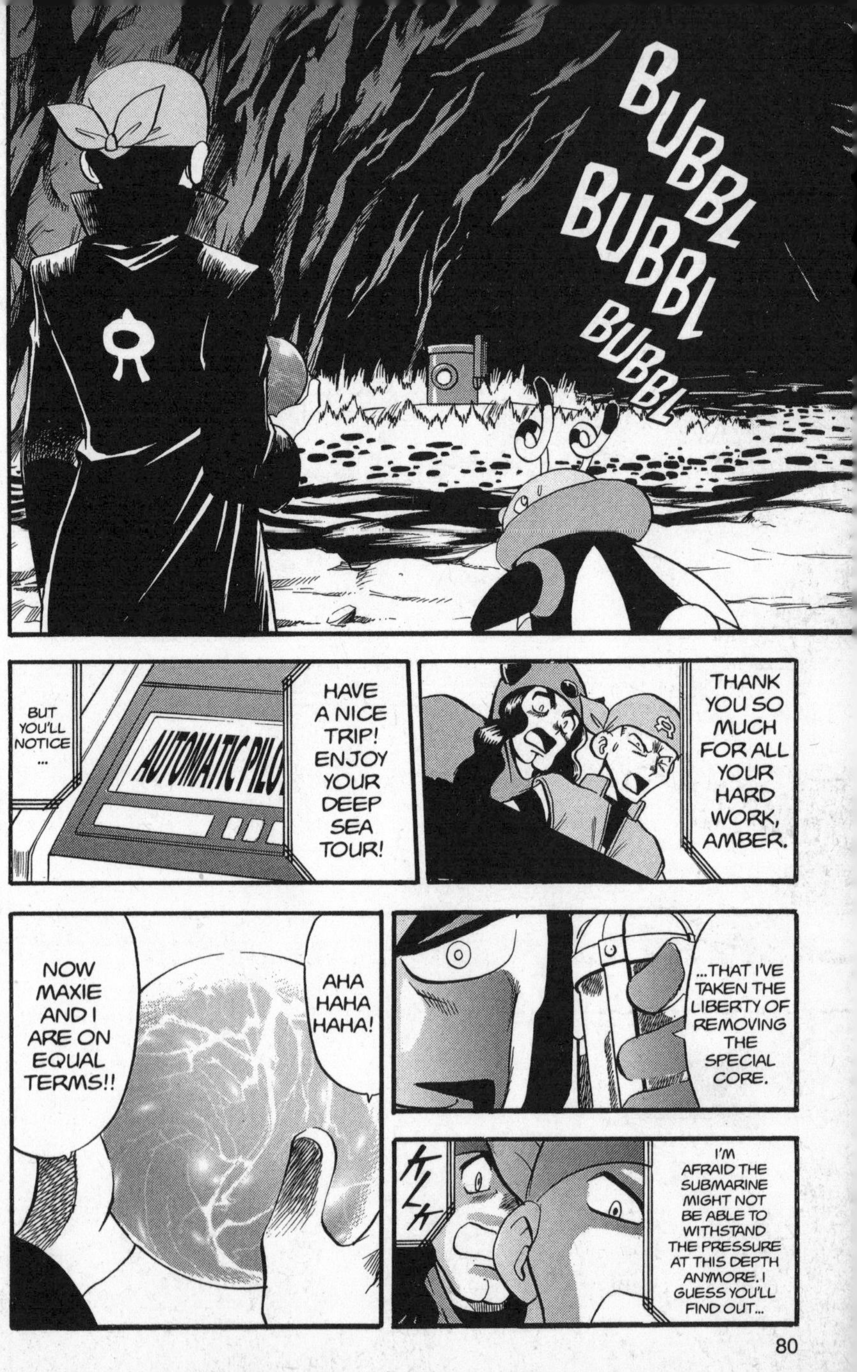
BUBBL
BUBBL
BUBBL
THANK YOU SO MUCH FOR ALL YOUR HARD WORK, AMBER.
HAVE A NICE TRIP! ENJOY YOUR DEEP SEA TOUR!
BUT YOU'LL NOTICE ...
AUTOMATIC PILO
...THAT I'VE TAKEN THE LIBERTY OF REMOVING THE SPECIAL CORE.
I'M AFRAID THE SUBMARINE MIGHT NOT BE ABLE TO WITHSTAND THE PRESSURE AT THIS DEPTH ANYMORE. I GUESS YOU'LL FIND OUT...
AHA HAHA HAHA!
NOW MAXIE AND I ARE ON EQUAL TERMS!!

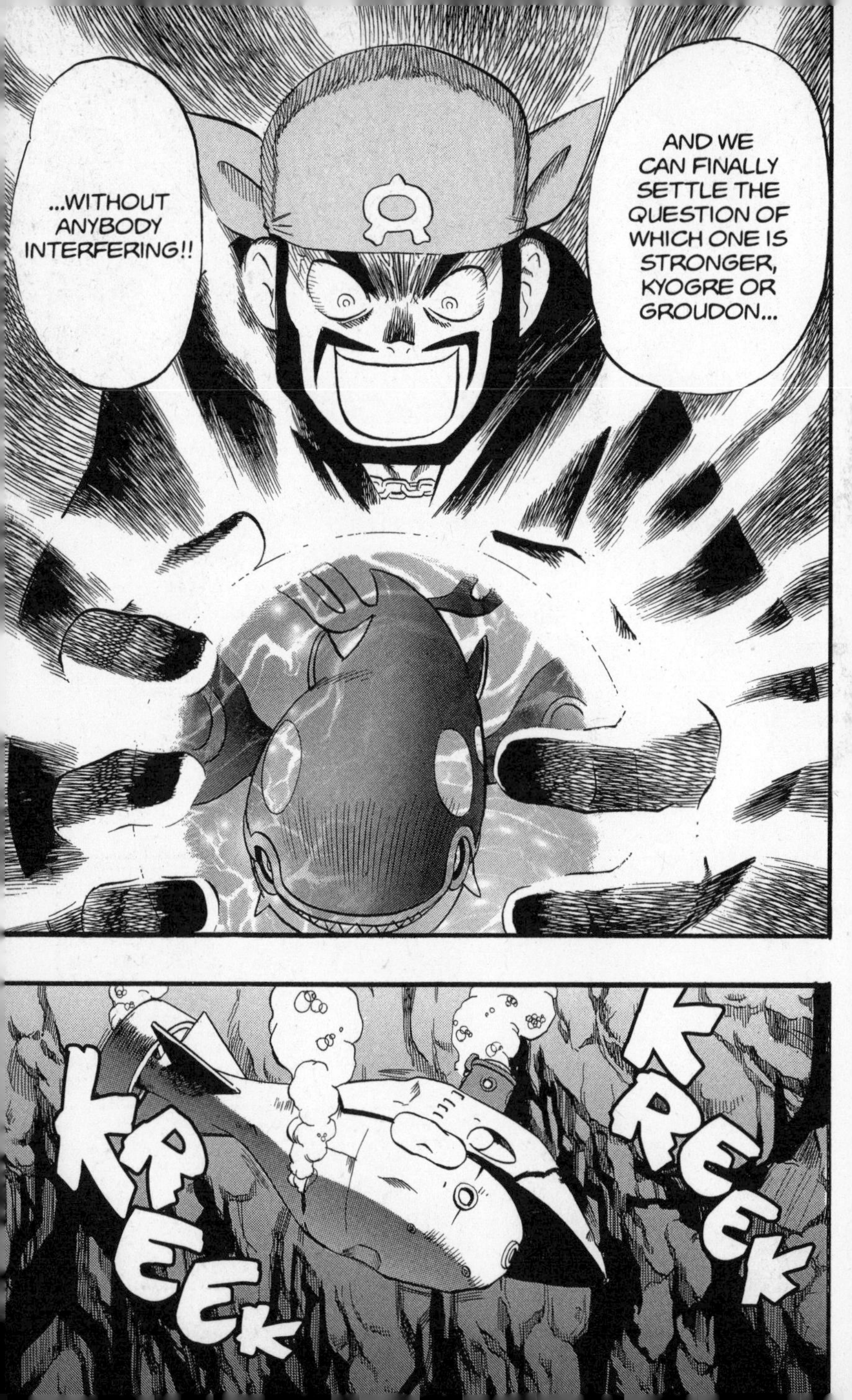
AND WE CAN FINALLY SETTLE THE QUESTION OF WHICH ONE IS STRONGER, KYOGRE OR GROUDON...
...WITHOUT ANYBODY INTERFERING!!
KREEK
KREEEK

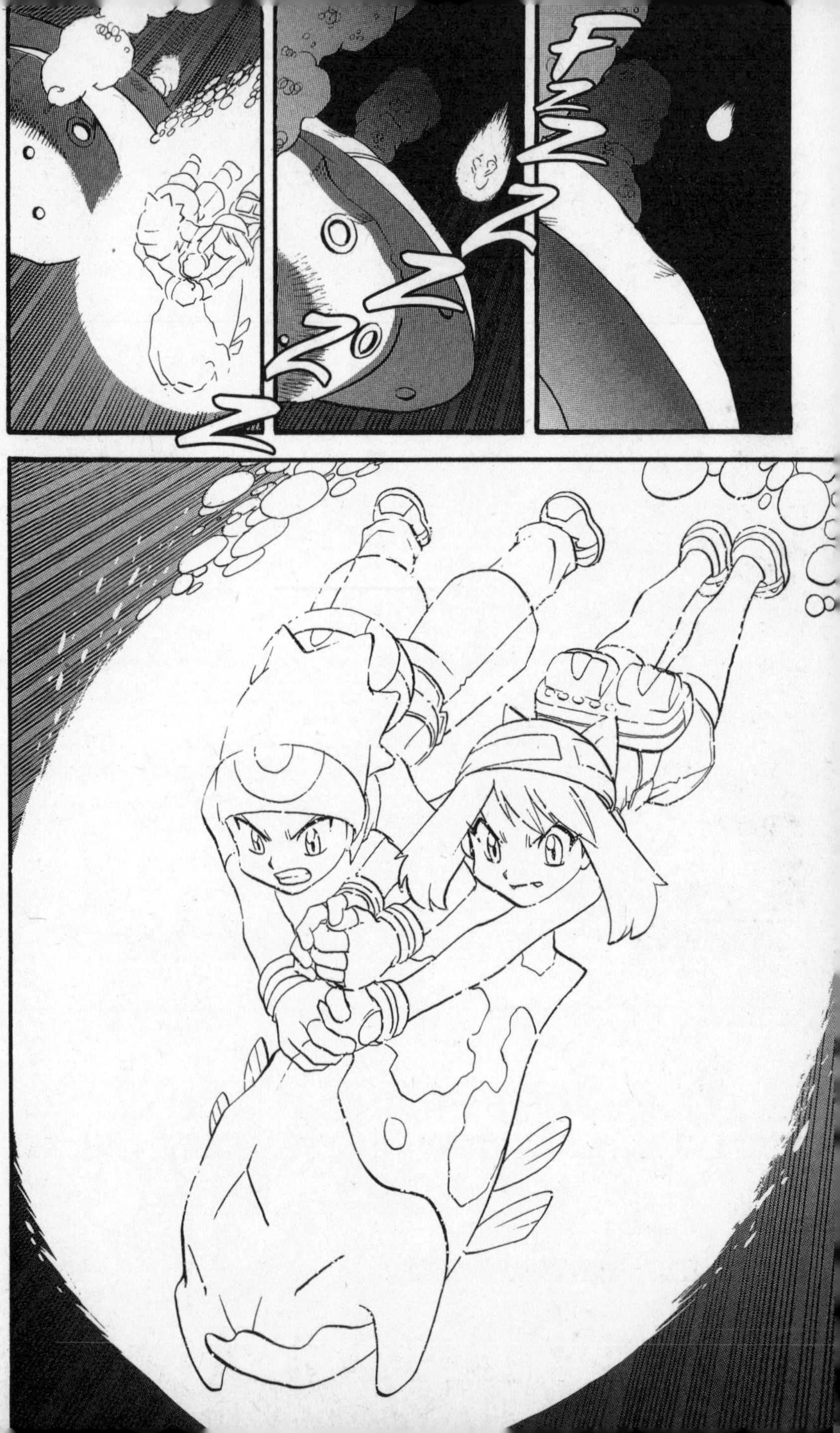
FZZZZZZZ

ADVENTURE MAP

SAPPHIRE

CHIC
Blaziken ♀
Lv40

RONO
Lairon ♂
Lv41

RELLY
Relicanth ♂
Lv47

PHADO
Donphan ♂
Lv48

TROPPY
Tropius ♂
Lv46

LORRY
Wailord ♂
Lv48

Fortree City

| Route 123 | Slateport City |

Route 126

Seafloor Cavern

RUBY

MUMU
Swampert ♂

NANA
Mightyena ♀

KIKI
Delcatty ♀

FOFO
Castform ♀

Stone Badge	Knuckle Badge	Dynamo Badge	Heat Badge
Balance Badge	Feather Badge	Mind Badge	Rain Badge

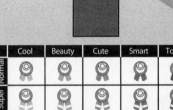

	Cool	Beauty	Cute	Smart	Tough
Normal					
Super					
Hyper					
Master					

● Chapter 243 ●
No Armaldo Is an Island

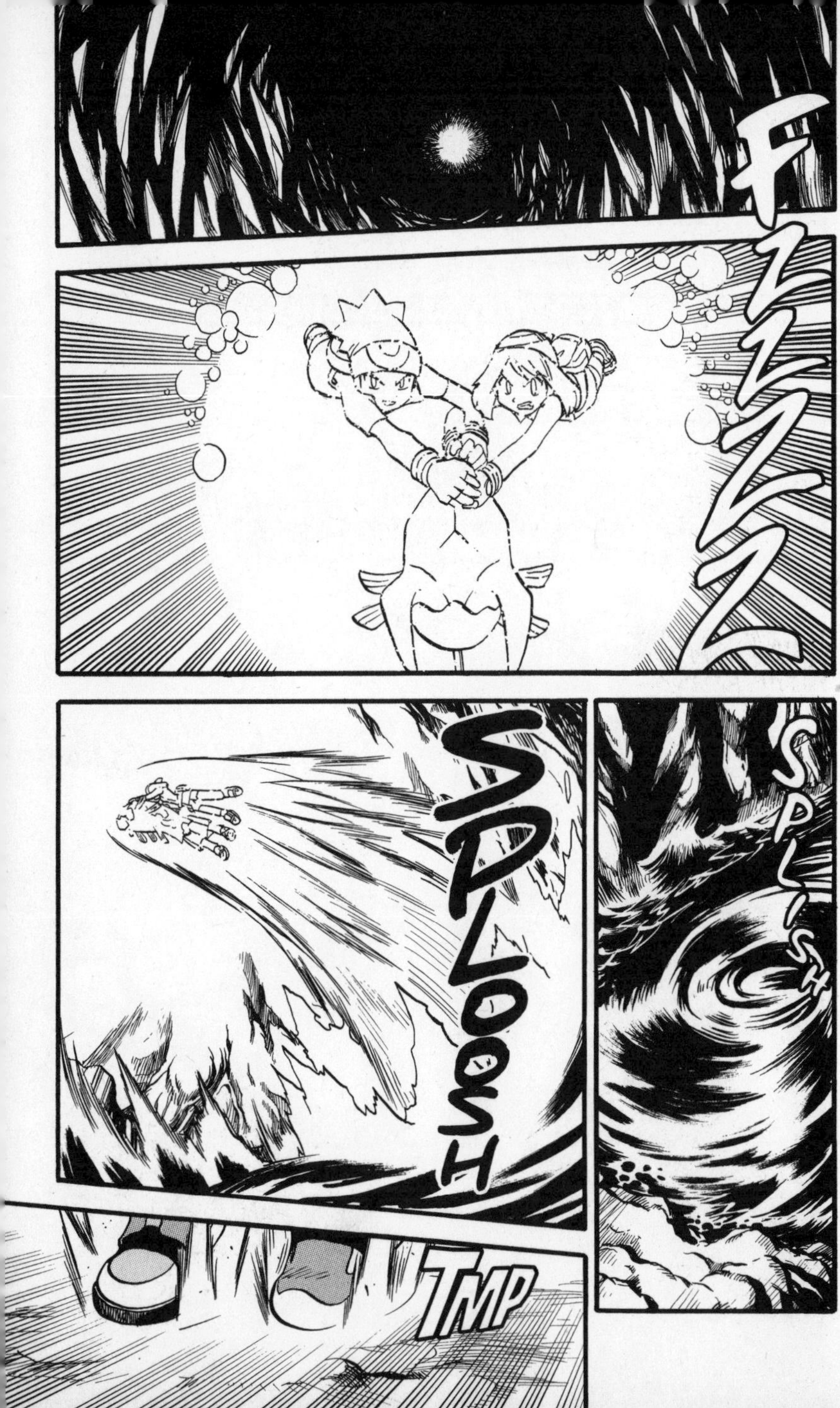
FZZZZZ
SPLISH
SPLOOSH
TMP

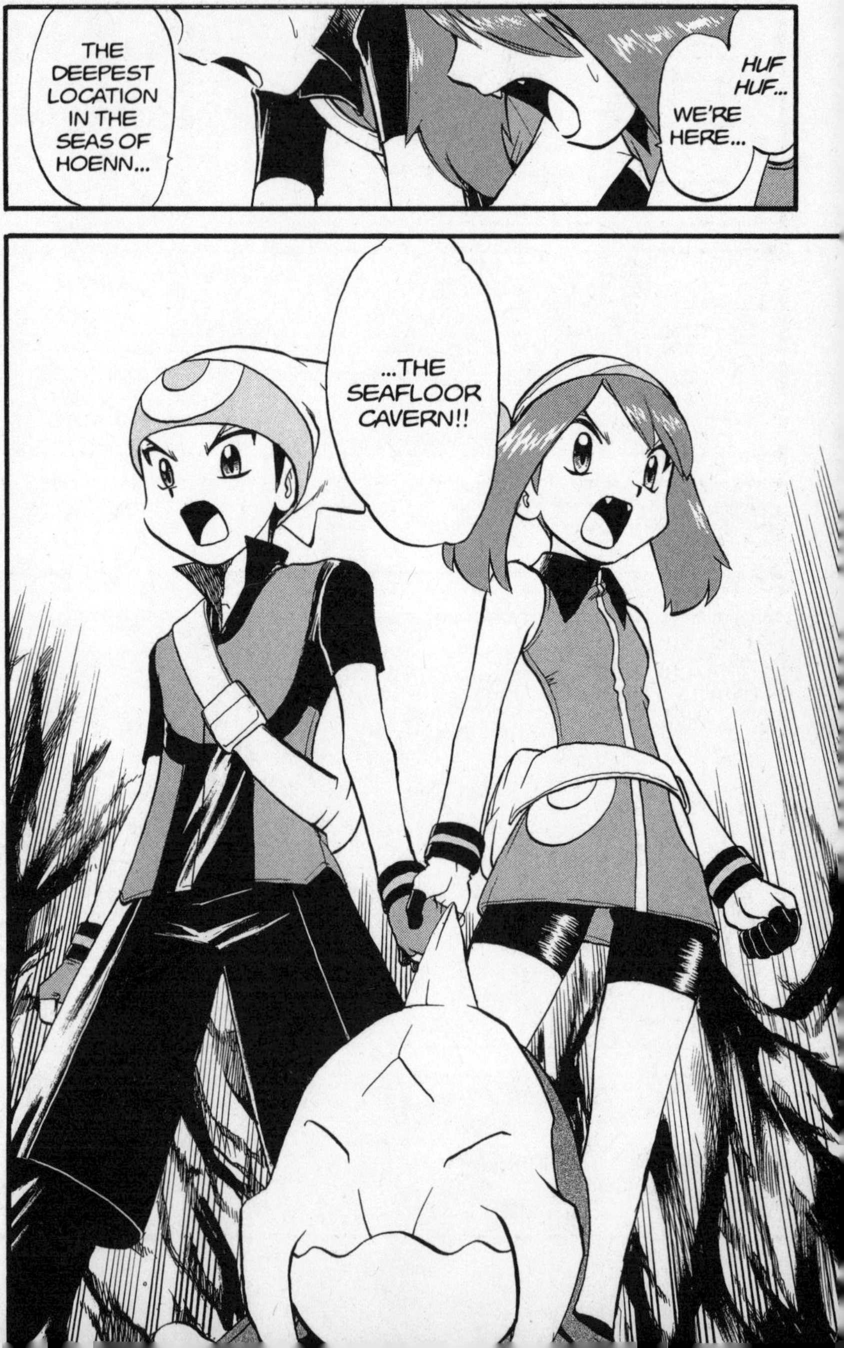
HUF HUF... WE'RE HERE...
THE DEEPEST LOCATION IN THE SEAS OF HOENN...
...THE SEAFLOOR CAVERN!!

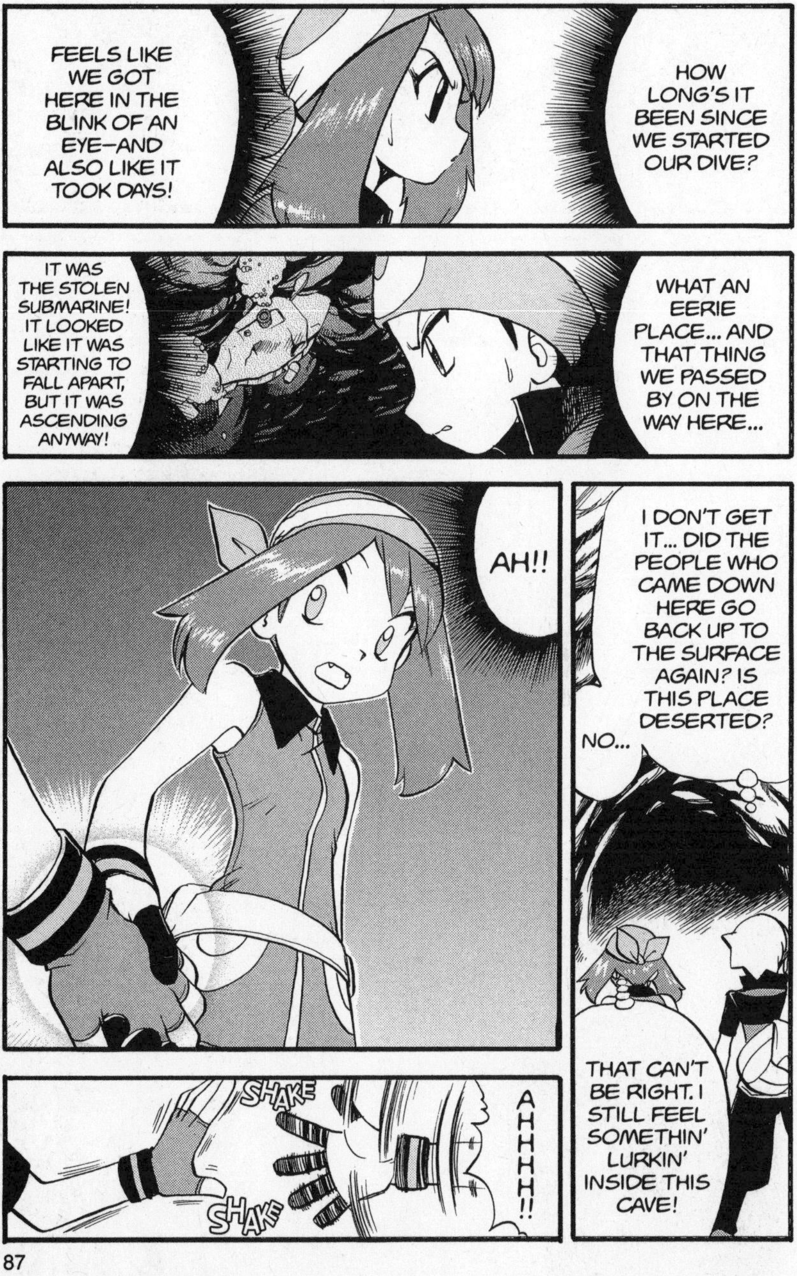
HOW LONG'S IT BEEN SINCE WE STARTED OUR DIVE?
FEELS LIKE WE GOT HERE IN THE BLINK OF AN EYE—AND ALSO LIKE IT TOOK DAYS!
WHAT AN EERIE PLACE... AND THAT THING WE PASSED BY ON THE WAY HERE...
IT WAS THE STOLEN SUBMARINE! IT LOOKED LIKE IT WAS STARTING TO FALL APART, BUT IT WAS ASCENDING ANYWAY!
I DON'T GET IT... DID THE PEOPLE WHO CAME DOWN HERE GO BACK UP TO THE SURFACE AGAIN? IS THIS PLACE DESERTED?
NO...
THAT CAN'T BE RIGHT. I STILL FEEL SOMETHIN' LURKIN' INSIDE THIS CAVE!
AH!!
SHAKE
SHAKE
AHHHH!!

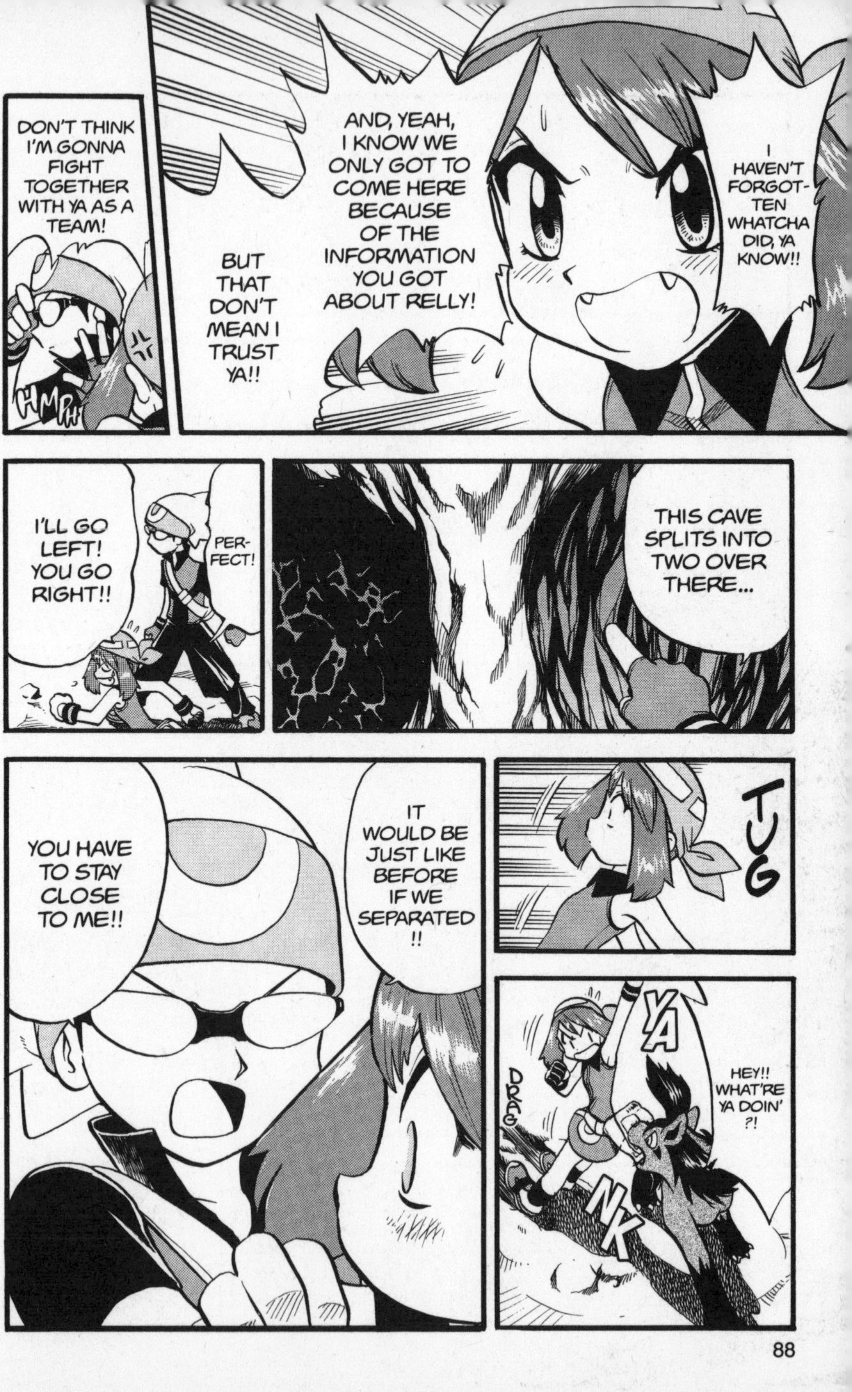
I HAVEN'T FORGOT-TEN WHATCHA DID, YA KNOW!!
AND, YEAH, I KNOW WE ONLY GOT TO COME HERE BECAUSE OF THE INFORMATION YOU GOT ABOUT RELLY!
BUT THAT DON'T MEAN I TRUST YA!!
DON'T THINK I'M GONNA FIGHT TOGETHER WITH YA AS A TEAM!
HMPH
THIS CAVE SPLITS INTO TWO OVER THERE...
PER-FECT!
I'LL GO LEFT! YOU GO RIGHT!!
TUG
YA
NK
HEY!! WHAT'RE YA DOIN' ?!
DRAG
IT WOULD BE JUST LIKE BEFORE IF WE SEPARATED !!
YOU HAVE TO STAY CLOSE TO ME!!

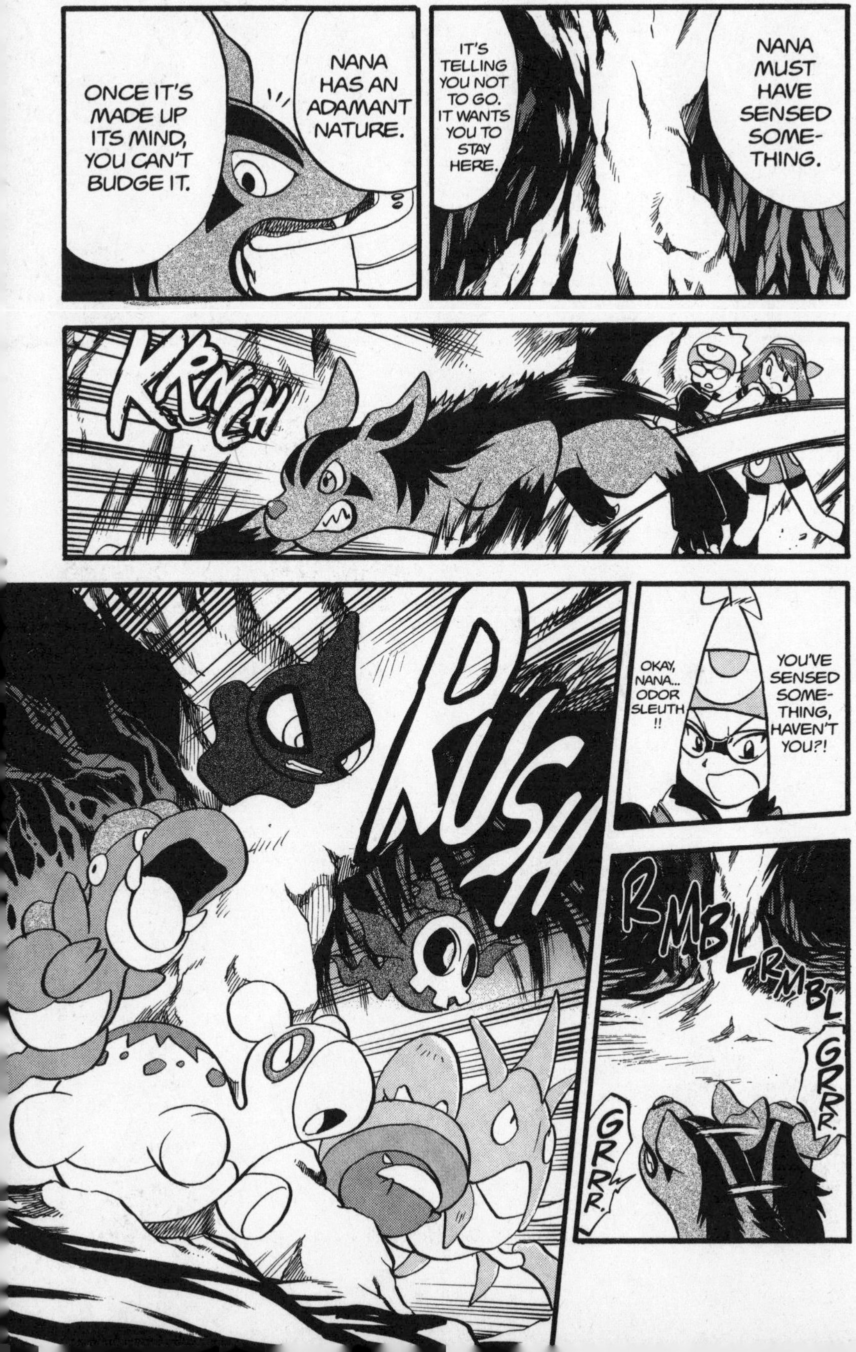
NANA MUST HAVE SENSED SOMETHING.
IT'S TELLING YOU NOT TO GO. IT WANTS YOU TO STAY HERE.
NANA HAS AN ADAMANT NATURE.
ONCE IT'S MADE UP ITS MIND, YOU CAN'T BUDGE IT.
KRNCH
YOU'VE SENSED SOMETHING, HAVEN'T YOU?!
OKAY, NANA... ODOR SLEUTH!!
RMBL RMBL
GRRR.
GRRR.
RUSH

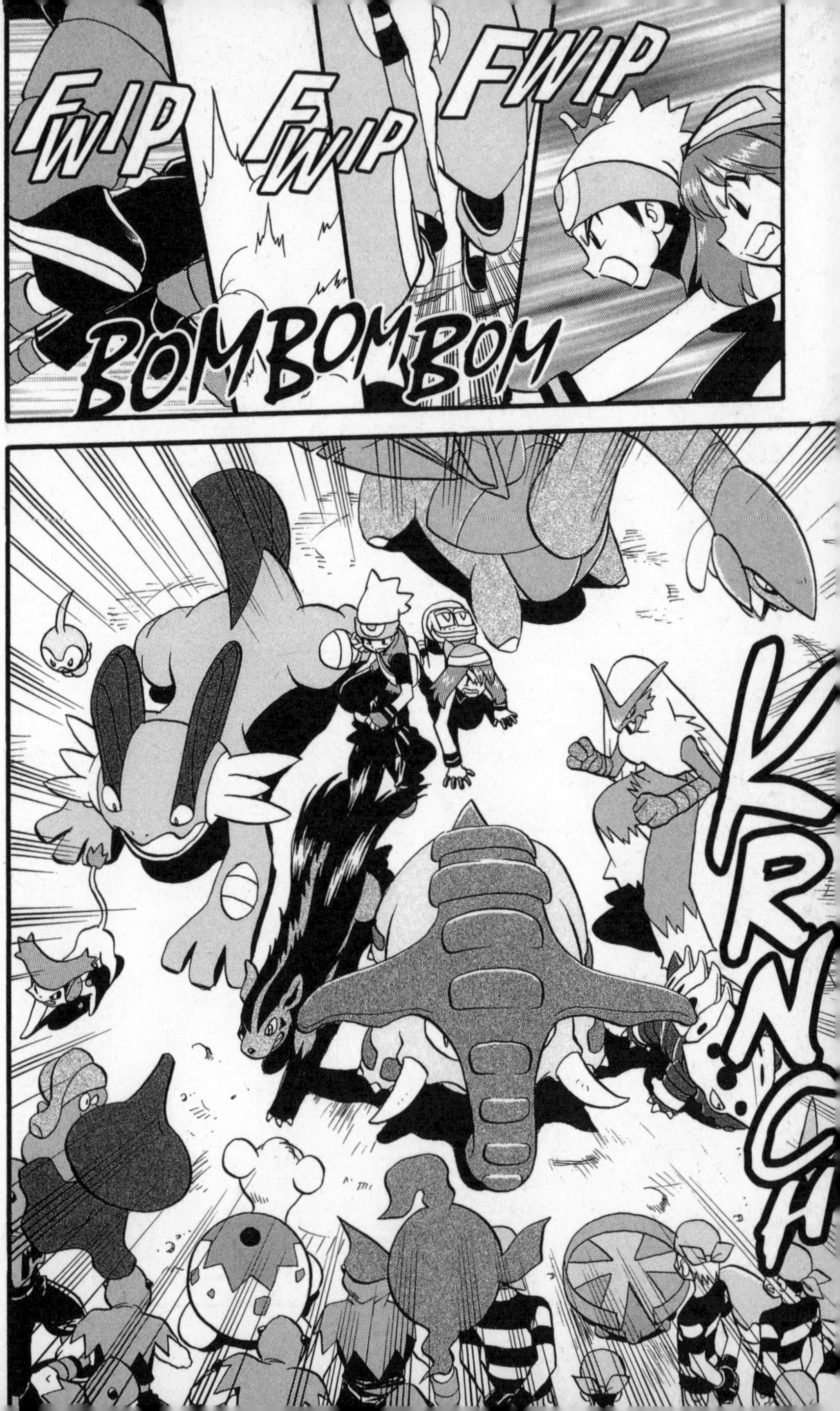
FWIP
FWIP
FWIP
BOMBOMBOM
KRNCH

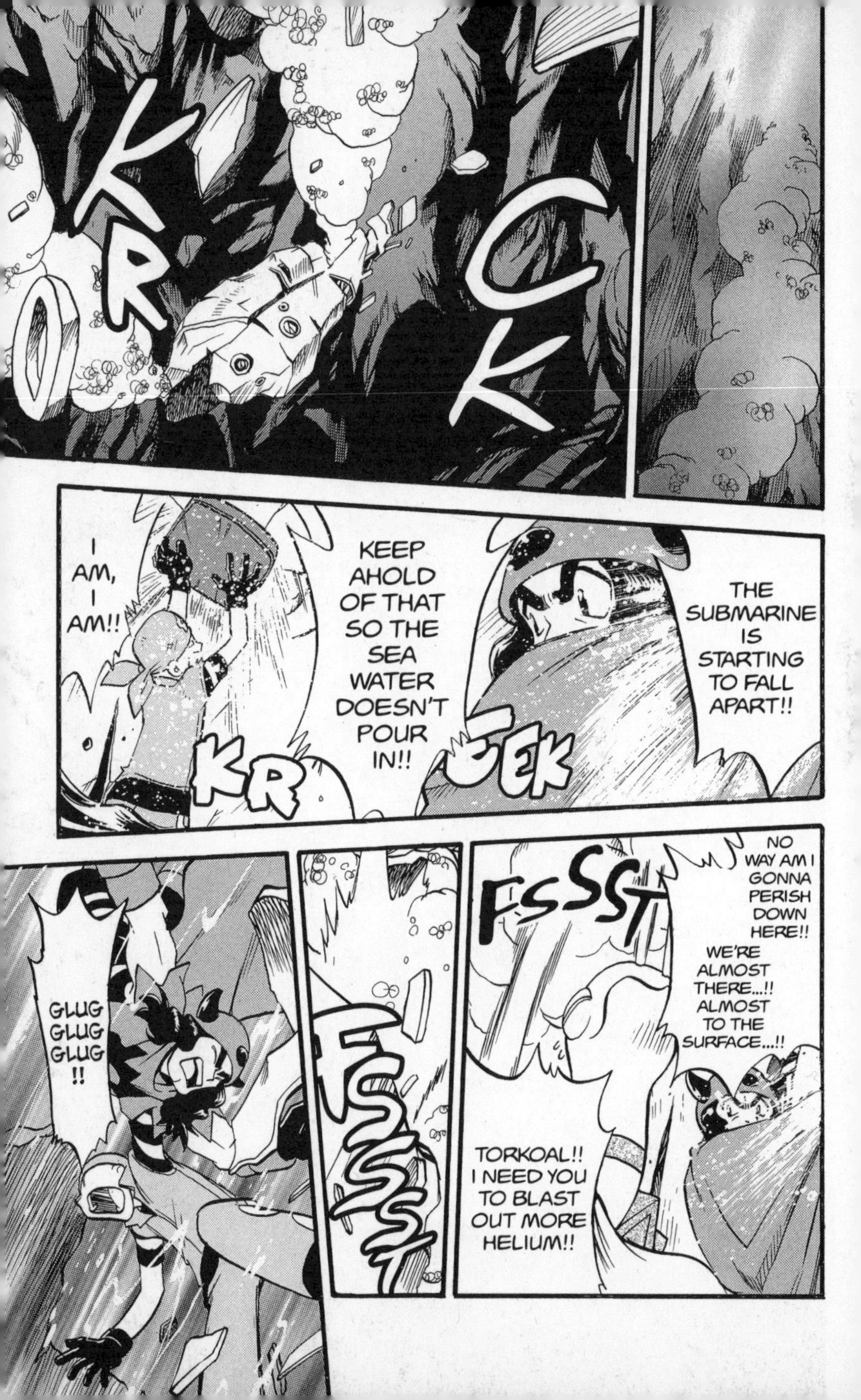
KROCK
THE SUBMARINE IS STARTING TO FALL APART!!
KEEP AHOLD OF THAT SO THE SEA WATER DOESN'T POUR IN!!
I AM, I AM!!
KR
EK
FSSST
NO WAY AM I GONNA PERISH DOWN HERE!!
WE'RE ALMOST THERE...!! ALMOST TO THE SURFACE...!!
TORKOAL!! I NEED YOU TO BLAST OUT MORE HELIUM!!
FSSST
GLUG GLUG GLUG!!

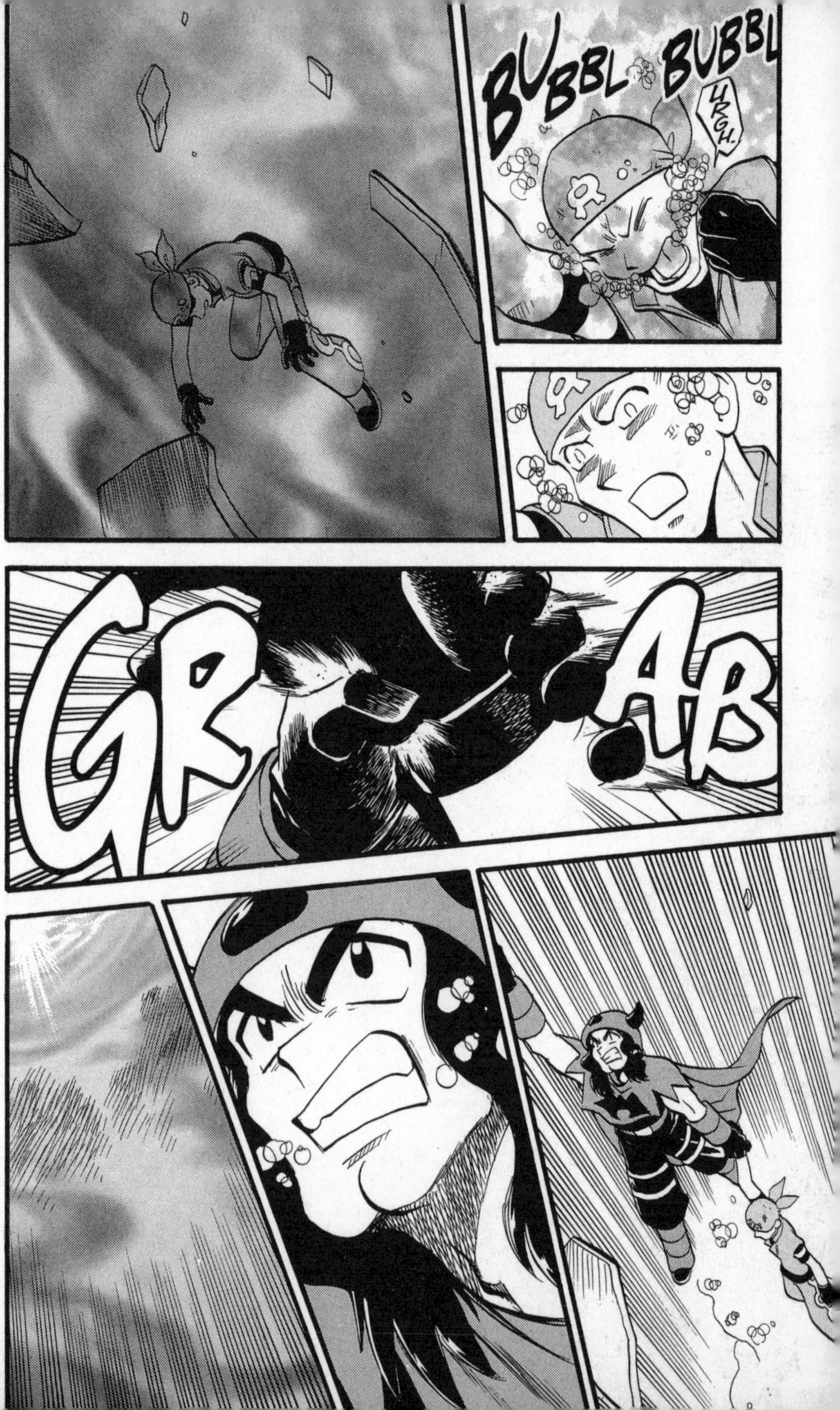
BUBBL BUBBL
URGH.
GRAB

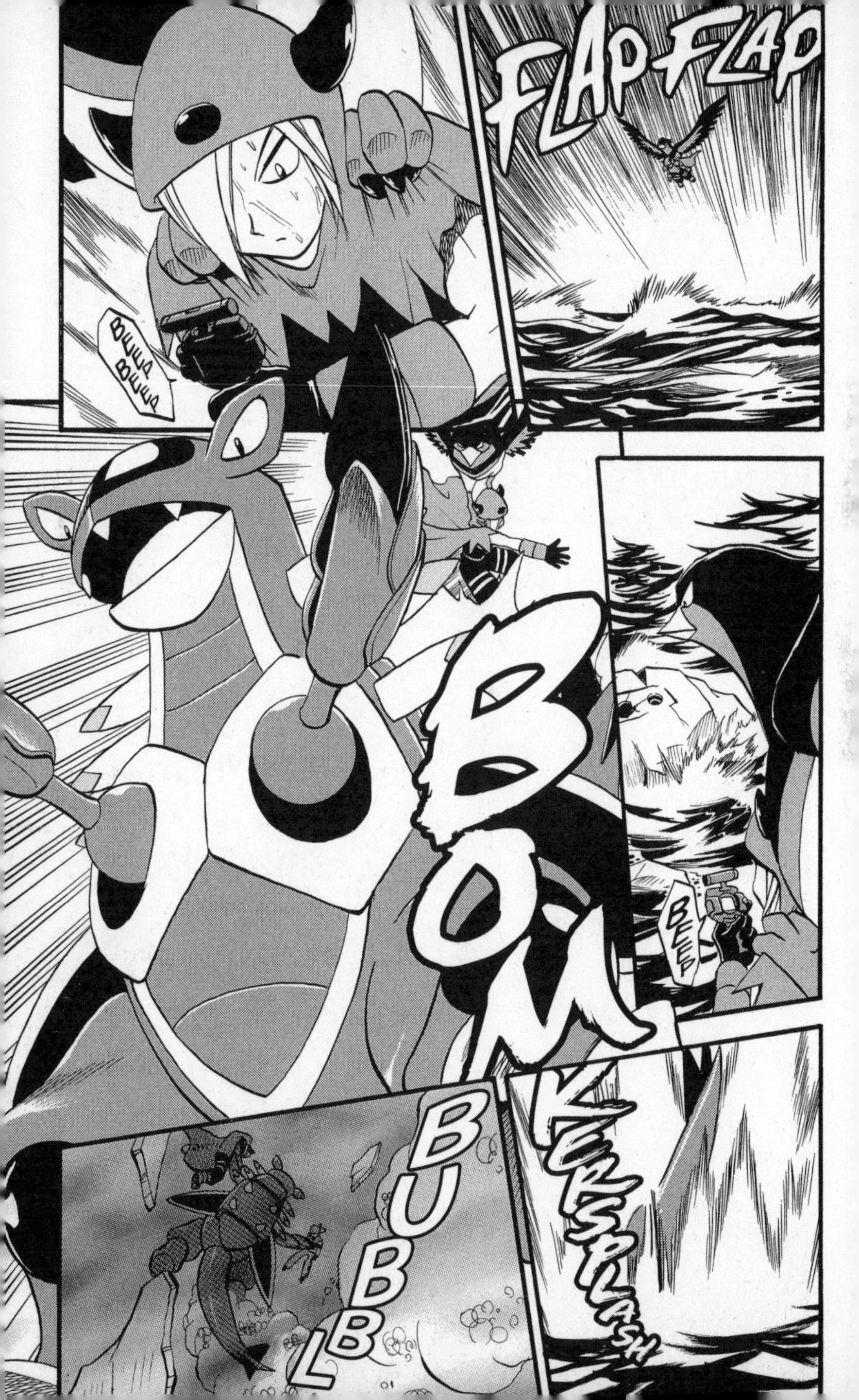
FLAP FLAP
BEEEP BEEEP
BEEP
BOOM
KERSPLASH
BUBBL

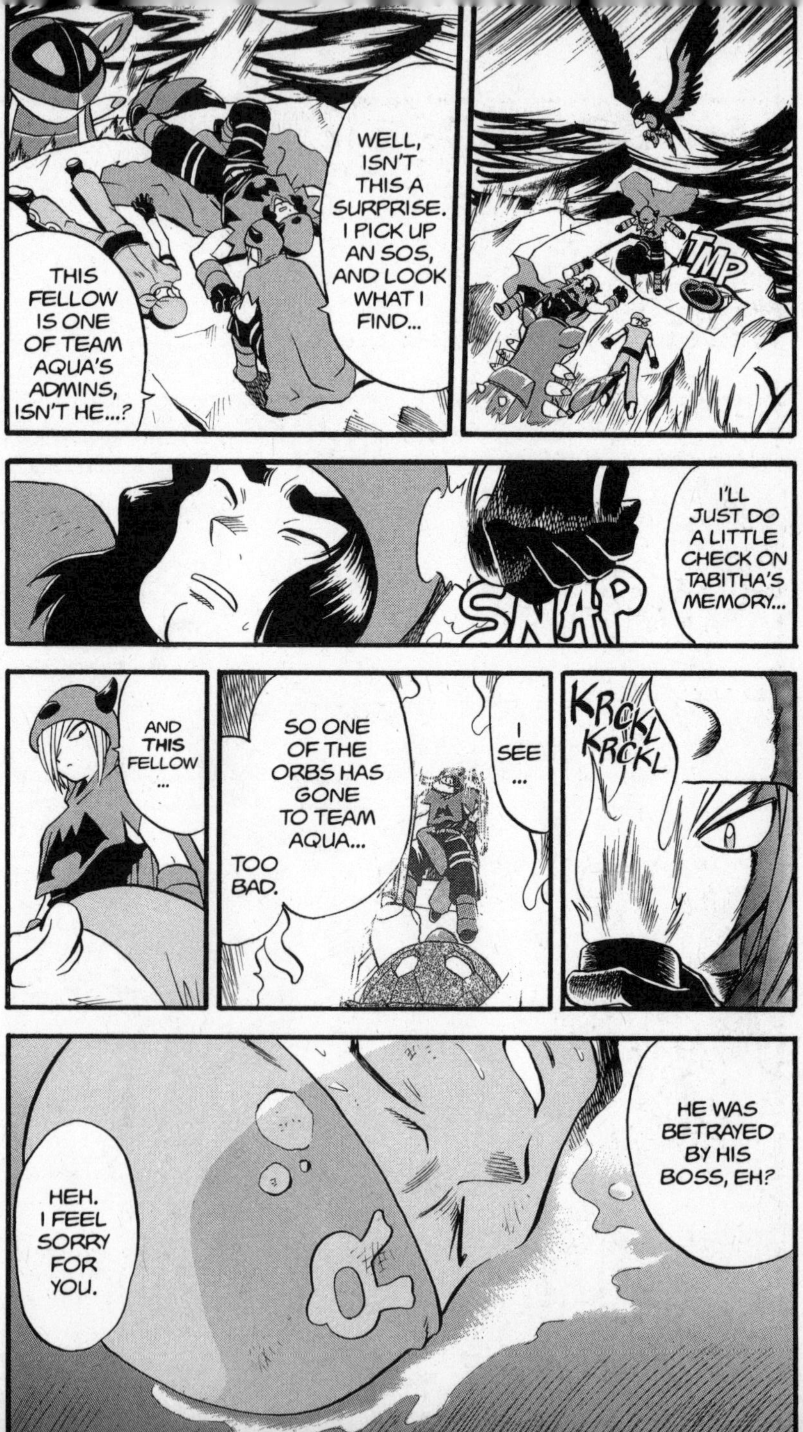
TMP
WELL, ISN'T THIS A SURPRISE. I PICK UP AN SOS, AND LOOK WHAT I FIND...
THIS FELLOW IS ONE OF TEAM AQUA'S ADMINS, ISN'T HE...?
I'LL JUST DO A LITTLE CHECK ON TABITHA'S MEMORY...
SNAP
KRCKL KRCKL
I SEE ...
SO ONE OF THE ORBS HAS GONE TO TEAM AQUA...
TOO BAD.
AND THIS FELLOW ...
HE WAS BETRAYED BY HIS BOSS, EH?
HEH. I FEEL SORRY FOR YOU.

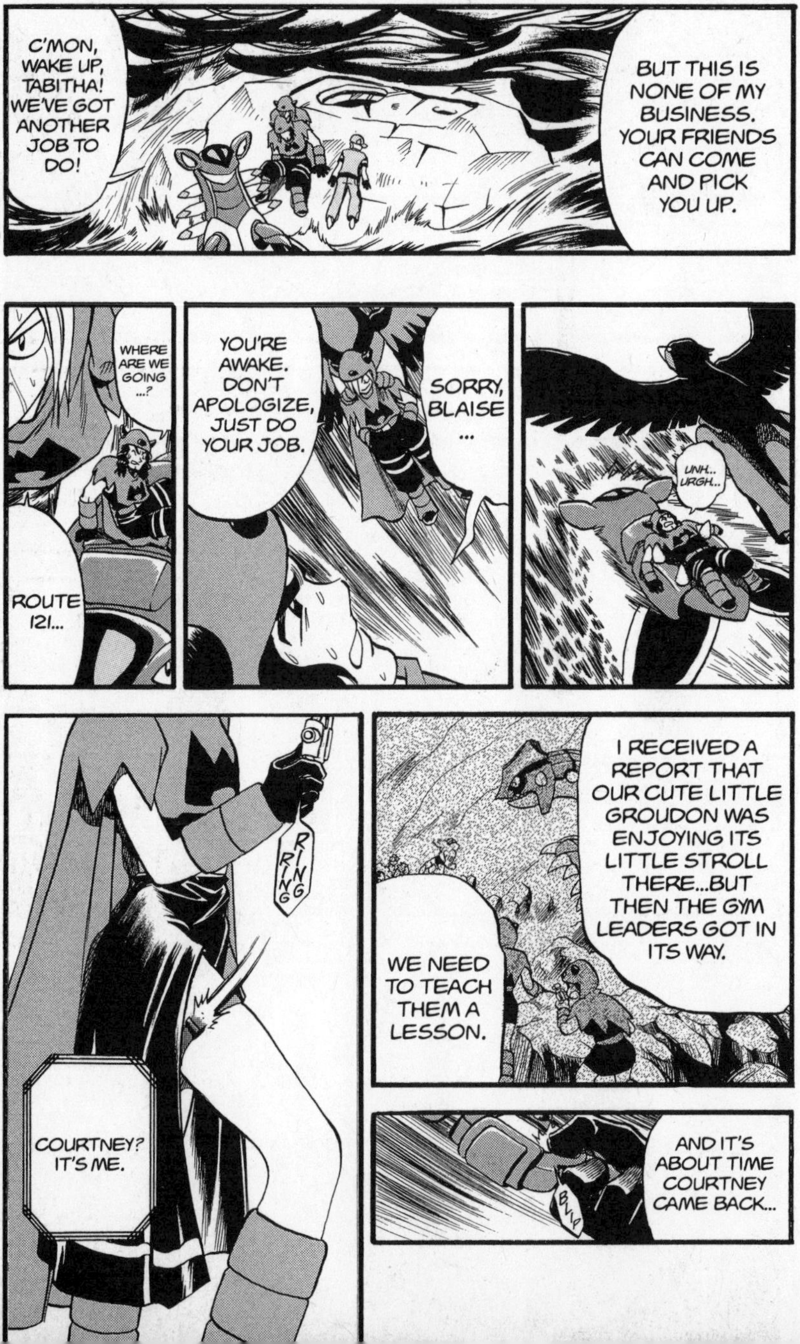
BUT THIS IS NONE OF MY BUSINESS. YOUR FRIENDS CAN COME AND PICK YOU UP.
C'MON, WAKE UP, TABITHA! WE'VE GOT ANOTHER JOB TO DO!
UNH... URGH...
SORRY, BLAISE ...
YOU'RE AWAKE. DON'T APOLOGIZE, JUST DO YOUR JOB.
WHERE ARE WE GOING ...?
ROUTE 121...
I RECEIVED A REPORT THAT OUR CUTE LITTLE GROUDON WAS ENJOYING ITS LITTLE STROLL THERE...BUT THEN THE GYM LEADERS GOT IN ITS WAY.
WE NEED TO TEACH THEM A LESSON.
BVVP
AND IT'S ABOUT TIME COURTNEY CAME BACK...
RING RING
COURTNEY? IT'S ME.

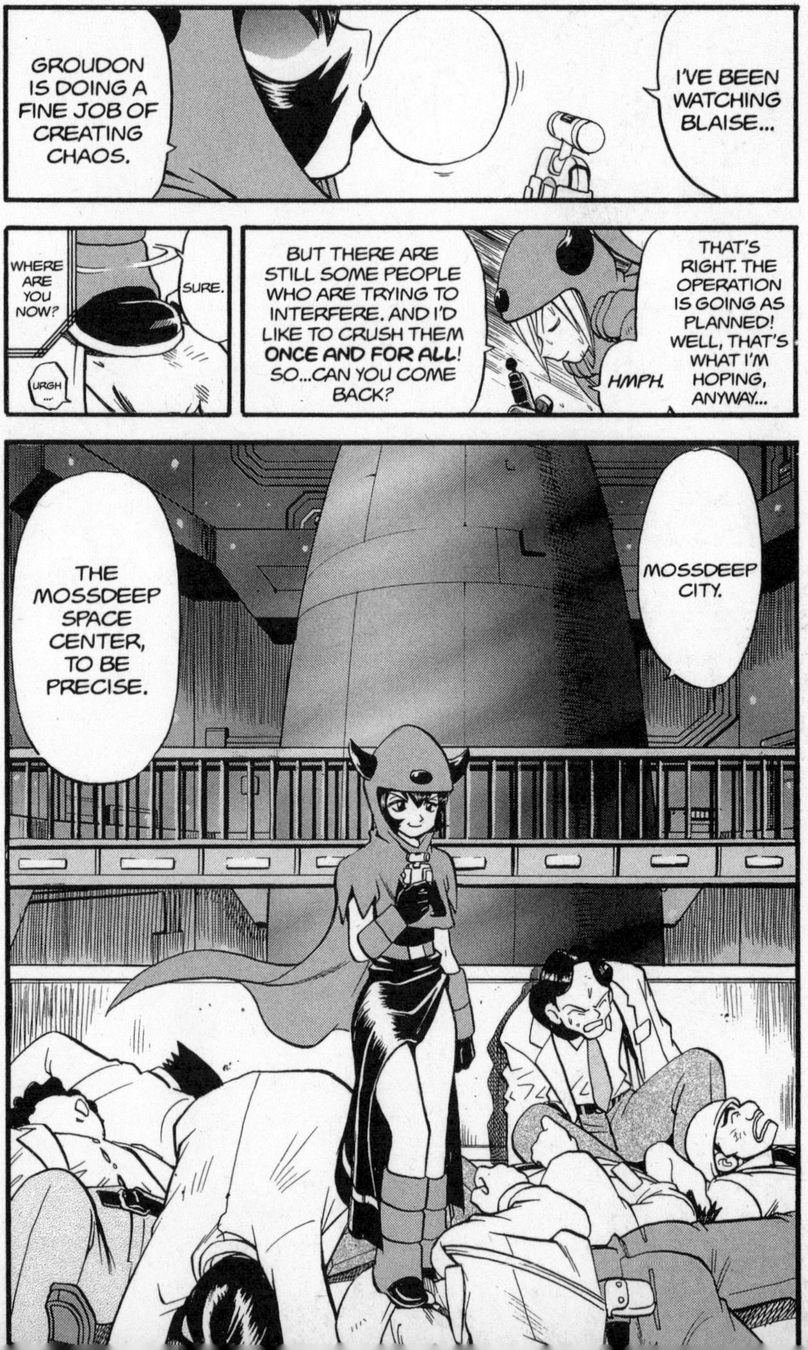
I'VE BEEN WATCHING BLAISE...
GROUDON IS DOING A FINE JOB OF CREATING CHAOS.
THAT'S RIGHT. THE OPERATION IS GOING AS PLANNED! WELL, THAT'S WHAT I'M HOPING, ANYWAY...
HMPH.
BUT THERE ARE STILL SOME PEOPLE WHO ARE TRYING TO INTERFERE. AND I'D LIKE TO CRUSH THEM **ONCE AND FOR ALL**! SO...CAN YOU COME BACK?
SURE.
WHERE ARE YOU NOW?
URGH...
MOSSDEEP CITY.
THE MOSSDEEP SPACE CENTER, TO BE PRECISE.

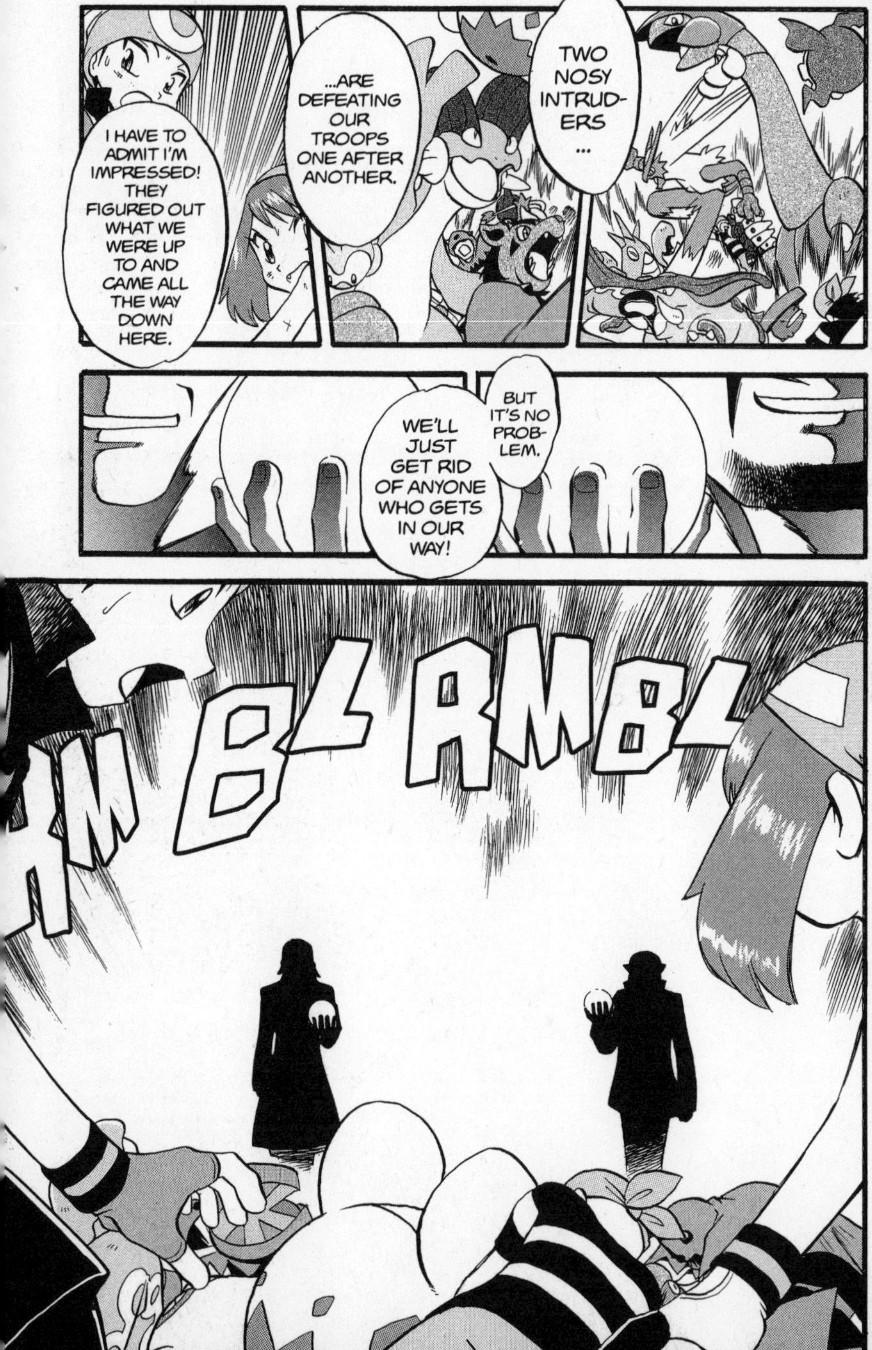
TWO NOSY INTRUDERS...
...ARE DEFEATING OUR TROOPS ONE AFTER ANOTHER.
I HAVE TO ADMIT I'M IMPRESSED! THEY FIGURED OUT WHAT WE WERE UP TO AND CAME ALL THE WAY DOWN HERE.
BUT IT'S NO PROBLEM.
WE'LL JUST GET RID OF ANYONE WHO GETS IN OUR WAY!
RMBL RMBL

● Chapter 244 ●

The Beginning of the End with Kyogre & Groudon VIII

Pokémon™ Adventures Ruby & Sapphire

The Fourth Chapter

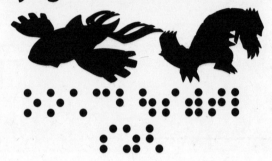

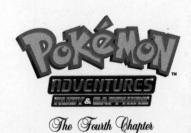

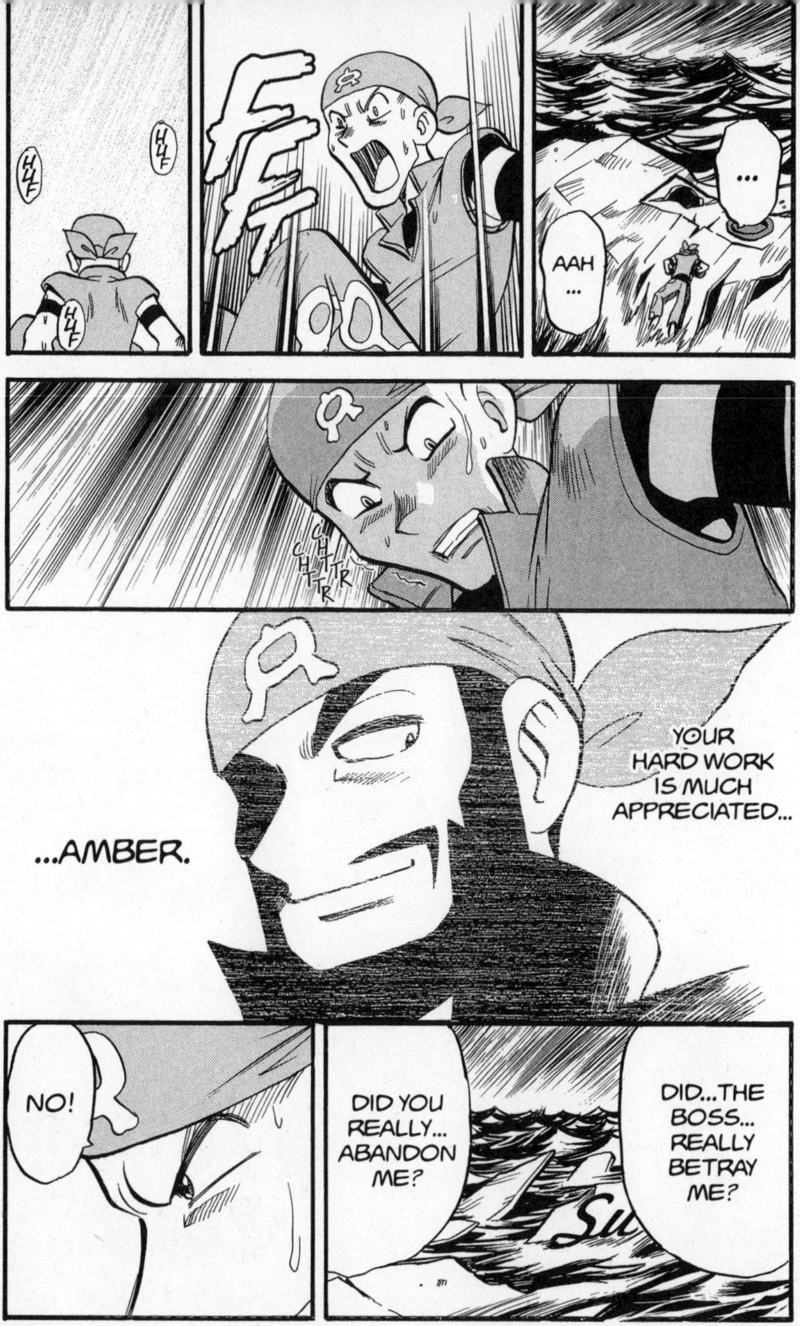
...
AAH ...
HUF
HUF
HUF
CHTTR
CHTTR
YOUR HARD WORK IS MUCH APPRECIATED...
...AMBER.
DID...THE BOSS... REALLY BETRAY ME?
DID YOU REALLY... ABANDON ME?
NO!

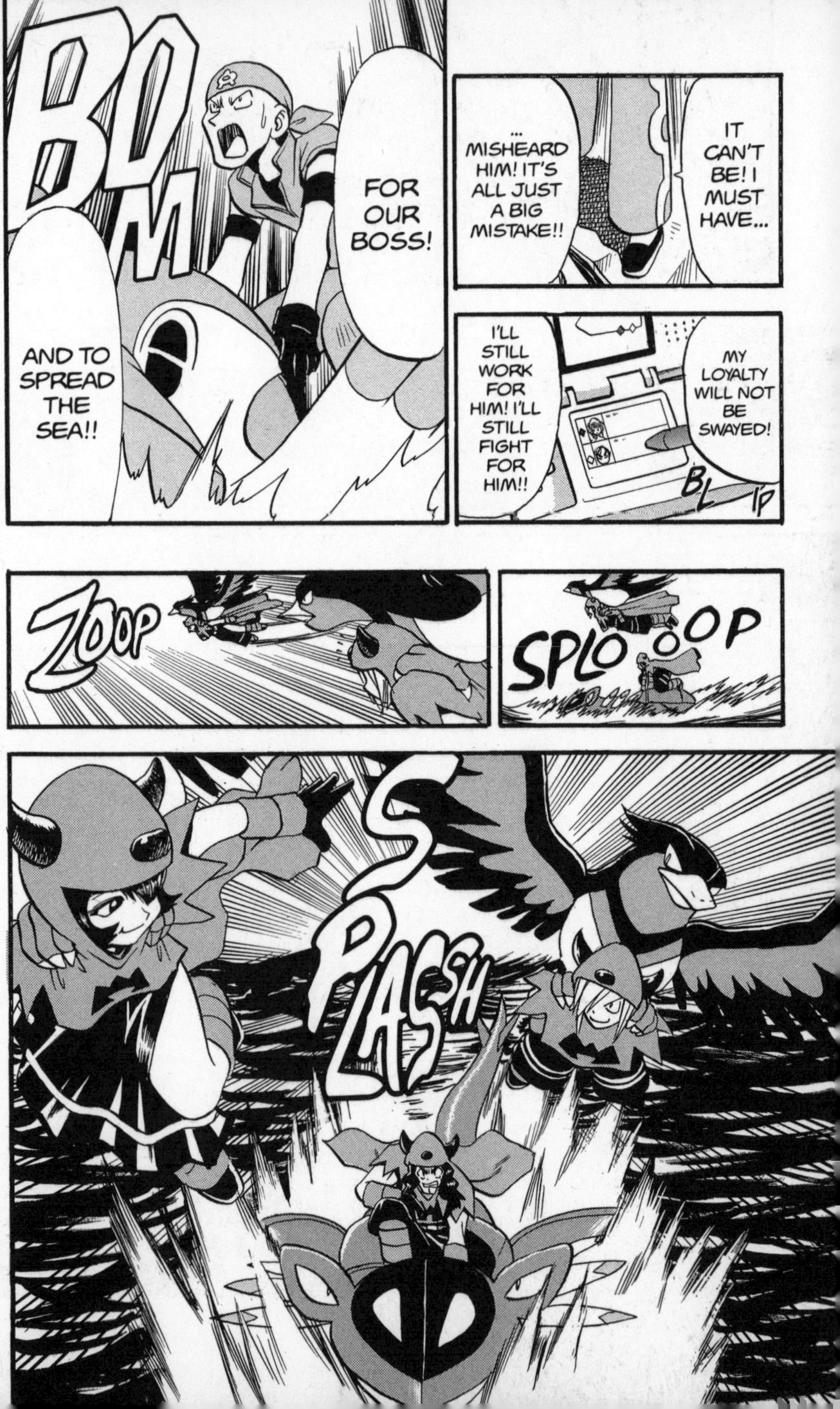
IT CAN'T BE! I MUST HAVE...
... MISHEARD HIM! IT'S ALL JUST A BIG MISTAKE!!
MY LOYALTY WILL NOT BE SWAYED!
I'LL STILL WORK FOR HIM! I'LL STILL FIGHT FOR HIM!!
BLIP
BOOM
FOR OUR BOSS!
AND TO SPREAD THE SEA!!
SPLOOOP
ZOOP
SPLASH

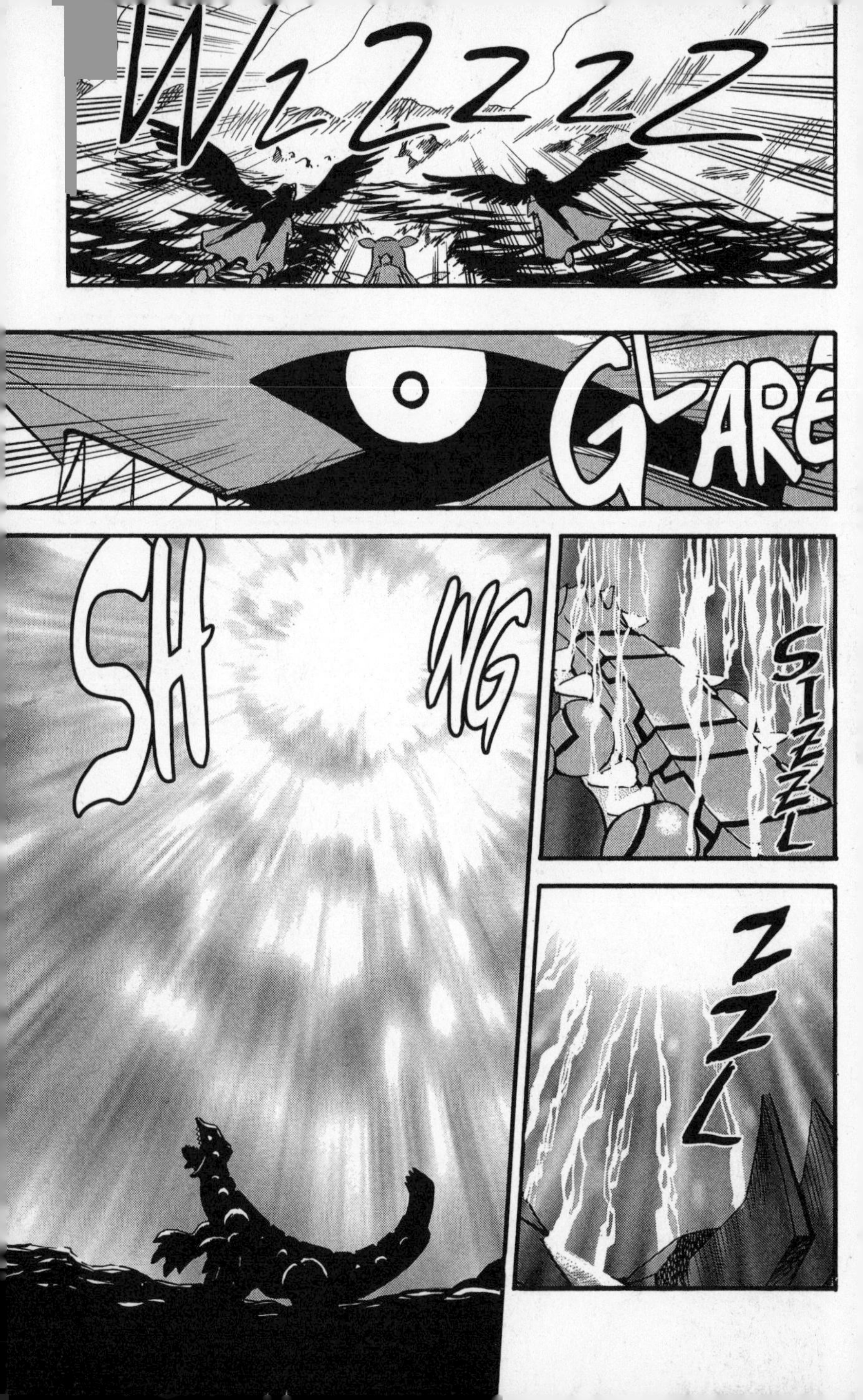
WZZZZZZ
GLARE
SIZZZL
ZZL
SH
NG

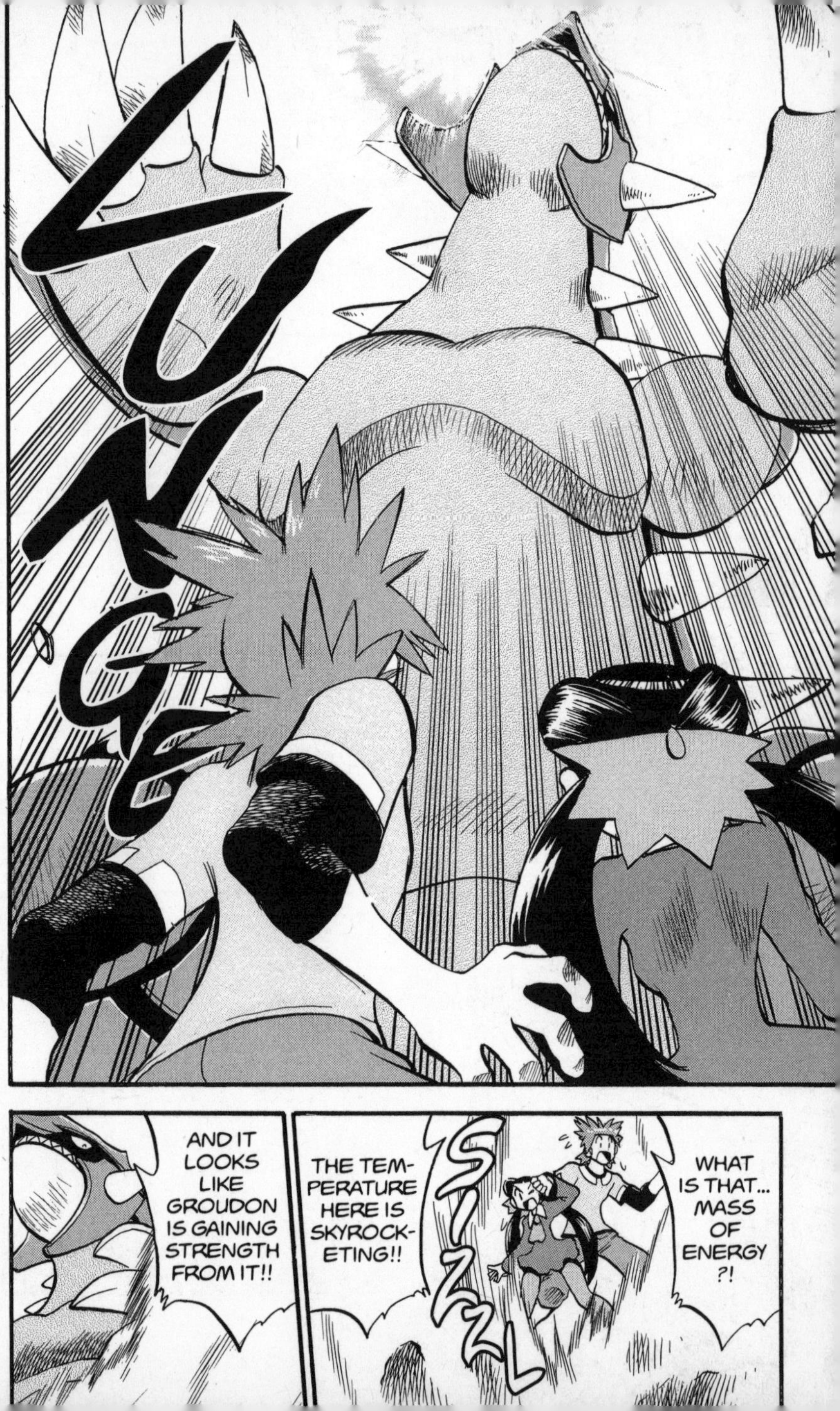
WHAT IS THAT... MASS OF ENERGY ?!
SIZZL
THE TEM-PERATURE HERE IS SKYROCK-ETING!!
AND IT LOOKS LIKE GROUDON IS GAINING STRENGTH FROM IT!!

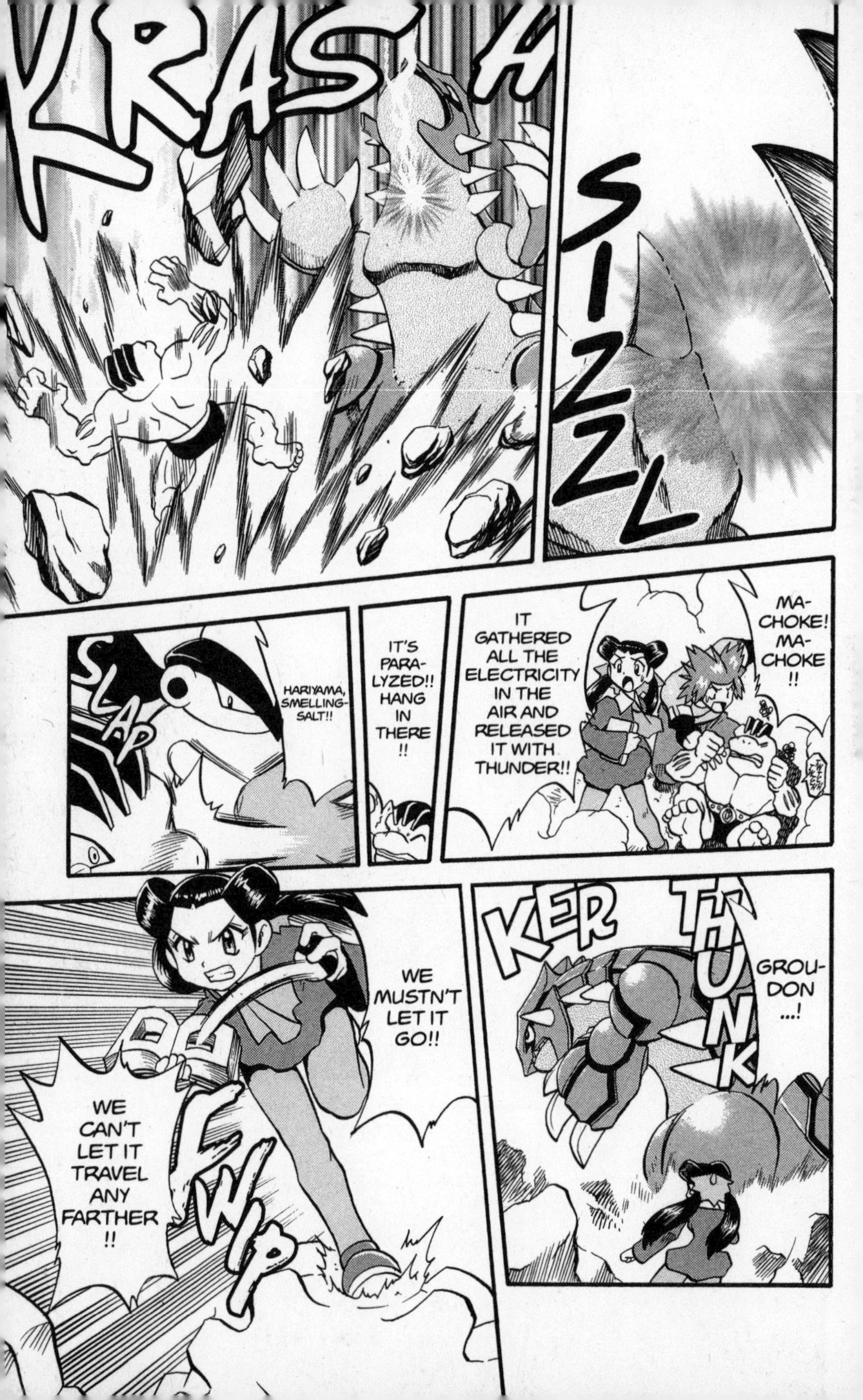
SIZZL
KRASH
MA-CHOKE! MA-CHOKE!!
IT GATHERED ALL THE ELECTRICITY IN THE AIR AND RELEASED IT WITH THUNDER!!
IT'S PARALYZED!! HANG IN THERE!!
HARIYAMA, SMELLING-SALT!!
SLAP
KER THUNK
GROU-DON...!
WE MUSTN'T LET IT GO!!
WE CAN'T LET IT TRAVEL ANY FARTHER!!
WHIP

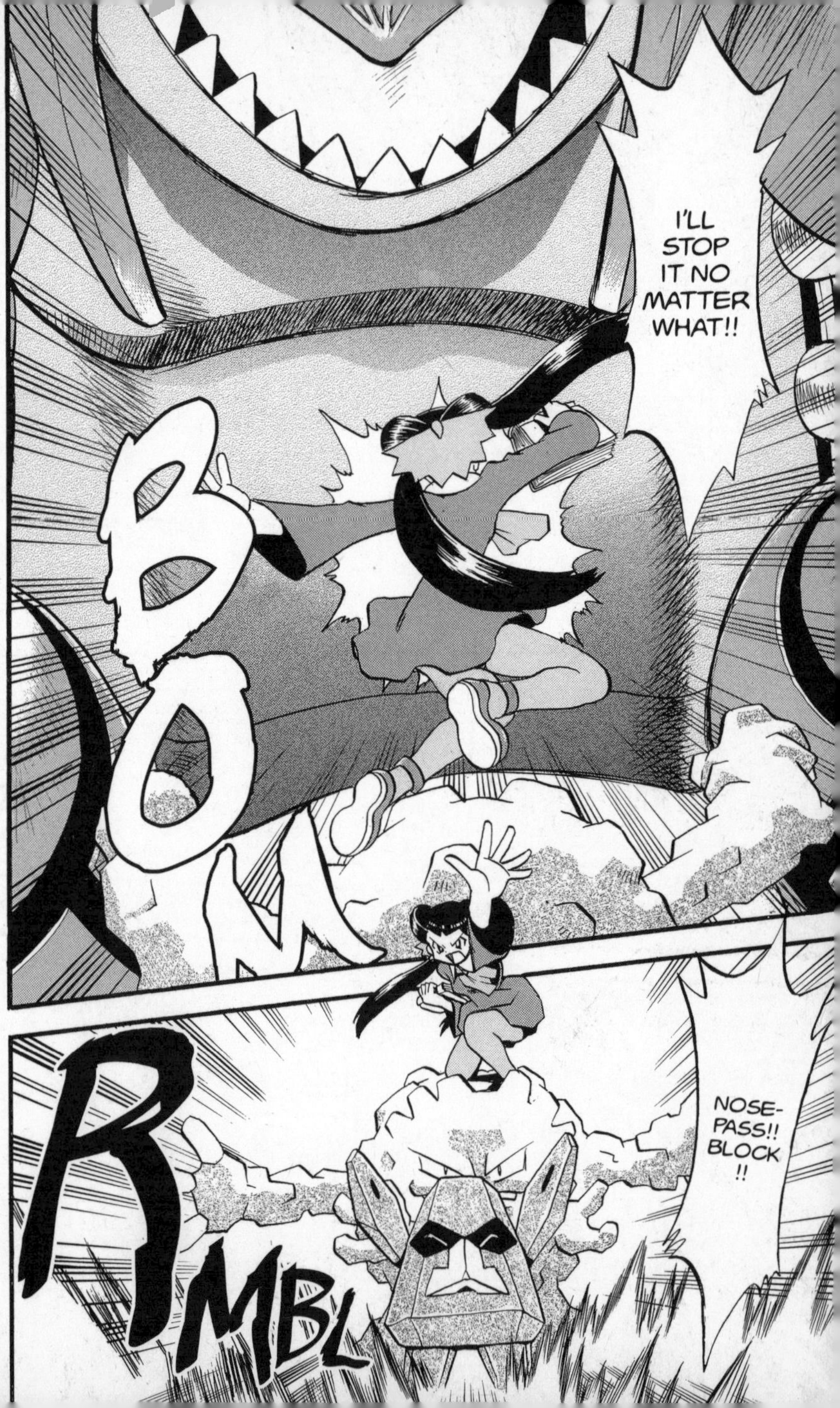
I'LL STOP IT NO MATTER WHAT!!
BOOM
NOSE-PASS!! BLOCK!!
RMBL

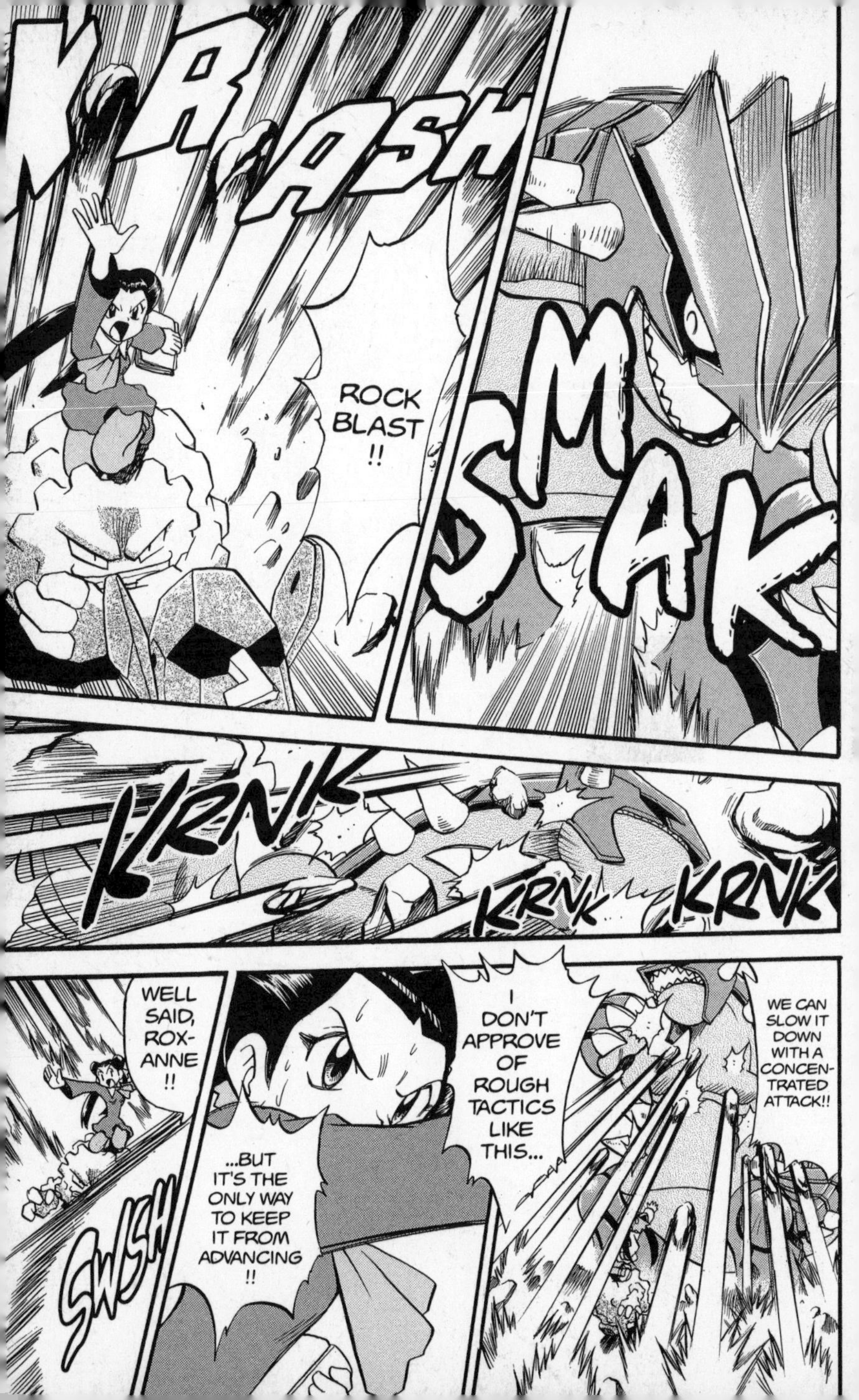
SMAK
KRASH
ROCK BLAST !!
KRNK
KRNK...
KRNK
WE CAN SLOW IT DOWN WITH A CONCEN-TRATED ATTACK!!
I DON'T APPROVE OF ROUGH TACTICS LIKE THIS...
...BUT IT'S THE ONLY WAY TO KEEP IT FROM ADVANCING !!
SWISH
WELL SAID, ROX-ANNE !!

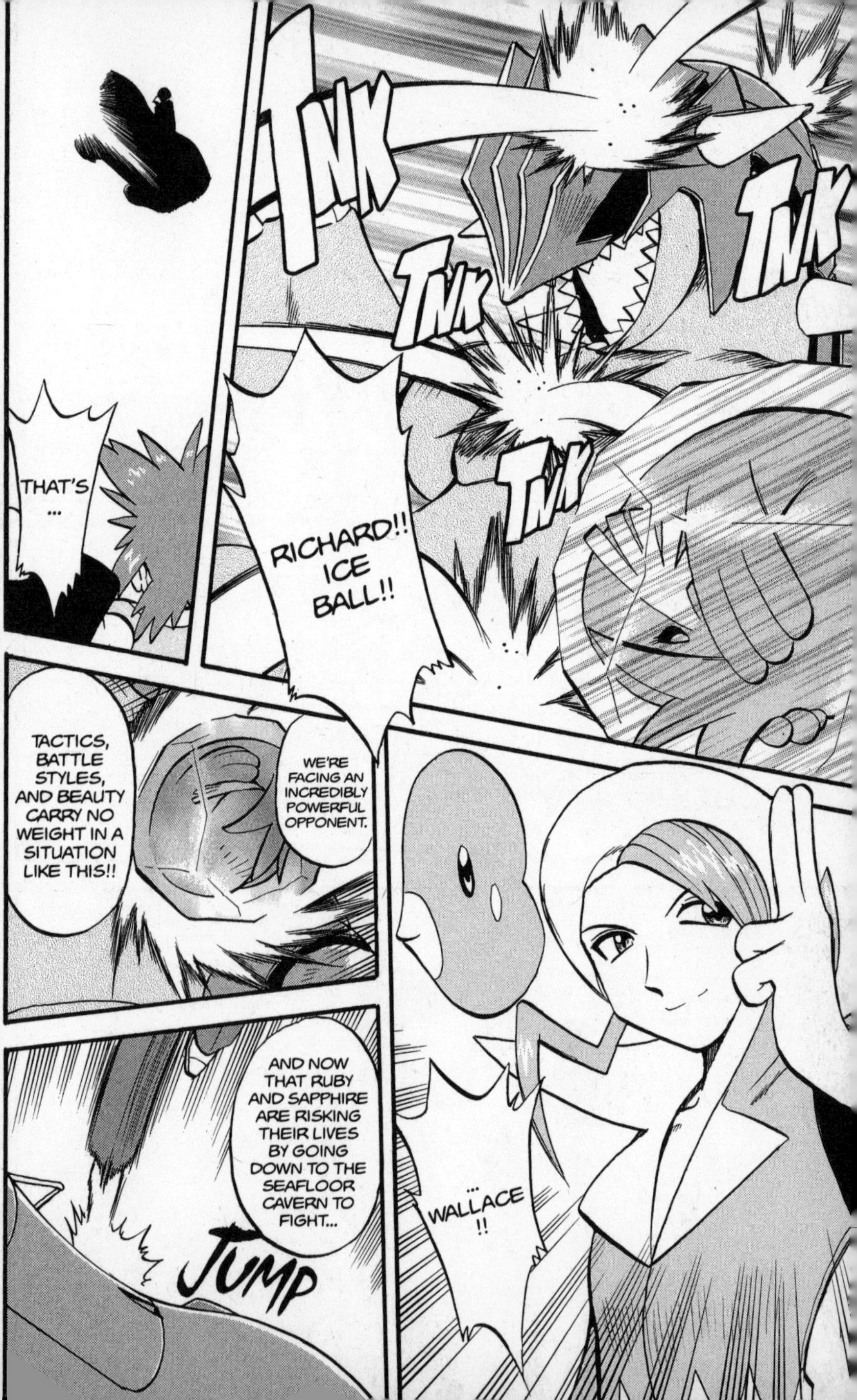
TINK
TNK
TNK
TNK
RICHARD!! ICE BALL!!
THAT'S ...
WE'RE FACING AN INCREDIBLY POWERFUL OPPONENT.
... WALLACE !!
TACTICS, BATTLE STYLES, AND BEAUTY CARRY NO WEIGHT IN A SITUATION LIKE THIS!!
AND NOW THAT RUBY AND SAPPHIRE ARE RISKING THEIR LIVES BY GOING DOWN TO THE SEAFLOOR CAVERN TO FIGHT...
JUMP

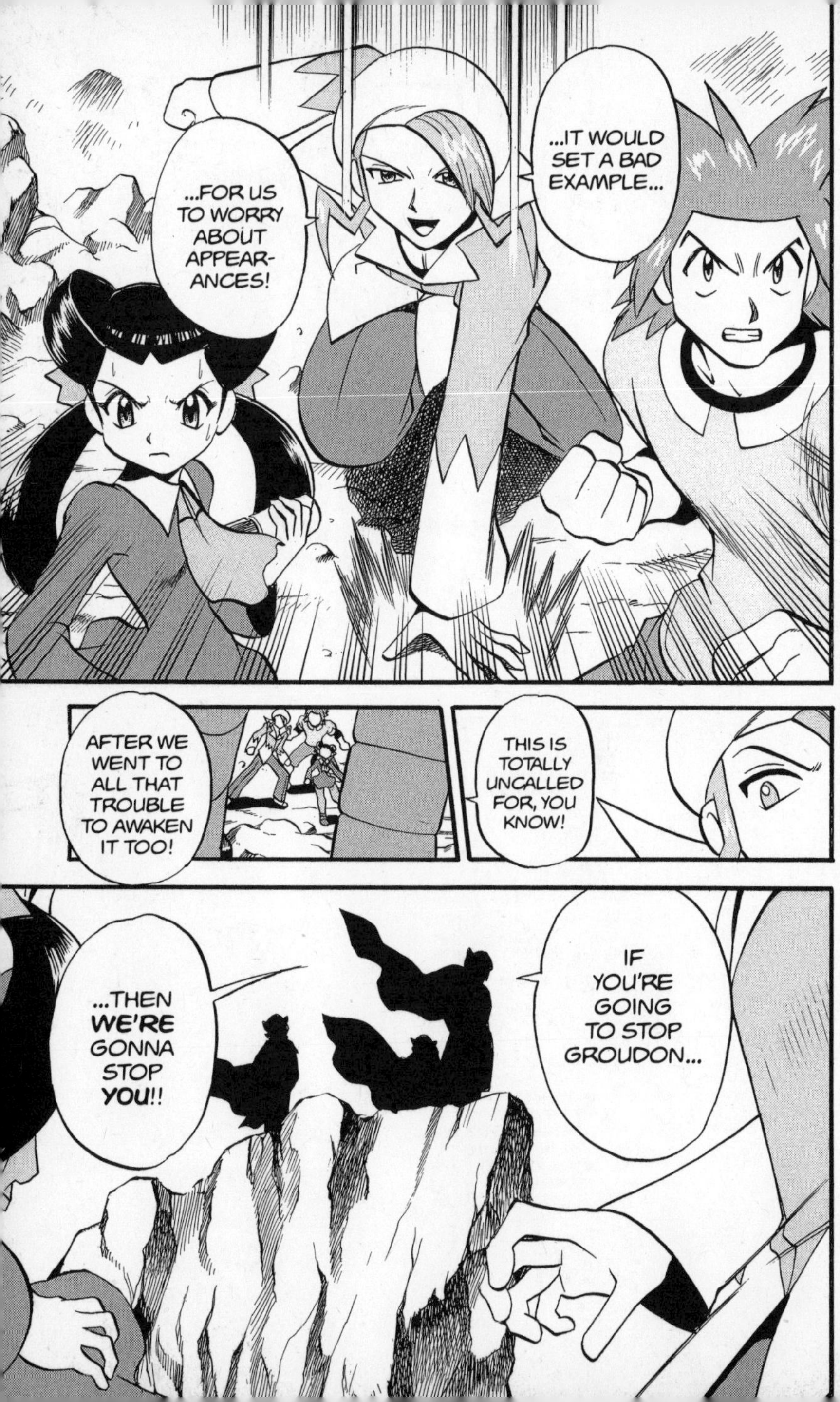
...IT WOULD SET A BAD EXAMPLE...
...FOR US TO WORRY ABOUT APPEARANCES!
THIS IS TOTALLY UNCALLED FOR, YOU KNOW!
AFTER WE WENT TO ALL THAT TROUBLE TO AWAKEN IT TOO!
IF YOU'RE GOING TO STOP GROUDON...
...THEN **WE'RE** GONNA STOP **YOU**!!

● Chapter 245 ●
Bravo, Vibrava

The Fourth Chapter

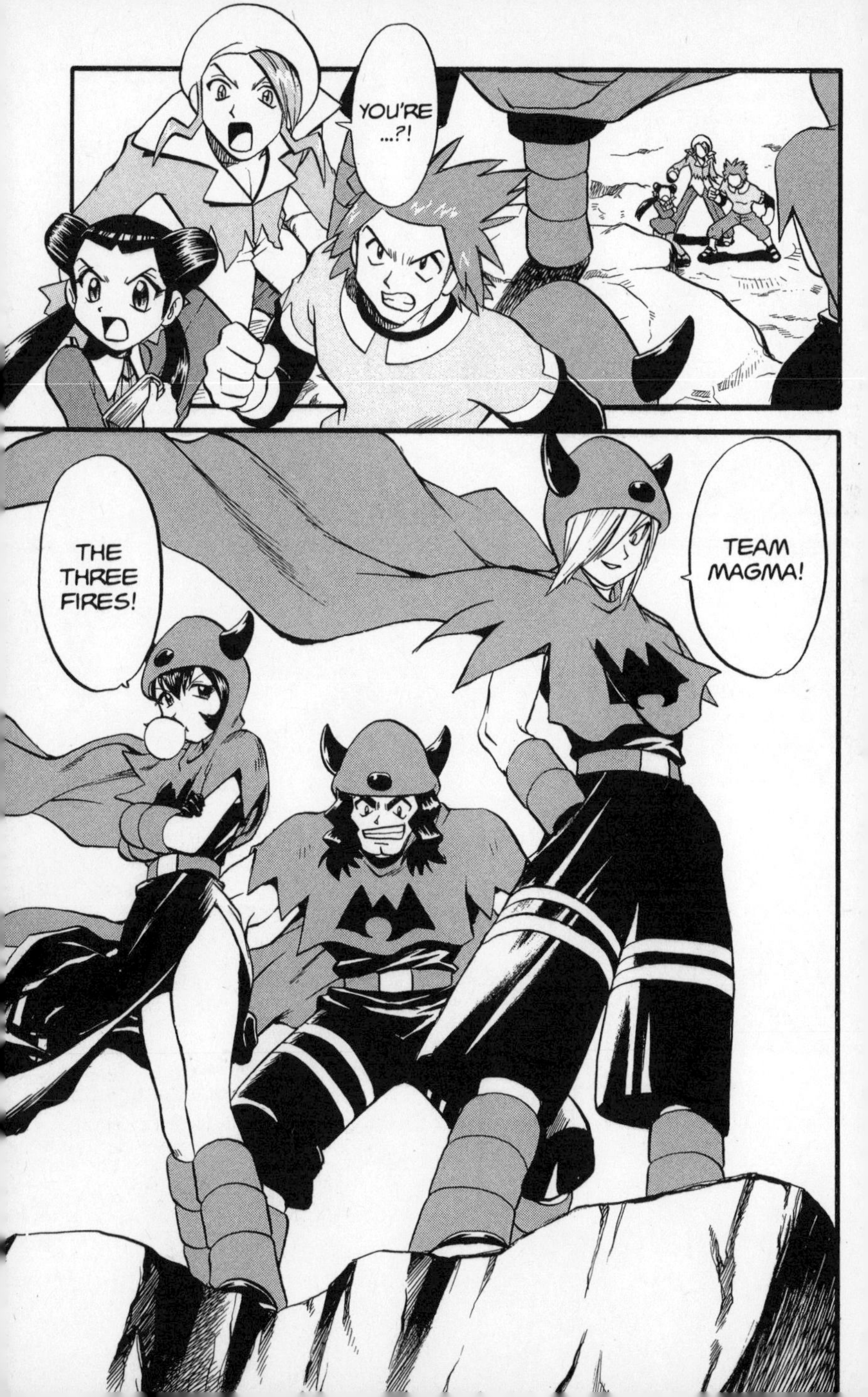

YOU'RE ...?!
TEAM MAGMA!
THE THREE FIRES!

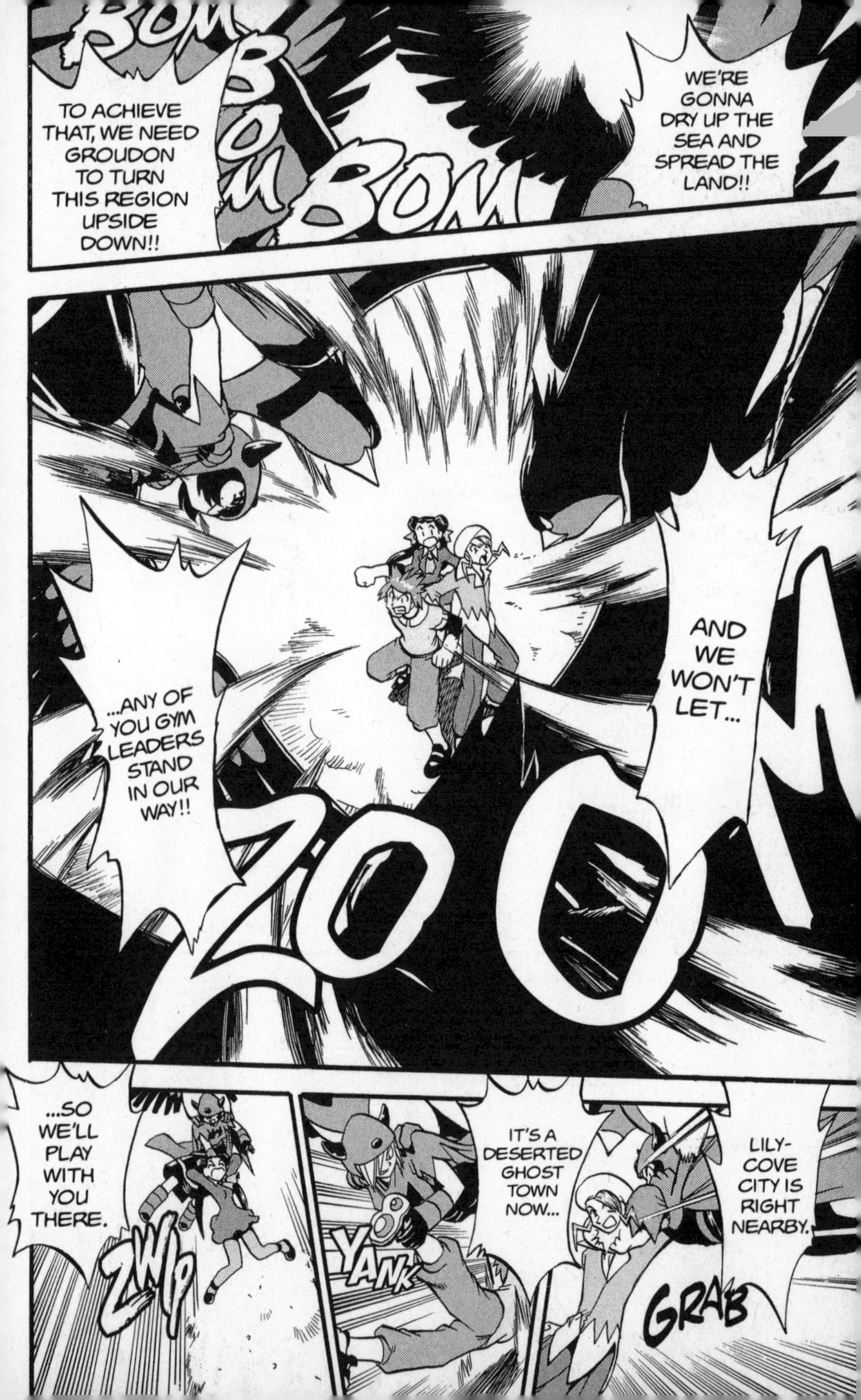
WE'RE GONNA DRY UP THE SEA AND SPREAD THE LAND!!
BOM BOM BOM
TO ACHIEVE THAT, WE NEED GROUDON TO TURN THIS REGION UPSIDE DOWN!!
AND WE WON'T LET...
...ANY OF YOU GYM LEADERS STAND IN OUR WAY!!
ZOOM
LILY-COVE CITY IS RIGHT NEARBY.
GRAB
IT'S A DESERTED GHOST TOWN NOW...
YANK
...SO WE'LL PLAY WITH YOU THERE.
ZWIP

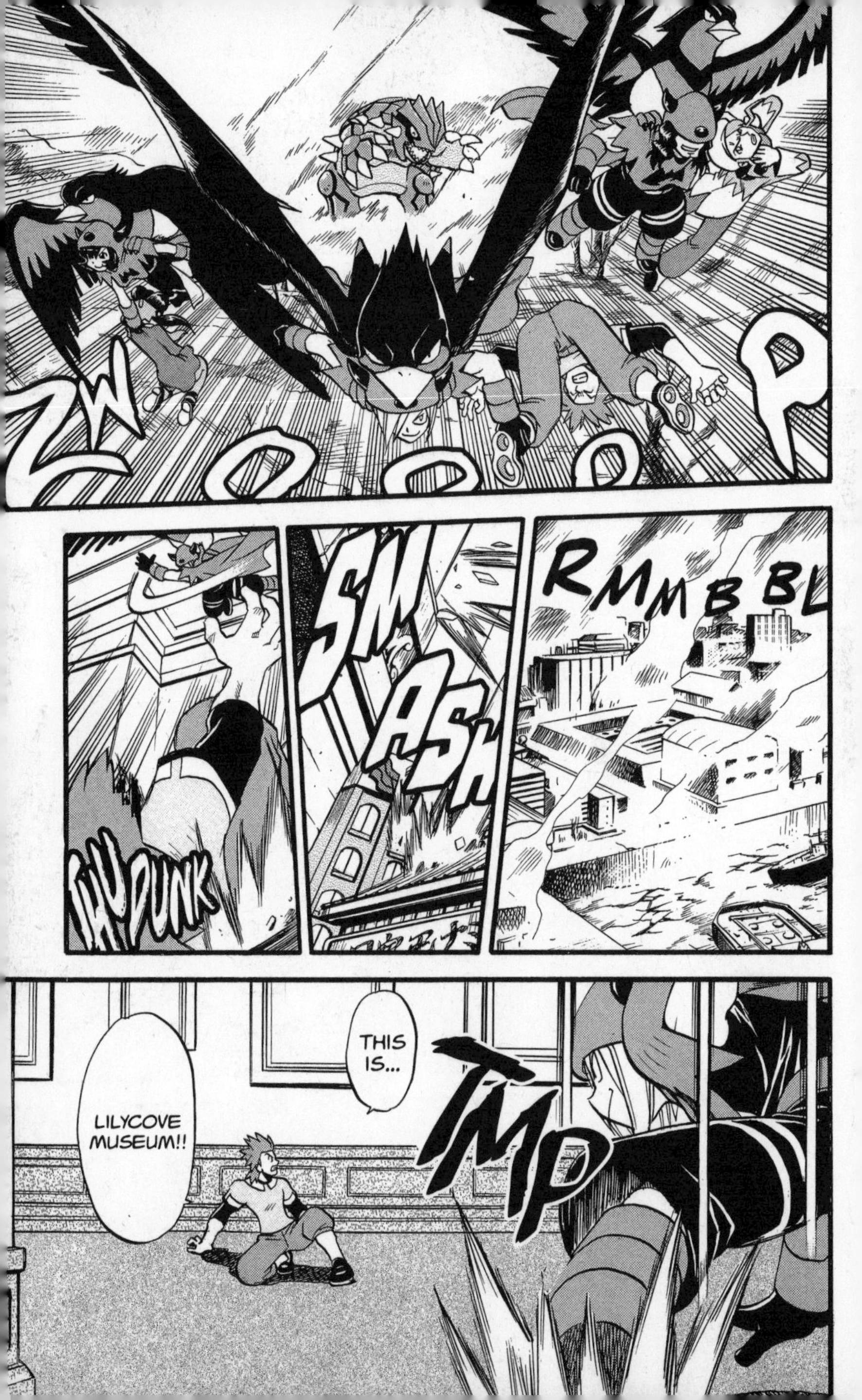
ZWOOOP
RMMBBL
SMASH
THUDUNK
TMP
THIS IS...
LILYCOVE MUSEUM!!

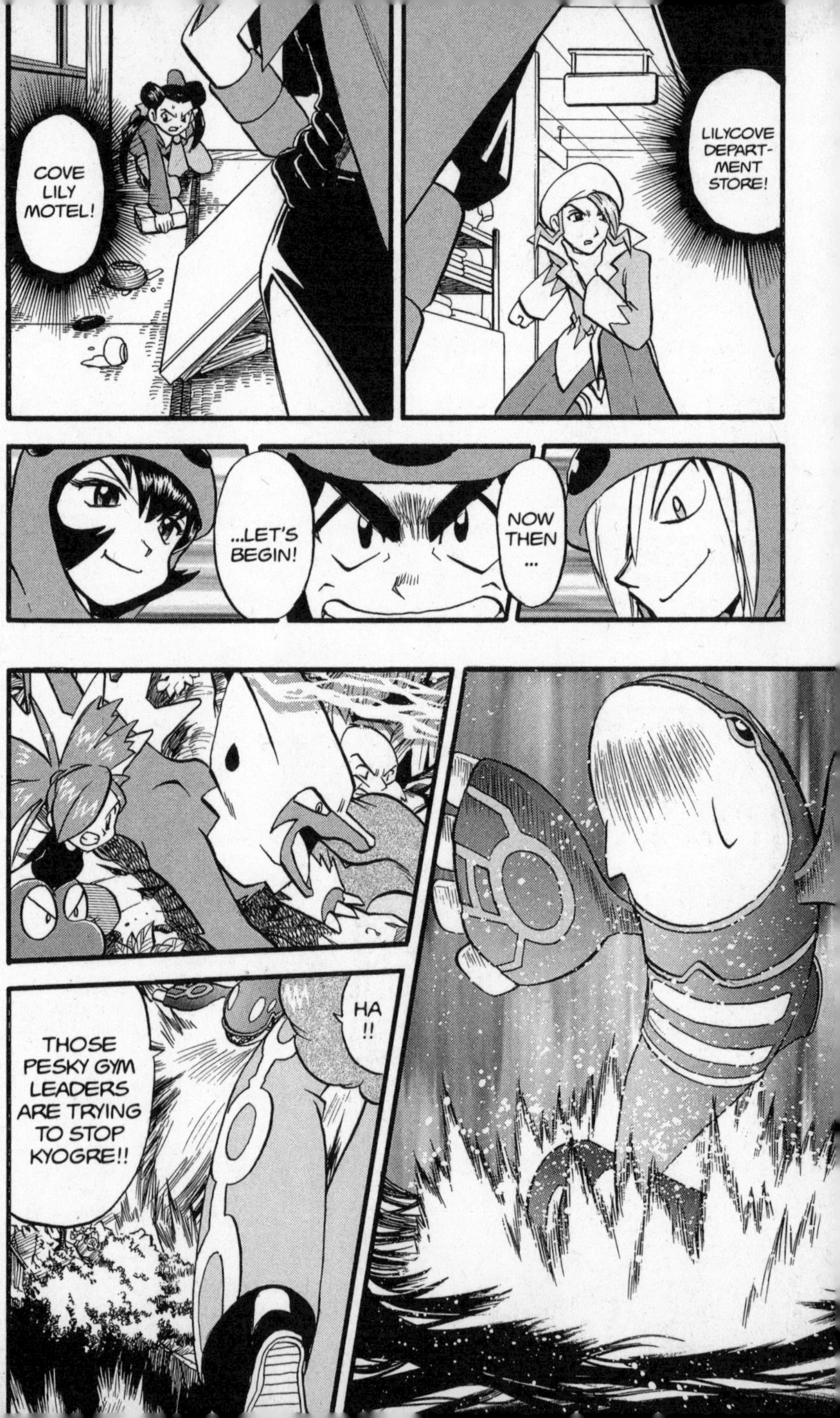
LILYCOVE DEPARTMENT STORE!
COVE LILY MOTEL!
NOW THEN ...
...LET'S BEGIN!
HA!!
THOSE PESKY GYM LEADERS ARE TRYING TO STOP KYOGRE!!

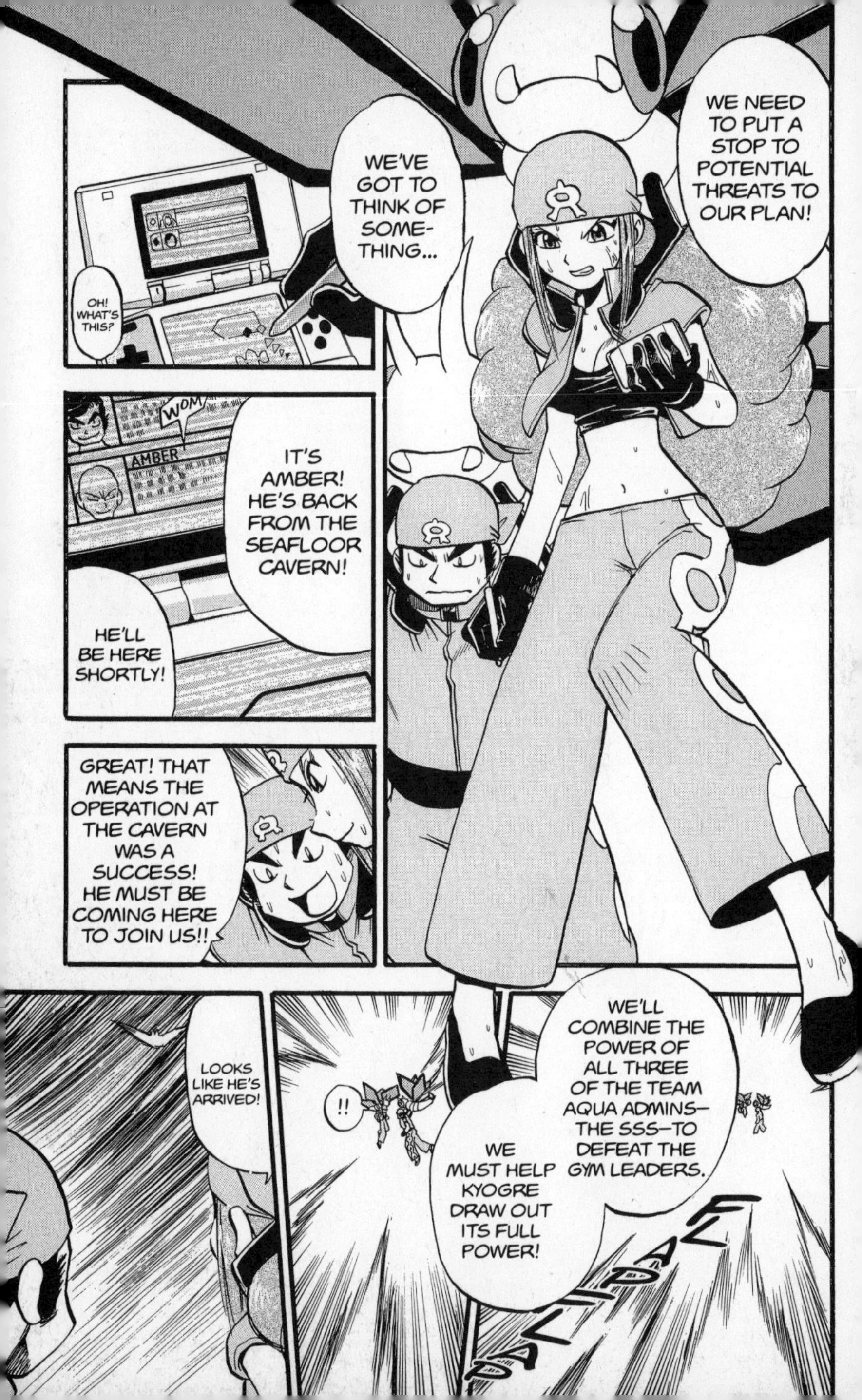
WE NEED TO PUT A STOP TO POTENTIAL THREATS TO OUR PLAN!
WE'VE GOT TO THINK OF SOME-THING...
OH! WHAT'S THIS?
WOM
AMBER
IT'S AMBER! HE'S BACK FROM THE SEAFLOOR CAVERN!
HE'LL BE HERE SHORTLY!
GREAT! THAT MEANS THE OPERATION AT THE CAVERN WAS A SUCCESS! HE MUST BE COMING HERE TO JOIN US!!
WE'LL COMBINE THE POWER OF ALL THREE OF THE TEAM AQUA ADMINS—THE SSS—TO DEFEAT THE GYM LEADERS.
WE MUST HELP KYOGRE DRAW OUT ITS FULL POWER!
!!
FLAP FLAP
LOOKS LIKE HE'S ARRIVED!

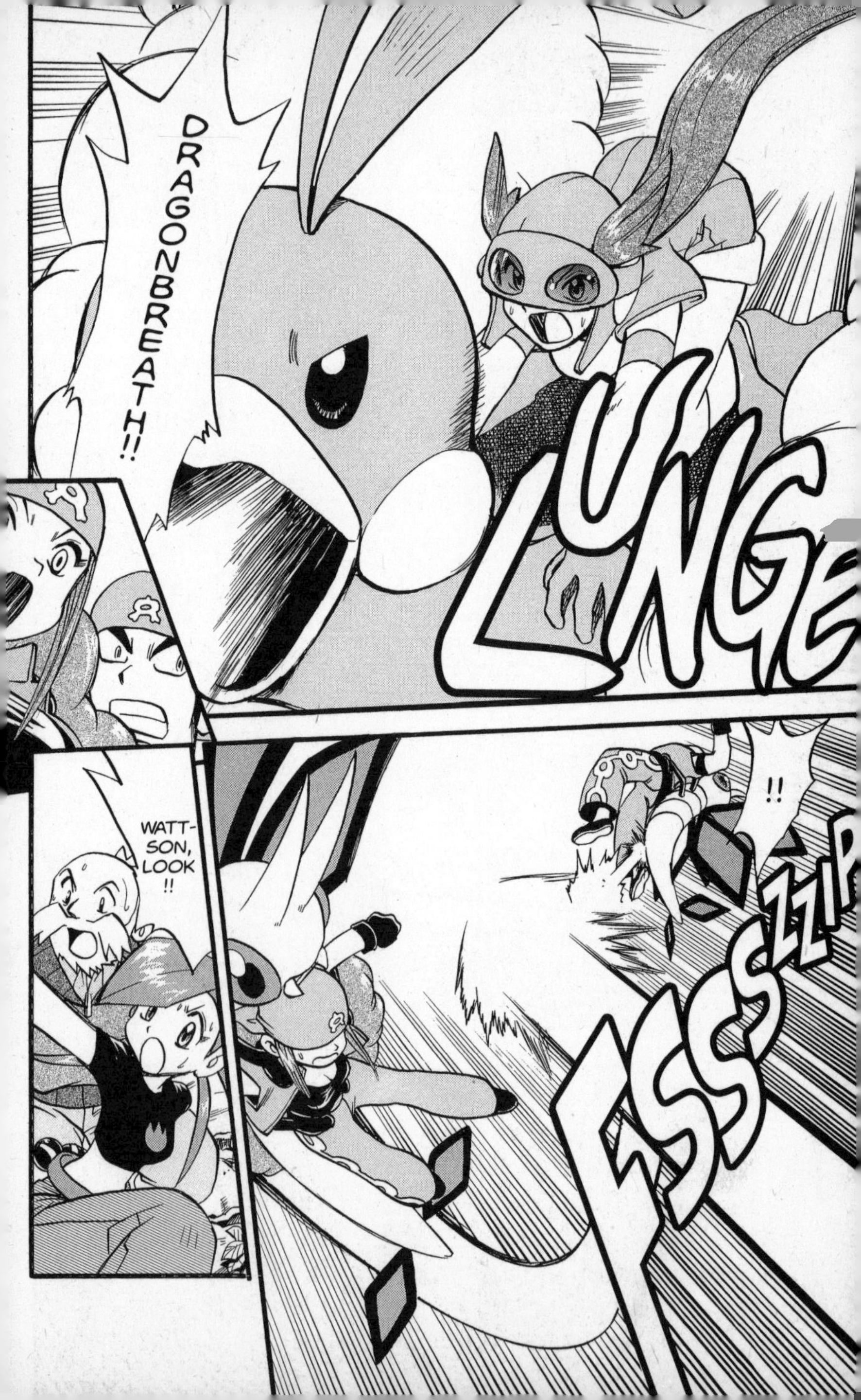
DRAGONBREATH!!
LUNGE
!!
FSSSZZIP
WATT-SON, LOOK!!

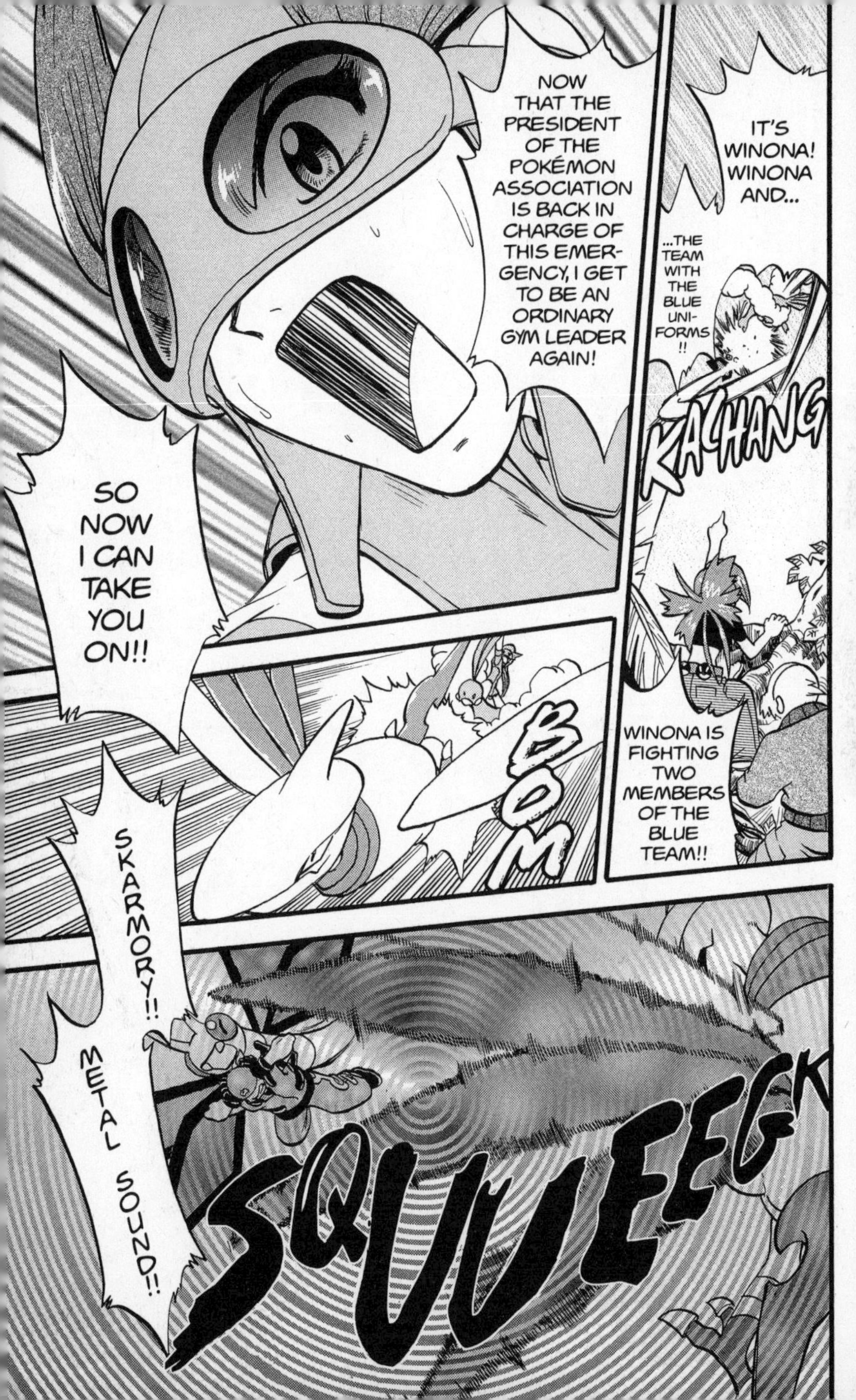
IT'S WINONA! WINONA AND...
...THE TEAM WITH THE BLUE UNIFORMS!!
KACHANG
WINONA IS FIGHTING TWO MEMBERS OF THE BLUE TEAM!!
NOW THAT THE PRESIDENT OF THE POKÉMON ASSOCIATION IS BACK IN CHARGE OF THIS EMERGENCY, I GET TO BE AN ORDINARY GYM LEADER AGAIN!
SO NOW I CAN TAKE YOU ON!!
BOOM
SKARMORY!!
METAL SOUND!!
SQUEEEGK

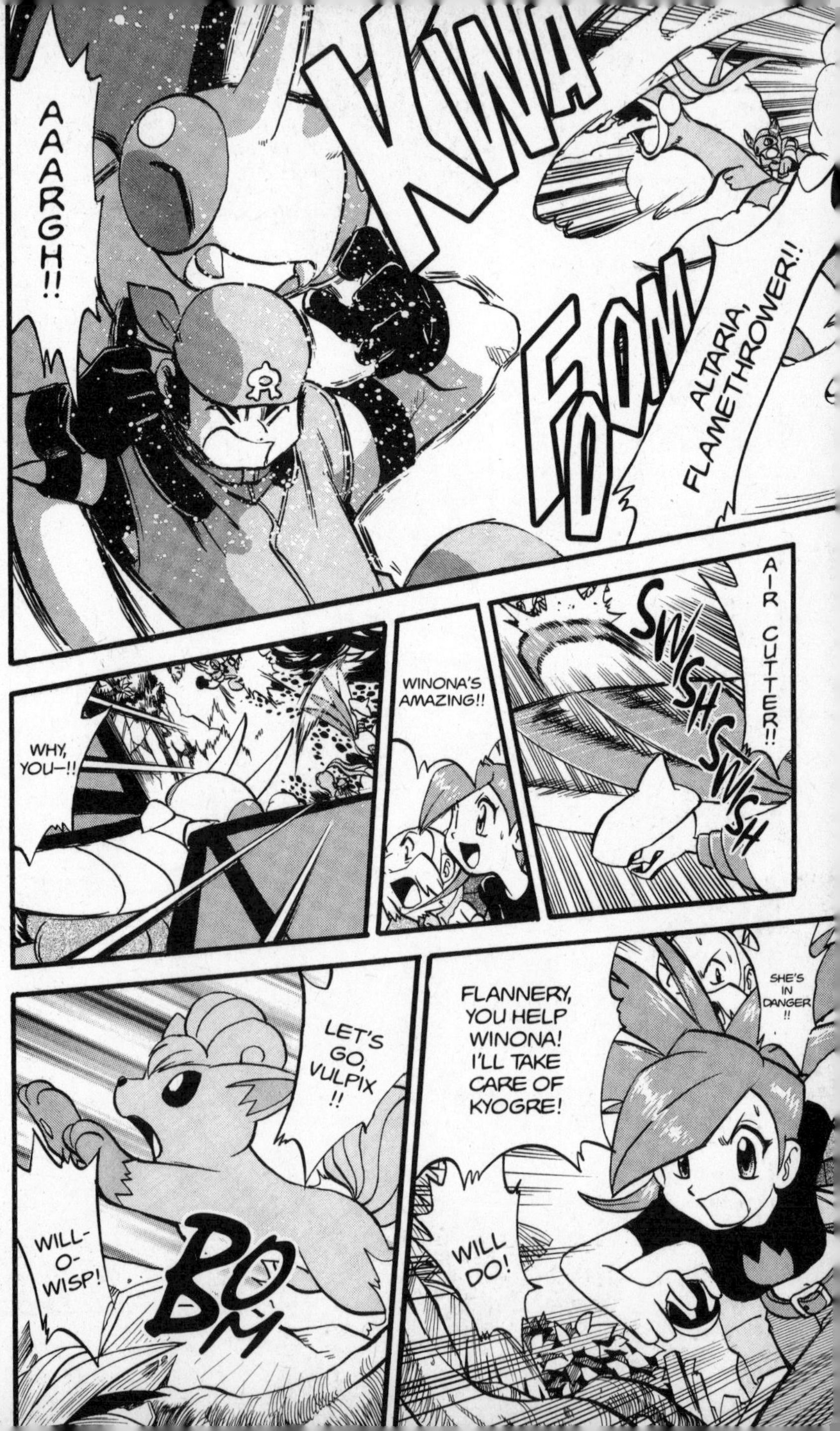
ALTARIA, FLAMETHROWER!!
KWA
FOOM
AAAARGH!!
AIR CUTTER!!
SWISH SWISH SWISH
WINONA'S AMAZING!!
WHY, YOU—!!
SHE'S IN DANGER!!
FLANNERY, YOU HELP WINONA! I'LL TAKE CARE OF KYOGRE!
WILL DO!
LET'S GO, VULPIX!!
WILL-O-WISP!
BOOM

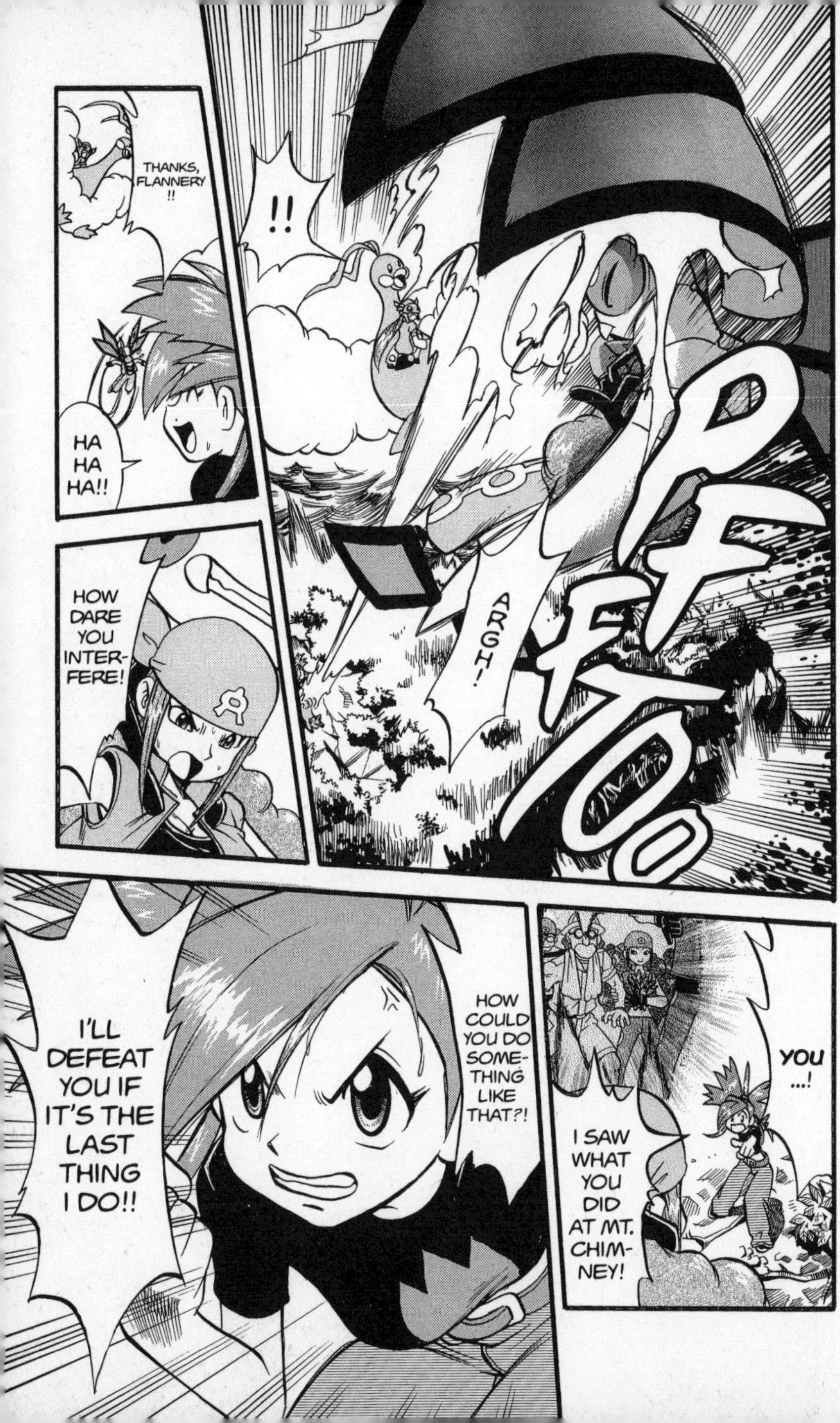
!!
ARGH!
THANKS, FLANNERY !!
HA HA HA!!
HOW DARE YOU INTERFERE!
YOU ...!
I SAW WHAT YOU DID AT MT. CHIMNEY!
HOW COULD YOU DO SOMETHING LIKE THAT?!
I'LL DEFEAT YOU IF IT'S THE LAST THING I DO!!

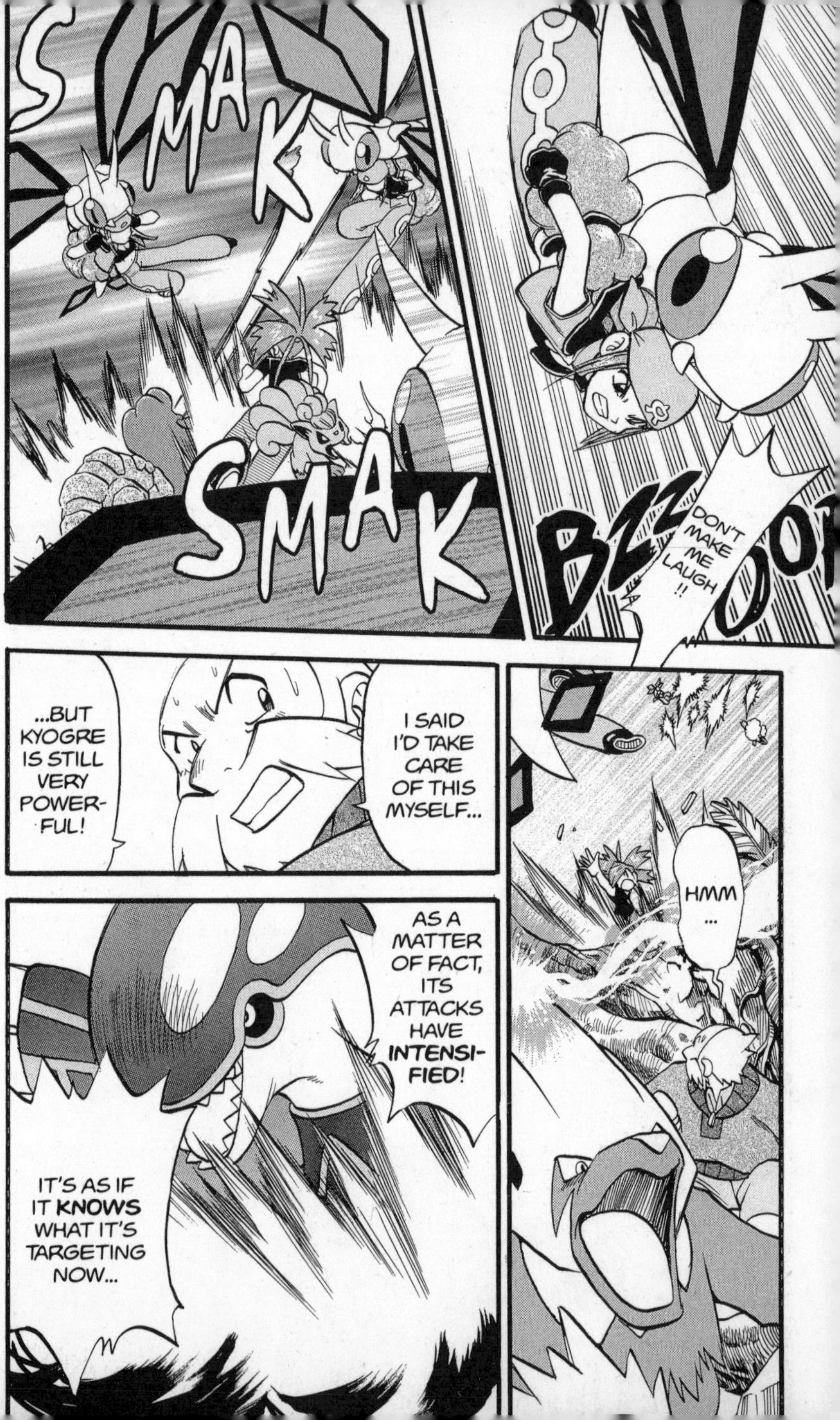

BZZ
DON'T MAKE ME LAUGH!!
SMAK
SMAK
HMM...
I SAID I'D TAKE CARE OF THIS MYSELF...
...BUT KYOGRE IS STILL VERY POWER-FUL!
AS A MATTER OF FACT, ITS ATTACKS HAVE **INTENSI-FIED**!
IT'S AS IF IT **KNOWS** WHAT IT'S TARGETING NOW...

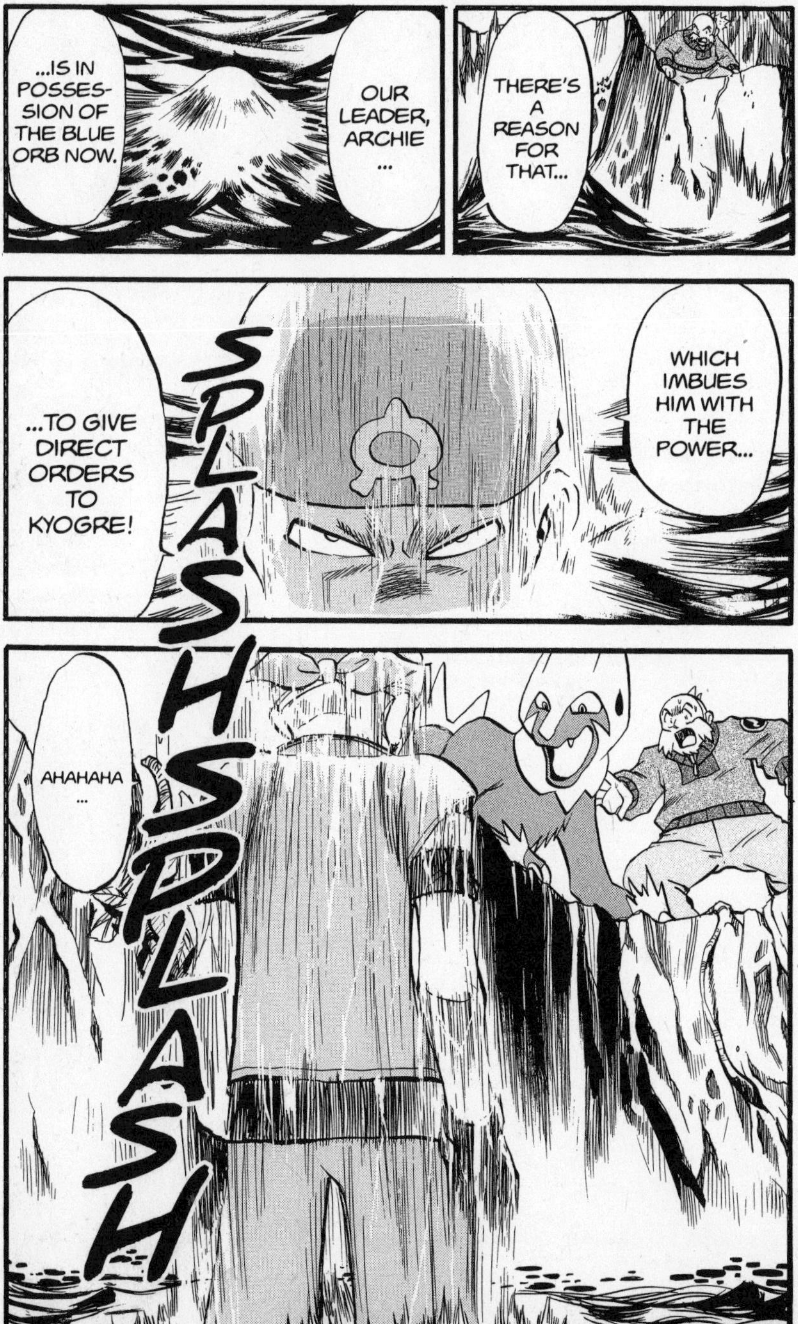
THERE'S A REASON FOR THAT...
OUR LEADER, ARCHIE ...
...IS IN POSSES-SION OF THE BLUE ORB NOW.
WHICH IMBUES HIM WITH THE POWER...
...TO GIVE DIRECT ORDERS TO KYOGRE!
SPLASH
SPLASH
AHAHAHA ...

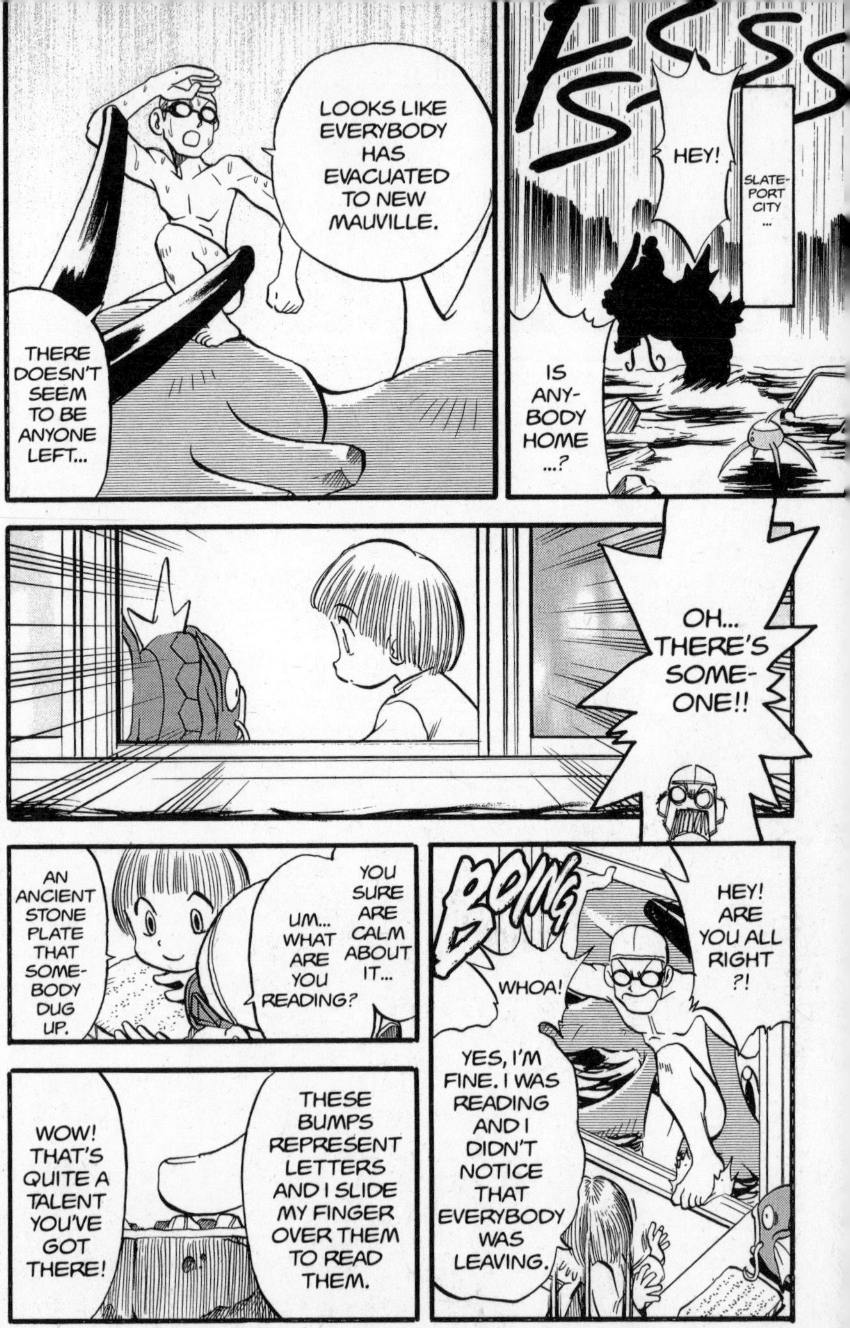
SLATEPORT CITY ...
HEY!
IS ANYBODY HOME ...?
LOOKS LIKE EVERYBODY HAS EVACUATED TO NEW MAUVILLE.
THERE DOESN'T SEEM TO BE ANYONE LEFT...
OH... THERE'S SOMEONE!!
HEY! ARE YOU ALL RIGHT ?!
BOING
WHOA!
YES, I'M FINE. I WAS READING AND I DIDN'T NOTICE THAT EVERYBODY WAS LEAVING.
YOU SURE ARE CALM ABOUT IT...
UM... WHAT ARE YOU READING?
AN ANCIENT STONE PLATE THAT SOMEBODY DUG UP.
THESE BUMPS REPRESENT LETTERS AND I SLIDE MY FINGER OVER THEM TO READ THEM.
WOW! THAT'S QUITE A TALENT YOU'VE GOT THERE!

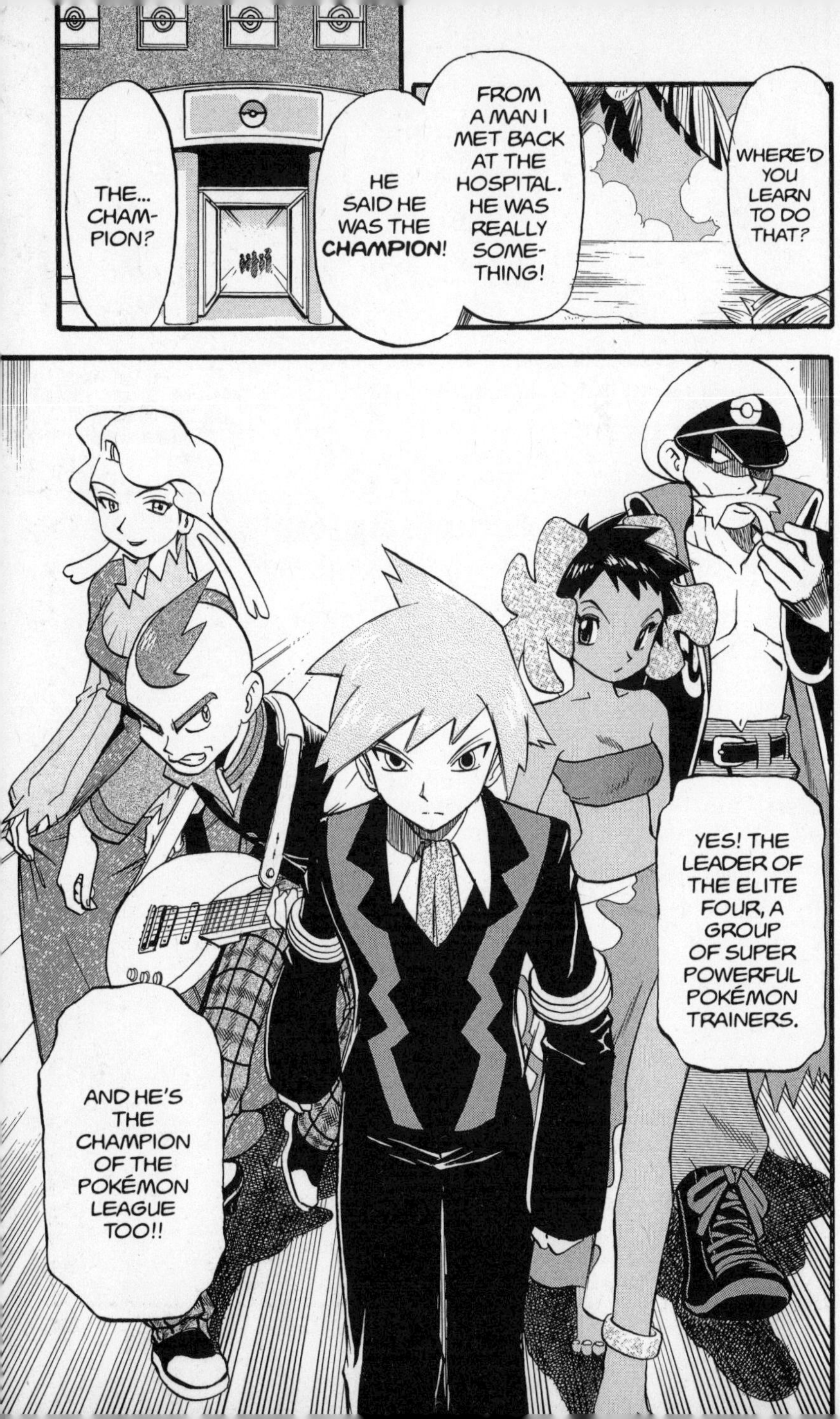
WHERE'D YOU LEARN TO DO THAT?
FROM A MAN I MET BACK AT THE HOSPITAL. HE WAS REALLY SOME-THING!
HE SAID HE WAS THE **CHAMPION**!
THE... CHAM-PION?
YES! THE LEADER OF THE ELITE FOUR, A GROUP OF SUPER POWERFUL POKÉMON TRAINERS.
AND HE'S THE CHAMPION OF THE POKÉMON LEAGUE TOO!!

ADVENTURE MAP

SAPPHIRE

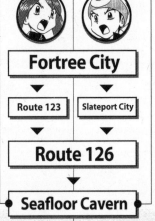

Fortree City

Route 123	Slateport City

Route 126

Seafloor Cavern

CHIC
Blaziken ♀
Lv40

RONO
Lairon ♂
Lv41

RELLY
Relicanth ♂
Lv47

PHADO
Donphan ♂
Lv48

TROPPY
Tropius ♂
Lv46

LORRY
Wailord ♂
Lv48

RUBY

MUMU
Swampert ♂

NANA
Mightyena ♀

KIKI
Delcatty ♀

FOFO
Castform ♀

	Stone Badge	Knuckle Badge	Dynamo Badge	Heat Badge
Balance Badge	Feather Badge	Mind Badge	Rain Badge

		Cool	Beauty	Cute	Smart	Tough
Normal		●	●	●	●	●
Super		●	●	●	●	●
Hyper		●	★	●	●	●
Master		★	★	★	★	★

● Chapter 246 ●
Can I Ninjask You a Question?

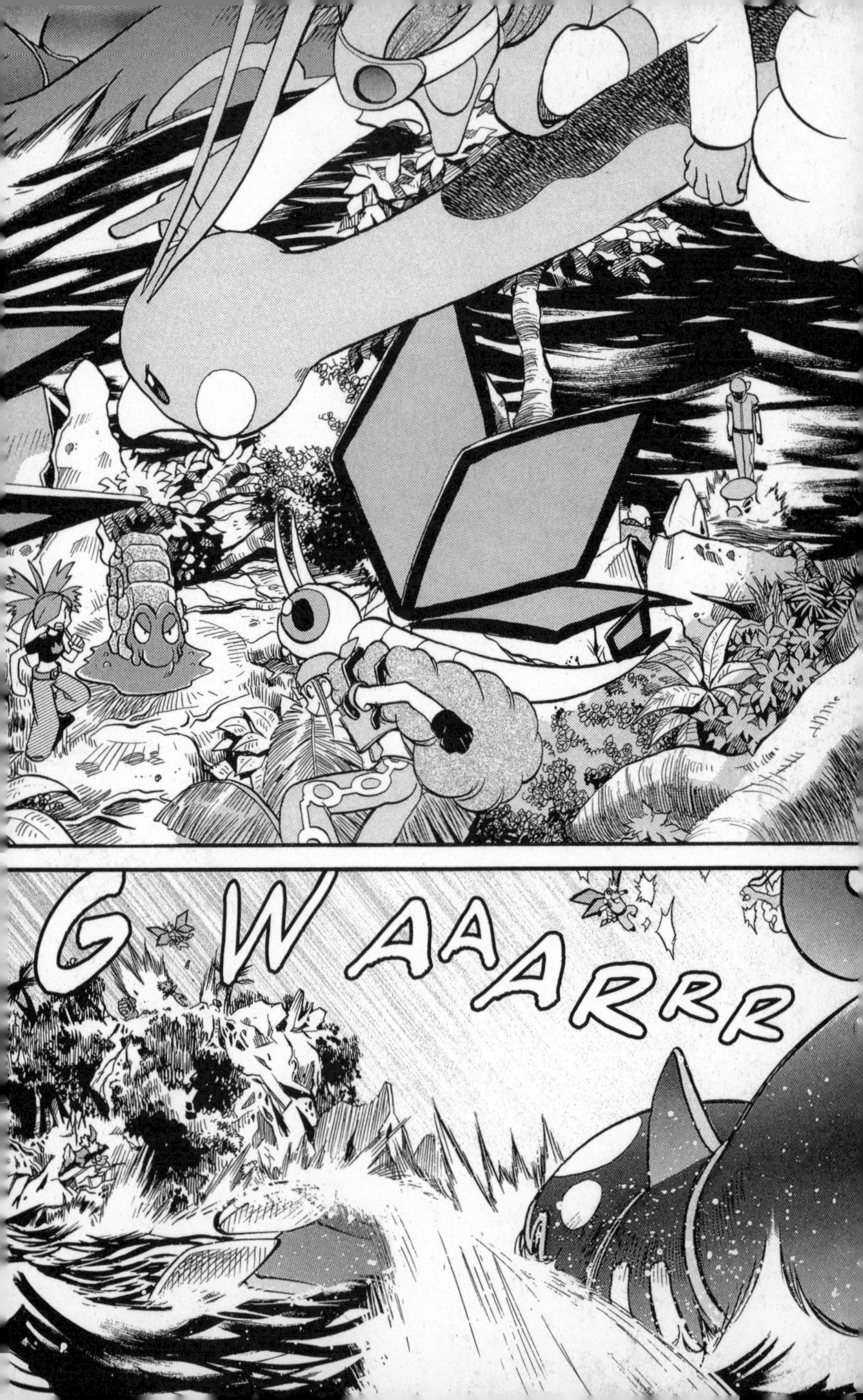
GWAAARRR

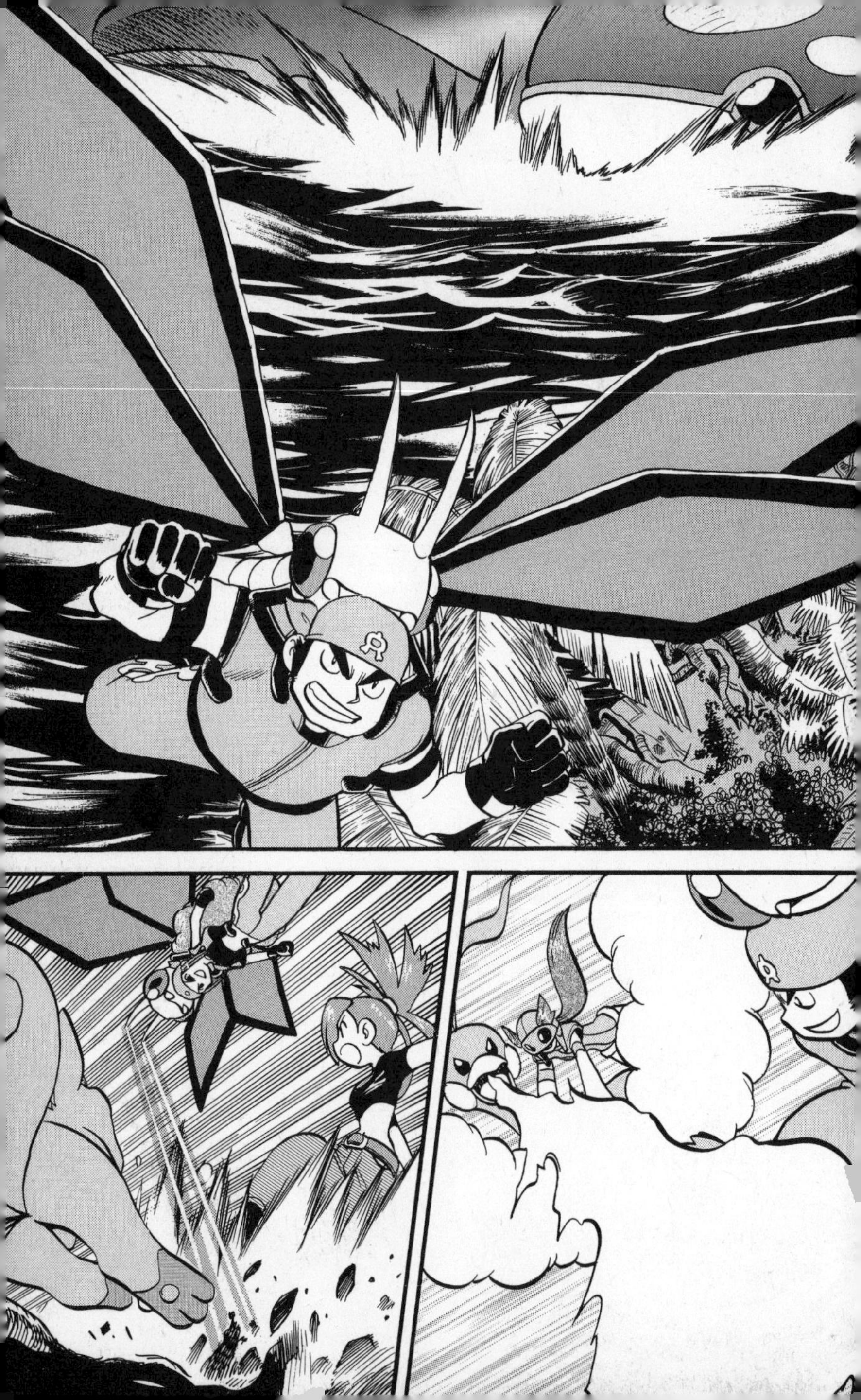

I "SEE" A "SEA" MAN!

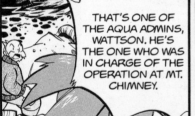

THAT'S ONE OF THE AQUA ADMINS, WATTSON. HE'S THE ONE WHO WAS IN CHARGE OF THE OPERATION AT MT. CHIMNEY.

AHA HA HA HA...

BLOOOP

...SPIT UP!!

PT TOO

STOCK-PILE AND...

...SWALLOW.

STOCK-PILE AND...

CLUB CLUB

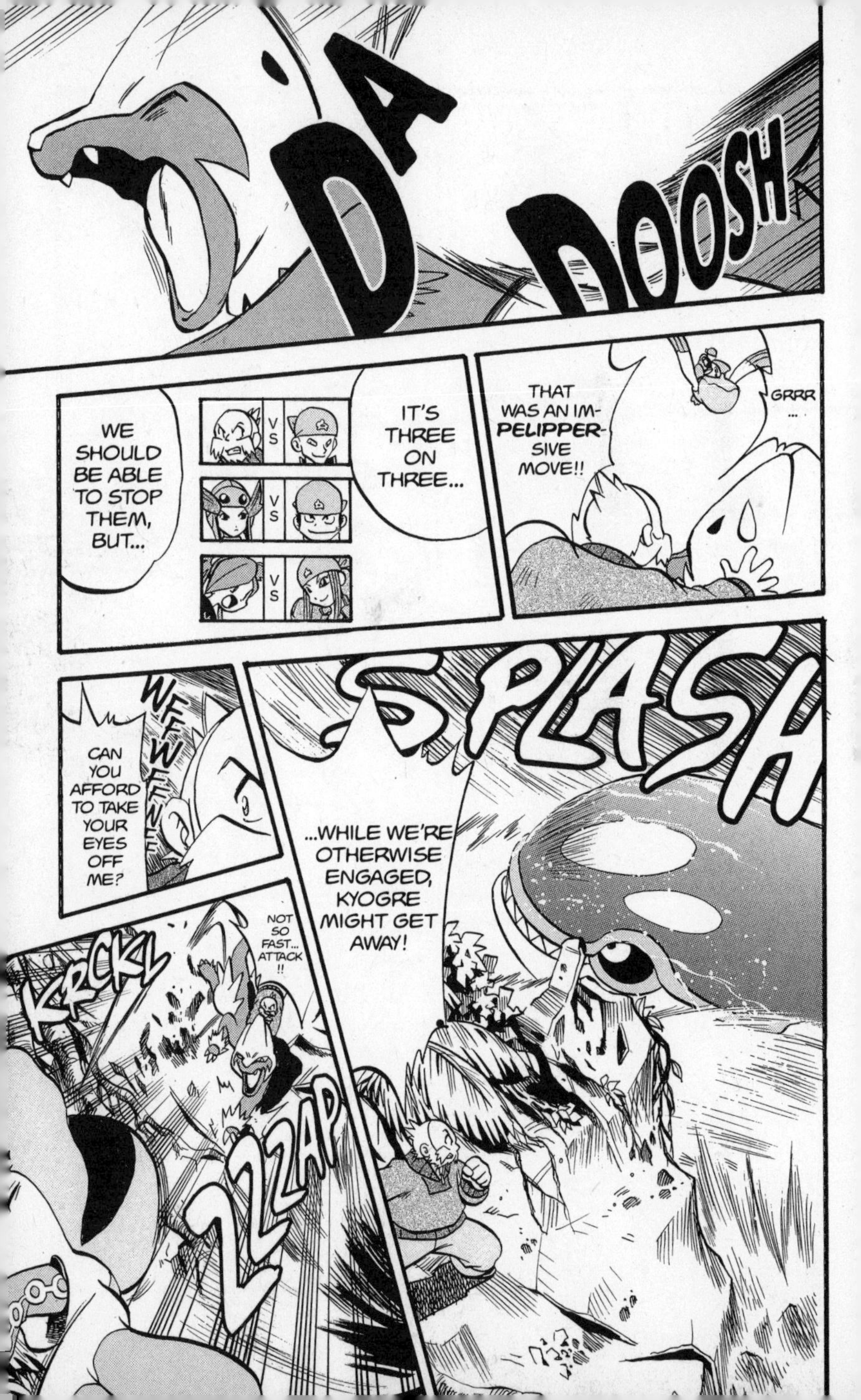

DA
DOOSH
THAT WAS AN IM-PELIPPER-SIVE MOVE!!
GRRR...
IT'S THREE ON THREE...
VS
VS
VS
WE SHOULD BE ABLE TO STOP THEM, BUT...
SPLASH
...WHILE WE'RE OTHERWISE ENGAGED, KYOGRE MIGHT GET AWAY!
WFFWFFWFF
CAN YOU AFFORD TO TAKE YOUR EYES OFF ME?
NOT SO FAST... ATTACK!!
KRCKL
ZZZAP

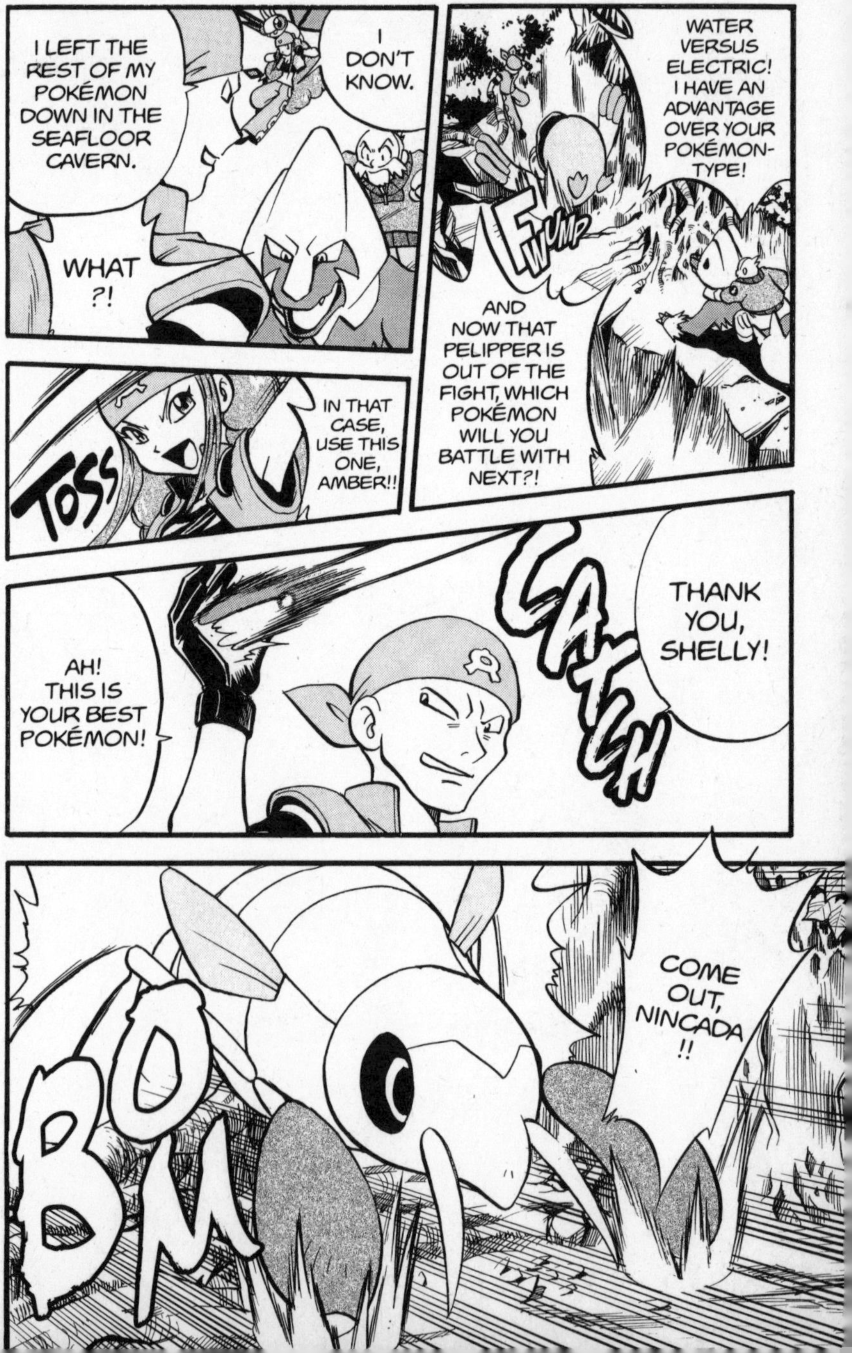
WATER VERSUS ELECTRIC! I HAVE AN ADVANTAGE OVER YOUR POKÉMON-TYPE!
FWUMP
AND NOW THAT PELIPPER IS OUT OF THE FIGHT, WHICH POKÉMON WILL YOU BATTLE WITH NEXT?!
I DON'T KNOW.
I LEFT THE REST OF MY POKÉMON DOWN IN THE SEAFLOOR CAVERN.
WHAT?!
IN THAT CASE, USE THIS ONE, AMBER!!
TOSS
THANK YOU, SHELLY!
CLAKUH
AH! THIS IS YOUR BEST POKÉMON!
COME OUT, NINCADA!!
BOOM

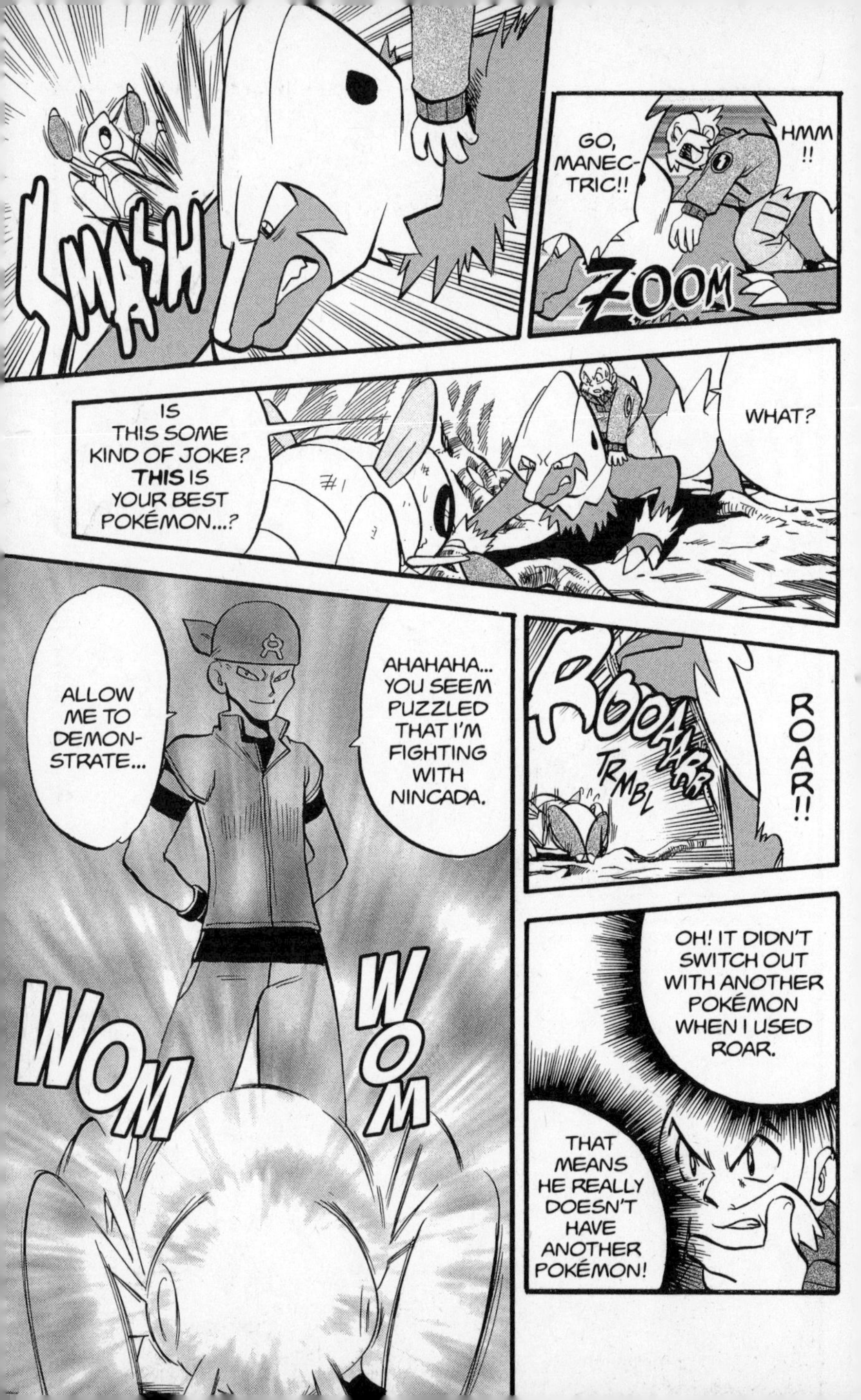
HMM!!
GO, MANECTRIC!!
ZOOM
SMASH
WHAT?
IS THIS SOME KIND OF JOKE? **THIS** IS YOUR BEST POKÉMON...?
ROAR!!
ROOAARR
TRMBL
OH! IT DIDN'T SWITCH OUT WITH ANOTHER POKÉMON WHEN I USED ROAR.
THAT MEANS HE REALLY DOESN'T HAVE ANOTHER POKÉMON!
AHAHAHA... YOU SEEM PUZZLED THAT I'M FIGHTING WITH NINCADA.
ALLOW ME TO DEMON-STRATE...
WOM
WOM

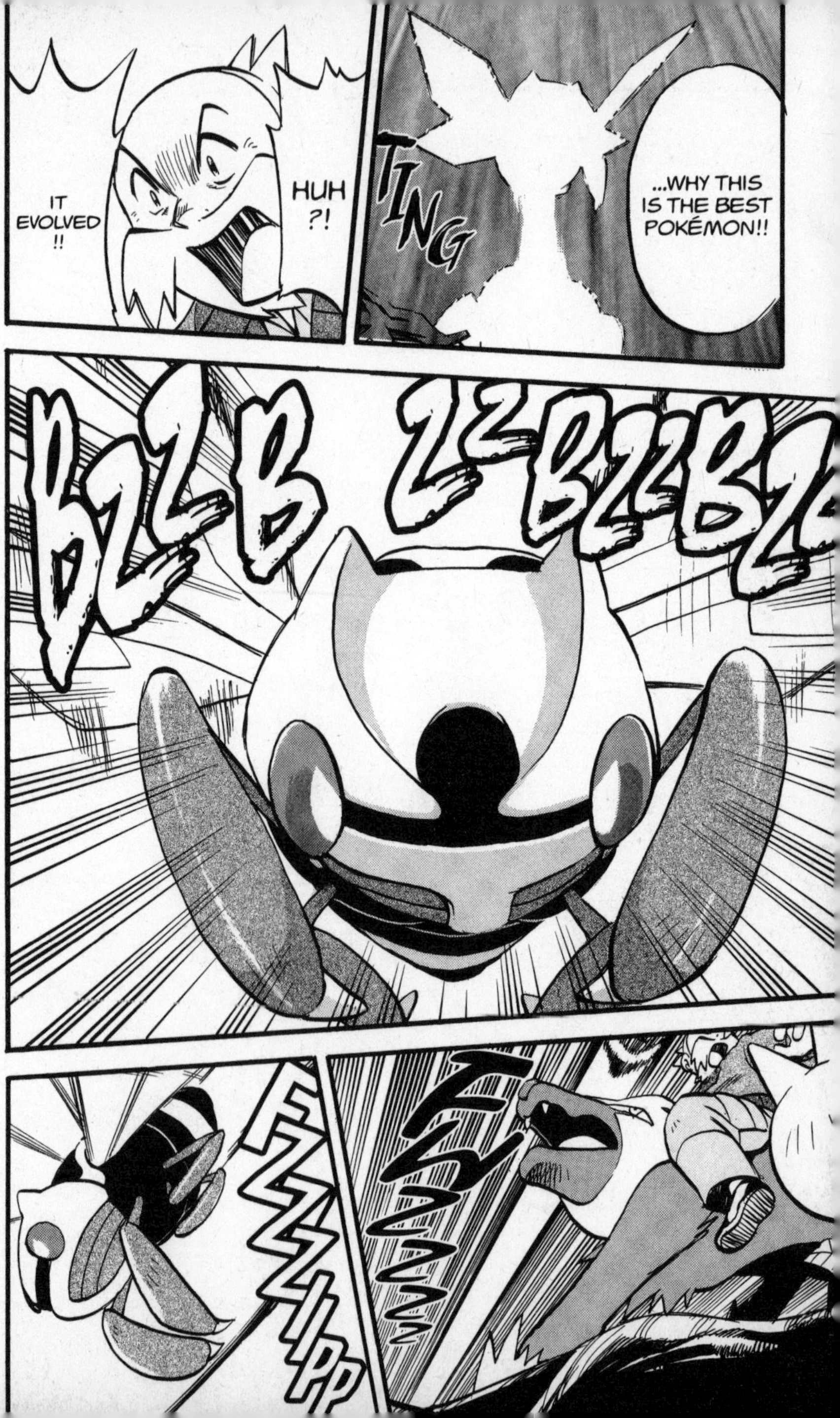
...WHY THIS IS THE BEST POKÉMON!!
TING
HUH ?!
IT EVOLVED !!
FZZZIPP

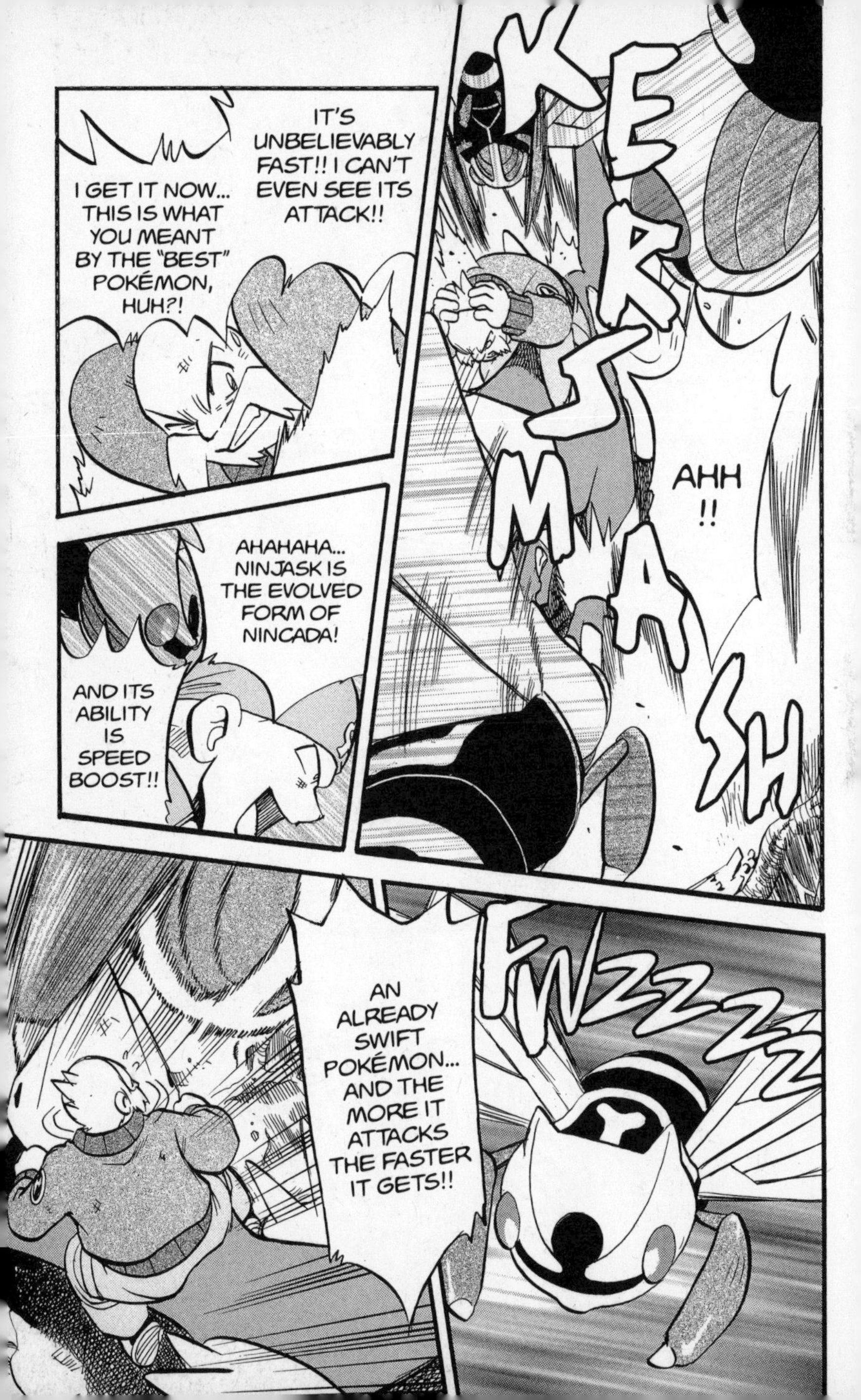
KERSMASH
AHH!!
IT'S UNBELIEVABLY FAST!! I CAN'T EVEN SEE ITS ATTACK!!
I GET IT NOW... THIS IS WHAT YOU MEANT BY THE "BEST" POKÉMON, HUH?!
AHAHAHA... NINJASK IS THE EVOLVED FORM OF NINCADA!
AND ITS ABILITY IS SPEED BOOST!!
FWZZZZZ
AN ALREADY SWIFT POKÉMON... AND THE MORE IT ATTACKS THE FASTER IT GETS!!

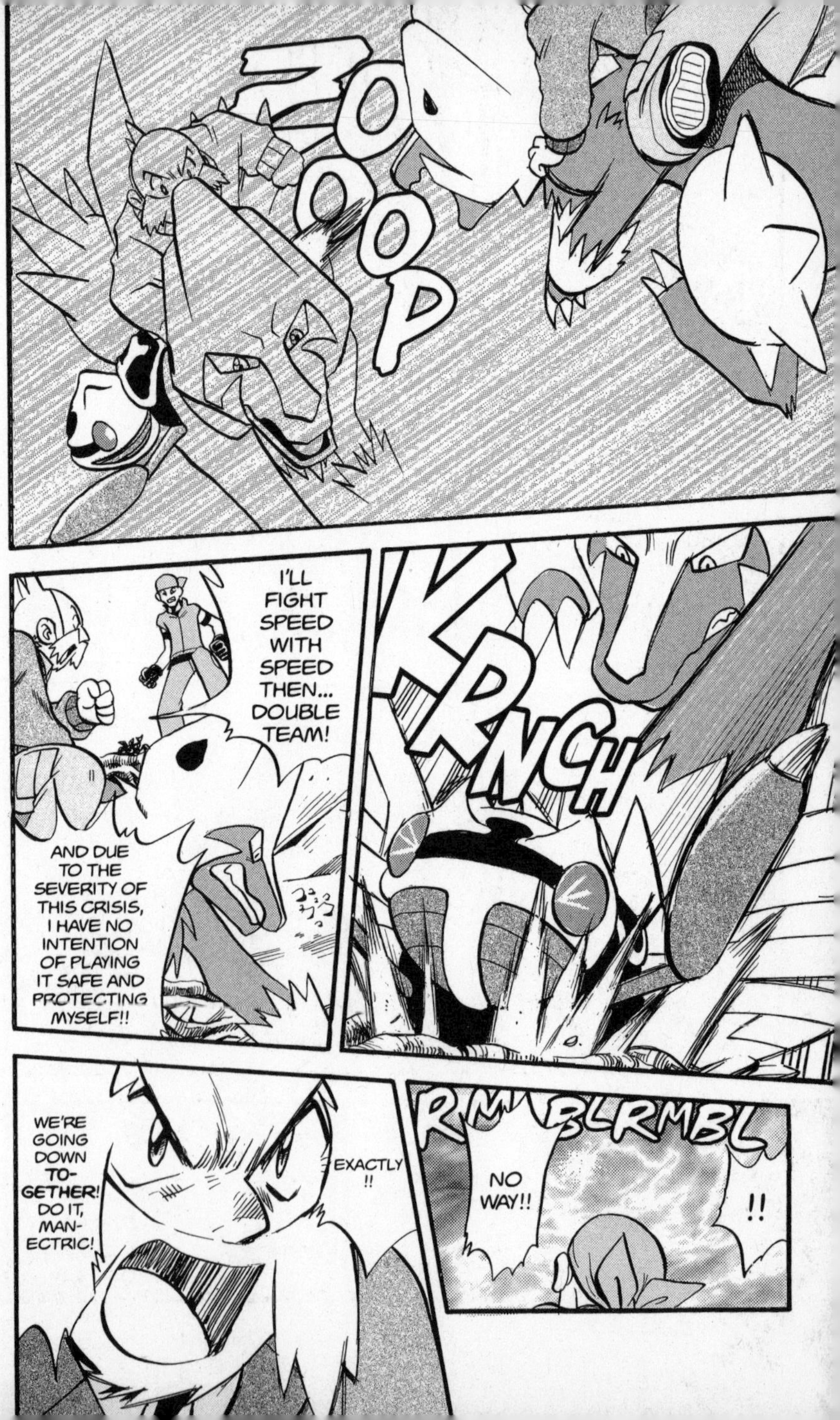
ZOOOOP
KRNCH
I'LL FIGHT SPEED WITH SPEED THEN... DOUBLE TEAM!
AND DUE TO THE SEVERITY OF THIS CRISIS, I HAVE NO INTENTION OF PLAYING IT SAFE AND PROTECTING MYSELF!!
RMMBLRMBL
!!
NO WAY!!
EXACTLY!!
WE'RE GOING DOWN TO-GETHER! DO IT, MAN-ECTRIC!

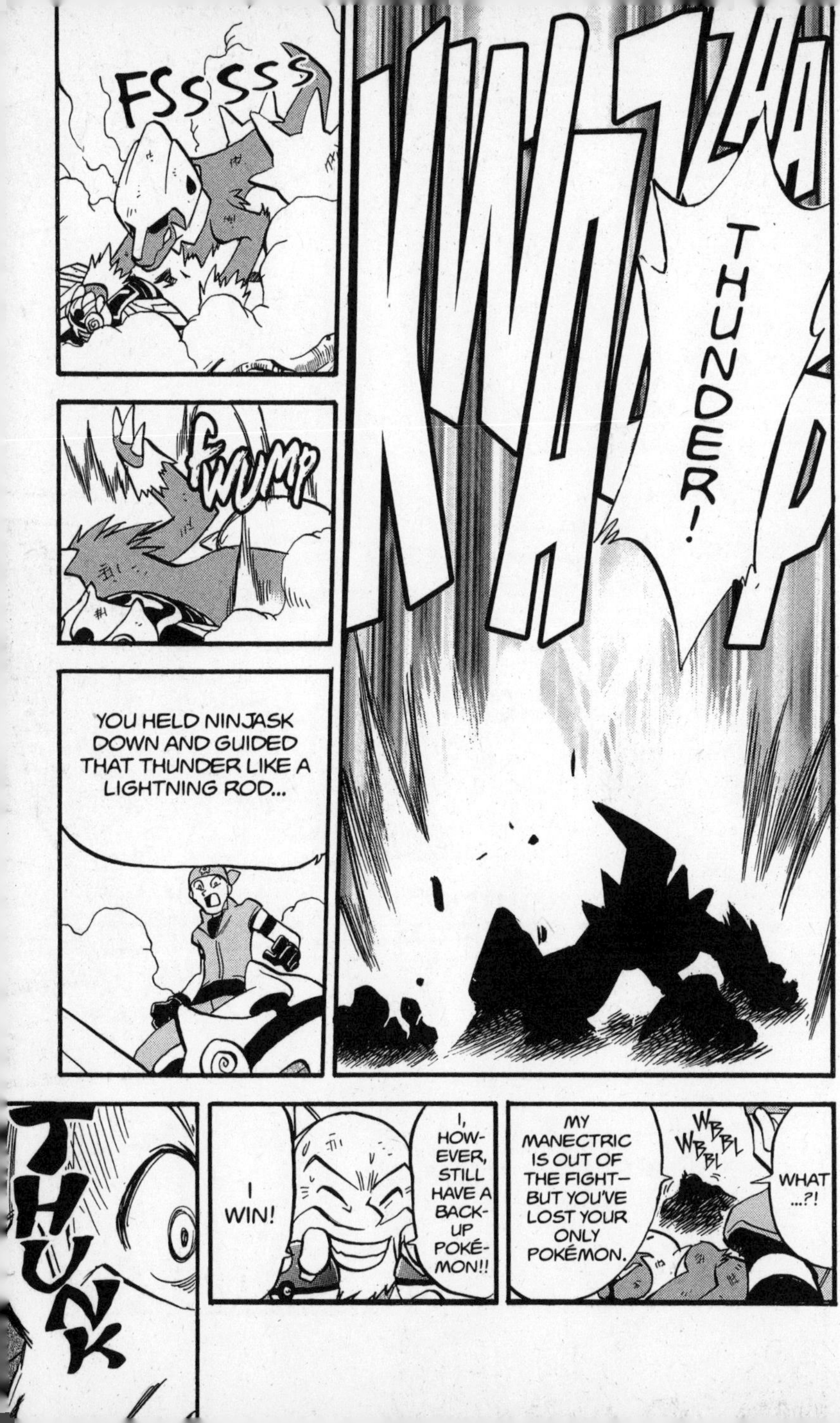
KWA-ZAAP
THUNDER!
FSSSSS
FWUMP
YOU HELD NINJASK DOWN AND GUIDED THAT THUNDER LIKE A LIGHTNING ROD...
MY MANECTRIC IS OUT OF THE FIGHT— BUT YOU'VE LOST YOUR ONLY POKÉMON.
WBBL WBBL
WHAT ...?!
I, HOW-EVER, STILL HAVE A BACK-UP POKÉ-MON!!
I WIN!
THUNK

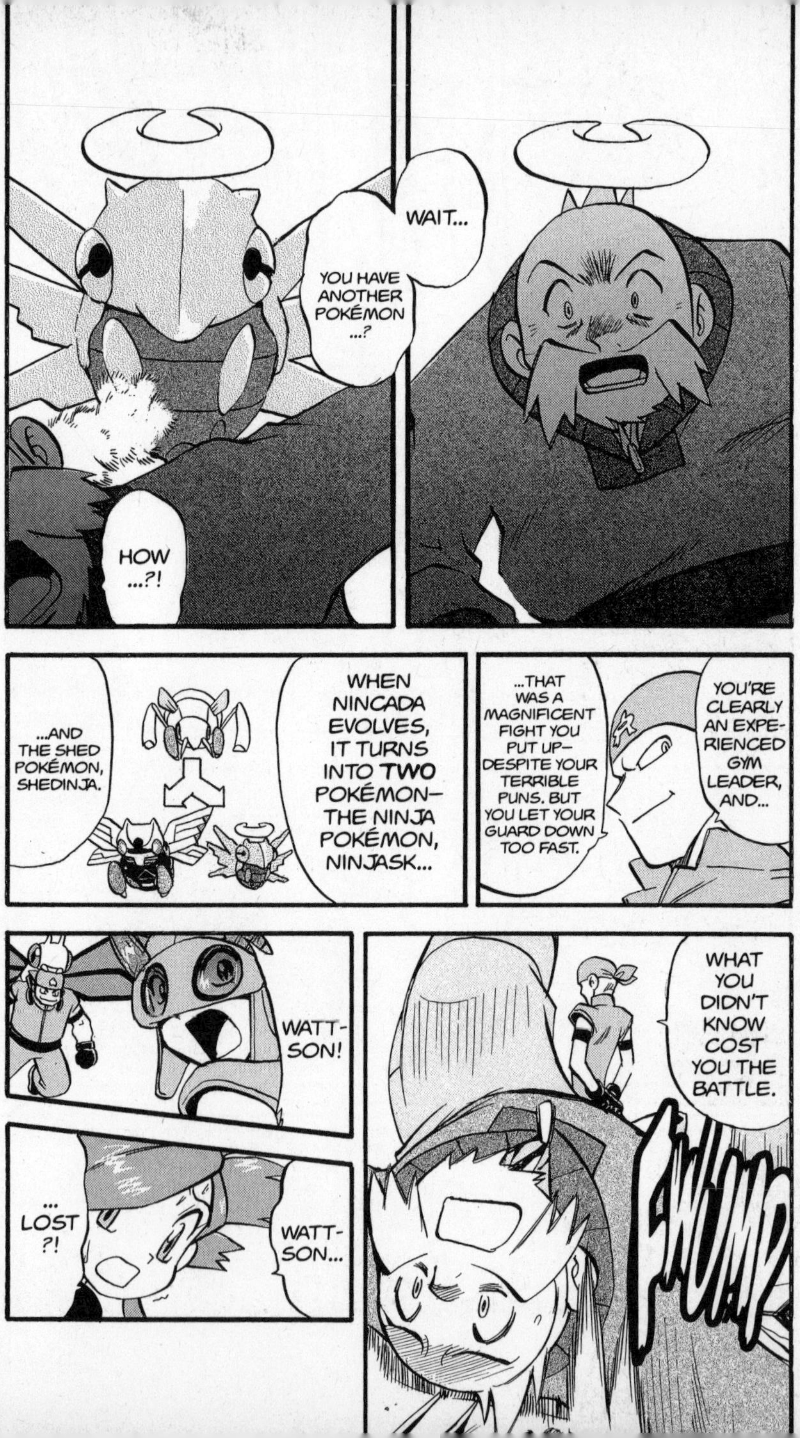
WAIT...
YOU HAVE ANOTHER POKÉMON ...?
HOW ...?!
YOU'RE CLEARLY AN EXPERIENCED GYM LEADER, AND...
...THAT WAS A MAGNIFICENT FIGHT YOU PUT UP—DESPITE YOUR TERRIBLE PUNS. BUT YOU LET YOUR GUARD DOWN TOO FAST.
WHEN NINCADA EVOLVES, IT TURNS INTO **TWO** POKÉMON—THE NINJA POKÉMON, NINJASK...
...AND THE SHED POKÉMON, SHEDINJA.
WHAT YOU DIDN'T KNOW COST YOU THE BATTLE.
FWUMP
WATT-SON!
WATT-SON...
...LOST?!

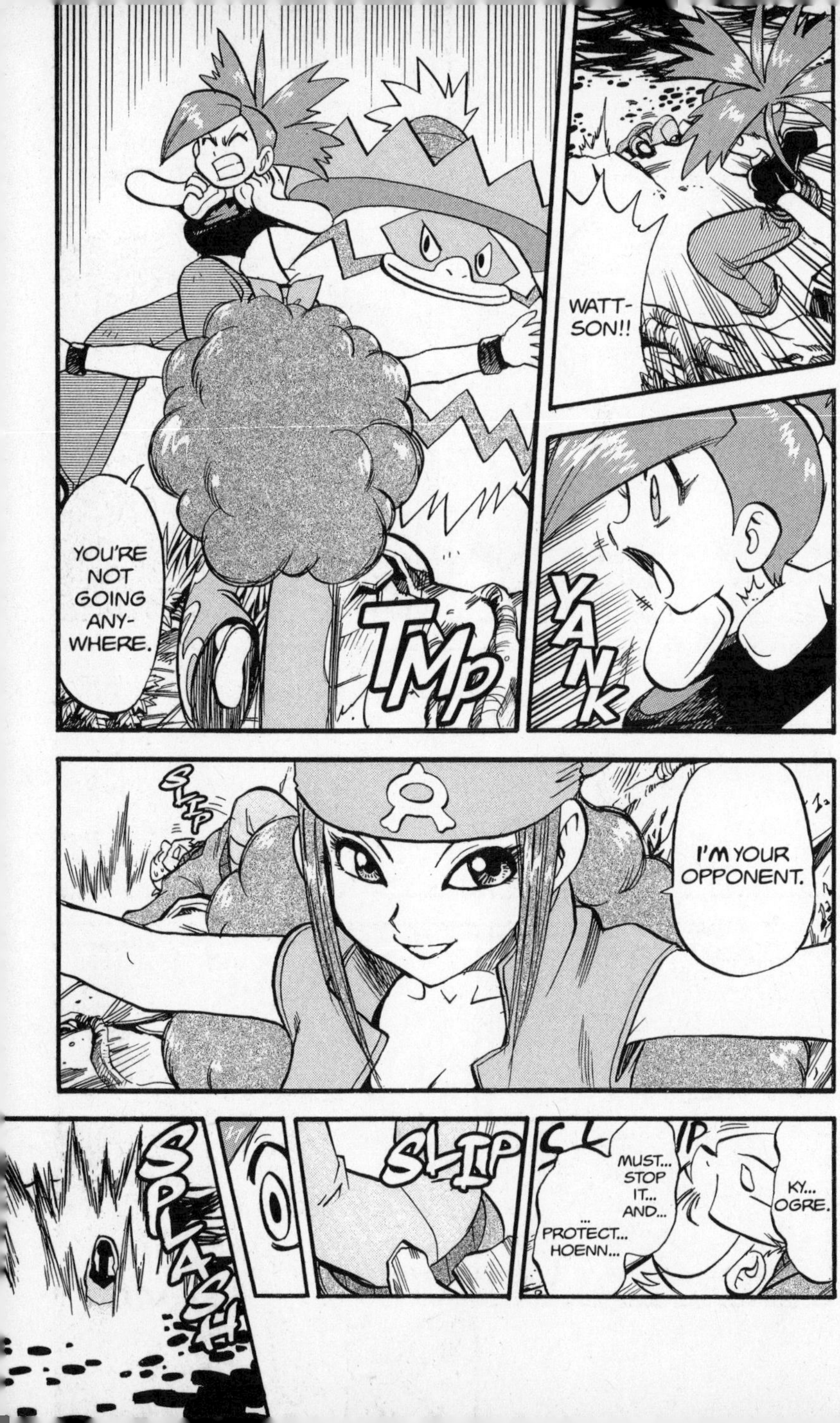
WATT-SON!!
YANK
YOU'RE NOT GOING ANY-WHERE.
TMP
I'M YOUR OPPONENT.
SLIP
KY... OGRE.
MUST... STOP IT... AND... ...PROTECT... HOENN...
SLIP
SPLASH

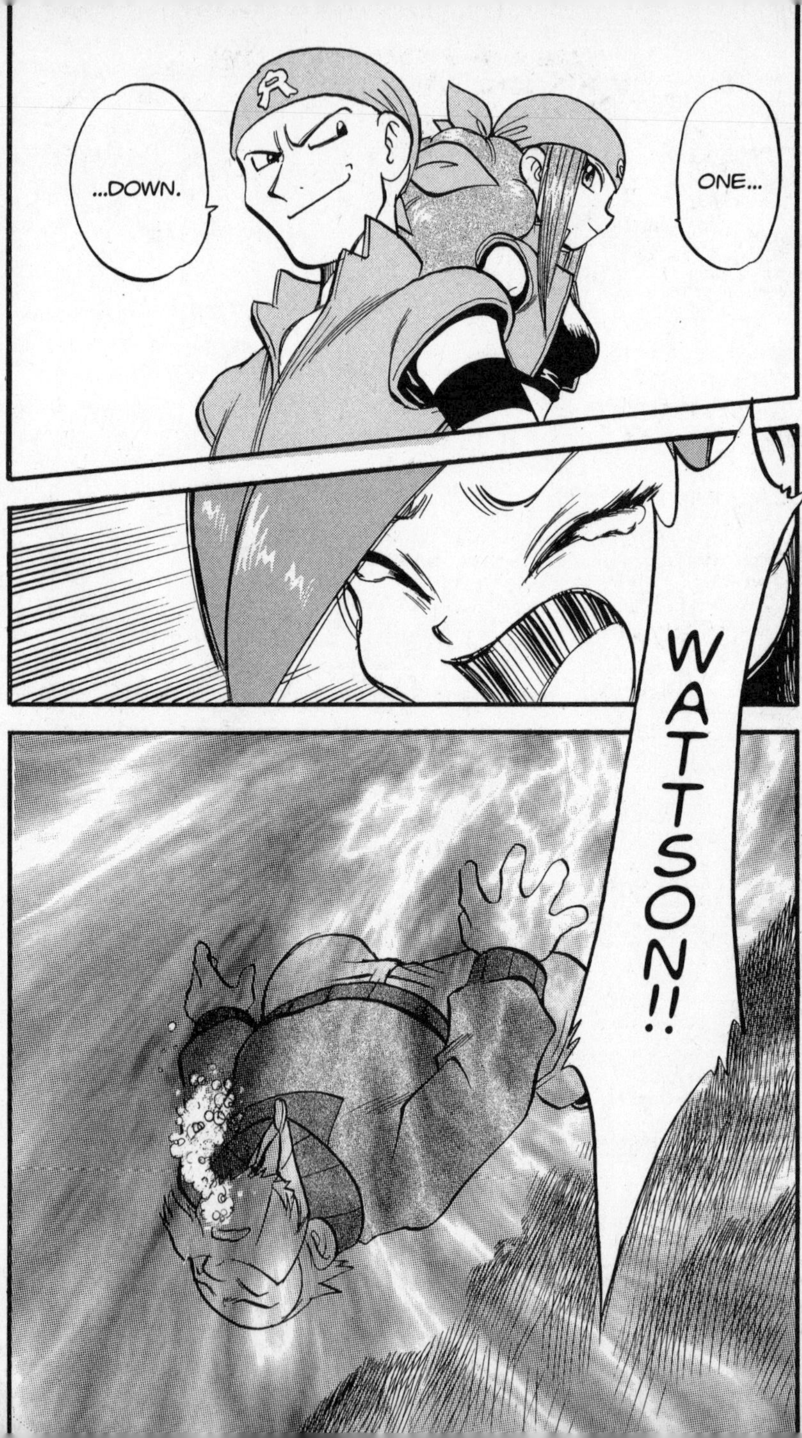
ONE...
...DOWN.
WATTSON!!

ADVENTURE MAP

SAPPHIRE

RUBY

Fortree City

▼ Route 123 (Sapphire) ▼ Slateport City (Ruby)

▼ **Route 126**

▼ **Seafloor Cavern**

SAPPHIRE

- CHIC — Blaziken ♀ — Lv40
- RONO — Lairon ♂ — Lv41
- RELLY — Relicanth ♂ — Lv47
- PHADO — Donphan ♂ — Lv48
- TROPPY — Tropius ♂ — Lv46
- LORRY — Wailord ♂ — Lv48

RUBY

- MUMU — Swampert ♂
- NANA — Mightyena ♀
- KIKI — Delcatty ♀
- FOFO — Castform ♀

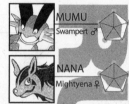

Stone Badge	Knuckle Badge	Dynamo Badge	Heat Badge
Balance Badge	Feather Badge	Mind Badge	Rain Badge

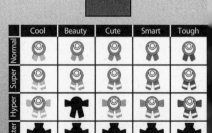

	Cool	Beauty	Cute	Smart	Tough
Normal					
Super					
Hyper					
Master					

● Chapter 247 ●
The Beginning of the End with Kyogre & Groudon IX

Pokémon
ADVENTURES™
RUBY & SAPPHIRE
The Fourth Chapter

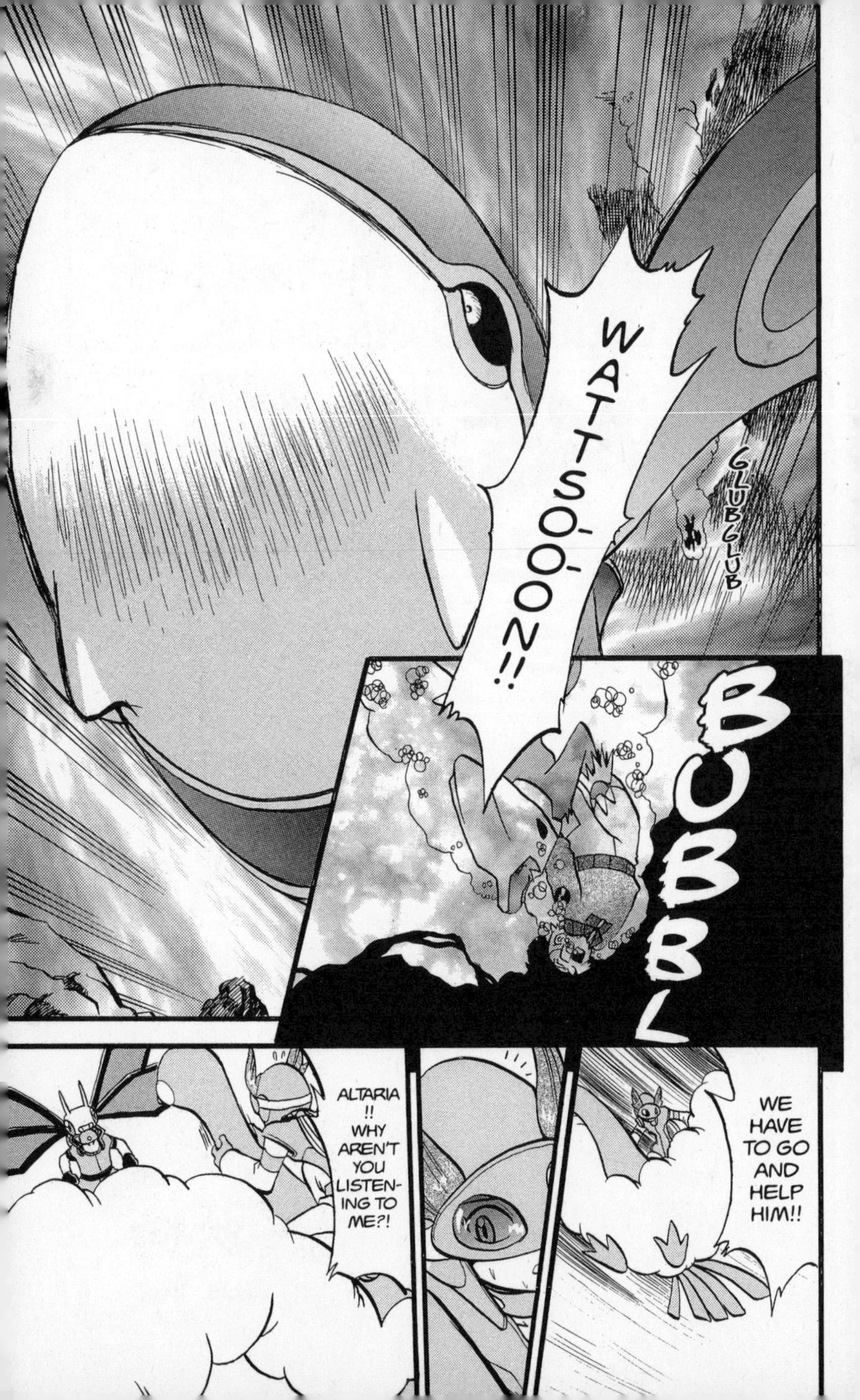
WATTSÓÓÓN!!
GLUB GLUB
BUBBL
WE HAVE TO GO AND HELP HIM!!
ALTARIA!! WHY AREN'T YOU LISTENING TO ME?!

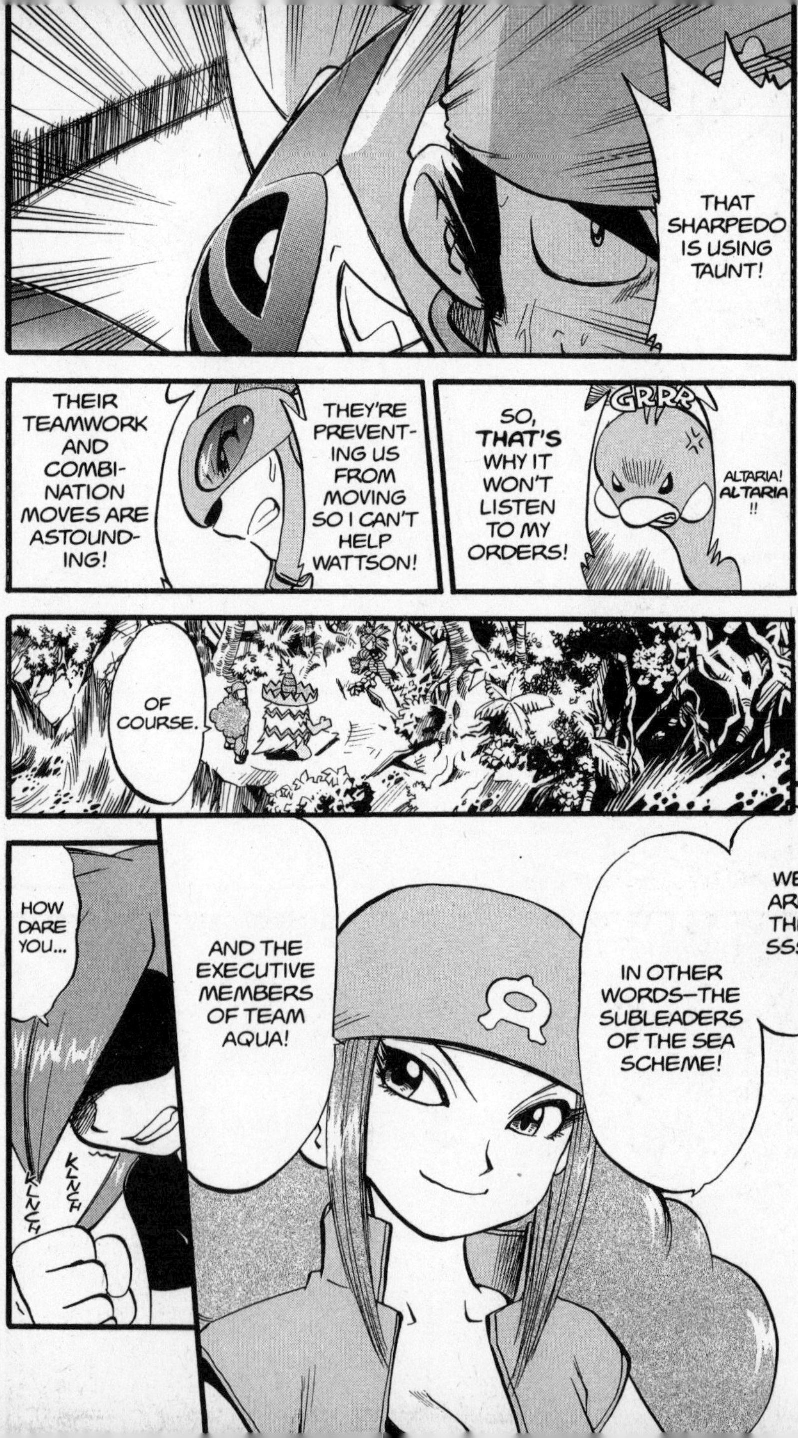

THAT SHARPEDO IS USING TAUNT!
GRRR
ALTARIA! ALTARIA!!
SO, **THAT'S** WHY IT WON'T LISTEN TO MY ORDERS!
THEY'RE PREVENTING US FROM MOVING SO I CAN'T HELP WATTSON!
THEIR TEAMWORK AND COMBINATION MOVES ARE ASTOUNDING!
OF COURSE.
WE ARE THE SSS.
IN OTHER WORDS—THE SUBLEADERS OF THE SEA SCHEME!
AND THE EXECUTIVE MEMBERS OF TEAM AQUA!
HOW DARE YOU...
KLNCH
KLNCH

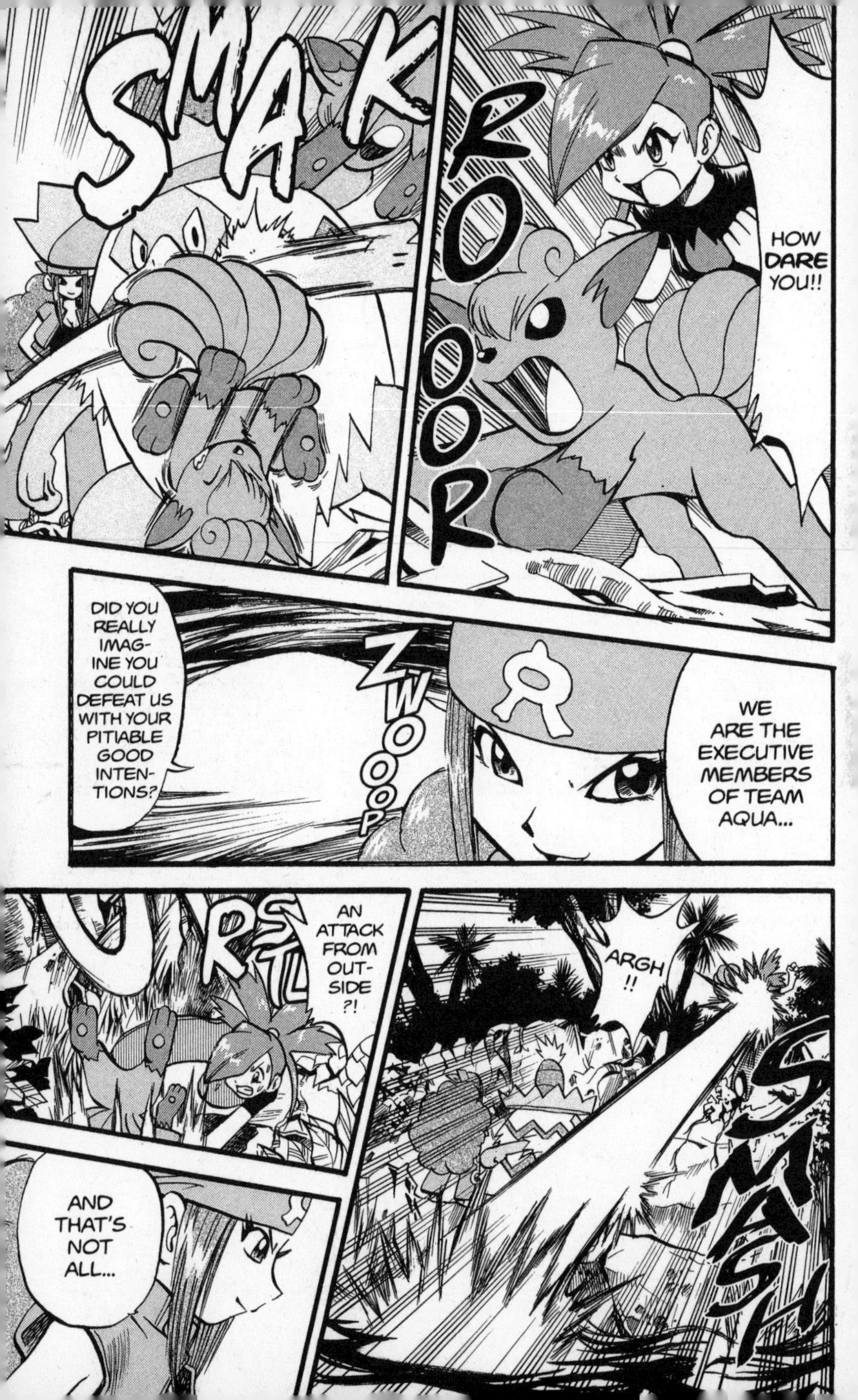
ROOOOR
HOW DARE YOU!!
SMAK
WE ARE THE EXECUTIVE MEMBERS OF TEAM AQUA...
ZWOOOOP
DID YOU REALLY IMAGINE YOU COULD DEFEAT US WITH YOUR PITIABLE GOOD INTENTIONS?
ARGH!!
SMASH
AN ATTACK FROM OUTSIDE?!
RSTL
AND THAT'S NOT ALL...

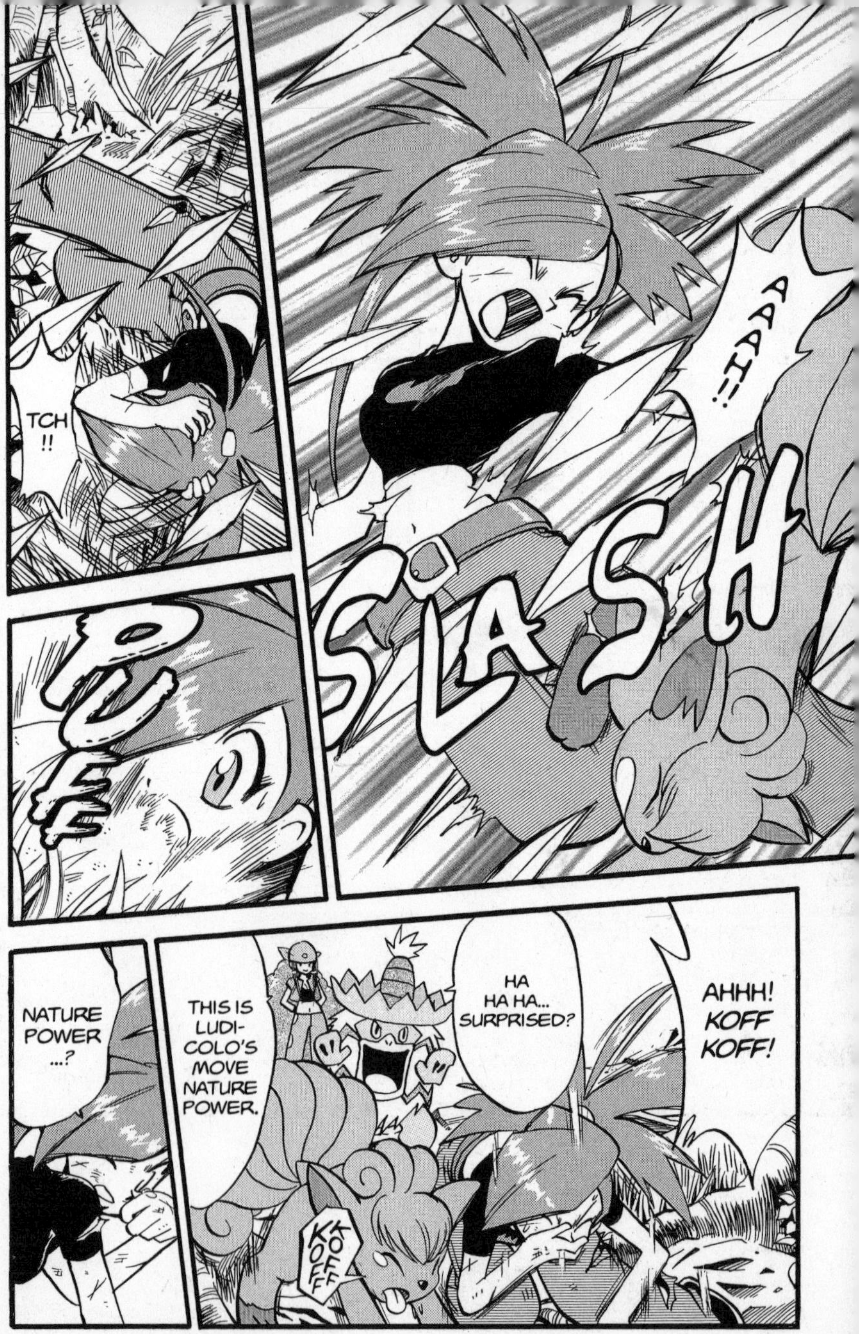
AAAAH!!
SLASH
TCH!!
PUFF
AHHH! KOFF KOFF!
HA HA HA... SURPRISED?
THIS IS LUDI-COLO'S MOVE NATURE POWER.
KOFF KOFF
NATURE POWER ...?

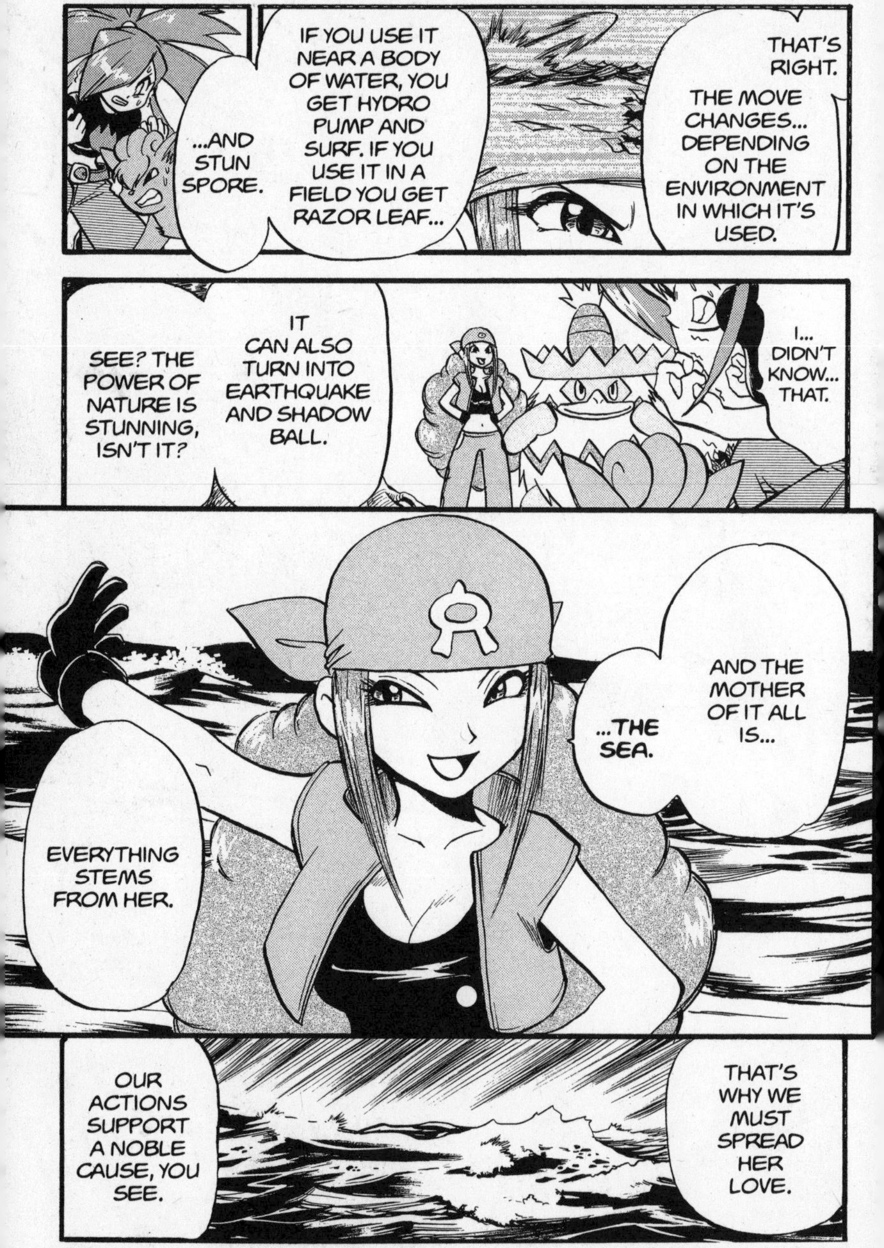
THAT'S RIGHT.
THE MOVE CHANGES... DEPENDING ON THE ENVIRONMENT IN WHICH IT'S USED.
IF YOU USE IT NEAR A BODY OF WATER, YOU GET HYDRO PUMP AND SURF. IF YOU USE IT IN A FIELD YOU GET RAZOR LEAF...
...AND STUN SPORE.
I... DIDN'T KNOW... THAT.
IT CAN ALSO TURN INTO EARTHQUAKE AND SHADOW BALL.
SEE? THE POWER OF NATURE IS STUNNING, ISN'T IT?
AND THE MOTHER OF IT ALL IS...
...THE SEA.
EVERYTHING STEMS FROM HER.
THAT'S WHY WE MUST SPREAD HER LOVE.
OUR ACTIONS SUPPORT A NOBLE CAUSE, YOU SEE.

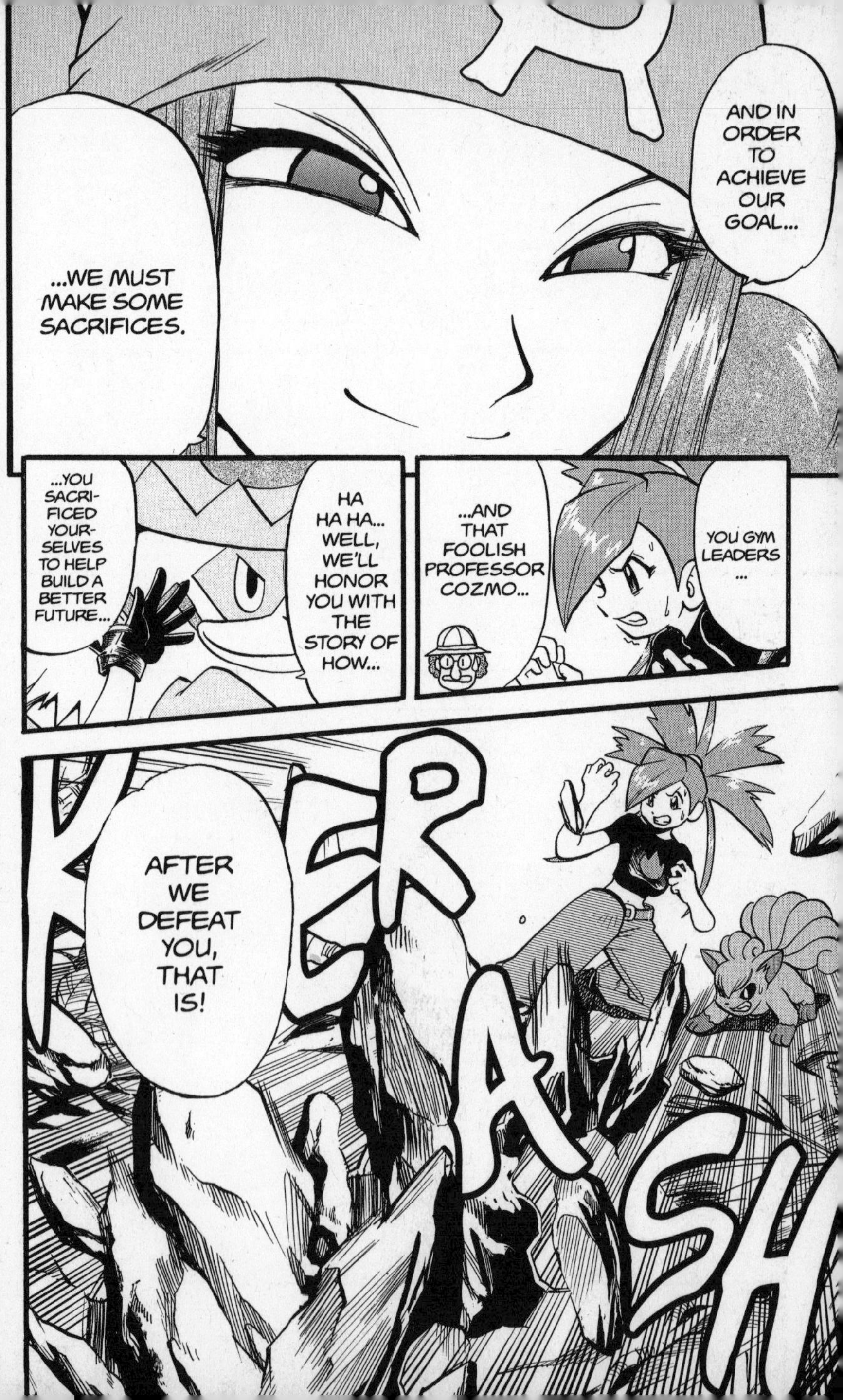
AND IN ORDER TO ACHIEVE OUR GOAL...
...WE MUST MAKE SOME SACRIFICES.
YOU GYM LEADERS ...
...AND THAT FOOLISH PROFESSOR COZMO...
HA HA HA... WELL, WE'LL HONOR YOU WITH THE STORY OF HOW...
...YOU SACRIFICED YOURSELVES TO HELP BUILD A BETTER FUTURE...
AFTER WE DEFEAT YOU, THAT IS!
KRASH

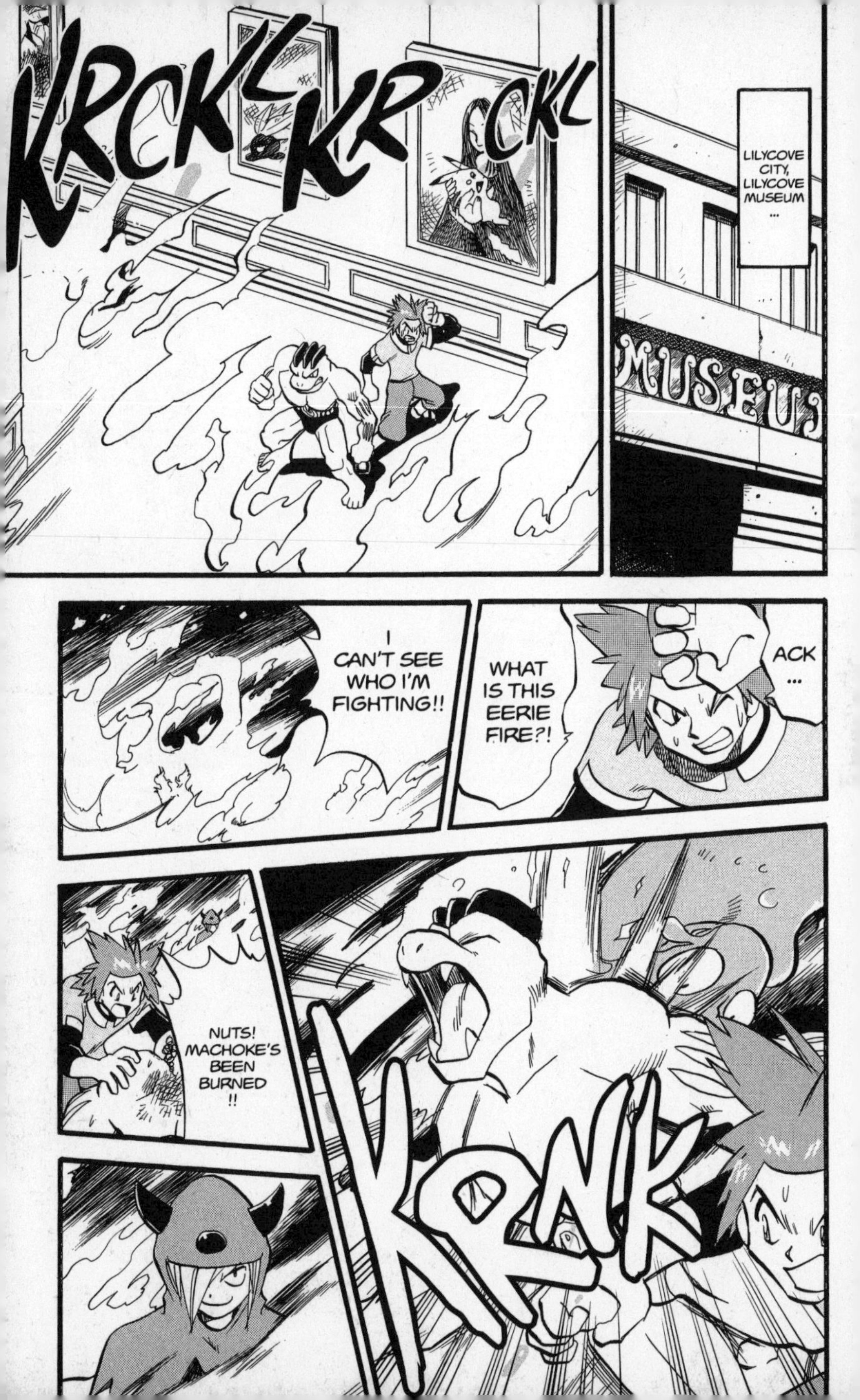
LILYCOVE CITY, LILYCOVE MUSEUM ...
MUSEU
KRCKL KR CKL
ACK ...
WHAT IS THIS EERIE FIRE?!
I CAN'T SEE WHO I'M FIGHTING!!
KONK
NUTS! MACHOKE'S BEEN BURNED !!

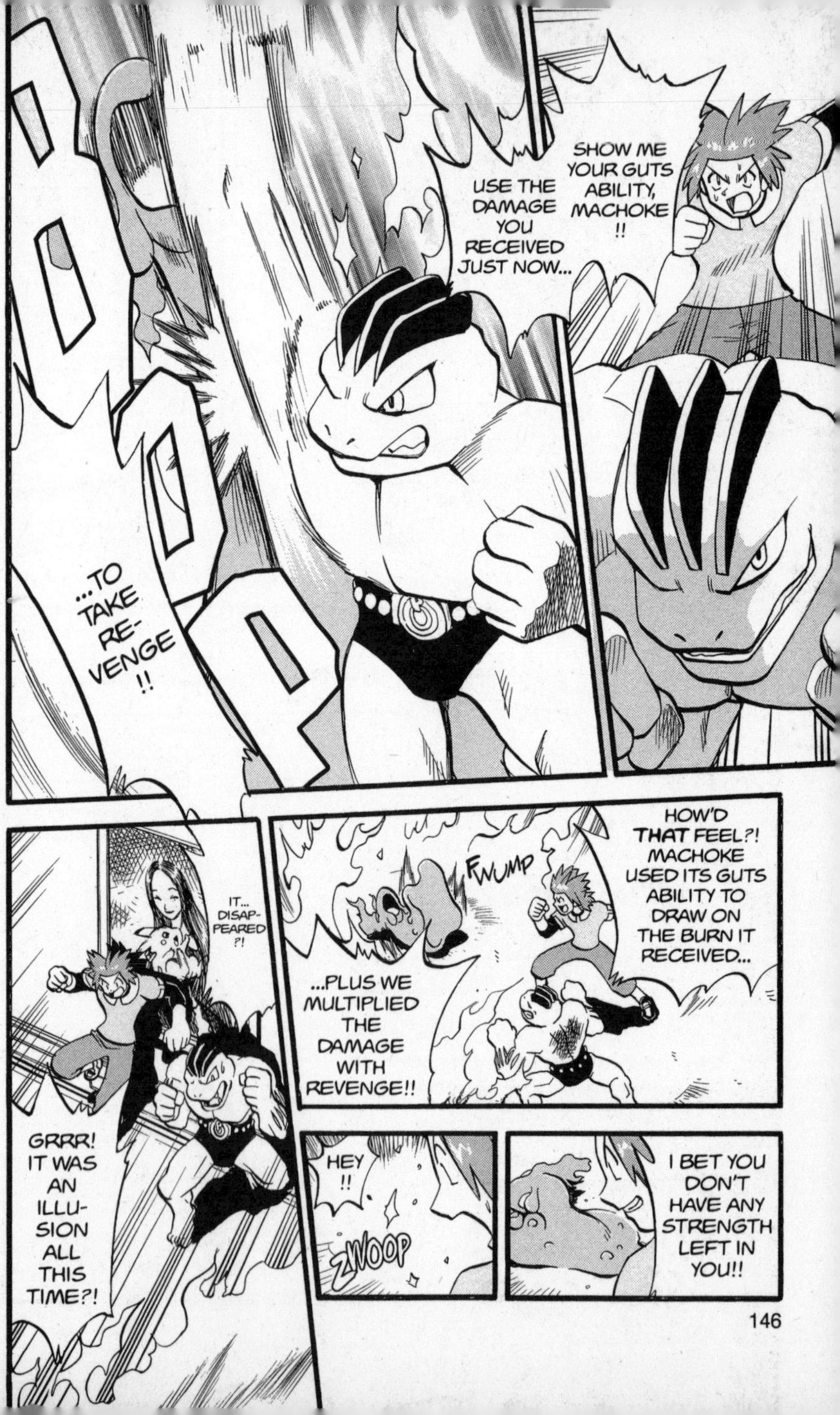
SHOW ME YOUR GUTS ABILITY, MACHOKE !!
USE THE DAMAGE YOU RECEIVED JUST NOW...
...TO TAKE RE-VENGE !!
HOW'D **THAT** FEEL?! MACHOKE USED ITS GUTS ABILITY TO DRAW ON THE BURN IT RECEIVED...
FWUMP
...PLUS WE MULTIPLIED THE DAMAGE WITH REVENGE!!
I BET YOU DON'T HAVE ANY STRENGTH LEFT IN YOU!!
HEY !!
ZWOOP
IT... DISAP-PEARED ?!
GRRR! IT WAS AN ILLU-SION ALL THIS TIME?!

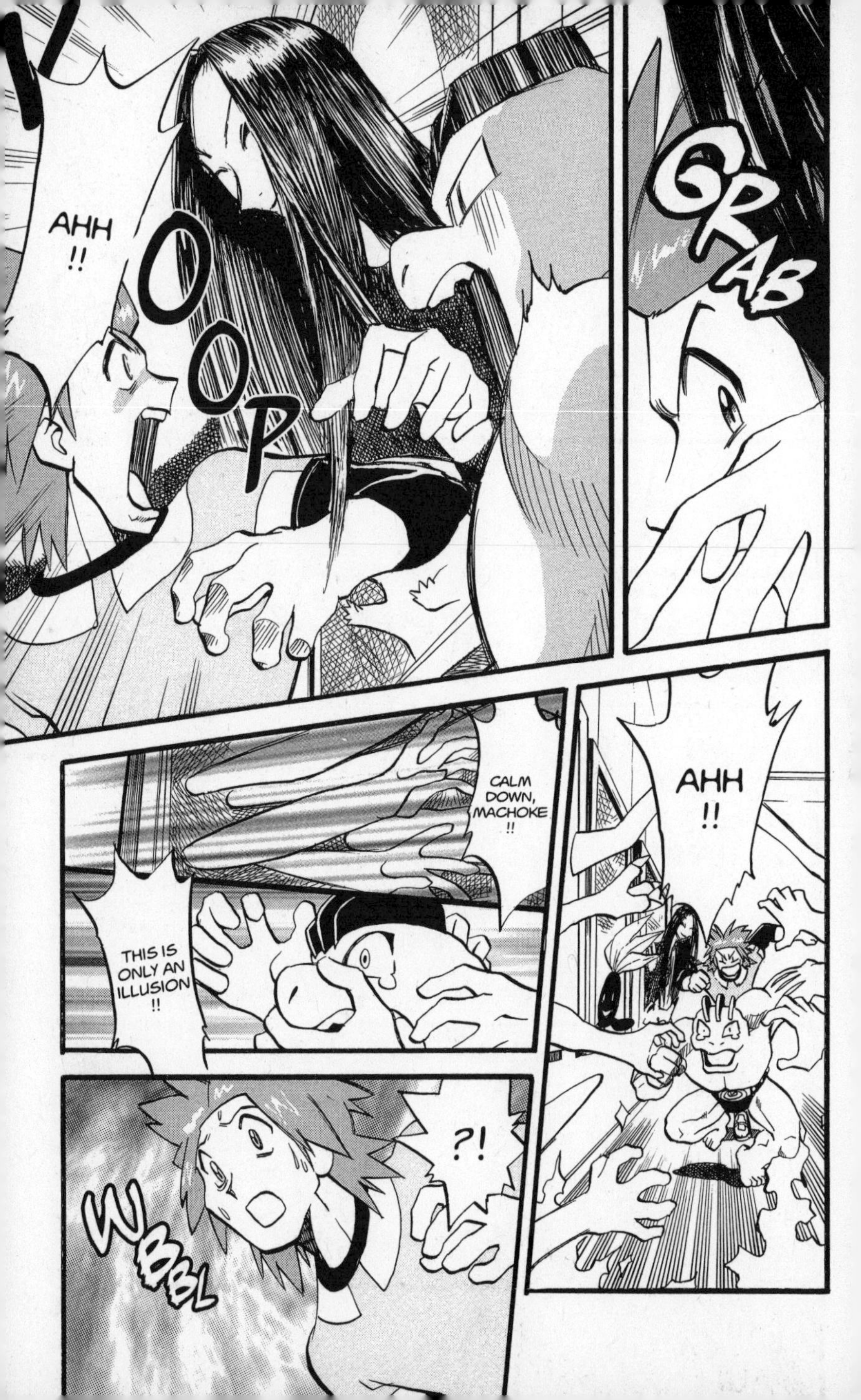
GRAB
AHH!!
OOP
AHH!!
CALM DOWN, MACHOKE!!
THIS IS ONLY AN ILLUSION!!
?!
WUBBL

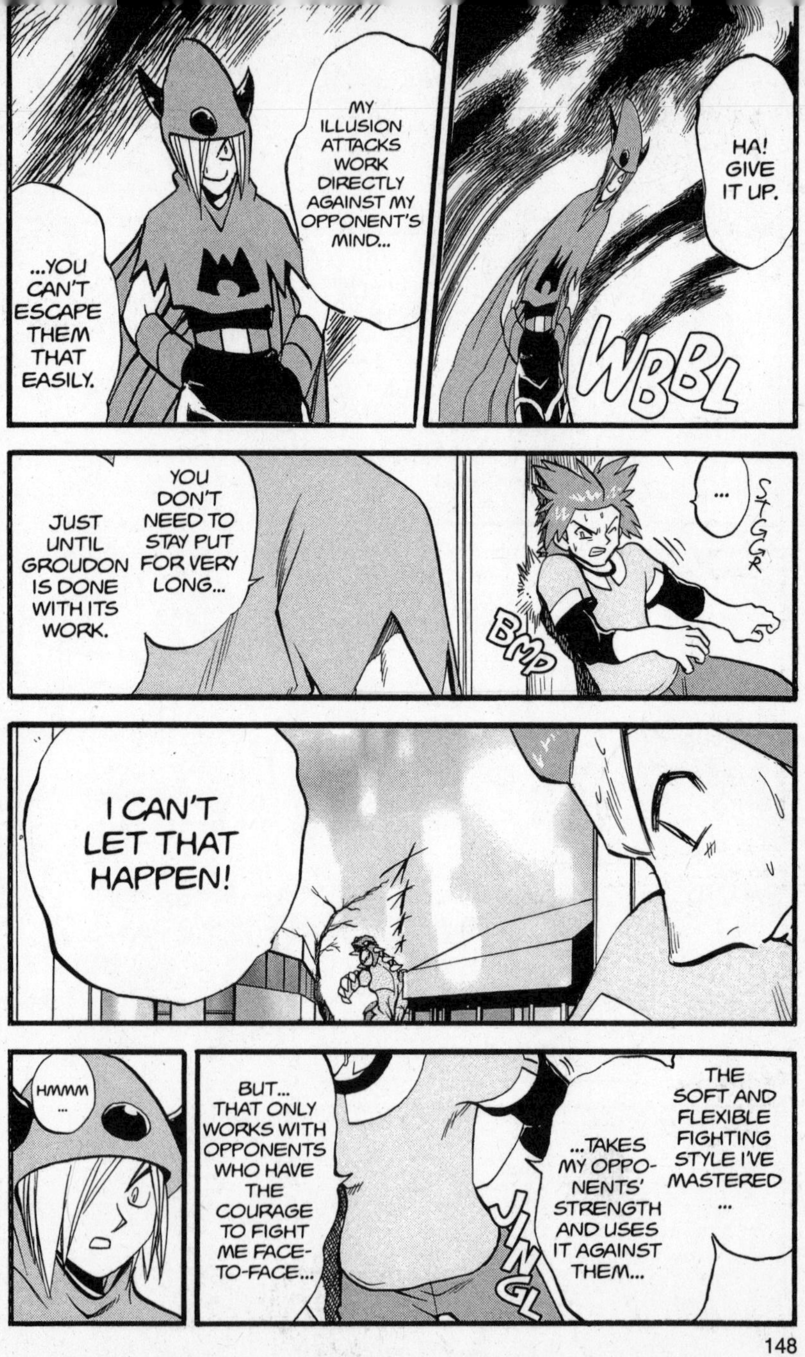
HA! GIVE IT UP.
WBBL
MY ILLUSION ATTACKS WORK DIRECTLY AGAINST MY OPPONENT'S MIND...
...YOU CAN'T ESCAPE THEM THAT EASILY.
...
STGGR
BMP
YOU DON'T NEED TO STAY PUT FOR VERY LONG...
JUST UNTIL GROUDON IS DONE WITH ITS WORK.
I CAN'T LET THAT HAPPEN!
THE SOFT AND FLEXIBLE FIGHTING STYLE I'VE MASTERED...
...TAKES MY OPPO-NENTS' STRENGTH AND USES IT AGAINST THEM...
JINGL
BUT... THAT ONLY WORKS WITH OPPONENTS WHO HAVE THE COURAGE TO FIGHT ME FACE-TO-FACE...
HMMM...

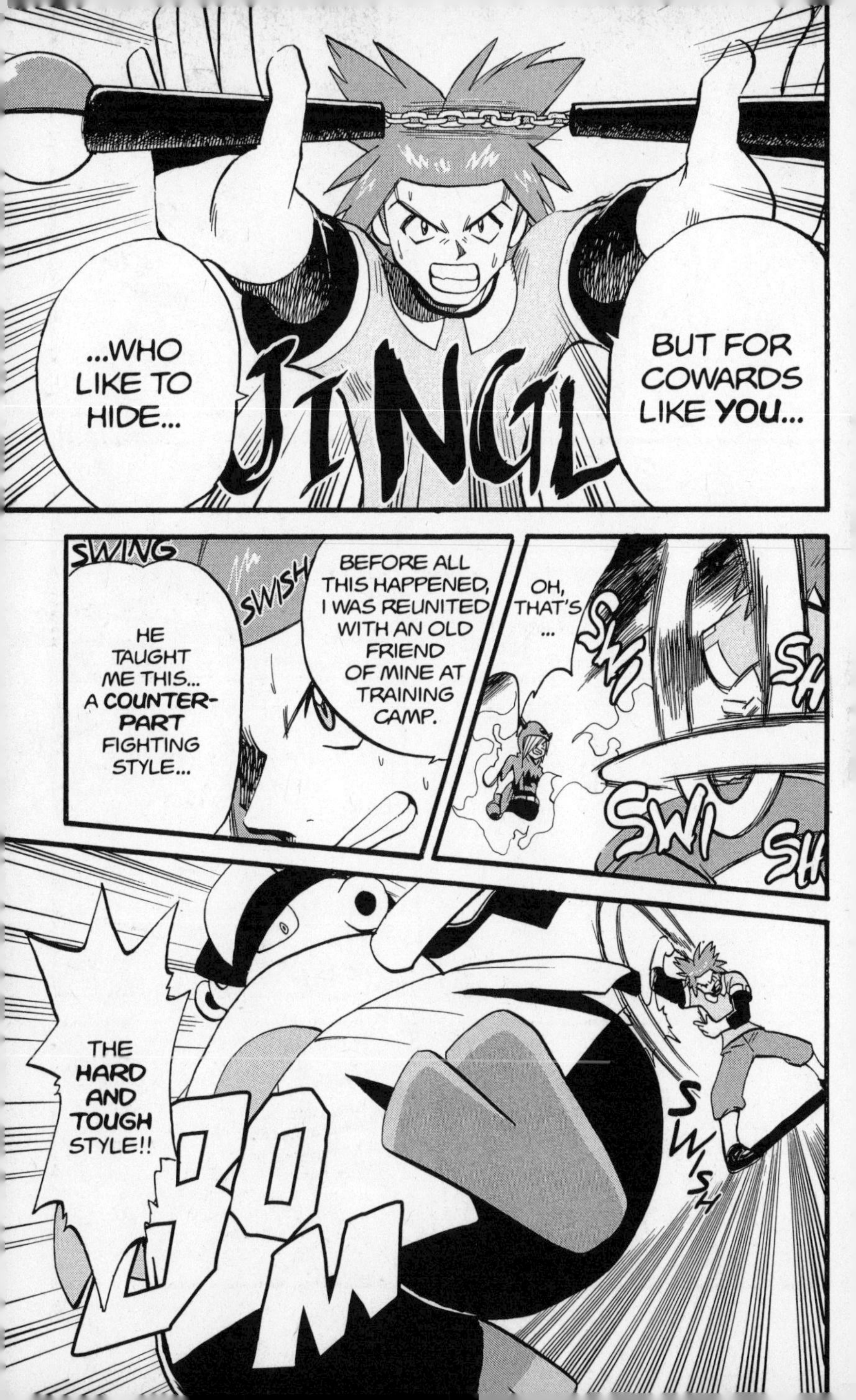
BUT FOR COWARDS LIKE YOU...
...WHO LIKE TO HIDE...
JINGL
OH, THAT'S ...
SWI
SH
SWI
SH
SWISH
BEFORE ALL THIS HAPPENED, I WAS REUNITED WITH AN OLD FRIEND OF MINE AT TRAINING CAMP.
SWING
HE TAUGHT ME THIS... A COUNTER-PART FIGHTING STYLE...
SWISH
THE HARD AND TOUGH STYLE!!

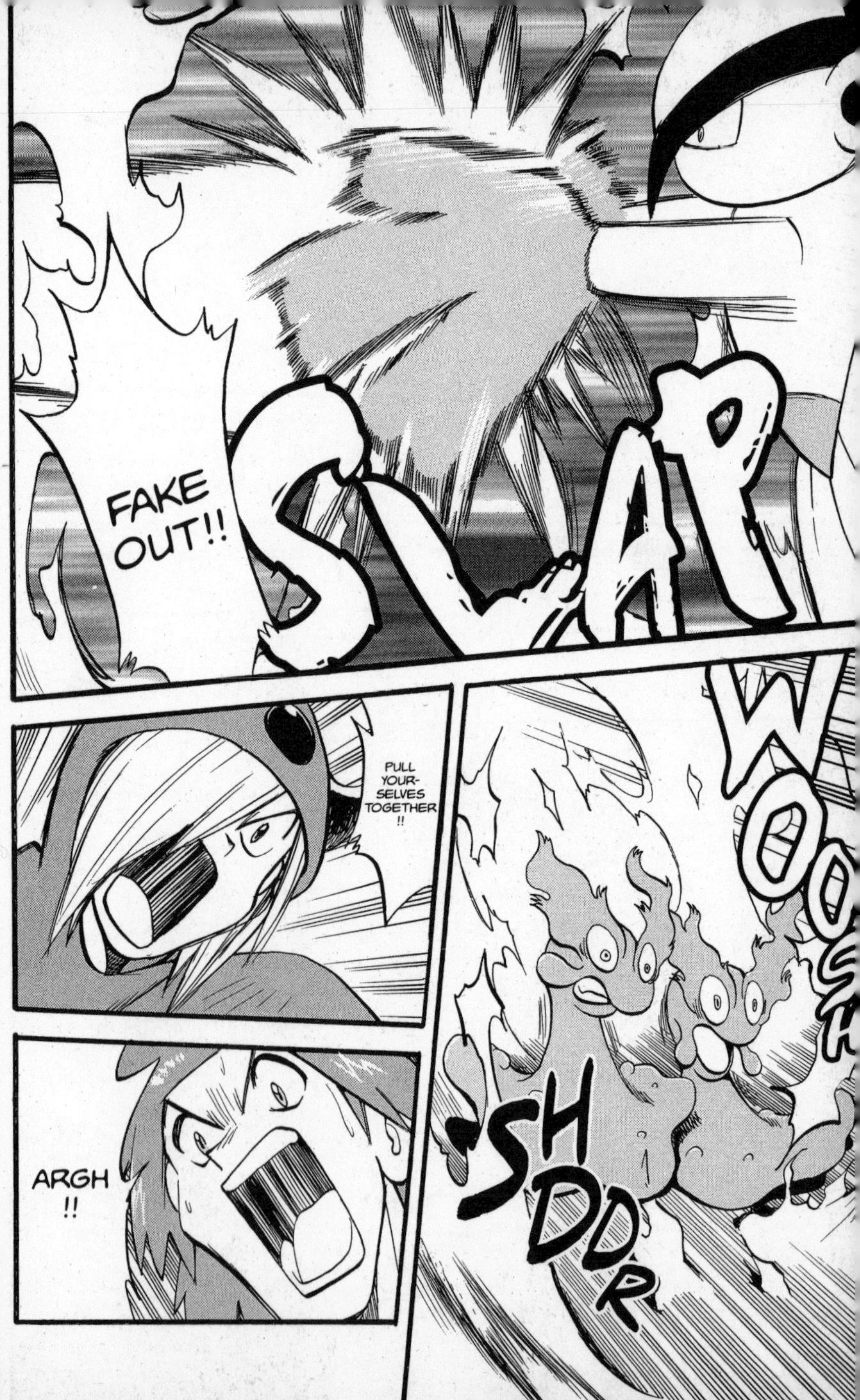
SLAP
FAKE OUT!!
WOOOSH
SHDDR
PULL YOUR-SELVES TOGETHER!!
ARGH!!

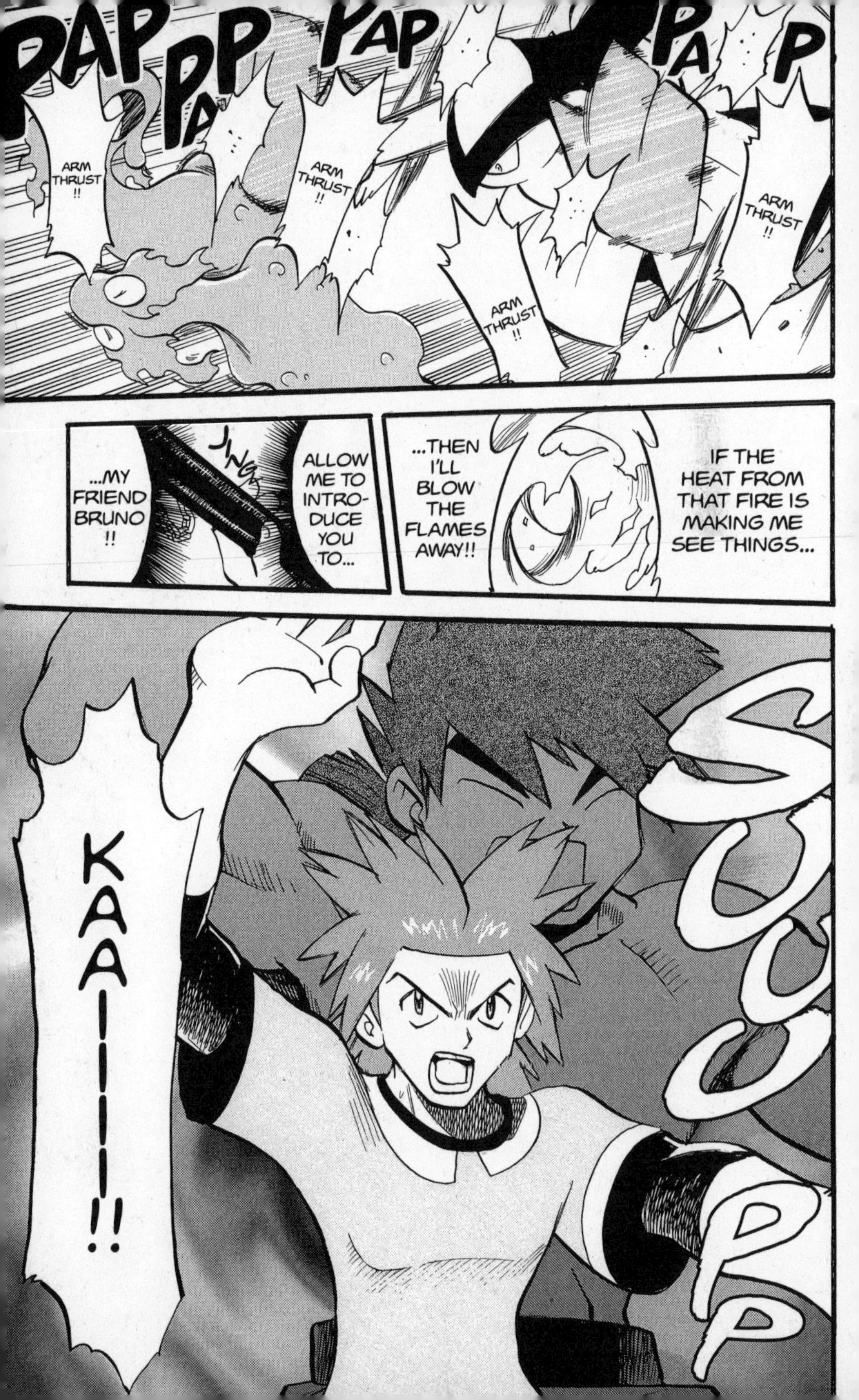

PAP
ARM THRUST !!
ARM THRUST !!
ARM THRUST !!
ARM THRUST !!
IF THE HEAT FROM THAT FIRE IS MAKING ME SEE THINGS...
...THEN I'LL BLOW THE FLAMES AWAY!!
ALLOW ME TO INTRO-DUCE YOU TO...
JING
...MY FRIEND BRUNO !!
KAAI!!

● Chapter 248 ●
The Beginning of the End with Kyogre & Groudon X

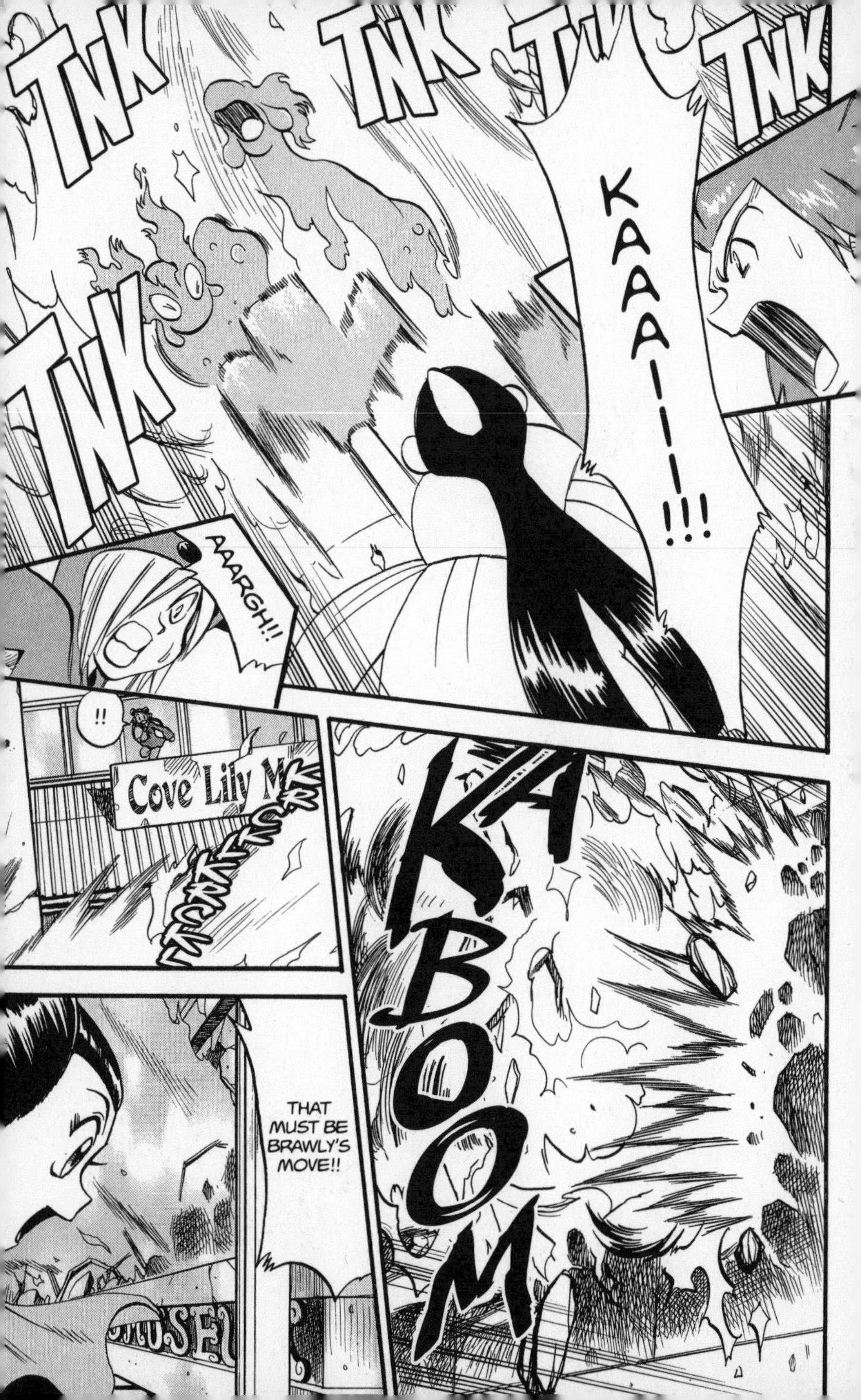
TNK
TNK
TNK
TNK
TNK
KAAA!!!
AAARGH!!
KABOOM
!!
Cove Lily M
KRCKL KRCKL
THAT MUST BE BRAWLY'S MOVE!!

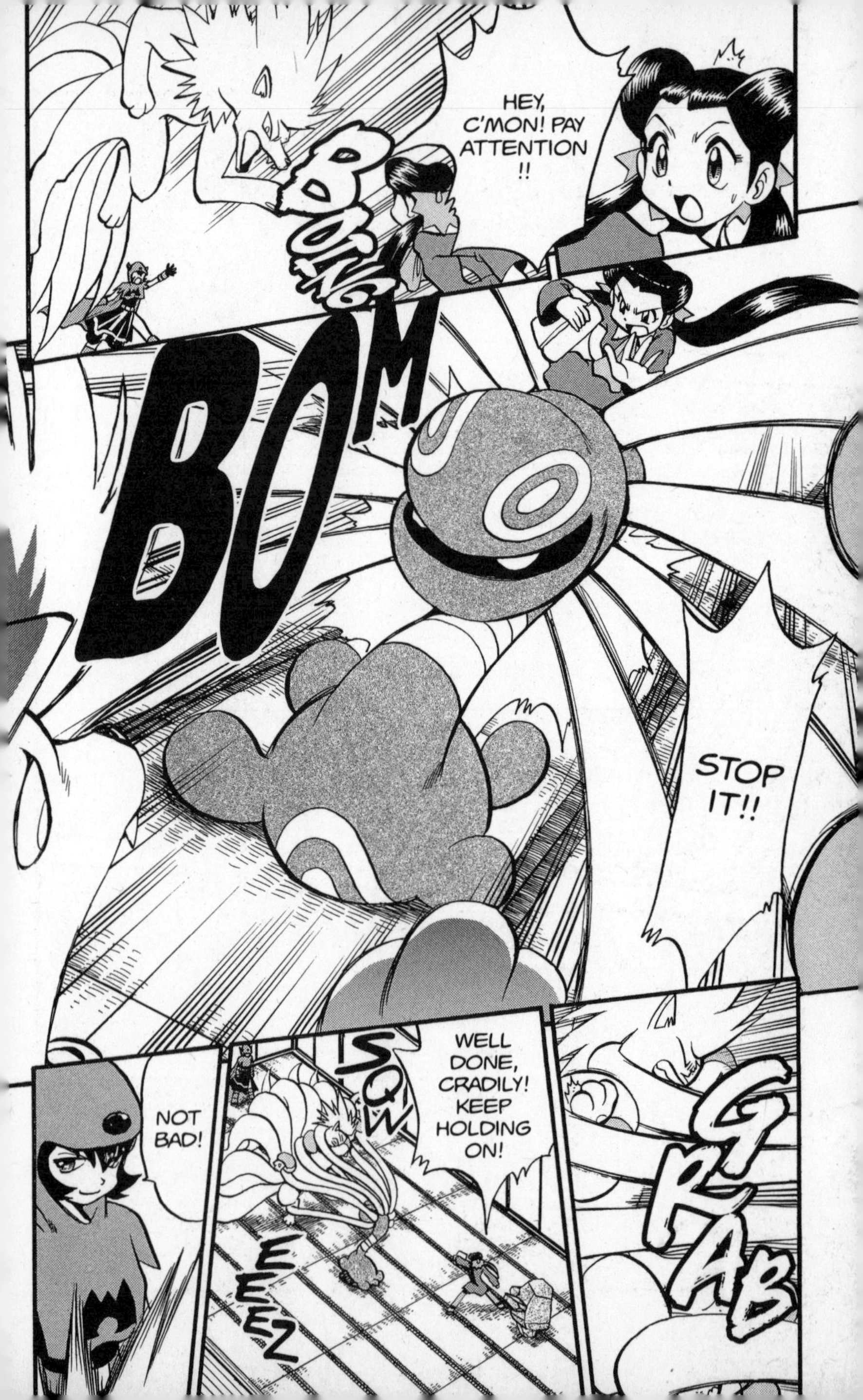
HEY, C'MON! PAY ATTENTION !!
BOING
BOM
STOP IT!!
GRAB
WELL DONE, CRADILY! KEEP HOLDING ON!
SQW
EEEZ
NOT BAD!

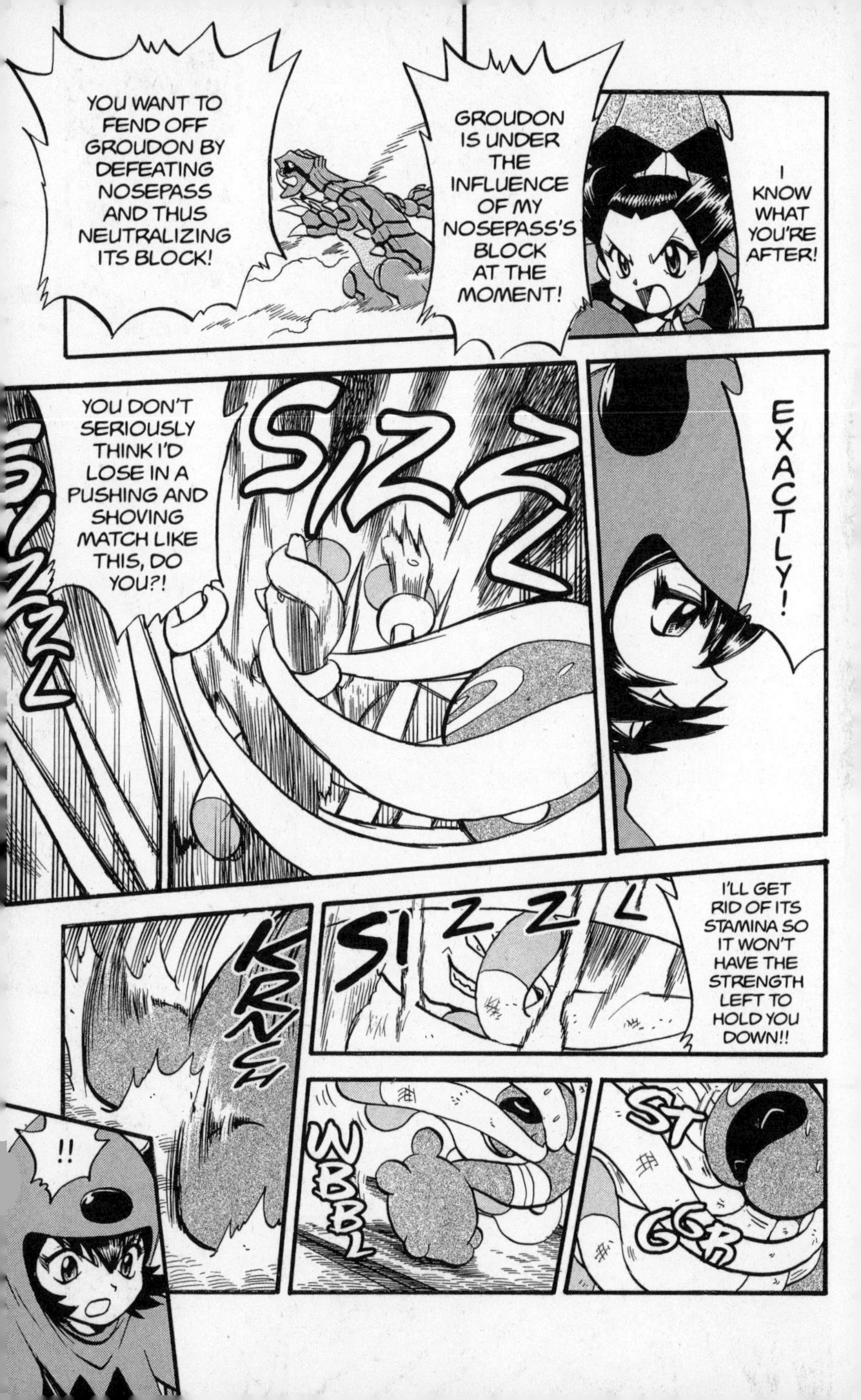
I KNOW WHAT YOU'RE AFTER!
GROUDON IS UNDER THE INFLUENCE OF MY NOSEPASS'S BLOCK AT THE MOMENT!
YOU WANT TO FEND OFF GROUDON BY DEFEATING NOSEPASS AND THUS NEUTRALIZING ITS BLOCK!
EXACTLY!
SIZZZ
YOU DON'T SERIOUSLY THINK I'D LOSE IN A PUSHING AND SHOVING MATCH LIKE THIS, DO YOU?!
I'LL GET RID OF ITS STAMINA SO IT WON'T HAVE THE STRENGTH LEFT TO HOLD YOU DOWN!!
SIZZZL
KRNCH
ST
GGR
WBBL
!!

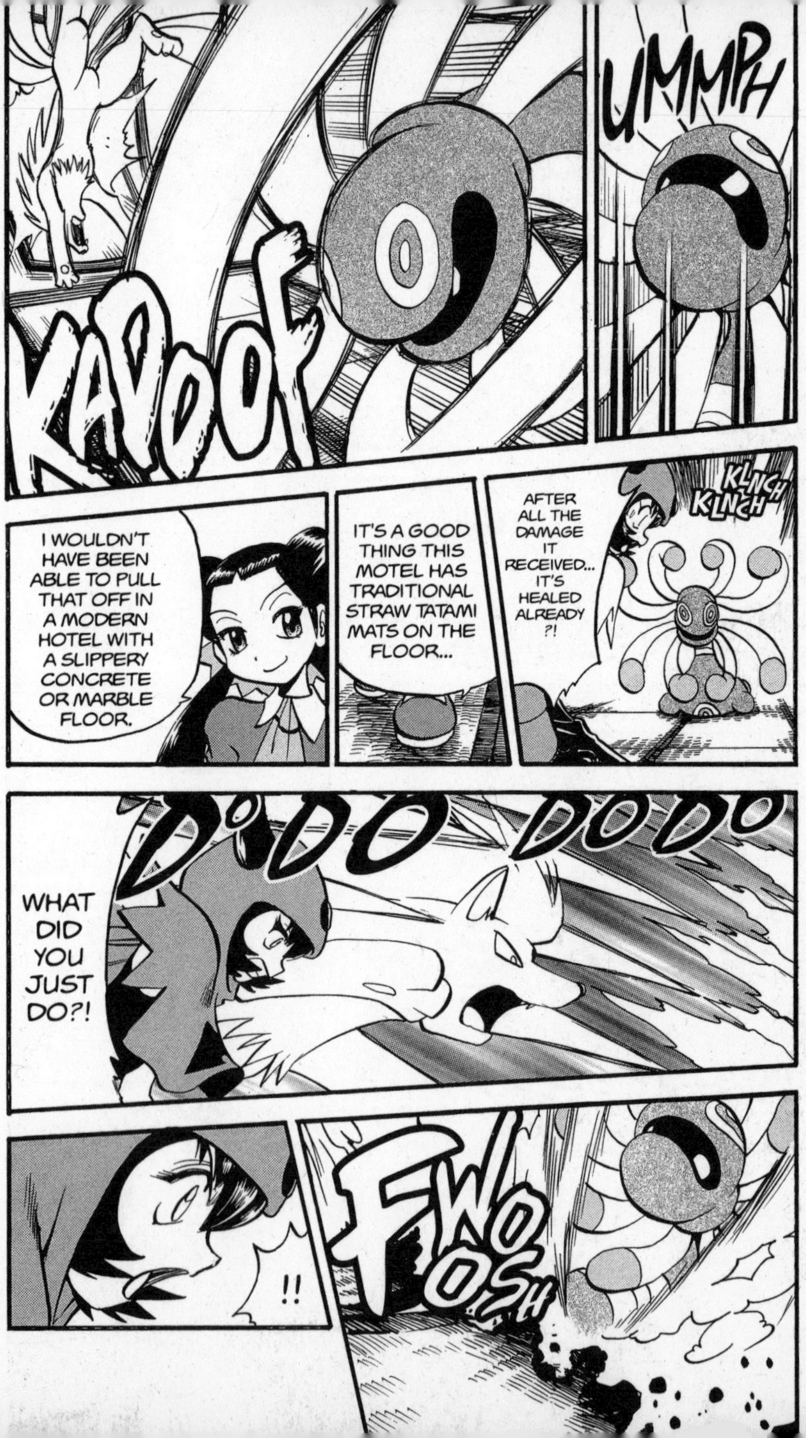
UMMPH
KAPOOF
KLNCH KLNCH
AFTER ALL THE DAMAGE IT RECEIVED... IT'S HEALED ALREADY ?!
IT'S A GOOD THING THIS MOTEL HAS TRADITIONAL STRAW TATAMI MATS ON THE FLOOR...
I WOULDN'T HAVE BEEN ABLE TO PULL THAT OFF IN A MODERN HOTEL WITH A SLIPPERY CONCRETE OR MARBLE FLOOR.
D'DO DO DO DO
WHAT DID YOU JUST DO?!
FWOOSH
!!

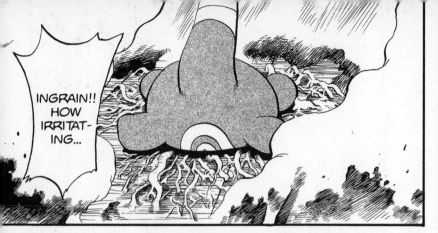

INGRAIN!! HOW IRRITATING...

KNOWLEDGE AND STRATEGY!

THAT'S MY BATTLE STYLE!!

THERE'RE STILL PEOPLE AROUND HERE...?!

KLTTR

KLTTR

!!

BZZT

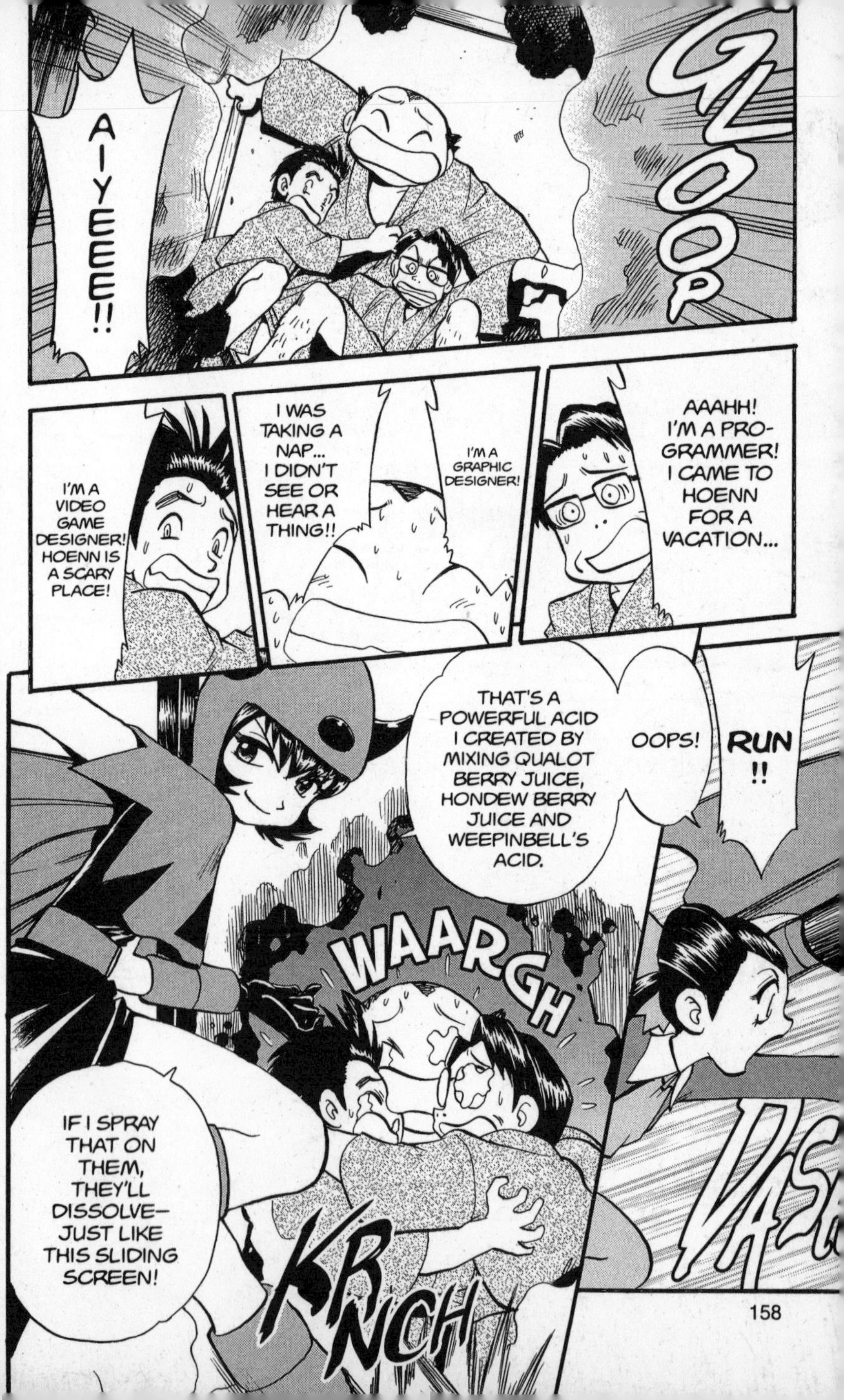
GLOOOP
AIYEEEE!!
AAAHH! I'M A PRO-GRAMMER! I CAME TO HOENN FOR A VACATION...
I'M A GRAPHIC DESIGNER!
I WAS TAKING A NAP... I DIDN'T SEE OR HEAR A THING!!
I'M A VIDEO GAME DESIGNER! HOENN IS A SCARY PLACE!
RUN!!
OOPS!
THAT'S A POWERFUL ACID I CREATED BY MIXING QUALOT BERRY JUICE, HONDEW BERRY JUICE AND WEEPINBELL'S ACID.
WAARGH
IF I SPRAY THAT ON THEM, THEY'LL DISSOLVE—JUST LIKE THIS SLIDING SCREEN!
KRNCH

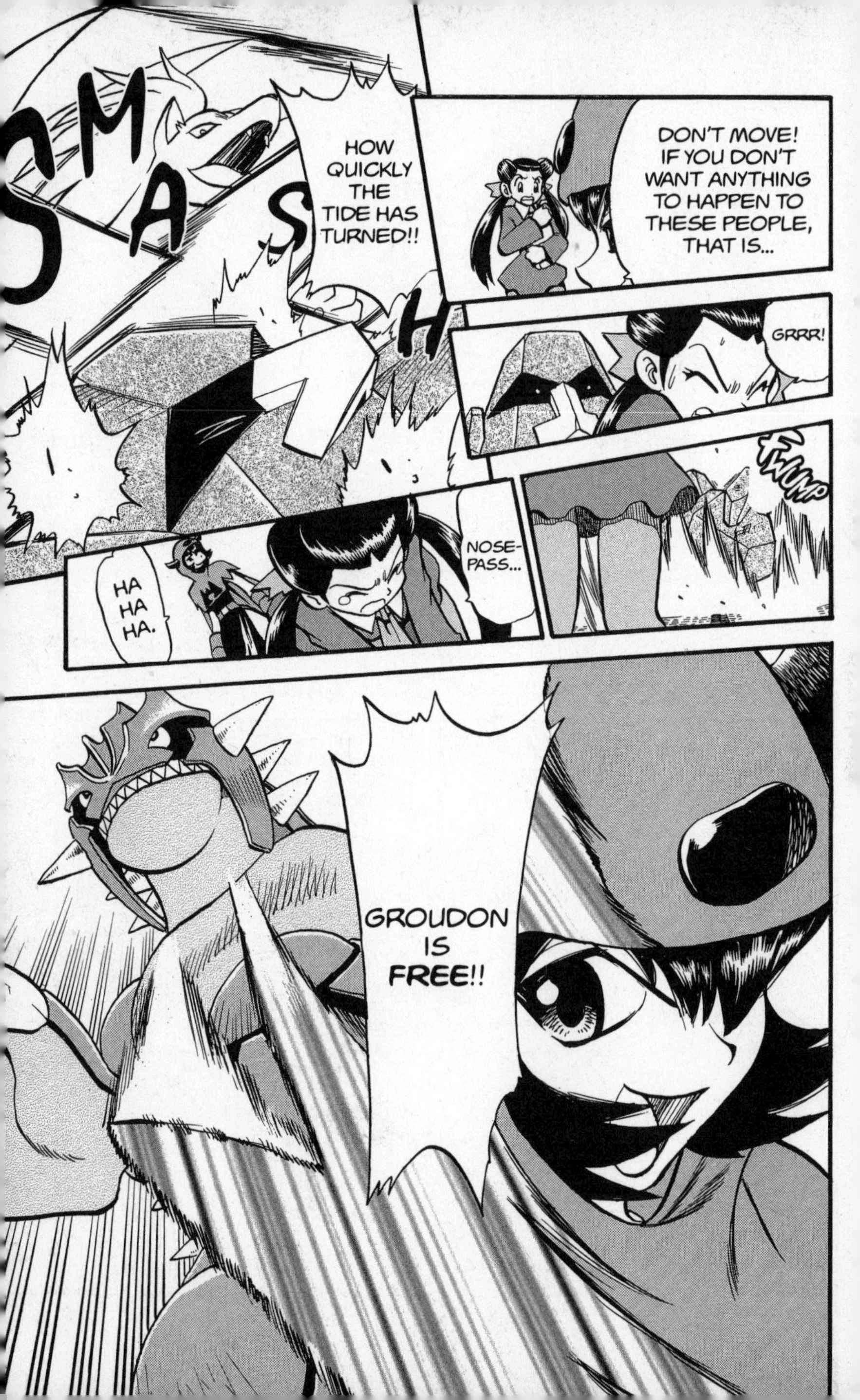
DON'T MOVE! IF YOU DON'T WANT ANYTHING TO HAPPEN TO THESE PEOPLE, THAT IS...
SMASH
HOW QUICKLY THE TIDE HAS TURNED!!
GRRR!
FWUMP
NOSE-PASS...
HA HA HA.
GROUDON IS FREE!!

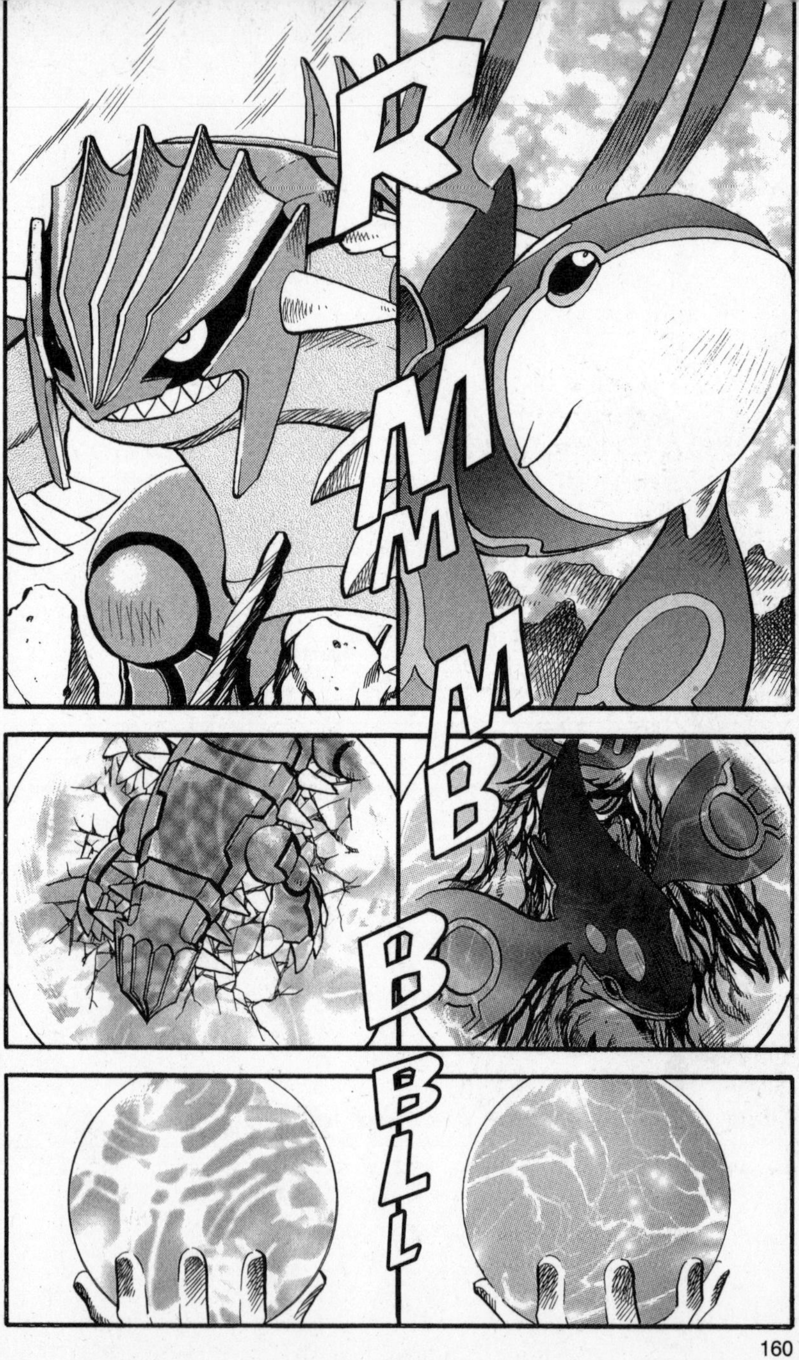
RMMMBBBLLL

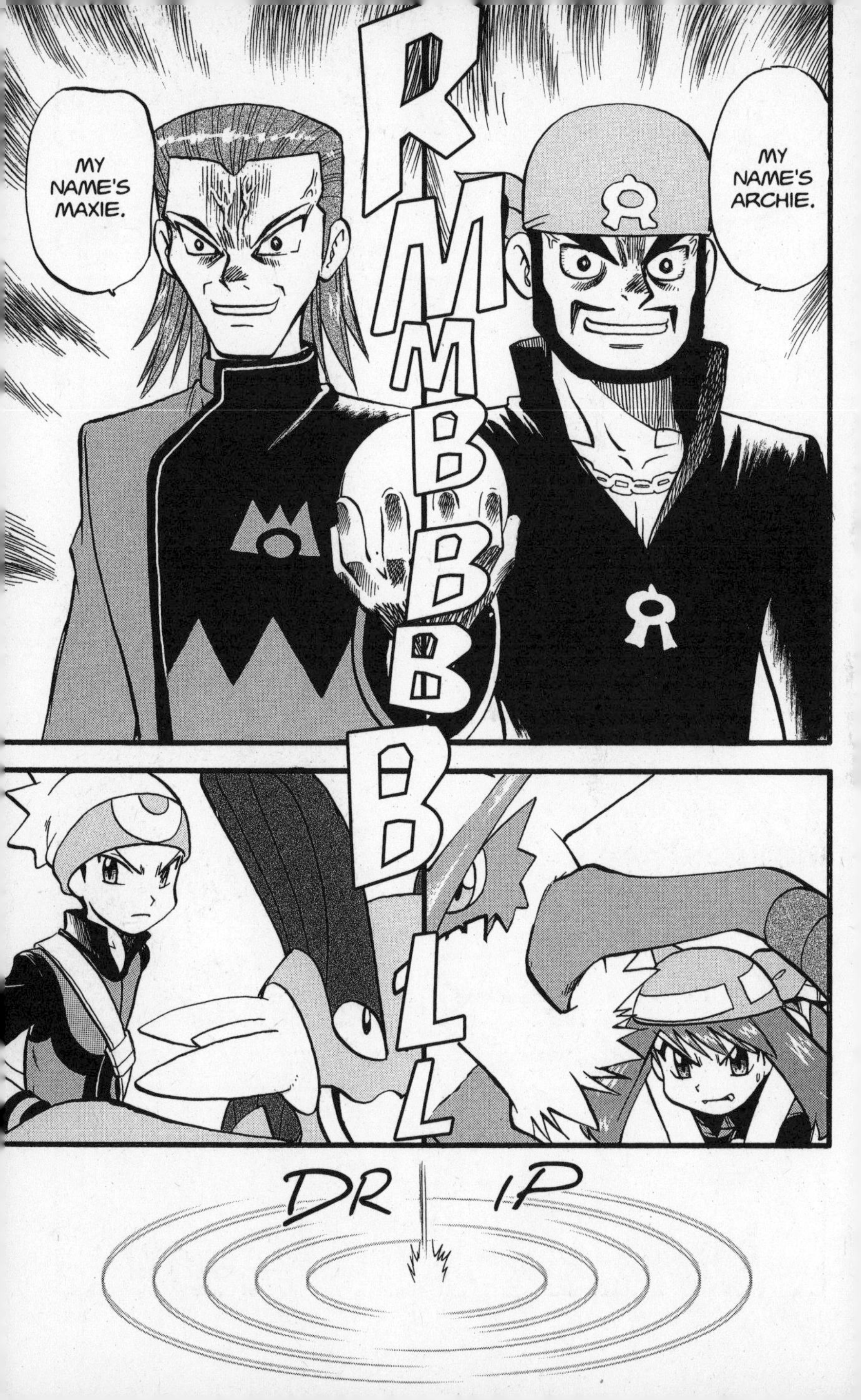
MY NAME'S ARCHIE.
MY NAME'S MAXIE.
RMMBBBBBLL
DRIP

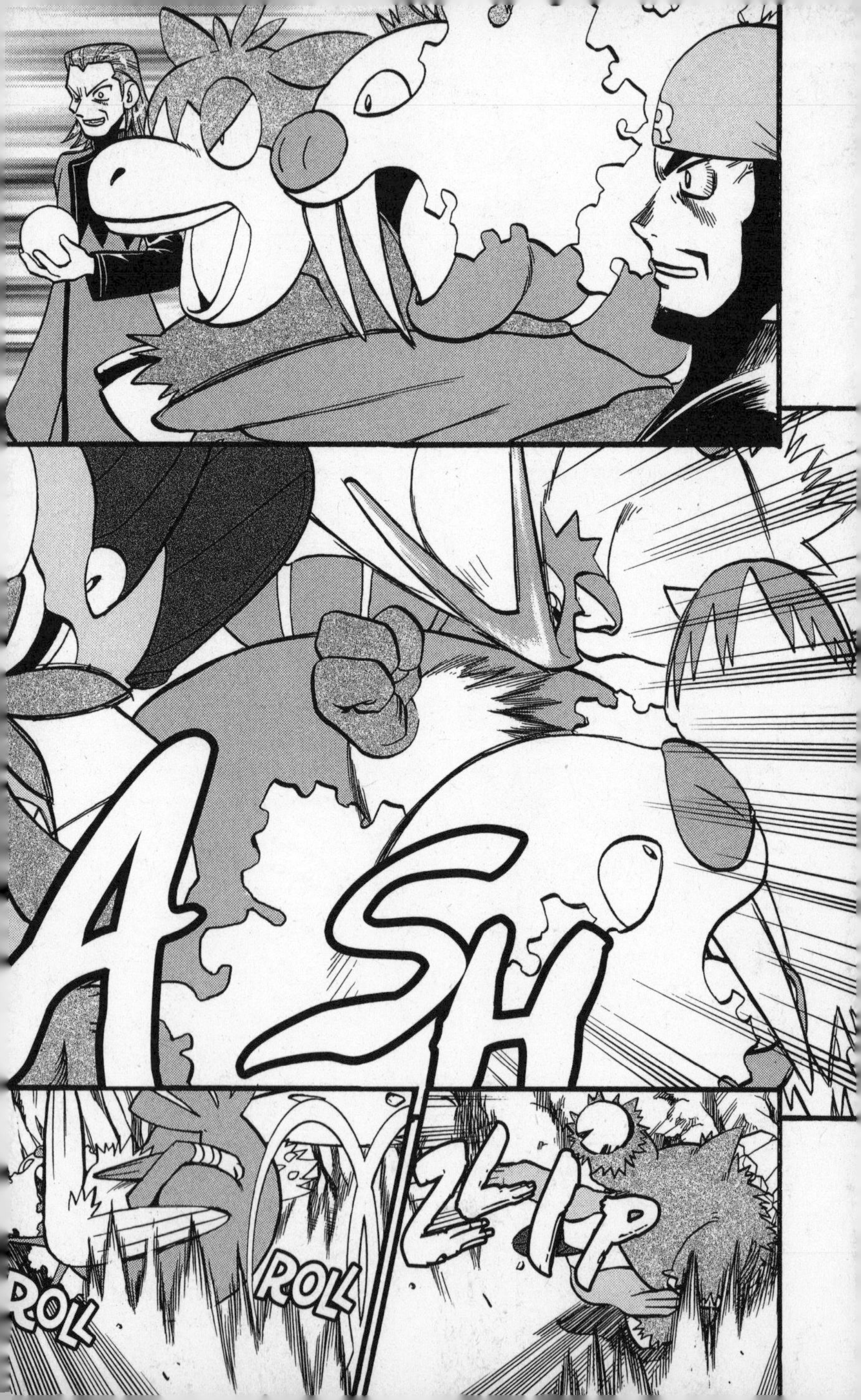
ASH
ZLIP
ROLL
ROLL

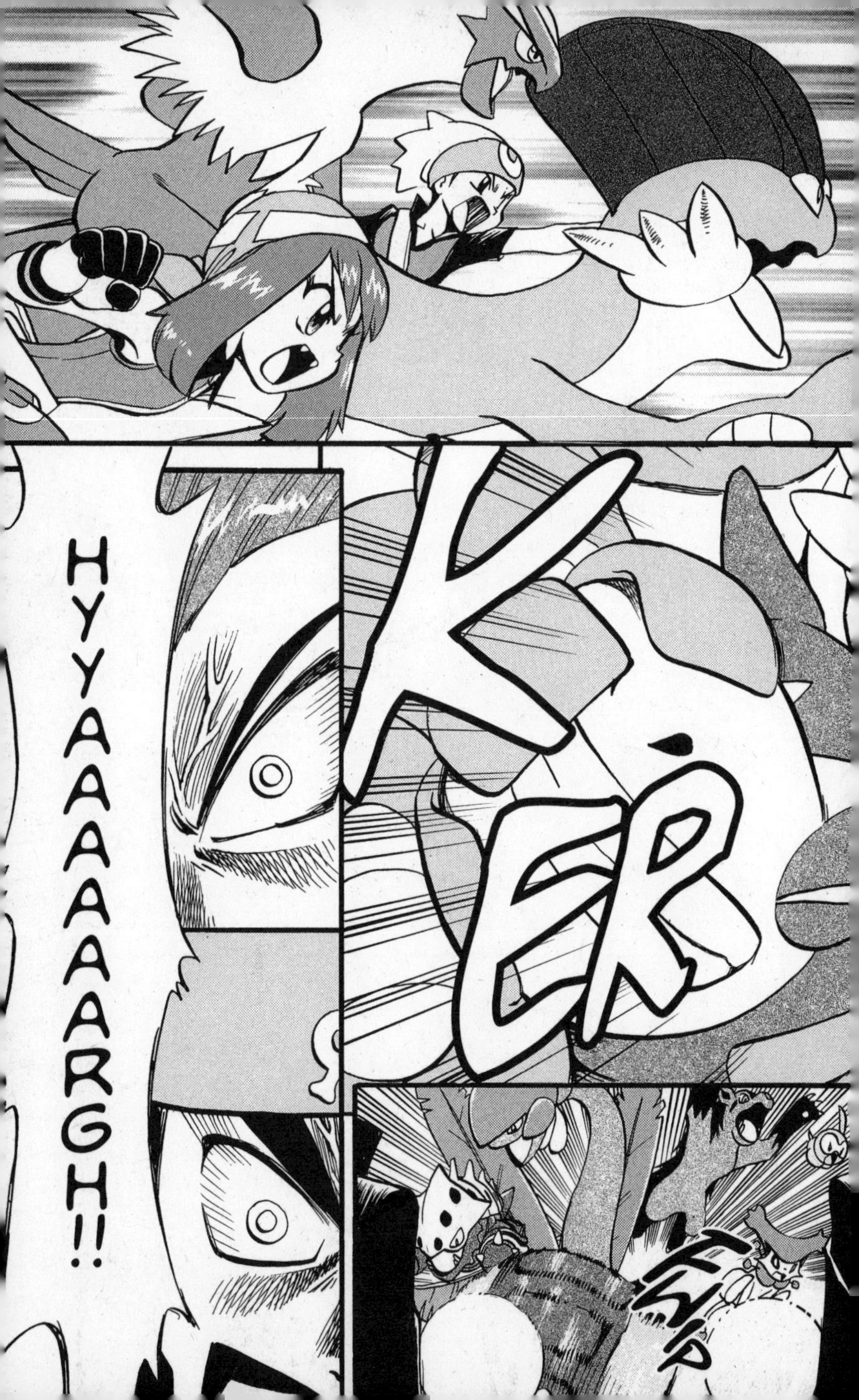
KER
FWIP
HYYAAAAAARGH!!

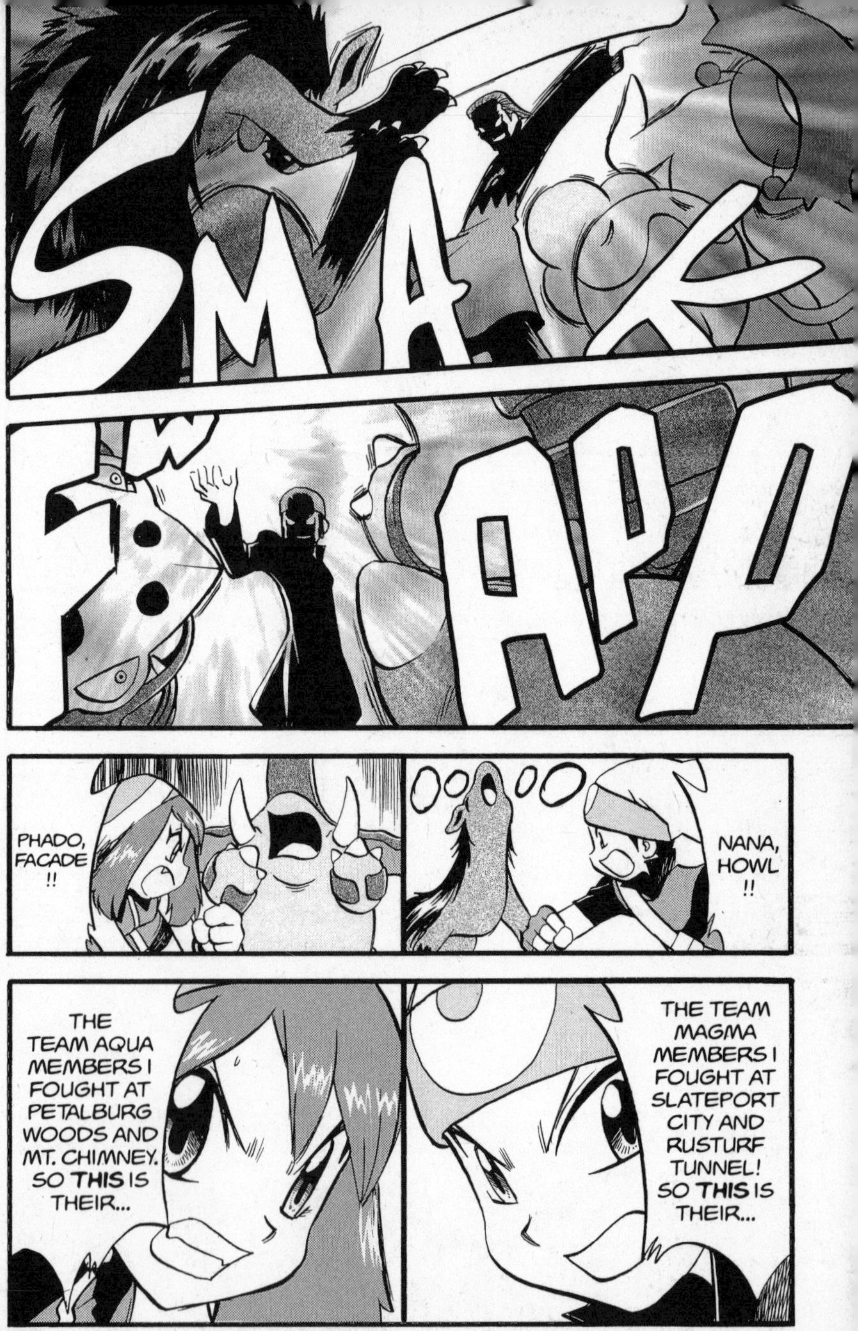
SMACK
NANA, HOWL!!
PHADO, FACADE!!
THE TEAM MAGMA MEMBERS I FOUGHT AT SLATEPORT CITY AND RUSTURF TUNNEL! SO THIS IS THEIR...
THE TEAM AQUA MEMBERS I FOUGHT AT PETALBURG WOODS AND MT. CHIMNEY. SO THIS IS THEIR...

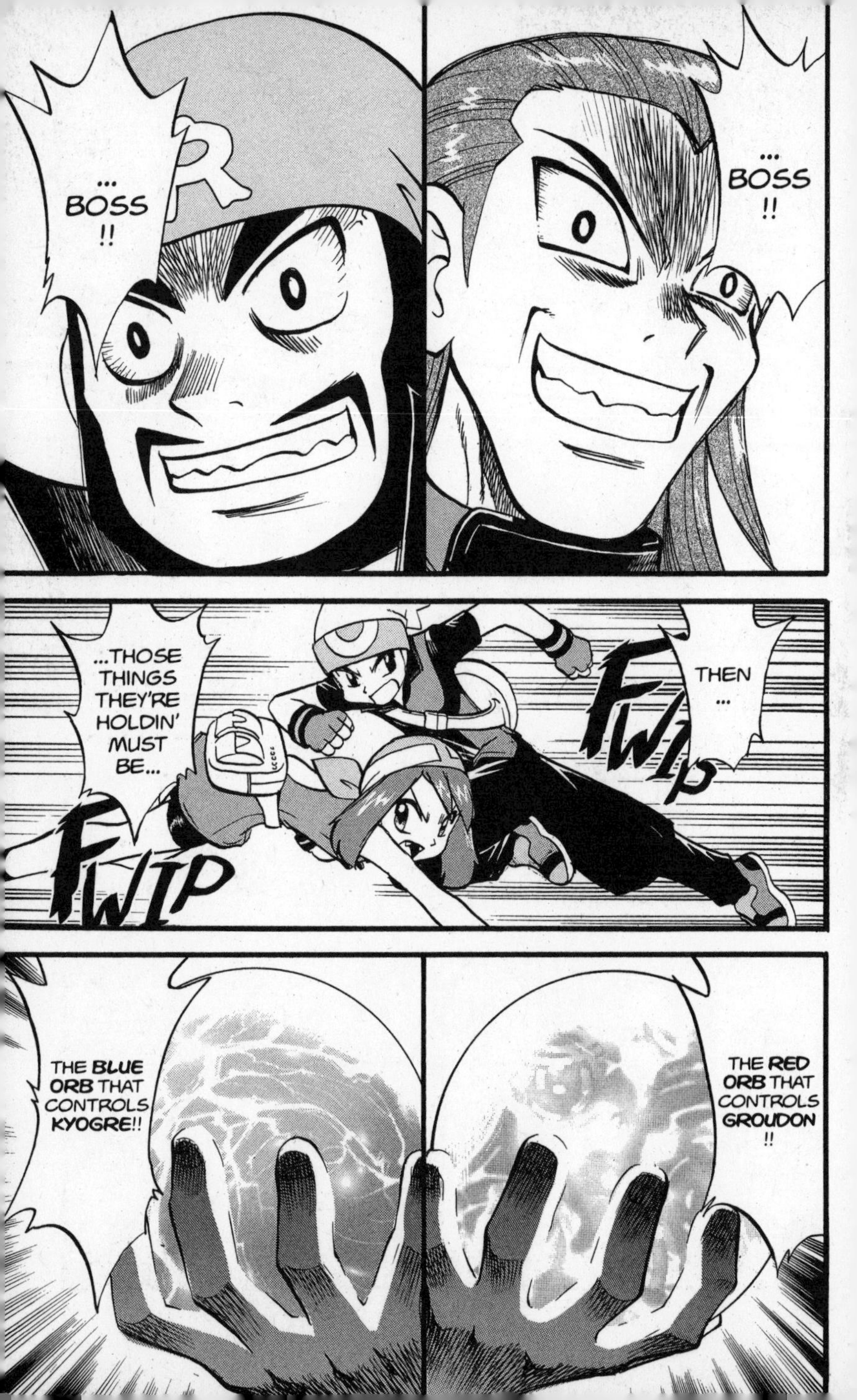
... BOSS !!
... BOSS !!
THEN ...
FWIP
...THOSE THINGS THEY'RE HOLDIN' MUST BE...
FWIP
THE RED ORB THAT CONTROLS GROUDON !!
THE BLUE ORB THAT CONTROLS KYOGRE!!

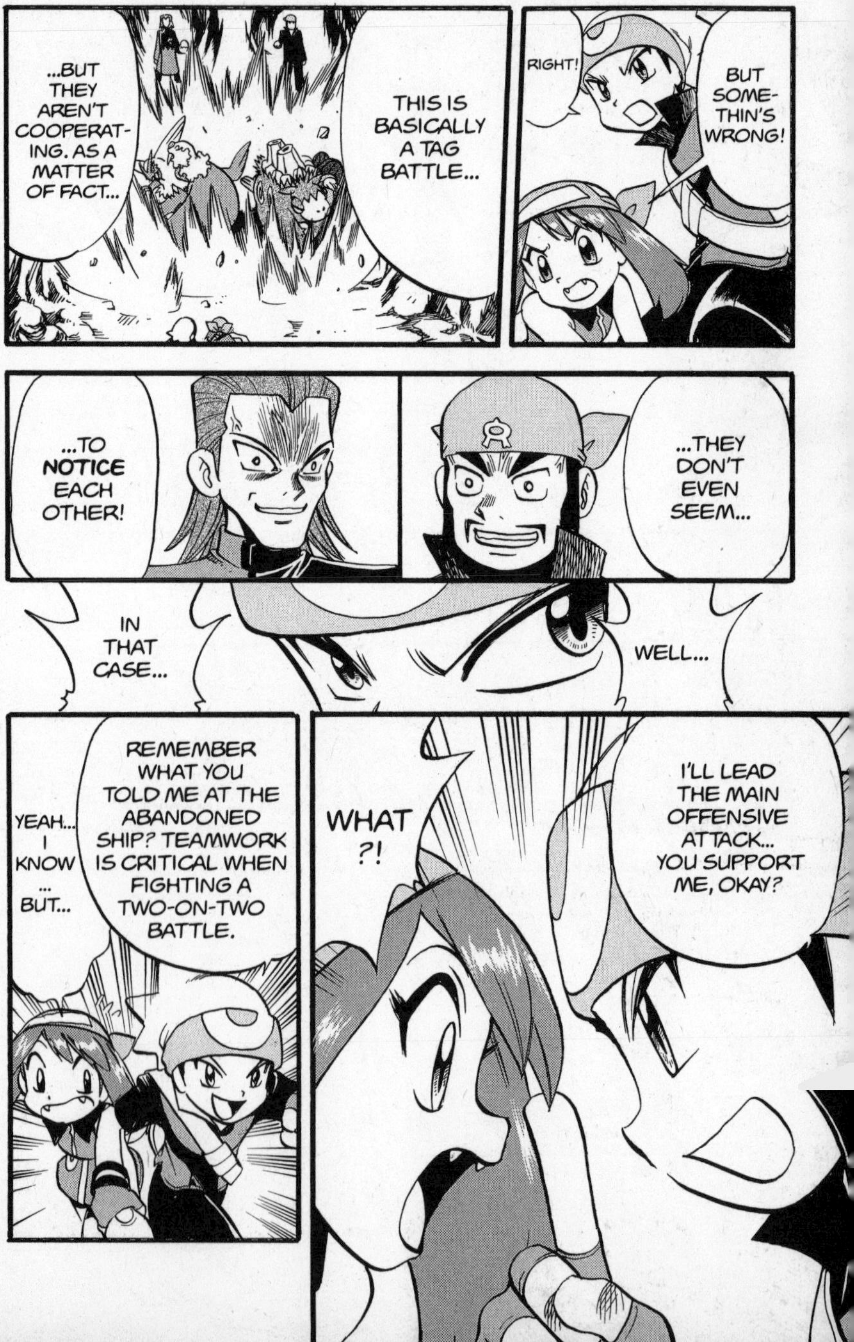
RIGHT!
BUT SOME-THIN'S WRONG!
THIS IS BASICALLY A TAG BATTLE...
...BUT THEY AREN'T COOPERAT-ING. AS A MATTER OF FACT...
...THEY DON'T EVEN SEEM...
...TO **NOTICE** EACH OTHER!
WELL...
IN THAT CASE...
I'LL LEAD THE MAIN OFFENSIVE ATTACK... YOU SUPPORT ME, OKAY?
WHAT ?!
REMEMBER WHAT YOU TOLD ME AT THE ABANDONED SHIP? TEAMWORK IS CRITICAL WHEN FIGHTING A TWO-ON-TWO BATTLE.
YEAH... I KNOW... BUT...

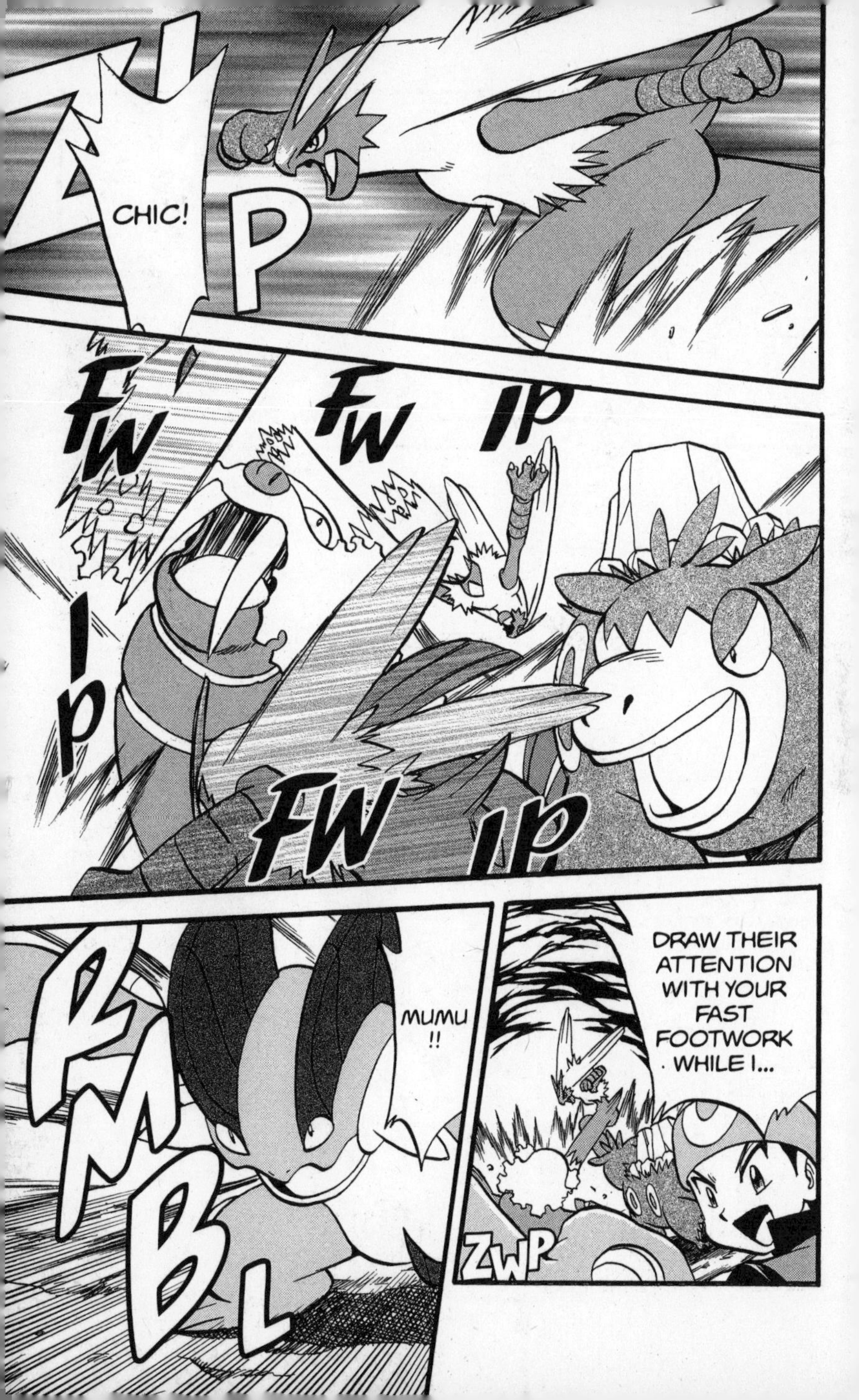
ZIP
CHIC!
FWIP
FWIP
FWIP
DRAW THEIR ATTENTION WITH YOUR FAST FOOTWORK WHILE I...
ZWP
MUMU!!
RUMBL

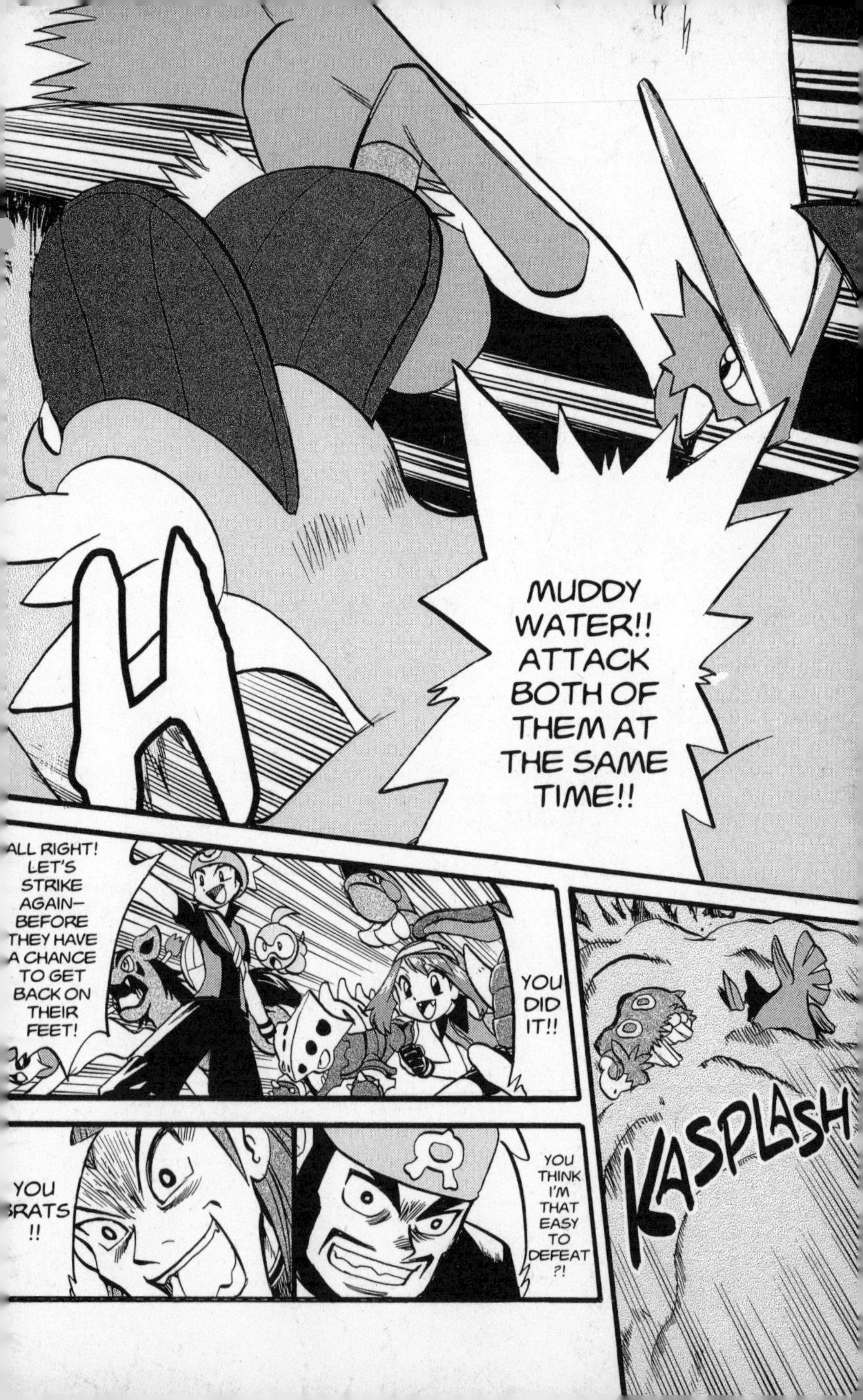
MUDDY WATER!! ATTACK BOTH OF THEM AT THE SAME TIME!!
KASPLASH
YOU DID IT!!
ALL RIGHT! LET'S STRIKE AGAIN—BEFORE THEY HAVE A CHANCE TO GET BACK ON THEIR FEET!
YOU THINK I'M THAT EASY TO DEFEAT ?!
YOU BRATS !!

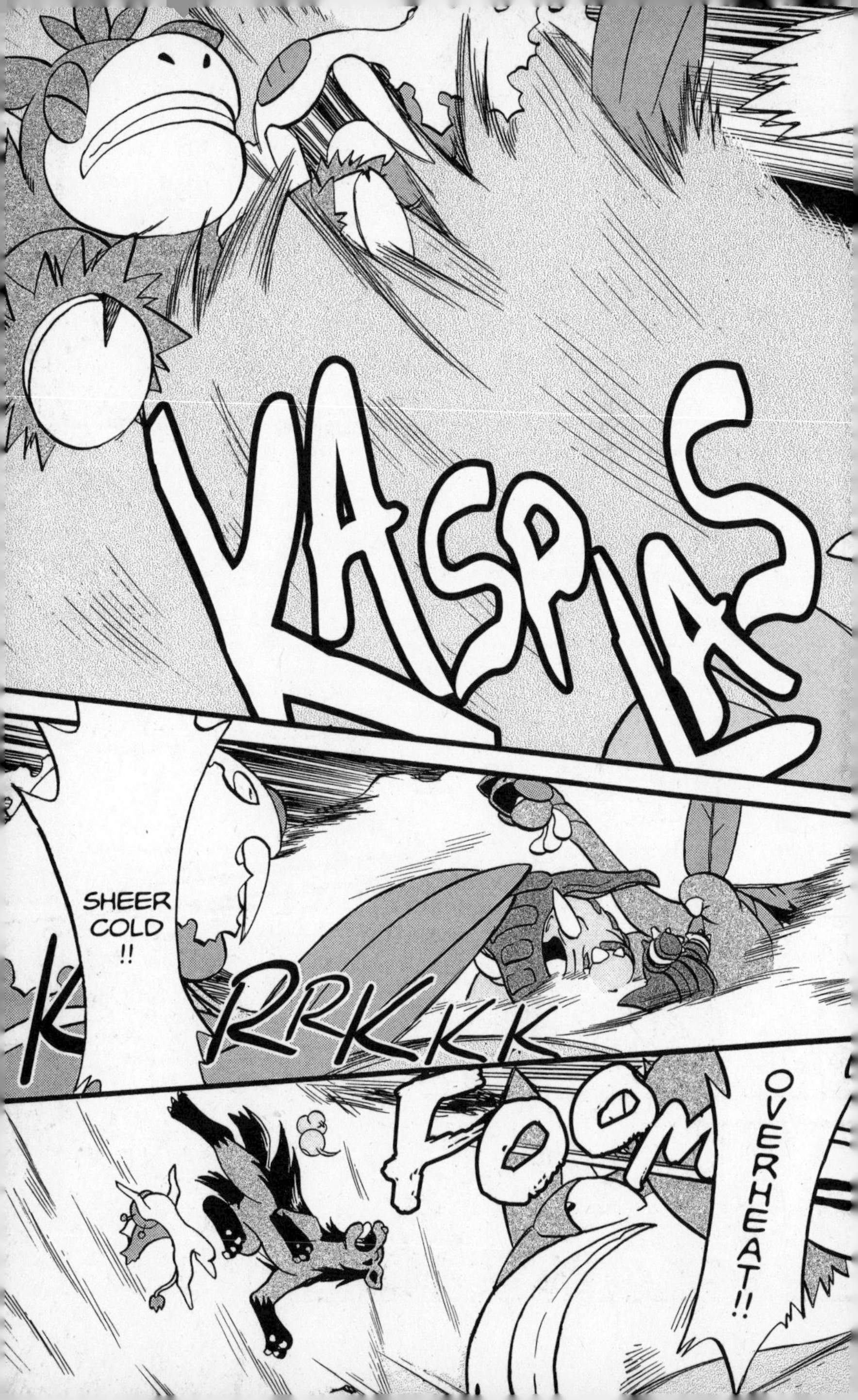
VASPLAS
SHEER COLD !!
KRRKKK
OVERHEAT!!
FOOM

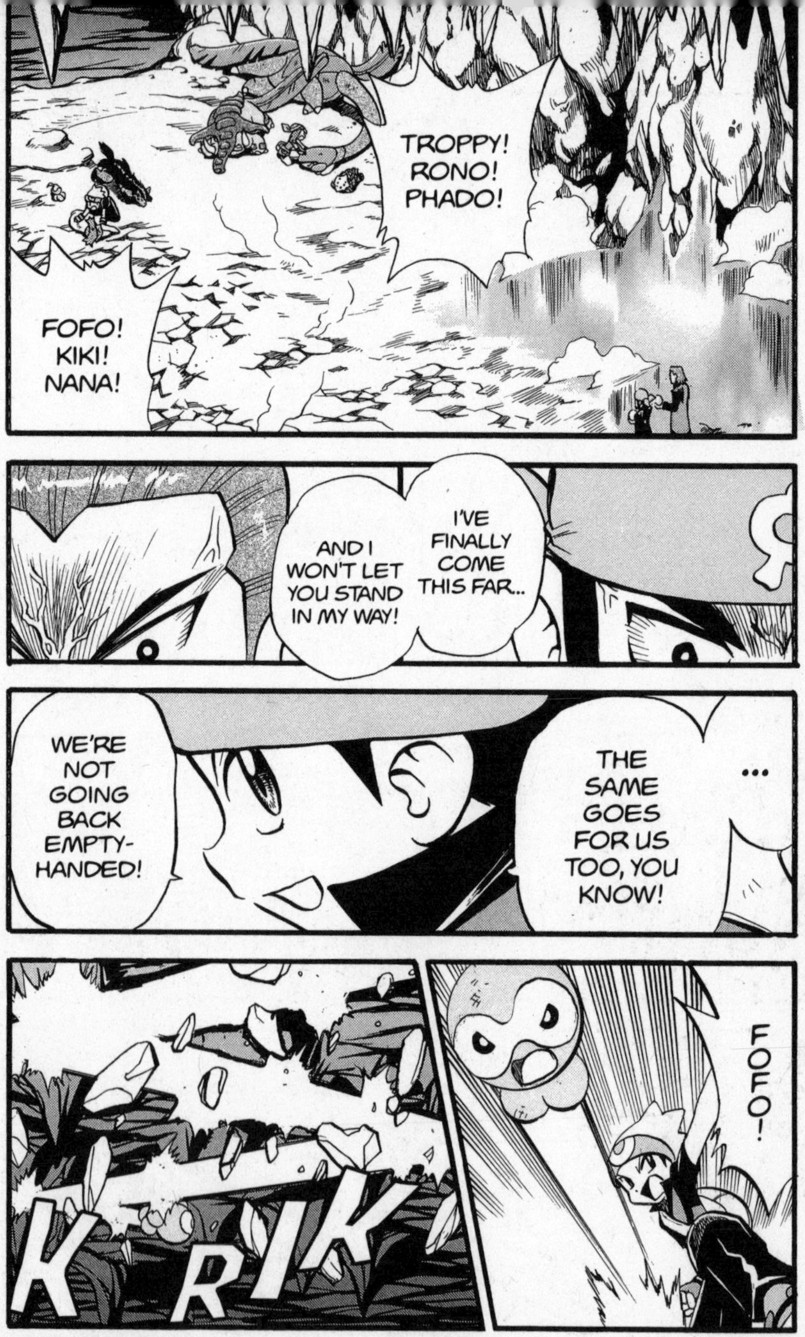
TROPPY! RONO! PHADO!
FOFO! KIKI! NANA!
I'VE FINALLY COME THIS FAR...
AND I WON'T LET YOU STAND IN MY WAY!
...
THE SAME GOES FOR US TOO, YOU KNOW!
WE'RE NOT GOING BACK EMPTY-HANDED!
FOFO!
KRIK

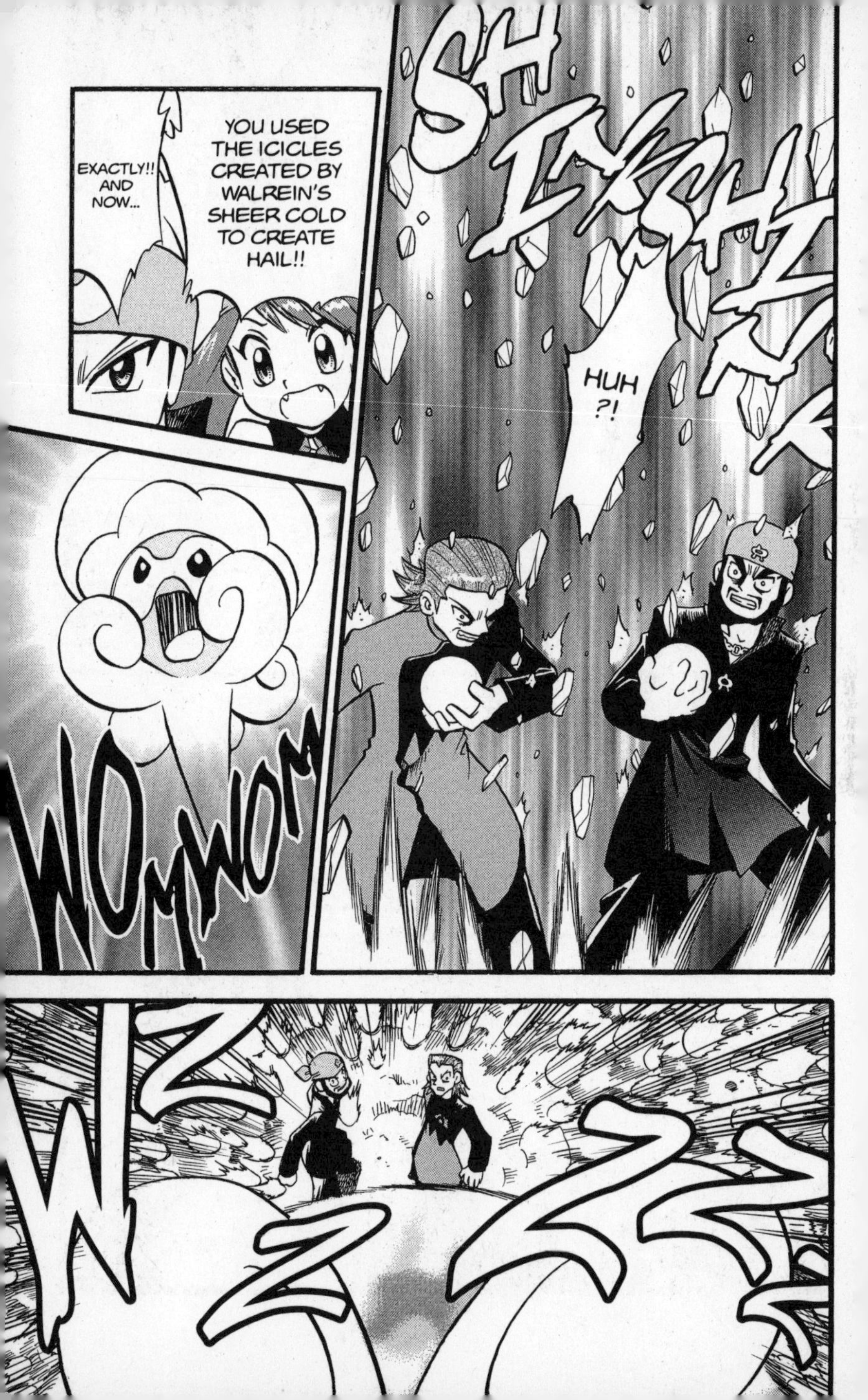
HUH ?!
YOU USED THE ICICLES CREATED BY WALREIN'S SHEER COLD TO CREATE HAIL!!
EXACTLY!! AND NOW...
WOMWOM

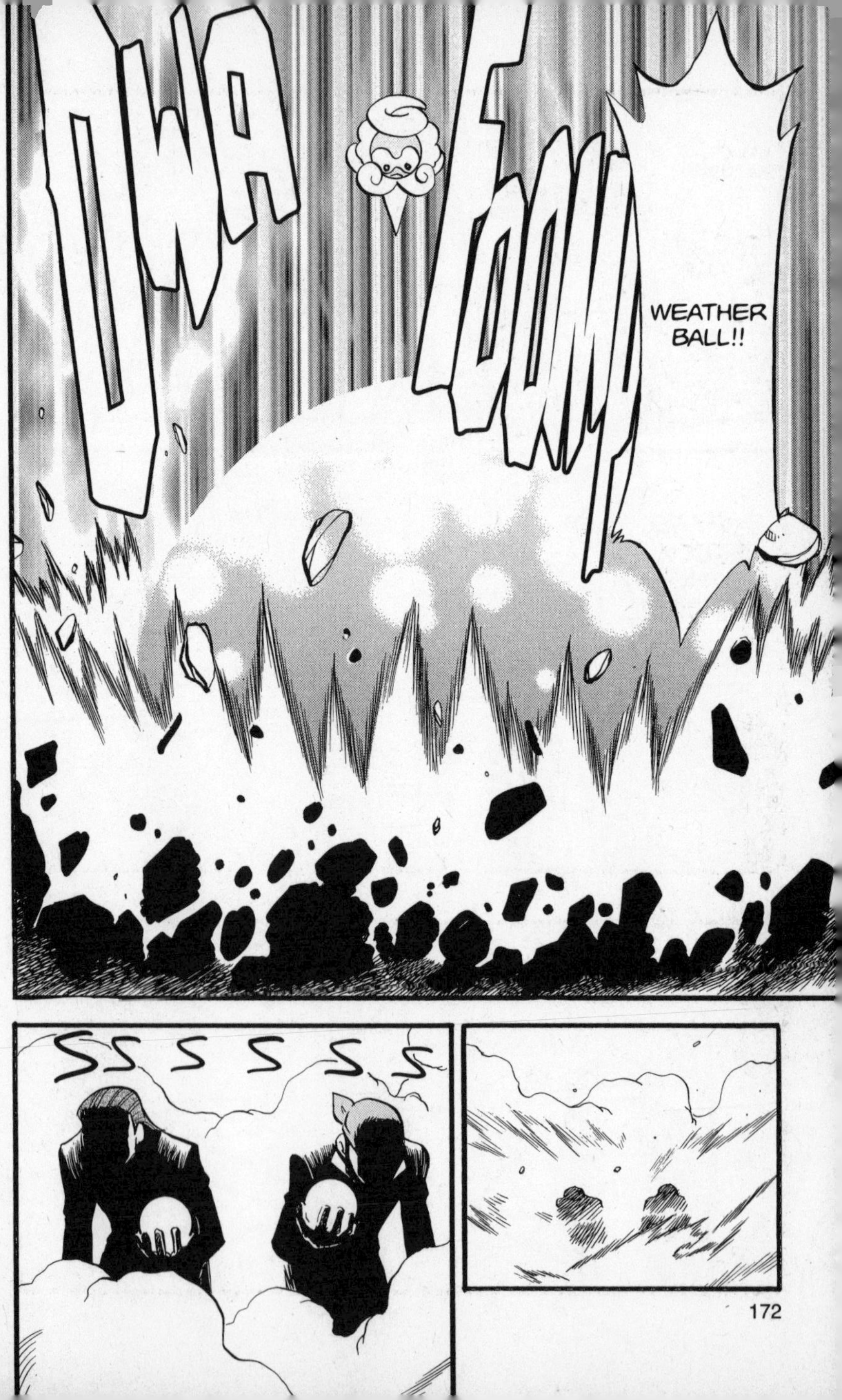
WEATHER BALL!!
SSSSSS

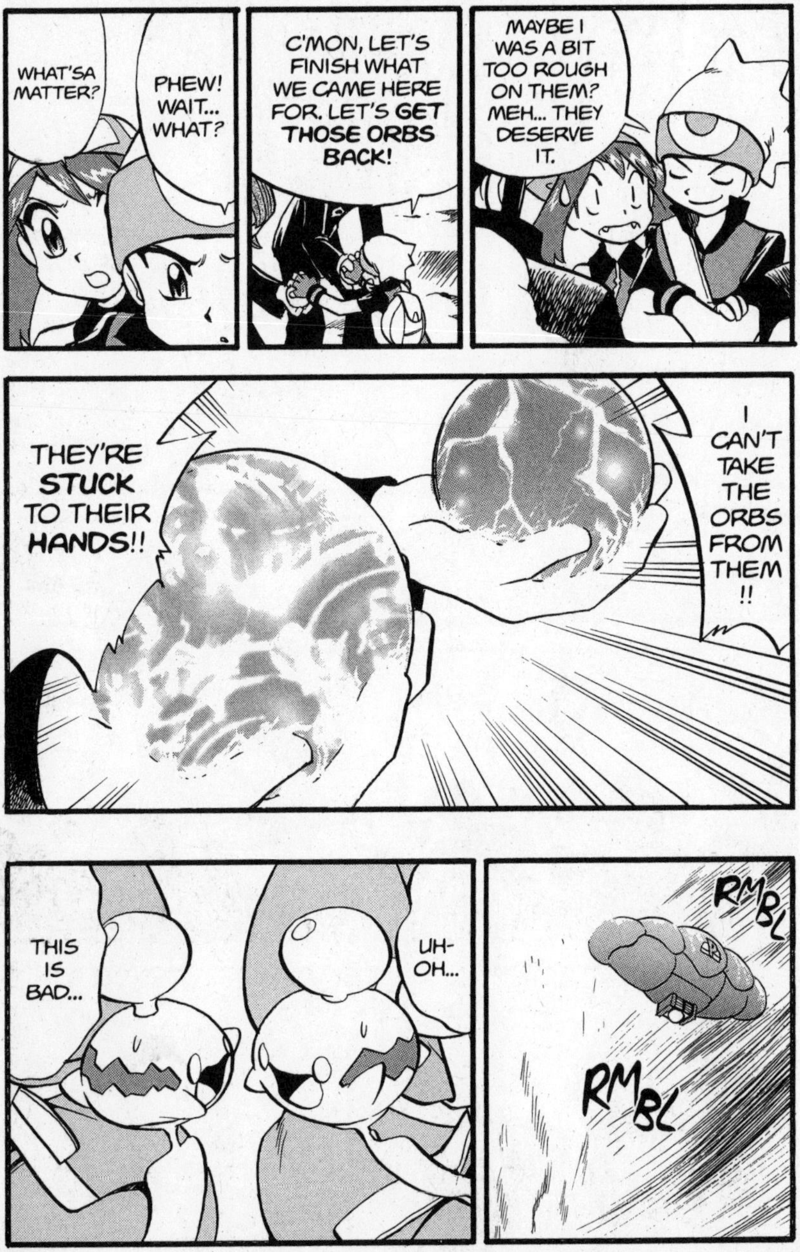
MAYBE I WAS A BIT TOO ROUGH ON THEM? MEH... THEY DESERVE IT.
C'MON, LET'S FINISH WHAT WE CAME HERE FOR. LET'S GET THOSE ORBS BACK!
PHEW! WAIT... WHAT?
WHAT'SA MATTER?
I CAN'T TAKE THE ORBS FROM THEM!!
THEY'RE STUCK TO THEIR HANDS!!
RMBL
RMBL
UH-OH...
THIS IS BAD...

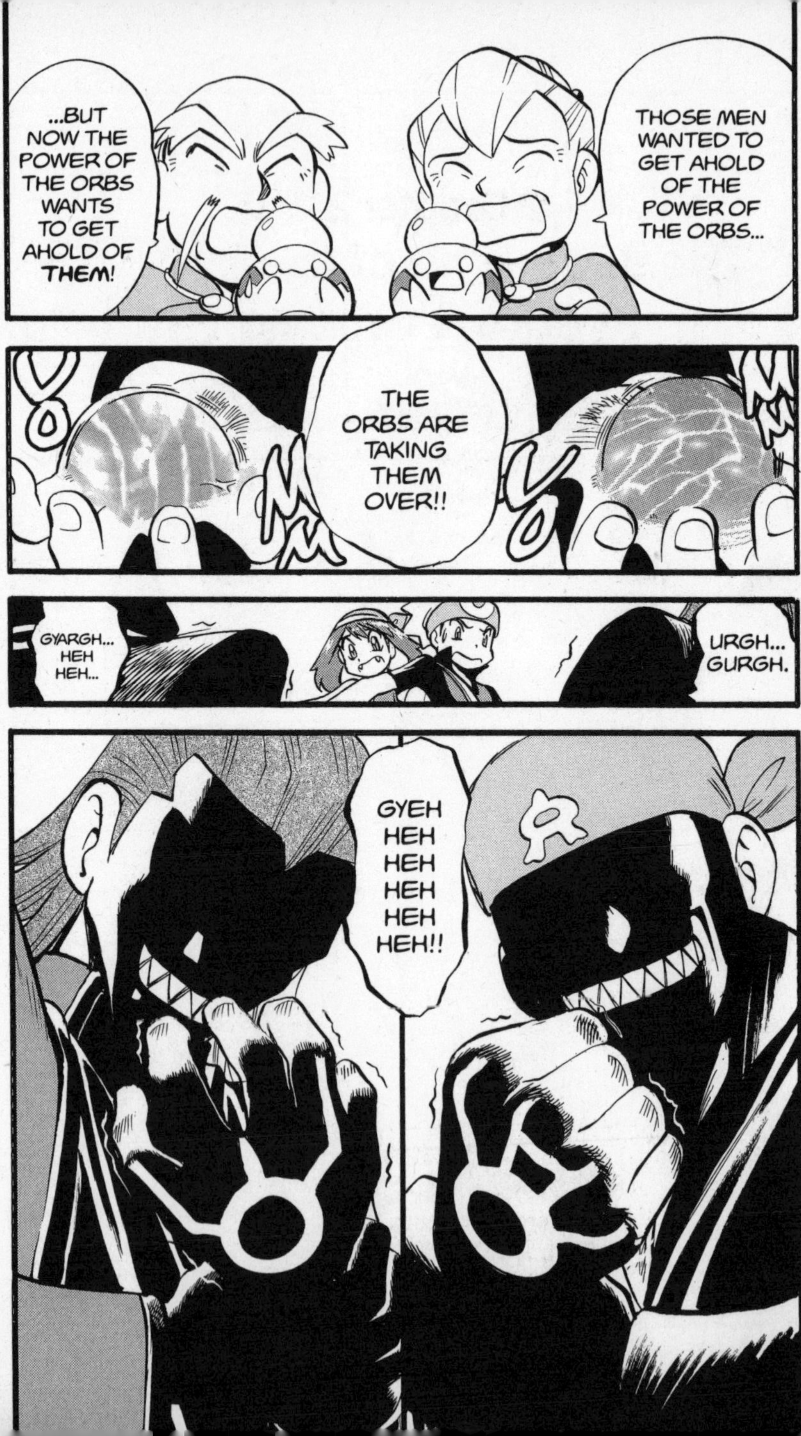
THOSE MEN WANTED TO GET AHOLD OF THE POWER OF THE ORBS...
...BUT NOW THE POWER OF THE ORBS WANTS TO GET AHOLD OF THEM!
THE ORBS ARE TAKING THEM OVER!!
URGH... GURGH.
GYARGH... HEH HEH...
GYEH HEH HEH HEH HEH HEH!!

● Chapter 249 ●
The Beginning of the End with Kyogre & Groudon XI

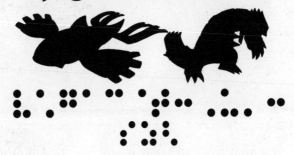

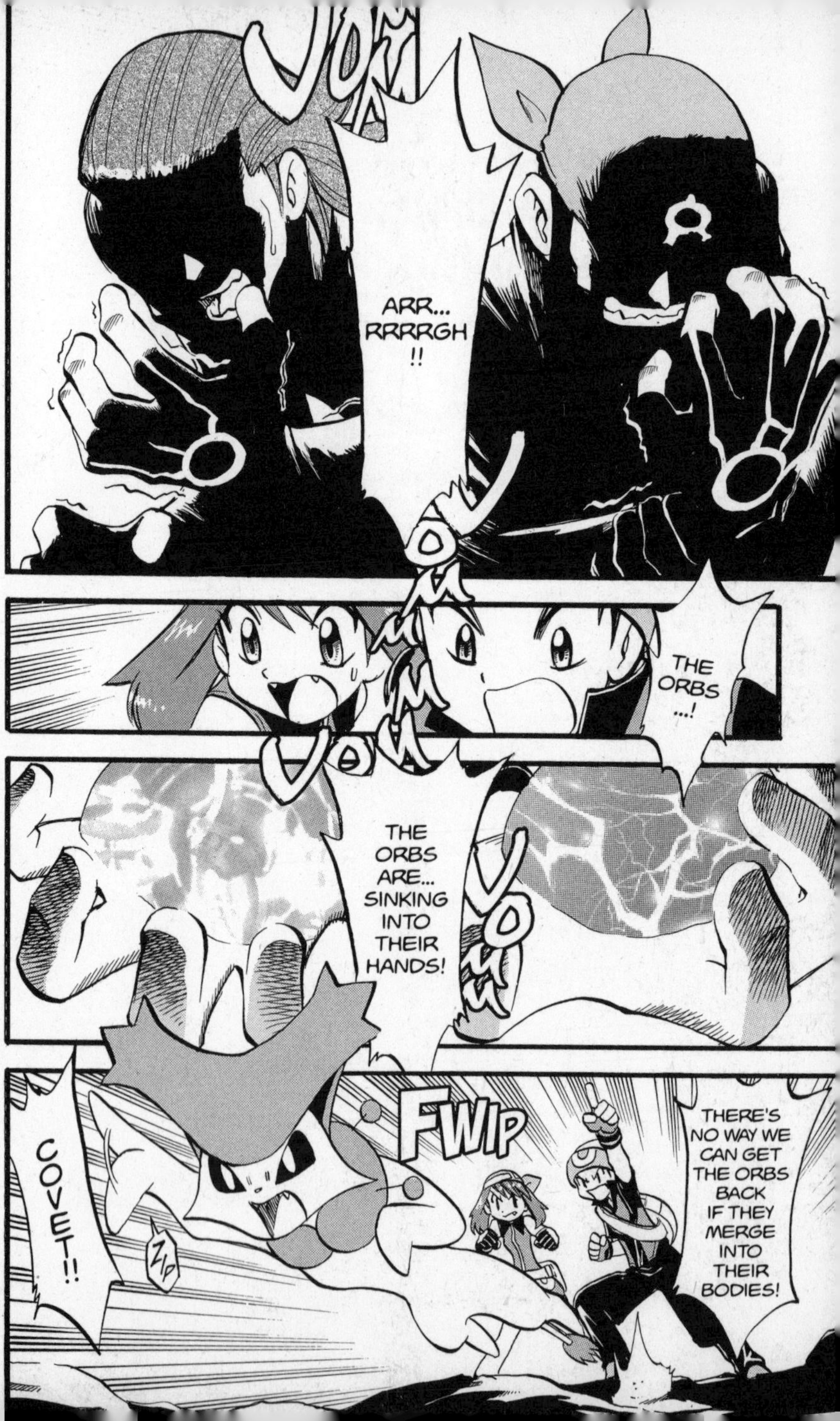
ARR... RRRRGH !!
THE ORBS ...!
THE ORBS ARE... SINKING INTO THEIR HANDS!
THERE'S NO WAY WE CAN GET THE ORBS BACK IF THEY MERGE INTO THEIR BODIES!
FWIP
COVET!!
ZIP

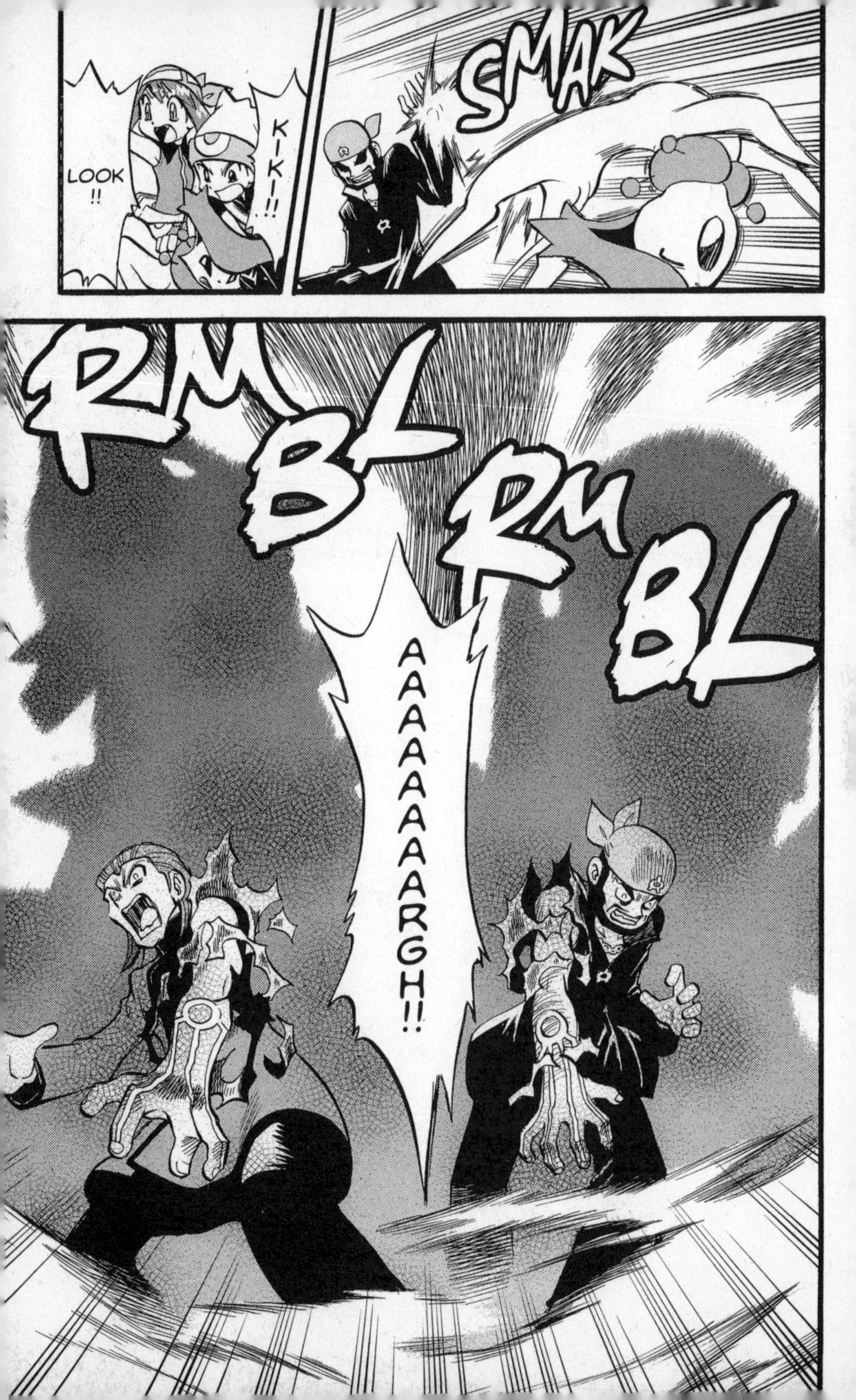
SMAK
KIKI!!
LOOK!!
RMBL RMBL
AAAAAAAAARGH!!

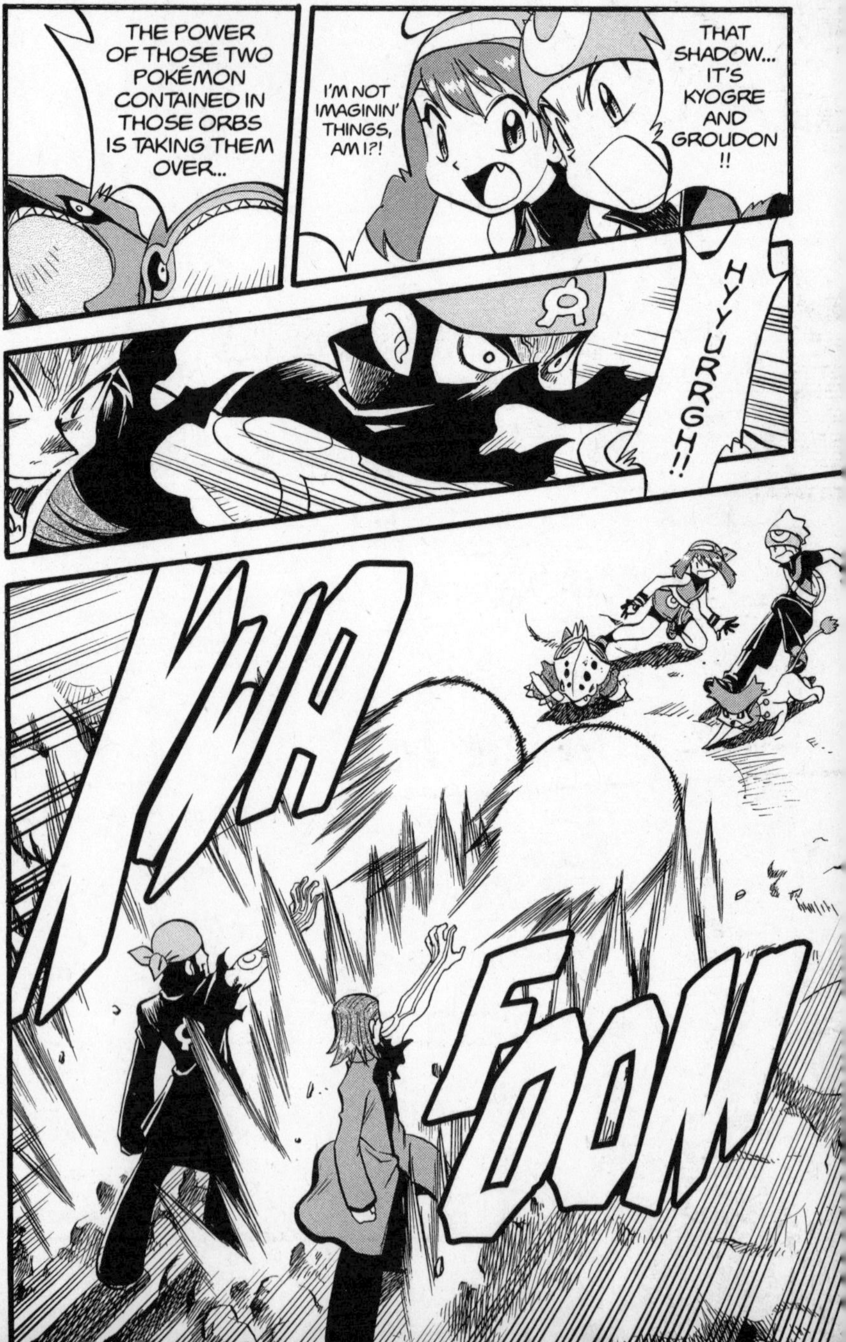
THAT SHADOW... IT'S KYOGRE AND GROUDON !!
I'M NOT IMAGININ' THINGS, AM I?!
THE POWER OF THOSE TWO POKÉMON CONTAINED IN THOSE ORBS IS TAKING THEM OVER...
HYYURRGH!!
VWA
FOOM

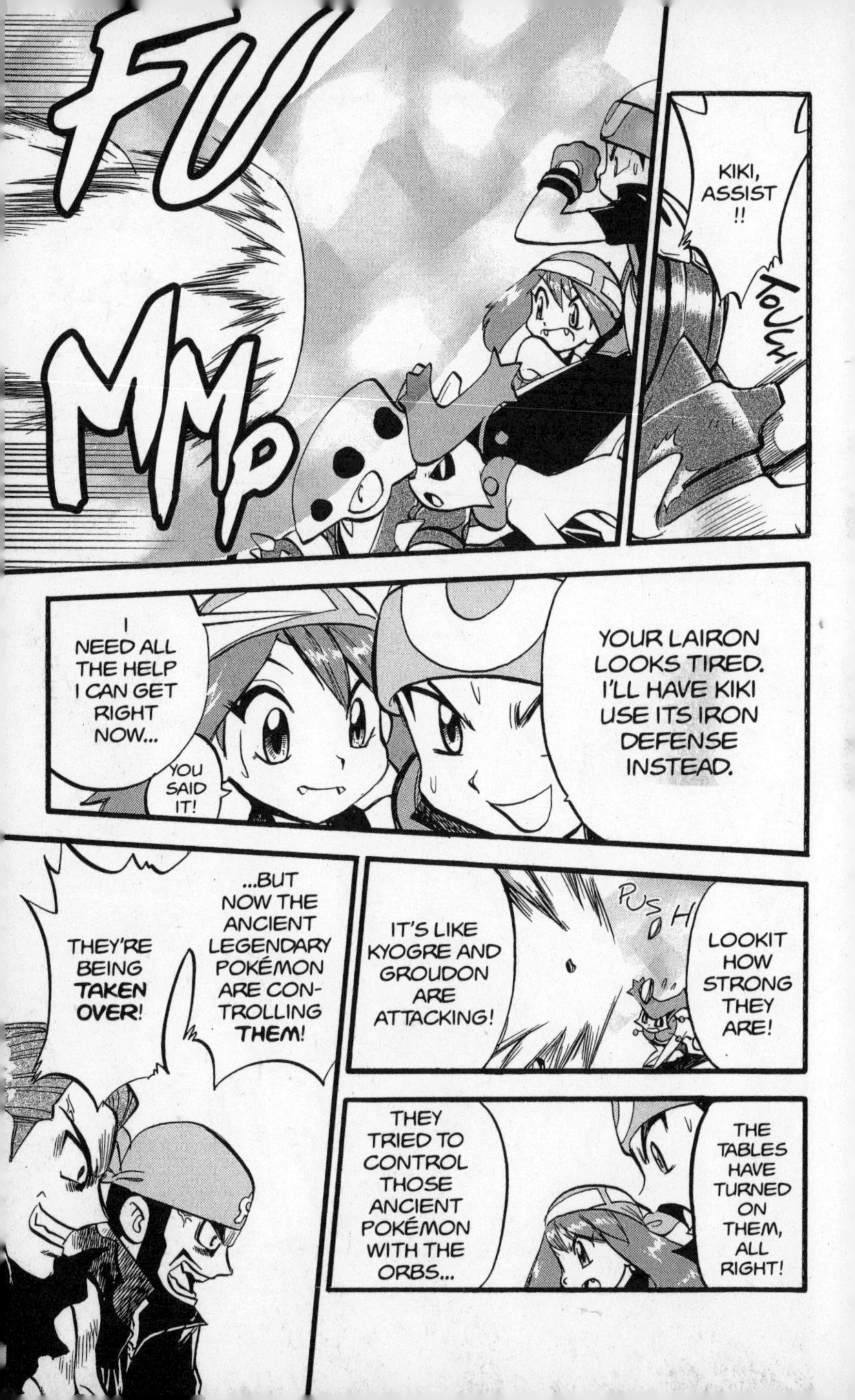
KIKI, ASSIST !!
TOUCH
FUMMP
YOUR LAIRON LOOKS TIRED. I'LL HAVE KIKI USE ITS IRON DEFENSE INSTEAD.
I NEED ALL THE HELP I CAN GET RIGHT NOW...
YOU SAID IT!
LOOKIT HOW STRONG THEY ARE!
PUSH
IT'S LIKE KYOGRE AND GROUDON ARE ATTACKING!
THE TABLES HAVE TURNED ON THEM, ALL RIGHT!
THEY TRIED TO CONTROL THOSE ANCIENT POKÉMON WITH THE ORBS...
...BUT NOW THE ANCIENT LEGENDARY POKÉMON ARE CON-TROLLING **THEM**!
THEY'RE BEING **TAKEN OVER**!

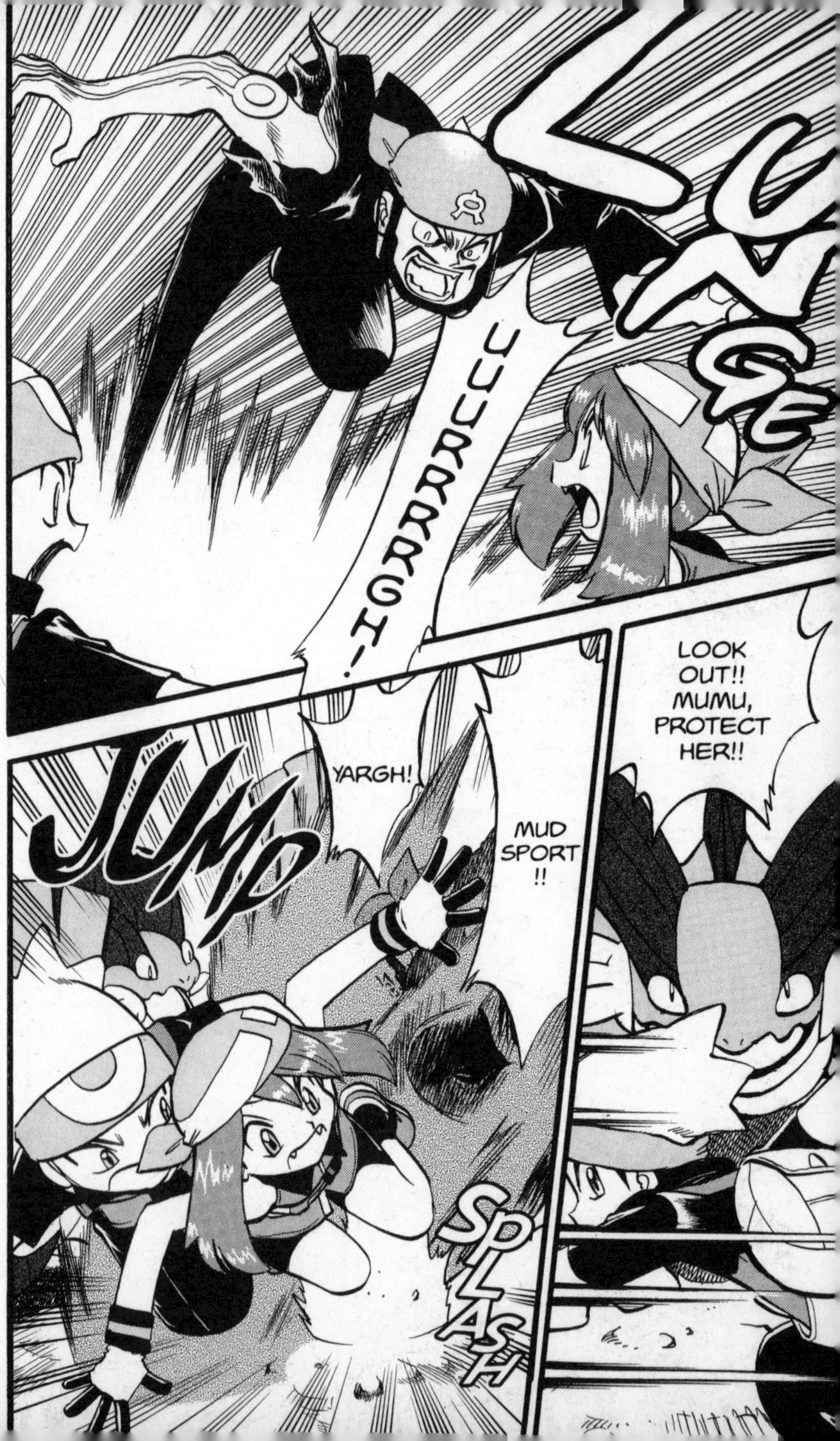
UUURRRRGH!
LOOK OUT!! MUMU, PROTECT HER!!
MUD SPORT !!
YARGH!
JUMP
SPLASH

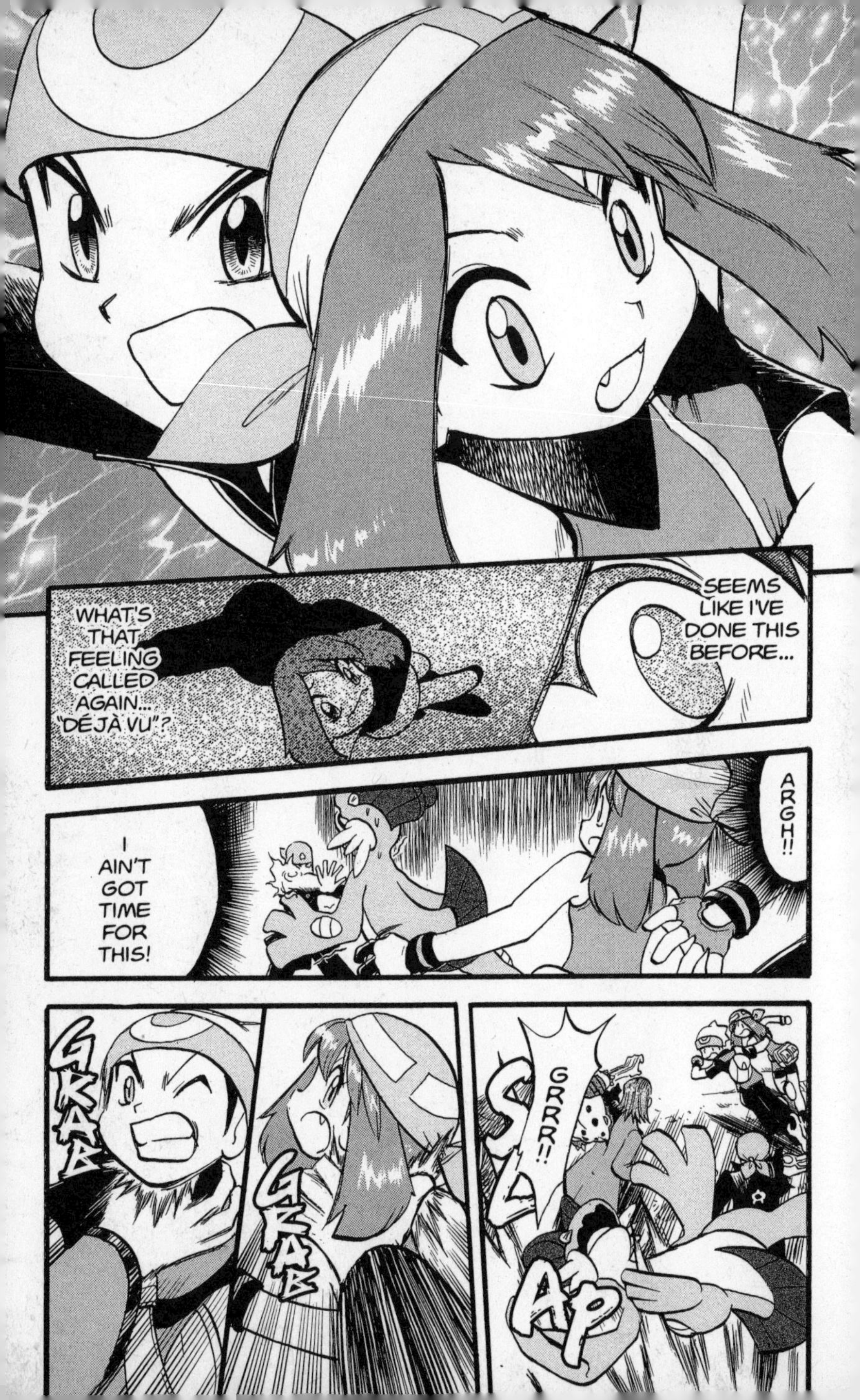
SEEMS LIKE I'VE DONE THIS BEFORE...
WHAT'S THAT FEELING CALLED AGAIN... "DÉJÀ VU"?
ARGH!!
I AIN'T GOT TIME FOR THIS!
GRRR!!
SLAP
GRAB
GRAB

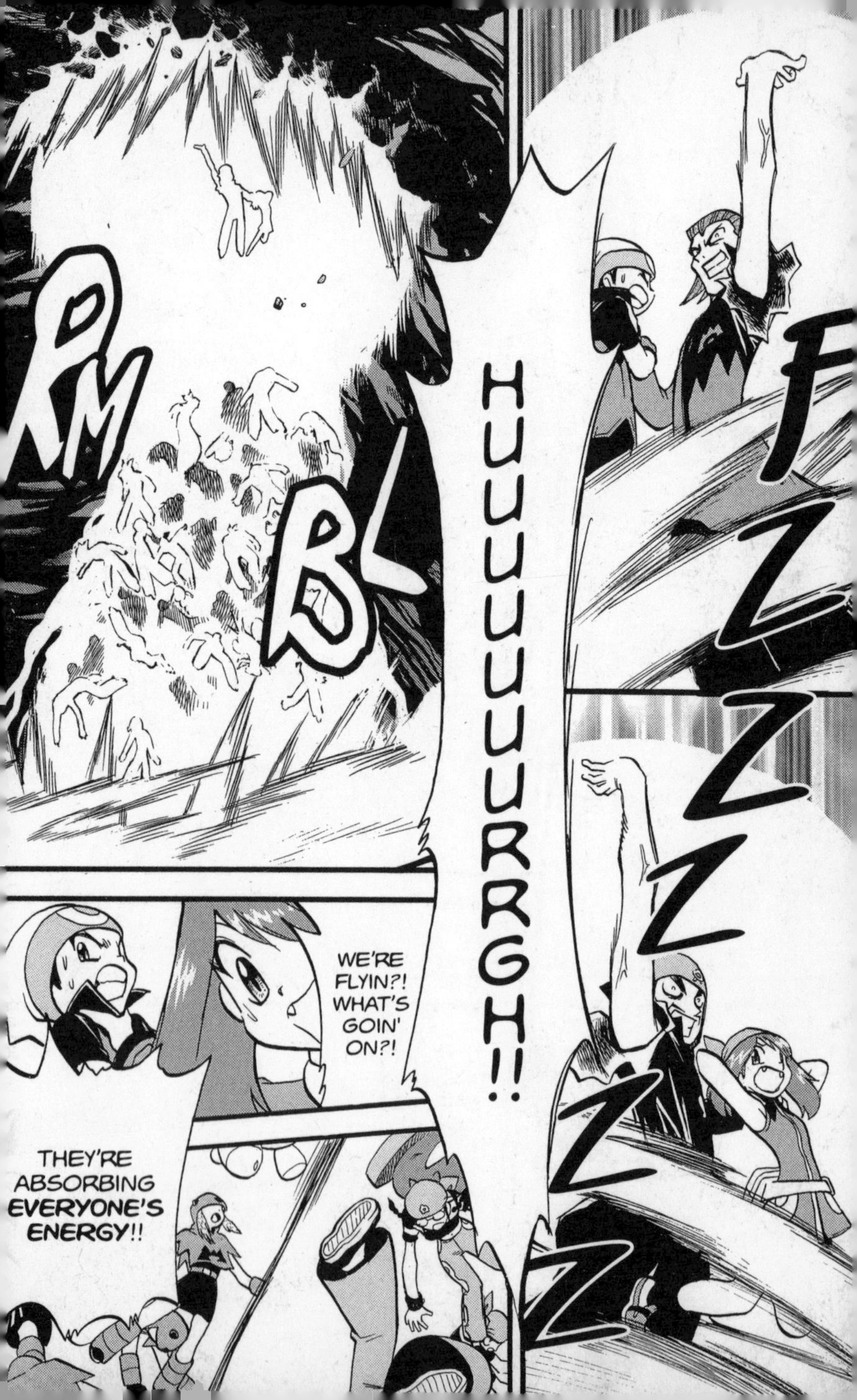
FIZZZZZ
HUUUUUURRGH!!
WE'RE FLYIN?! WHAT'S GOIN' ON?!
THEY'RE ABSORBING EVERYONE'S ENERGY!!

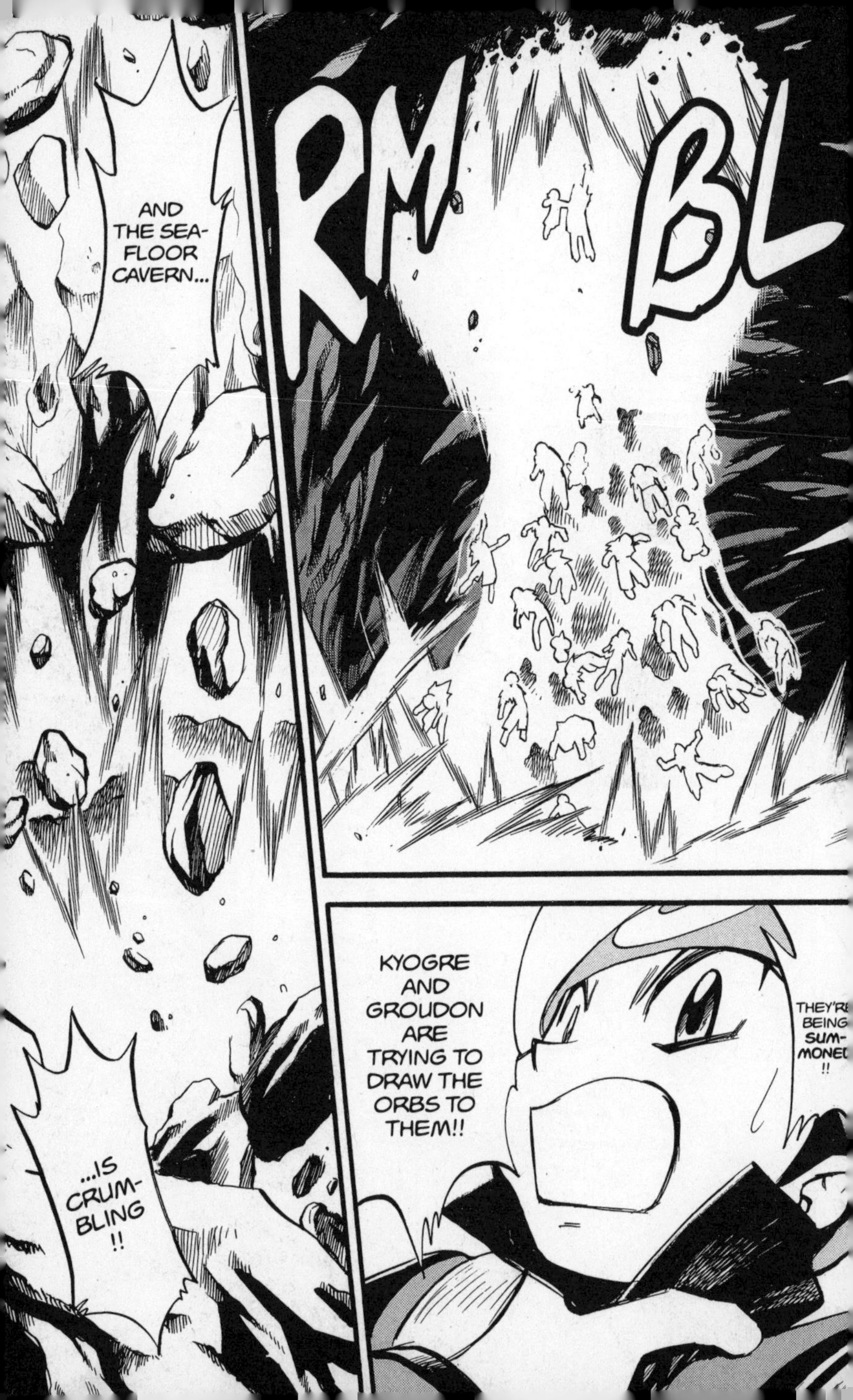
RM BL
THEY'RE BEING SUM-MONED !!
KYOGRE AND GROUDON ARE TRYING TO DRAW THE ORBS TO THEM!!
AND THE SEA-FLOOR CAVERN...
...IS CRUM-BLING !!

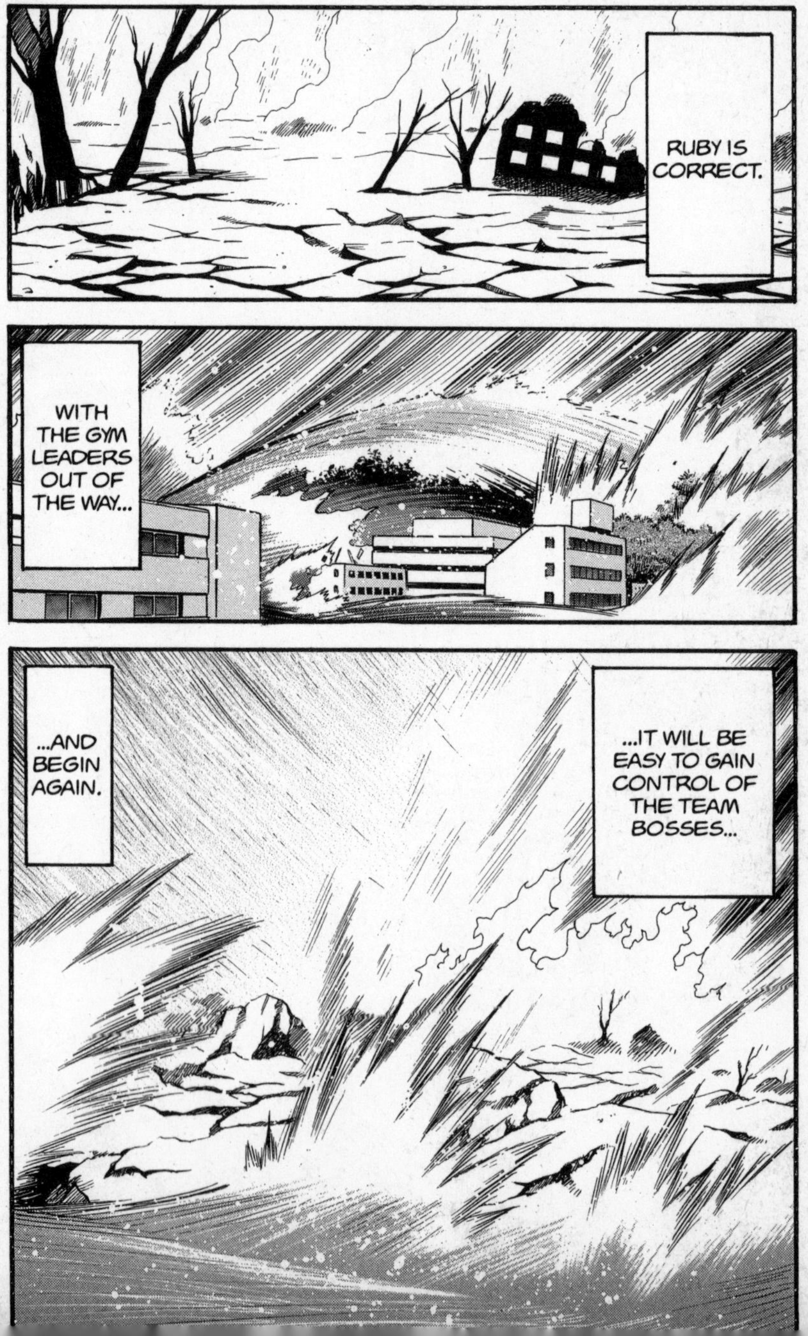
RUBY IS CORRECT.
WITH THE GYM LEADERS OUT OF THE WAY...
...IT WILL BE EASY TO GAIN CONTROL OF THE TEAM BOSSES...
...AND BEGIN AGAIN.

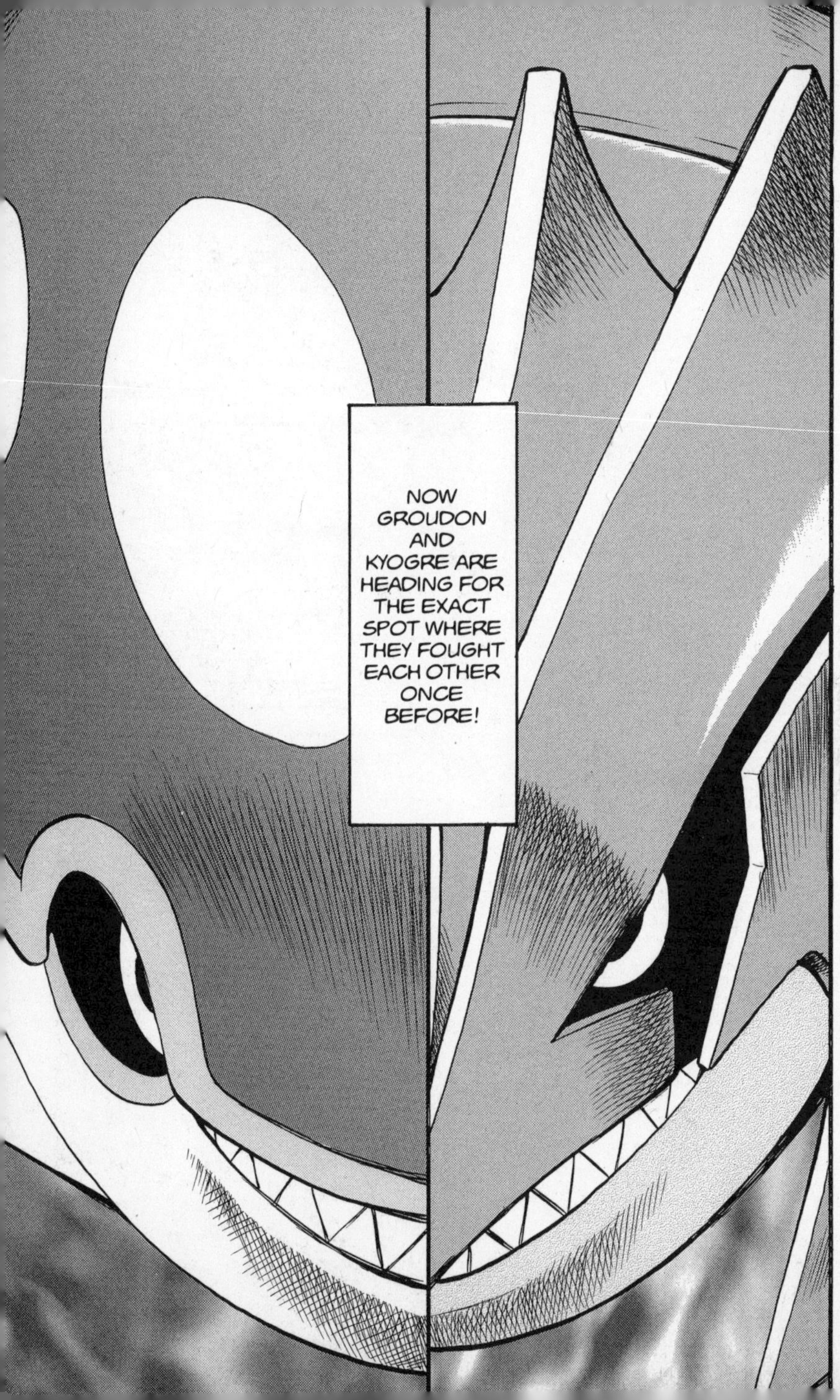
NOW GROUDON AND KYOGRE ARE HEADING FOR THE EXACT SPOT WHERE THEY FOUGHT EACH OTHER ONCE BEFORE!

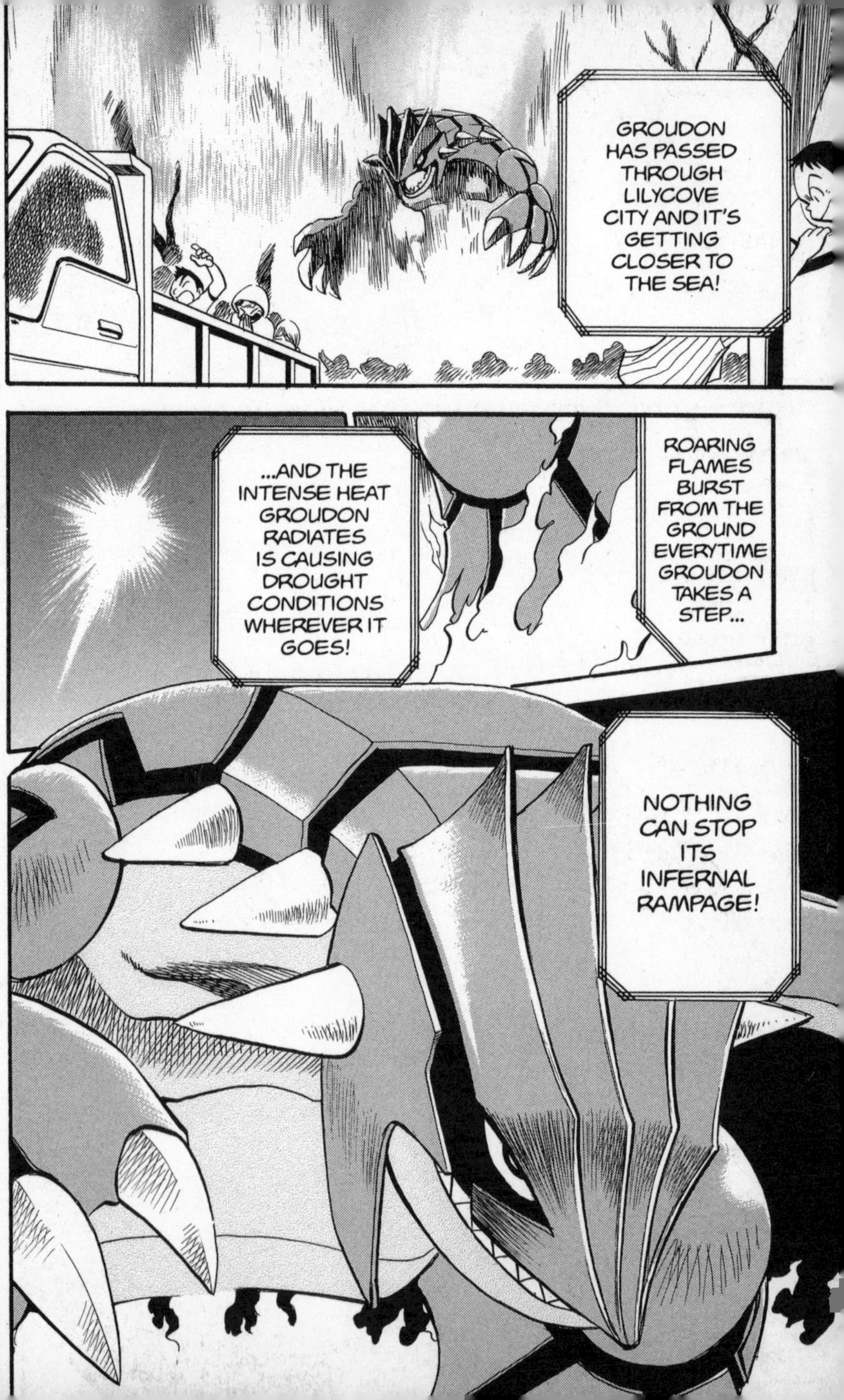
GROUDON HAS PASSED THROUGH LILYCOVE CITY AND IT'S GETTING CLOSER TO THE SEA!
ROARING FLAMES BURST FROM THE GROUND EVERYTIME GROUDON TAKES A STEP...
...AND THE INTENSE HEAT GROUDON RADIATES IS CAUSING DROUGHT CONDITIONS WHEREVER IT GOES!
NOTHING CAN STOP ITS INFERNAL RAMPAGE!

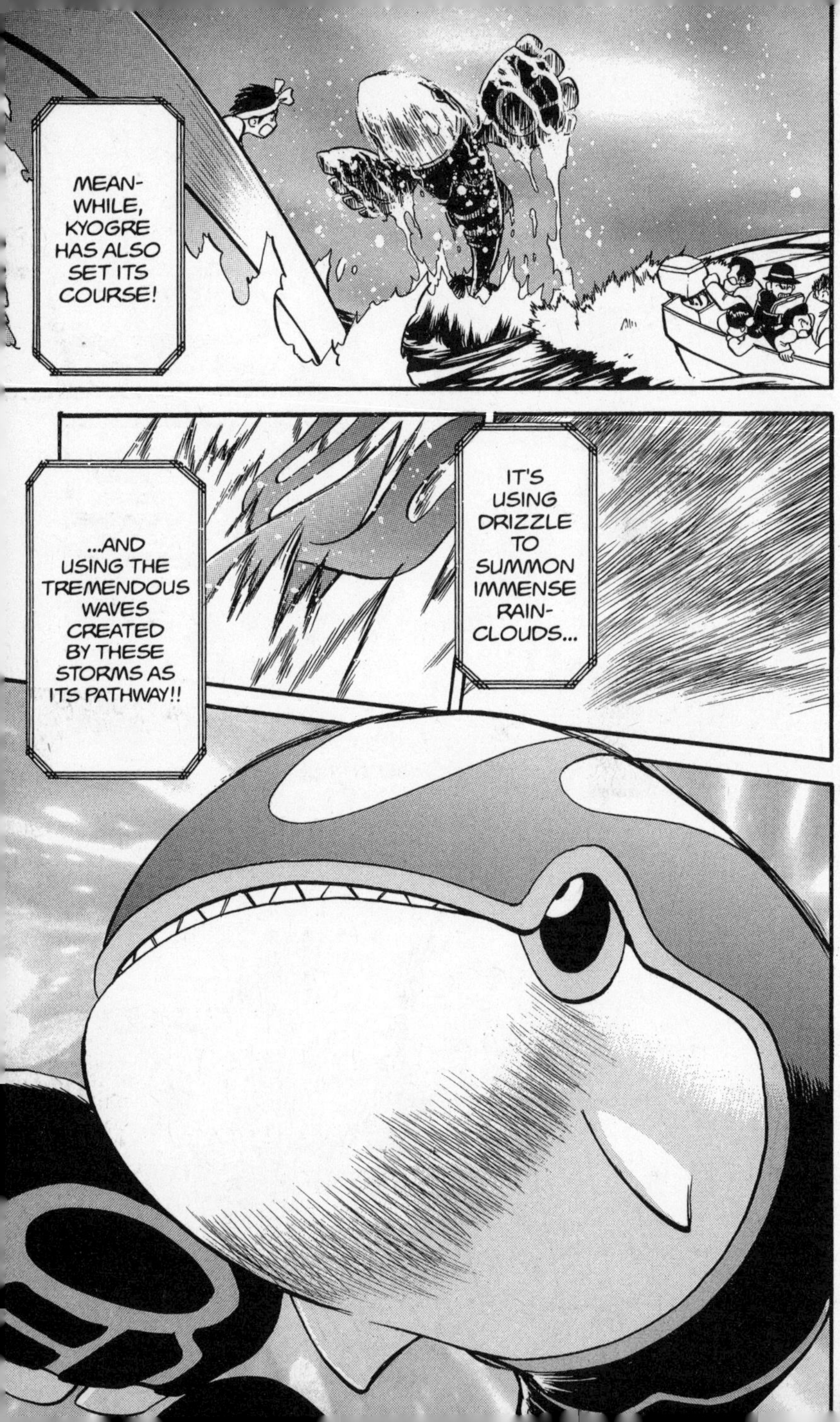
MEANWHILE, KYOGRE HAS ALSO SET ITS COURSE!
IT'S USING DRIZZLE TO SUMMON IMMENSE RAINCLOUDS...
...AND USING THE TREMENDOUS WAVES CREATED BY THESE STORMS AS ITS PATHWAY!!

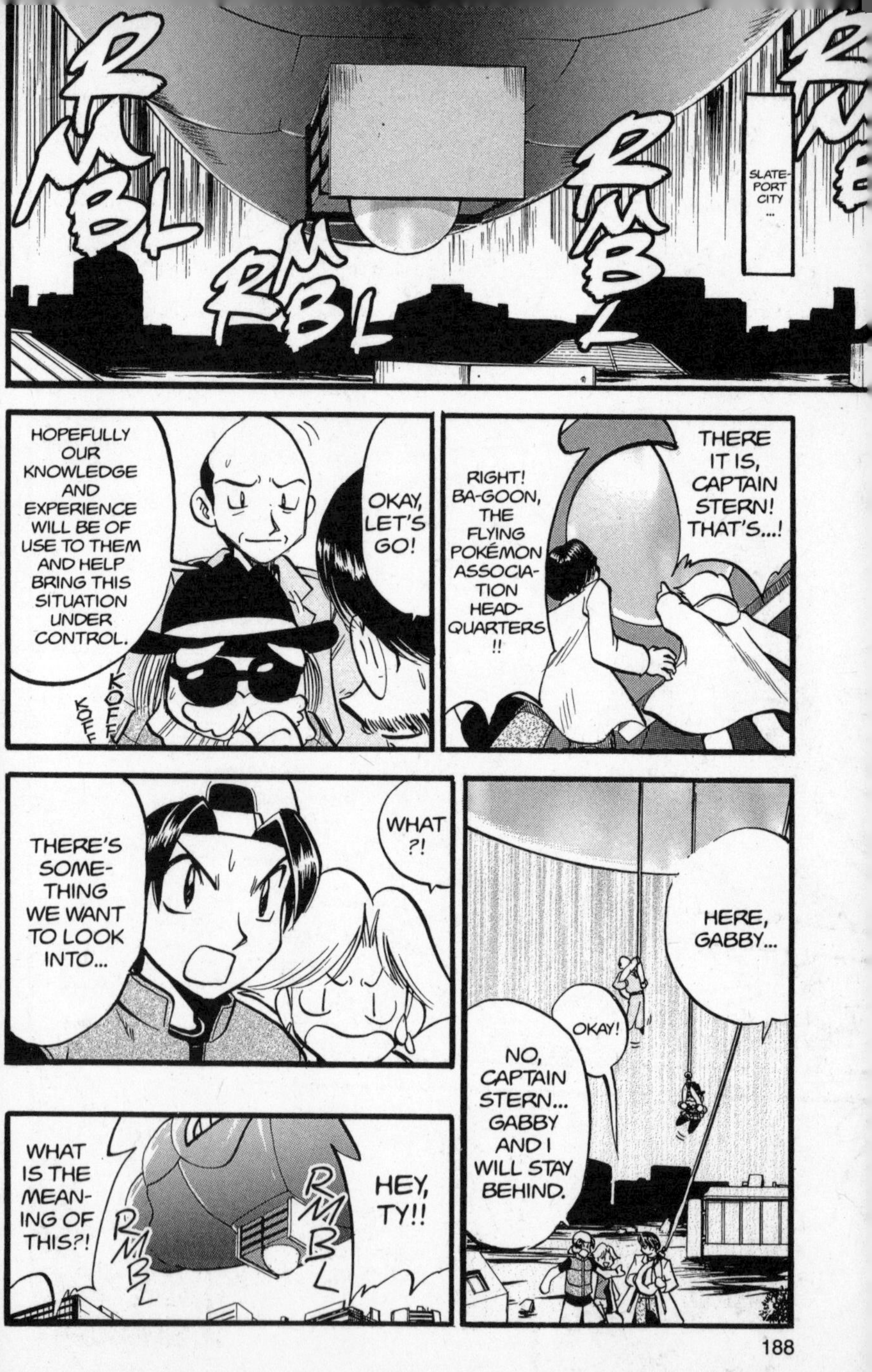
RMBL
RMBL
SLATEPORT CITY...
RMBL
RMBL
THERE IT IS, CAPTAIN STERN! THAT'S...!
RIGHT! BA-GOON, THE FLYING POKÉMON ASSOCIATION HEADQUARTERS!!
OKAY, LET'S GO!
HOPEFULLY OUR KNOWLEDGE AND EXPERIENCE WILL BE OF USE TO THEM AND HELP BRING THIS SITUATION UNDER CONTROL.
KOFF KOFF
HERE, GABBY...
OKAY!
NO, CAPTAIN STERN... GABBY AND I WILL STAY BEHIND.
WHAT?!
THERE'S SOMETHING WE WANT TO LOOK INTO...
HEY, TY!!
RMBL
WHAT IS THE MEANING OF THIS?!
RMBL

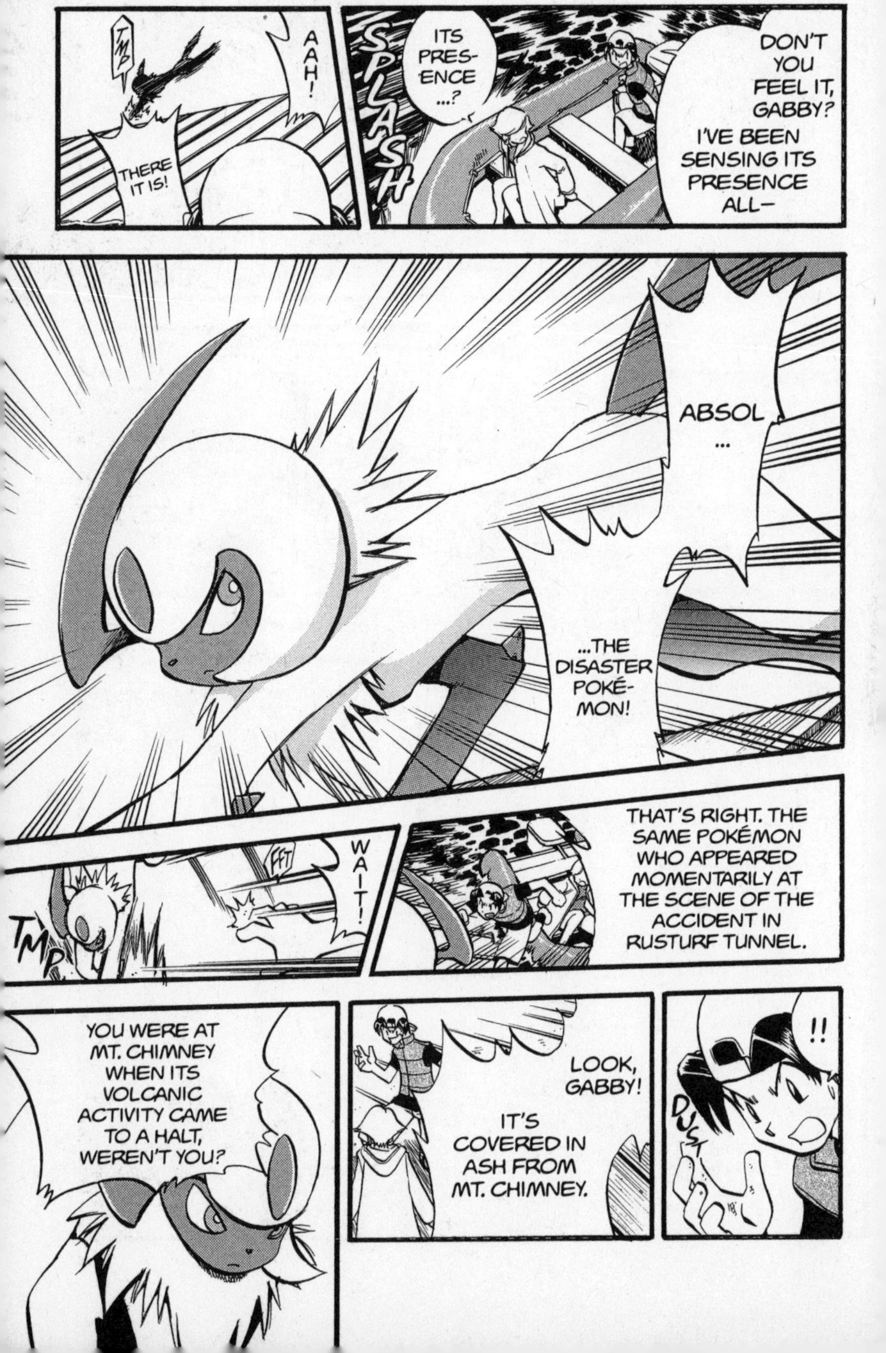
DON'T YOU FEEL IT, GABBY?
I'VE BEEN SENSING ITS PRESENCE ALL—
ITS PRESENCE...?
SPLASH
AAH!
TMP
THERE IT IS!
ABSOL...
...THE DISASTER POKÉMON!
THAT'S RIGHT. THE SAME POKÉMON WHO APPEARED MOMENTARILY AT THE SCENE OF THE ACCIDENT IN RUSTURF TUNNEL.
WAIT!
FFT
TMP
!!
DUST
LOOK, GABBY!
IT'S COVERED IN ASH FROM MT. CHIMNEY.
YOU WERE AT MT. CHIMNEY WHEN ITS VOLCANIC ACTIVITY CAME TO A HALT, WEREN'T YOU?

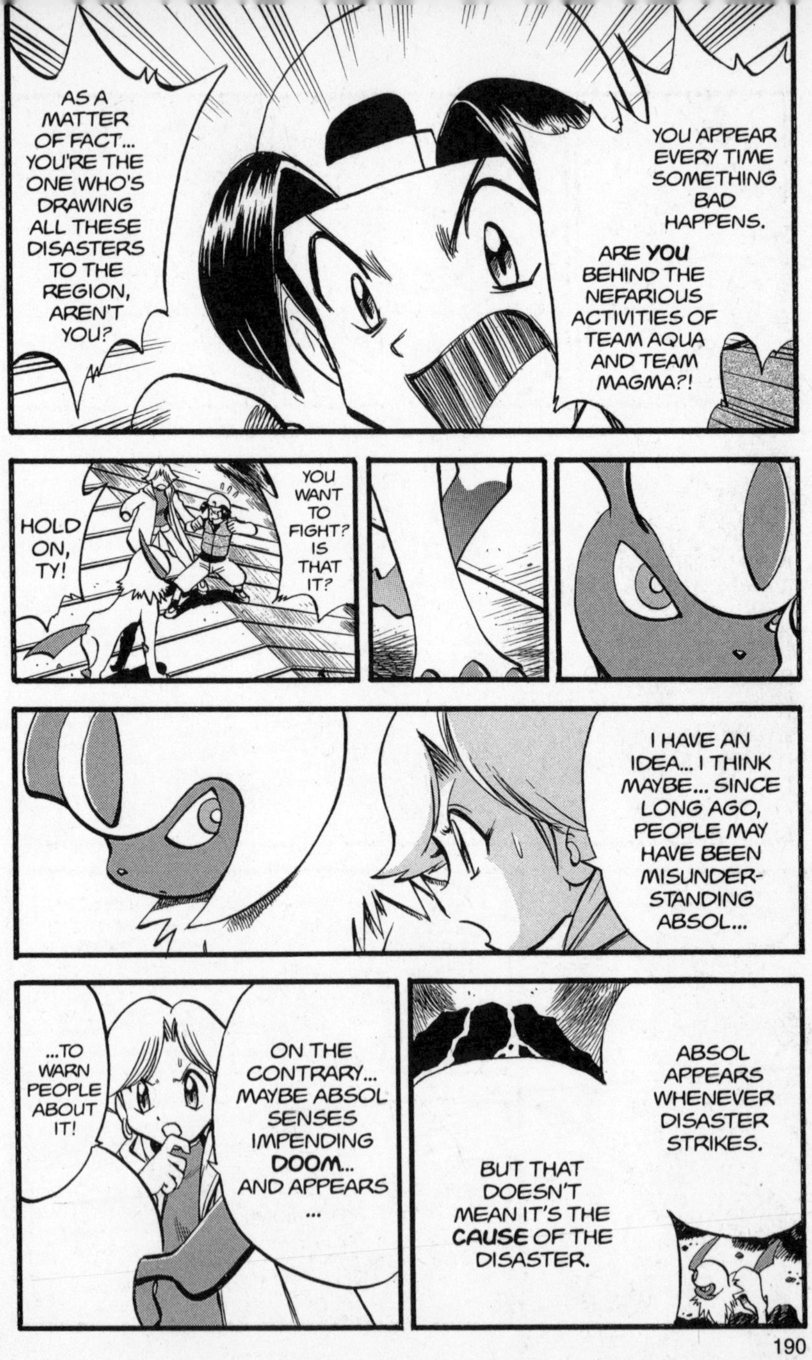
YOU APPEAR EVERY TIME SOMETHING BAD HAPPENS.
ARE **YOU** BEHIND THE NEFARIOUS ACTIVITIES OF TEAM AQUA AND TEAM MAGMA?!
AS A MATTER OF FACT... YOU'RE THE ONE WHO'S DRAWING ALL THESE DISASTERS TO THE REGION, AREN'T YOU?
YOU WANT TO FIGHT? IS THAT IT?
HOLD ON, TY!
I HAVE AN IDEA... I THINK MAYBE... SINCE LONG AGO, PEOPLE MAY HAVE BEEN MISUNDER-STANDING ABSOL...
ABSOL APPEARS WHENEVER DISASTER STRIKES.
BUT THAT DOESN'T MEAN IT'S THE **CAUSE** OF THE DISASTER.
ON THE CONTRARY... MAYBE ABSOL SENSES IMPENDING **DOOM**... AND APPEARS ...
...TO WARN PEOPLE ABOUT IT!

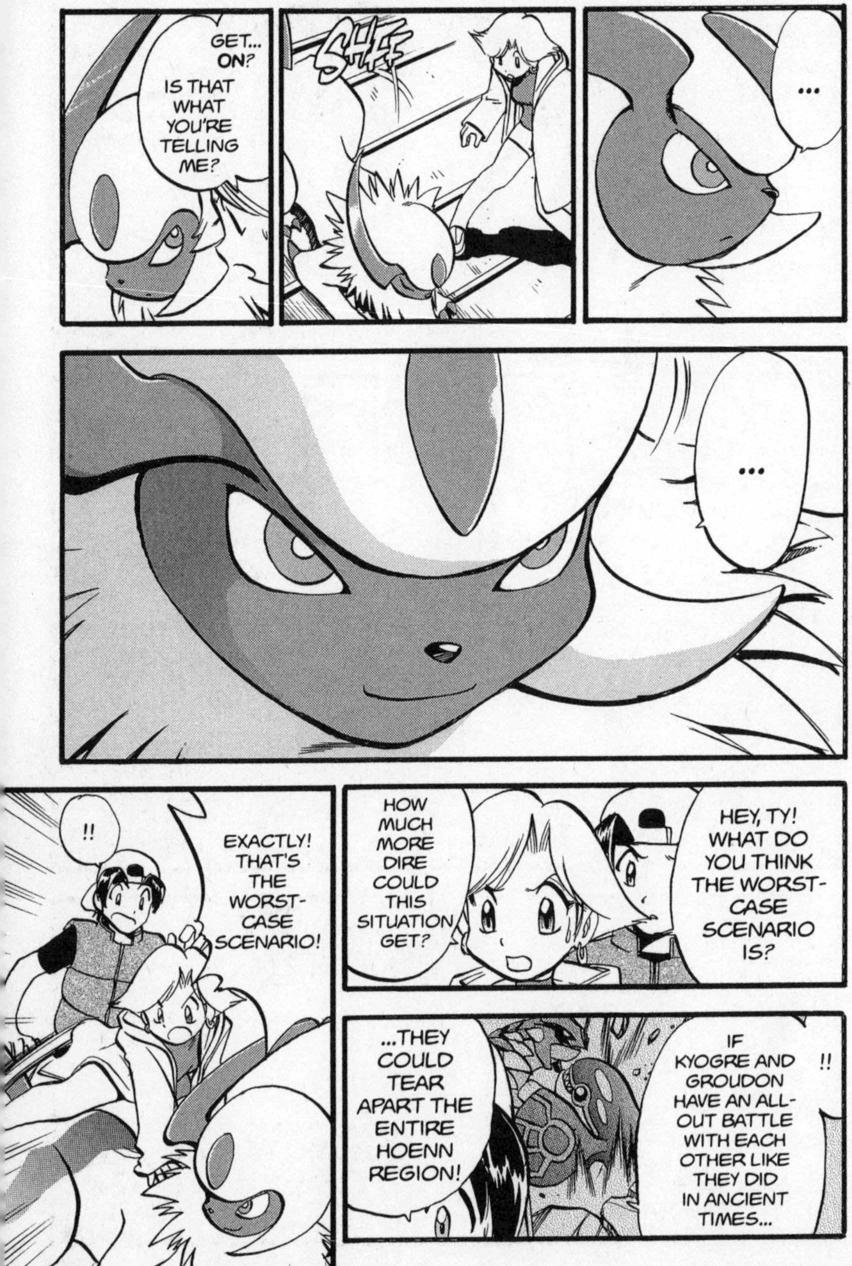
...
SHFF
GET... ON?
IS THAT WHAT YOU'RE TELLING ME?
...
HEY, TY! WHAT DO YOU THINK THE WORST-CASE SCENARIO IS?
HOW MUCH MORE DIRE COULD THIS SITUATION GET?
IF KYOGRE AND GROUDON HAVE AN ALL-OUT BATTLE WITH EACH OTHER LIKE THEY DID IN ANCIENT TIMES...
!!
...THEY COULD TEAR APART THE ENTIRE HOENN REGION!
EXACTLY! THAT'S THE WORST-CASE SCENARIO!
!!

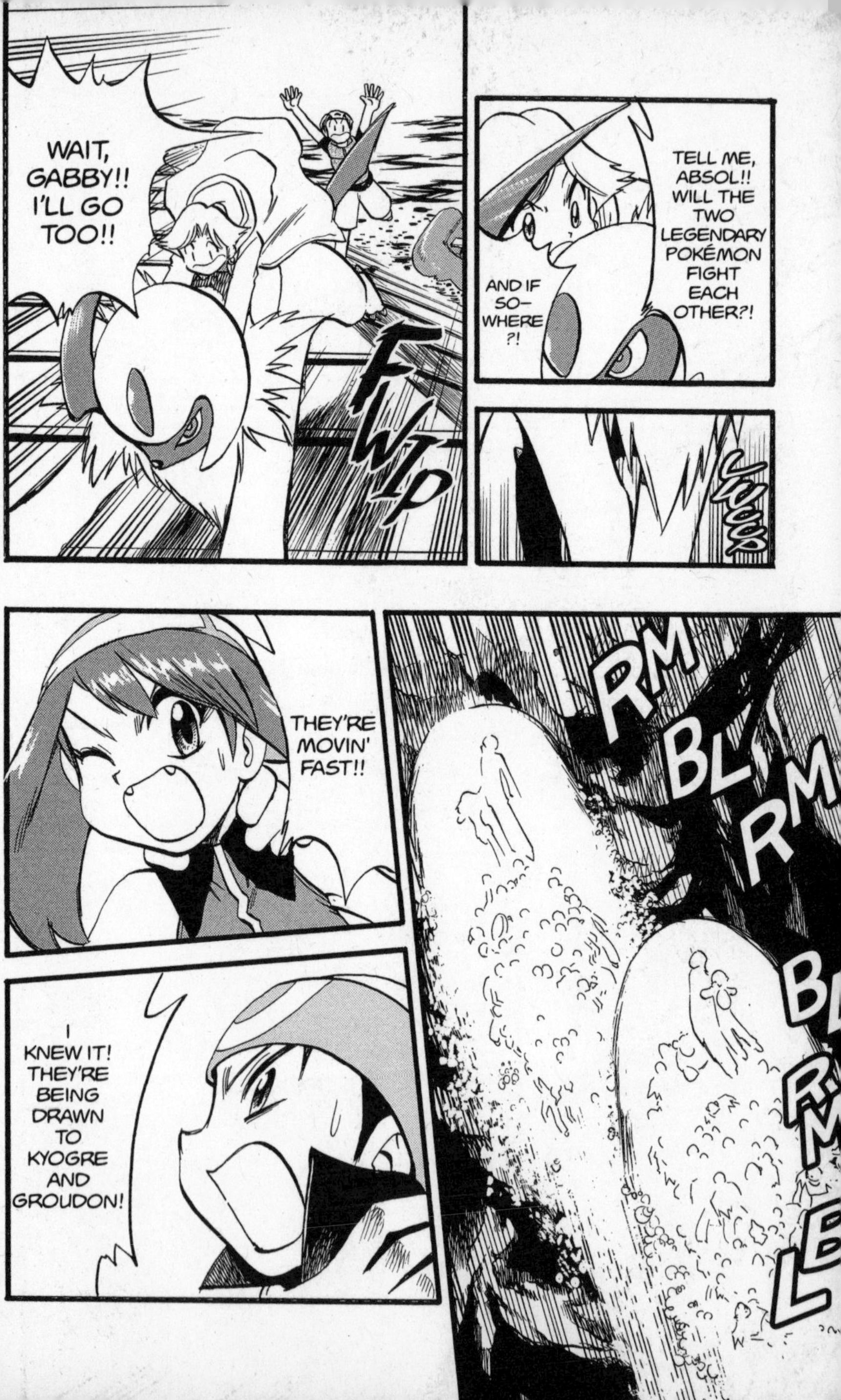
TELL ME, ABSOL!! WILL THE TWO LEGENDARY POKéMON FIGHT EACH OTHER?!
AND IF SO—WHERE?!
WAIT, GABBY!! I'LL GO TOO!!
FWIP
RMBL RMBL RMBL
THEY'RE MOVIN' FAST!!
I KNEW IT! THEY'RE BEING DRAWN TO KYOGRE AND GROUDON!

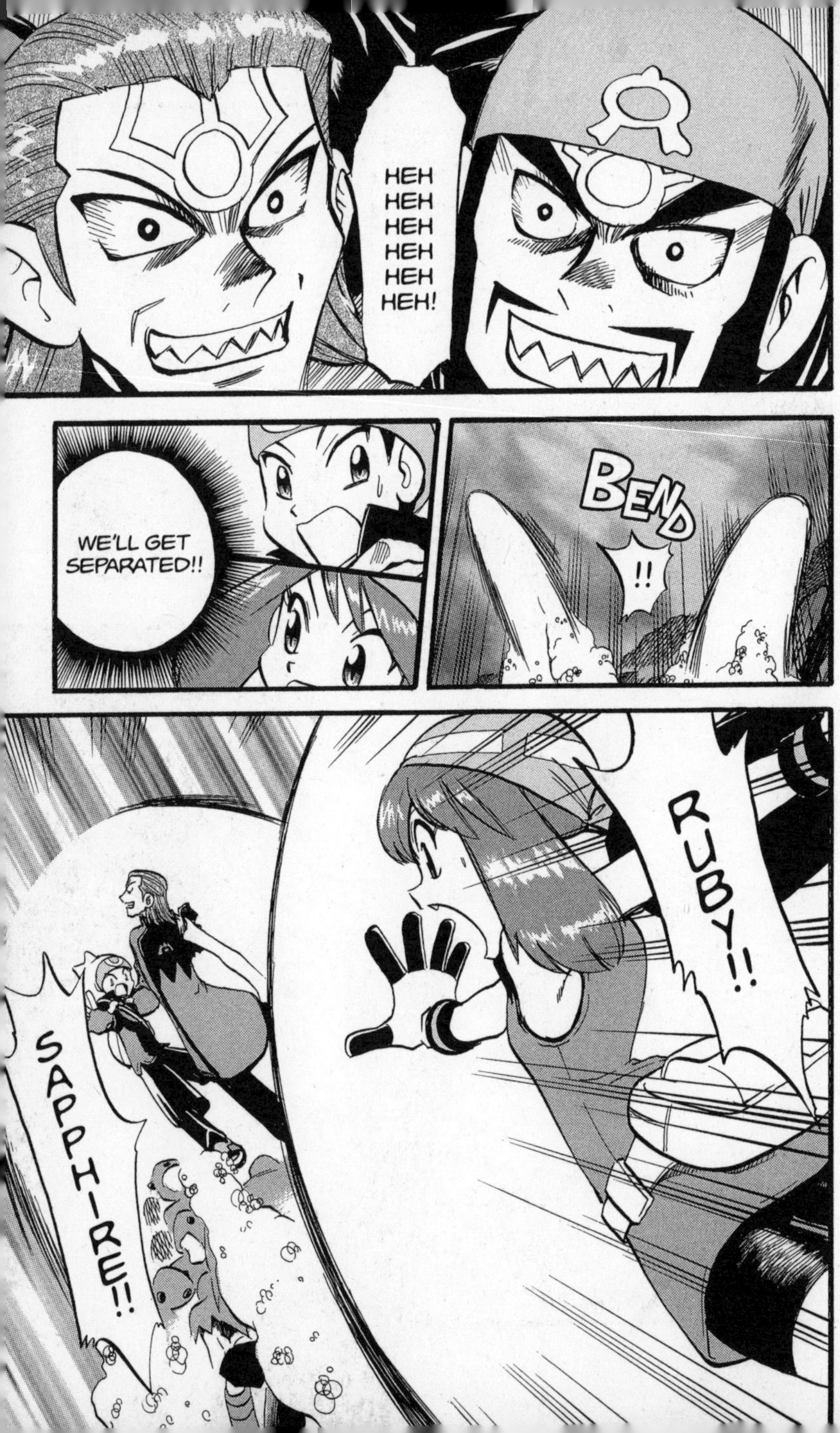
HEH HEH HEH HEH HEH HEH!
BEND
!!
WE'LL GET SEPARATED!!
RUBY!!
SAPPHIRE!!

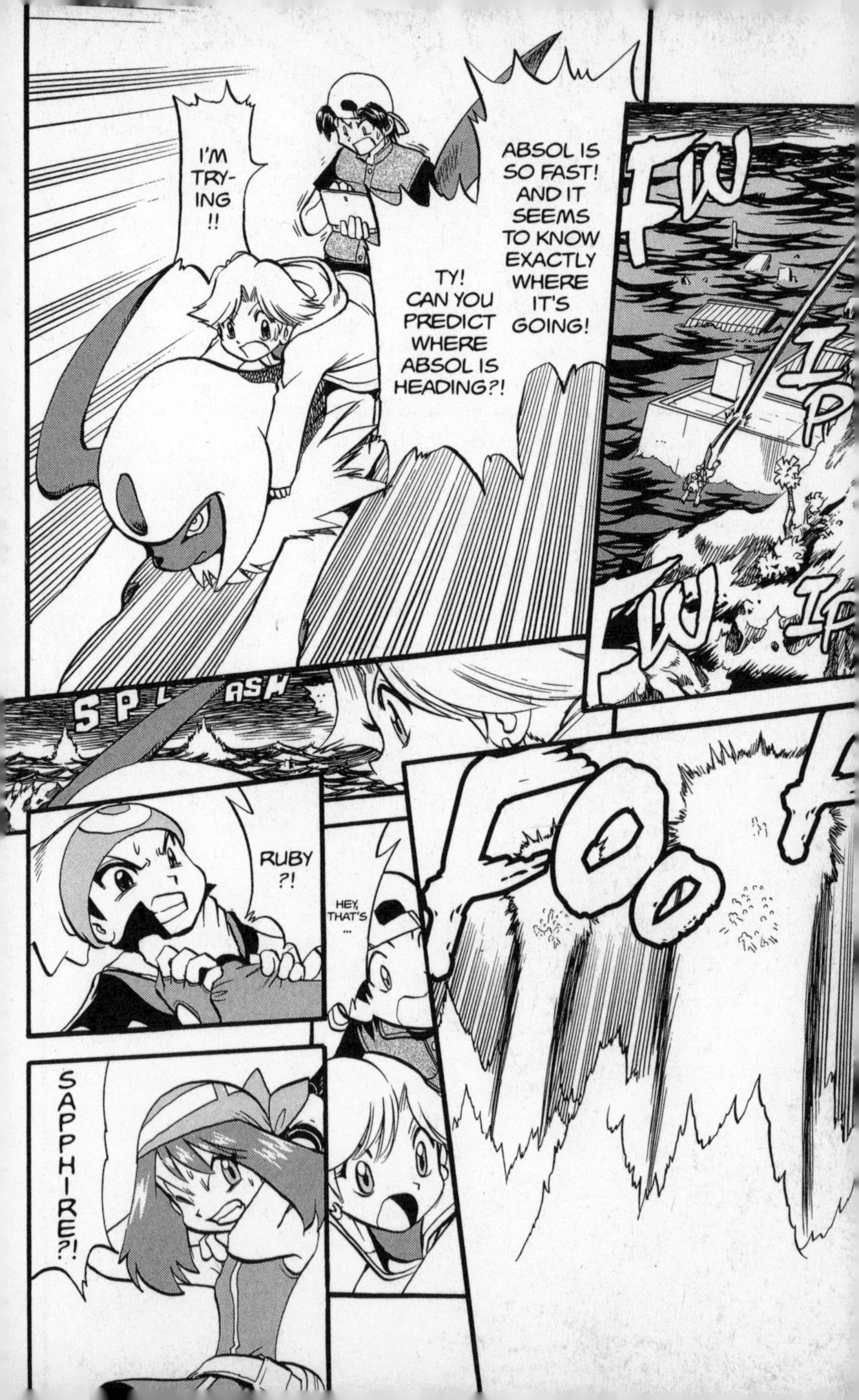
FW
FW
ABSOL IS SO FAST! AND IT SEEMS TO KNOW EXACTLY WHERE IT'S GOING!
TY! CAN YOU PREDICT WHERE ABSOL IS HEADING?!
I'M TRY-ING !!
SPLASH
FOO
HEY, THAT'S ...
RUBY ?!
SAPPHIRE?!

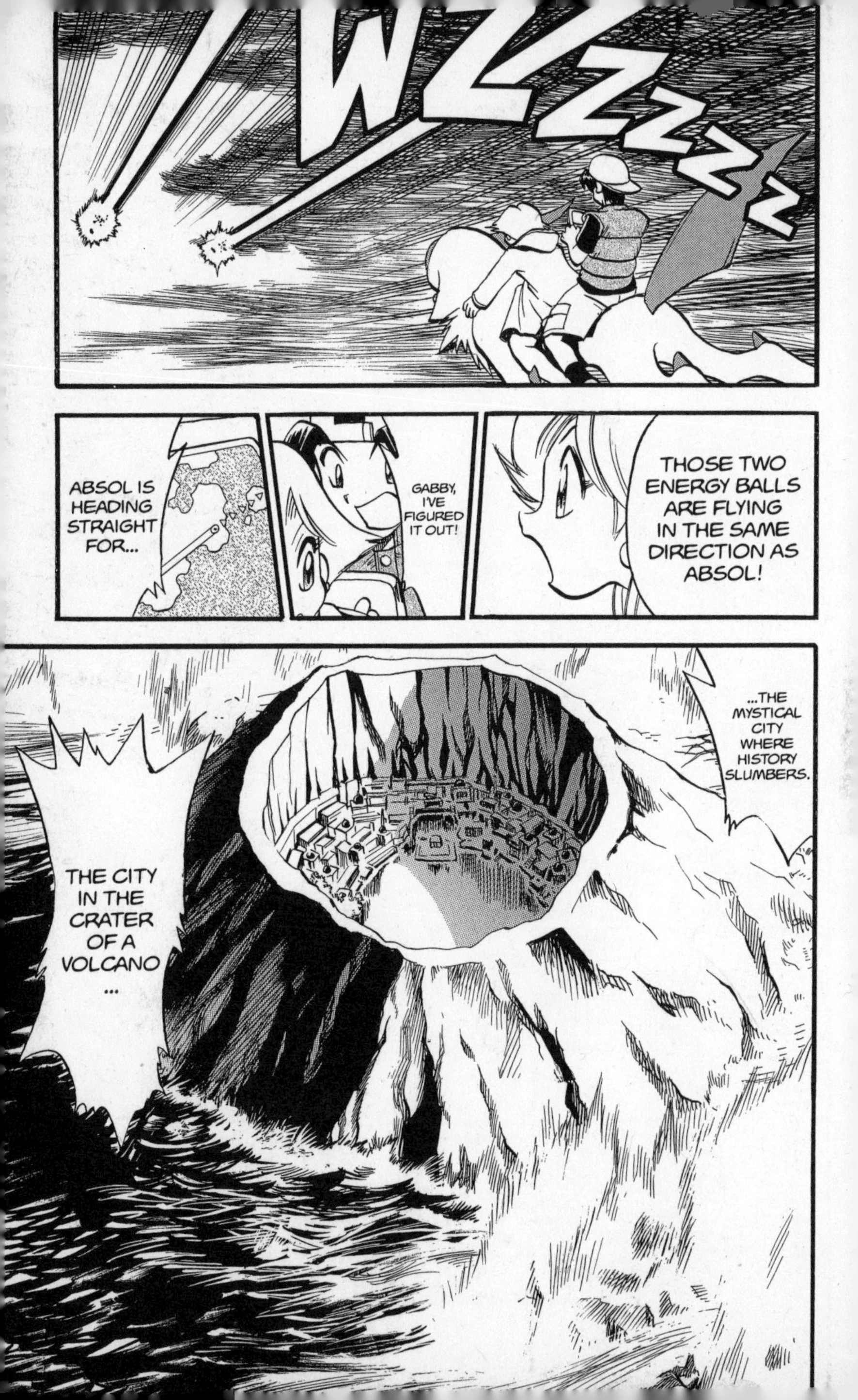
WZZZZZ
THOSE TWO ENERGY BALLS ARE FLYING IN THE SAME DIRECTION AS ABSOL!
GABBY, I'VE FIGURED IT OUT!
ABSOL IS HEADING STRAIGHT FOR...
THE CITY IN THE CRATER OF A VOLCANO...
...THE MYSTICAL CITY WHERE HISTORY SLUMBERS.

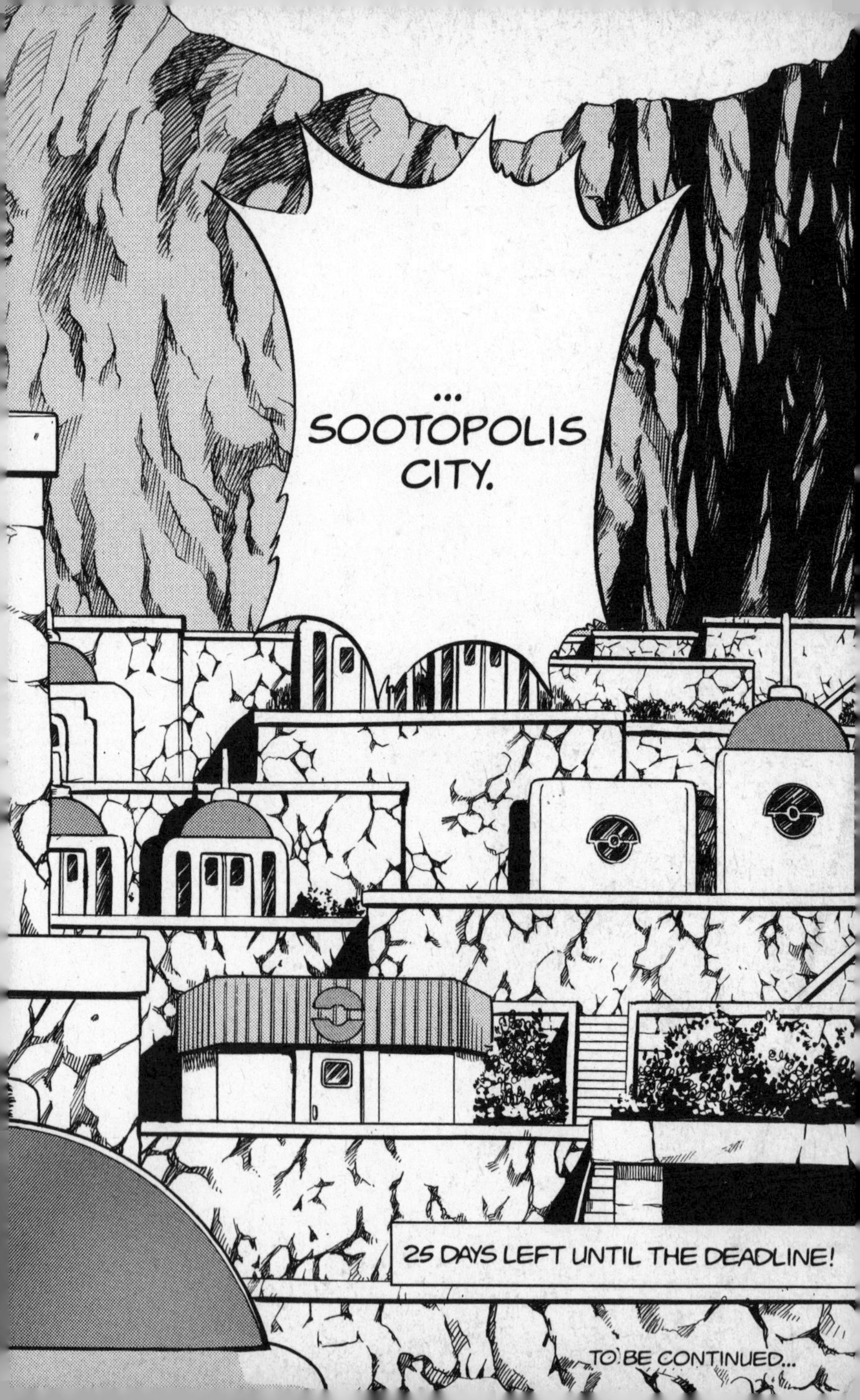
...SOOTOPOLIS CITY.
25 DAYS LEFT UNTIL THE DEADLINE!
TO BE CONTINUED...

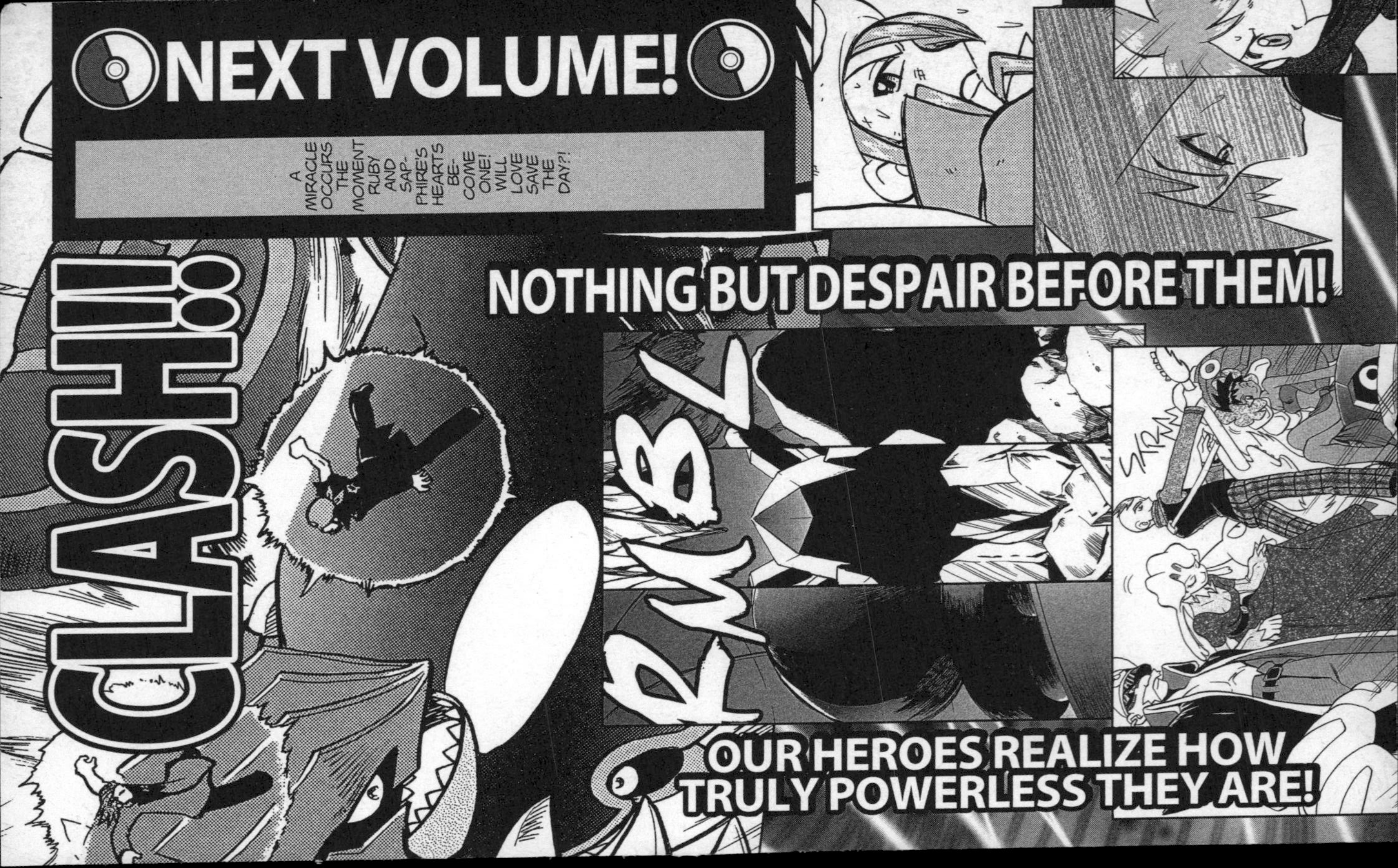
NEXT VOLUME!
A MIRACLE OCCURS THE MOMENT RUBY AND SAPPHIRE'S HEARTS BECOME ONE! WILL LOVE SAVE THE DAY?!
CLASH!!
NOTHING BUT DESPAIR BEFORE THEM!
RMBL
OUR HEROES REALIZE HOW TRULY POWERLESS THEY ARE!

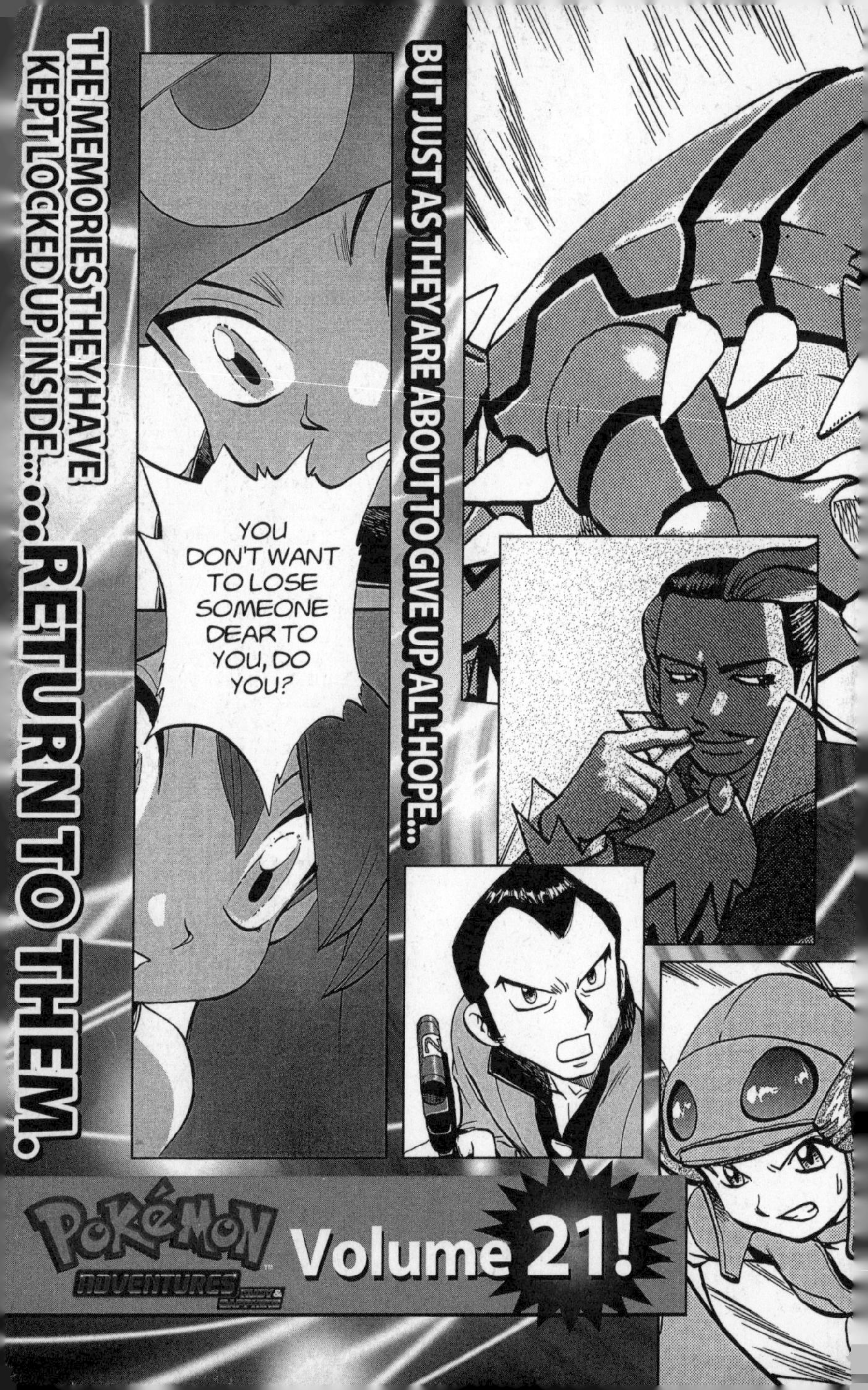

BUT JUST AS THEY ARE ABOUT TO GIVE UP ALL HOPE...
YOU DON'T WANT TO LOSE SOMEONE DEAR TO YOU, DO YOU?
THE MEMORIES THEY HAVE KEPT LOCKED UP INSIDE...
...RETURN TO THEM.
POKÉMON ADVENTURES RUBY & SAPPHIRE
Volume 21!

Special Feature: The Source of the Cosmic Power!

The Orbs and Stones hold the key to this battle... Let's take a look at the incredible power hidden inside them.

THE MYSTERY OF THE MYSTICAL ORBS AND STONES

ORBS AND STONES ARE VALUED AS WORKS OF ART IN THE HOENN REGION. THE TYPE OF ENERGY EMANATING FROM THE ORBS AND STONES IS STILL A COMPLETE MYSTERY. BUT SINCE THEY ARE DEEPLY CONNECTED TO ANCIENT POKÉMON AND THE CURRENT ENVIRONMENTAL CATASTROPHE, IT IS OF THE UTMOST IMPORTANCE TO UNDERSTAND THEIR SECRET.

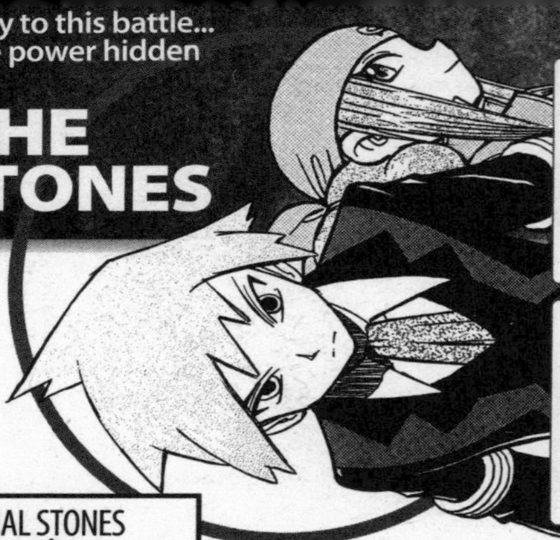

STONE COLLECTOR: STEVEN

THE POKÉMON CHAMPION. HE IS KNOWLEDGEABLE ABOUT ANCIENT RUINS.

TEAM AQUA: SSS SHELLY

SKILLED AT USING STONES TO EVOLVE POKÉMON.

ORBS

CAN BE USED TO CONTROL LEGENDARY POKÉMON'S BEHAVIOR.

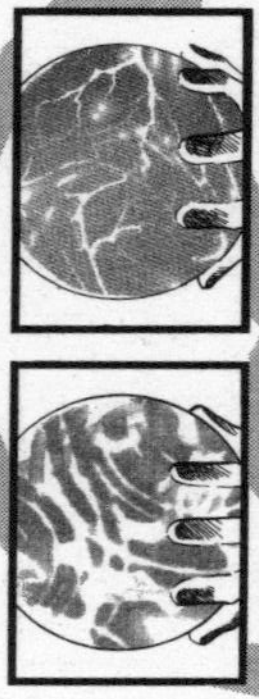

BLUE ORB

RED ORB

THE RED AND BLUE ORBS CONTROL KYOGRE AND GROUDON—AT A PRICE. THE ORBS TAKE OVER THE MINDS OF THOSE WHO WIELD THEM AND ABSORB THEIR LIFE ENERGY!

STONES

THESE SPECIAL STONES INFLUENCE POKÉMON EVOLUTION.

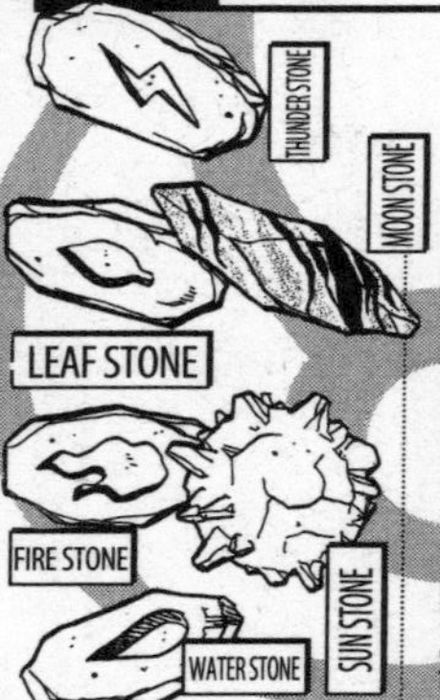
THUNDER STONE
MOON STONE
LEAF STONE
FIRE STONE
SUN STONE
WATER STONE

IT'S WIDELY KNOWN THAT THE STONES EXCAVATED THROUGHOUT THE HOENN REGION ARE CONNECTED TO POKÉMON TYPES, SUCH AS FIRE AND WATER, AND INFLUENCE POKÉMON EVOLUTION. CONVERSELY, A STONE CALLED THE EVERSTONE INHIBITS POKÉMON EVOLUTION.

METEORITE

A ROCK FULL OF MYSTICAL ENERGY THAT FELL FROM SPACE.

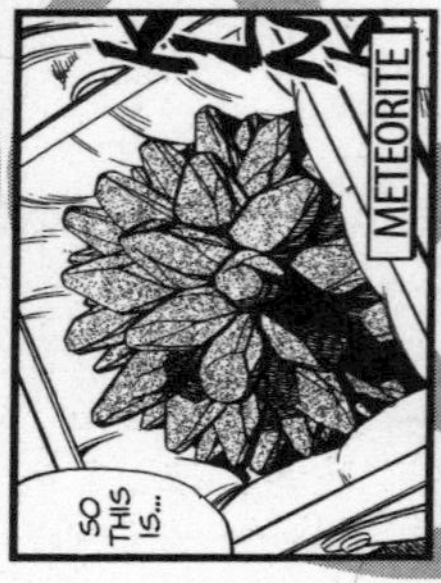
SO THIS IS...

METEORITE

ALTHOUGH ONLY THE SIZE OF A SOCCER BALL, THIS METEORITE IS POWERFUL ENOUGH TO HALT THE ACTIVITY OF A VOLCANO. THE SOURCE OF ITS POWER IS THOUGHT TO BE SOME KIND OF SPECIAL ENERGY IT ABSORBED IN ITS JOURNEY THROUGH OUTER SPACE. THE MYSTERIES OF SPACE ARE ENDLESS...

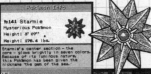

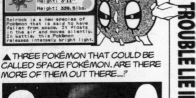

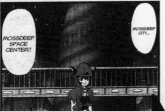

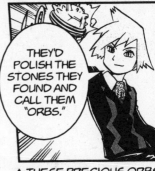

THEY'D POLISH THE STONES THEY FOUND AND CALL THEM "ORBS."

▲ THESE PRECIOUS ORBS WERE ORIGINALLY STONES.

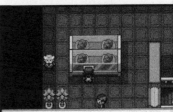

A Stone that fell on Mt. Moon, thus probably a Moon Stone...

▲OF ALL THE STONES, ONLY THE MOON STONE HAS AN UNKNOWN DERIVATION. SOME THEORIZE THAT IT MIGHT BE A FRAGMENT OF A METEORITE THAT FELL FROM SPACE.

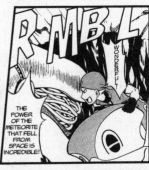

R-M-B-L
WONDERFUL!
THE POWER OF THE METEORITE THAT FELL FROM SPACE IS INCREDIBLE!

▲ TEAM AQUA USED THE ENERGY OF THIS STONE TO ACCOMPLISH THEIR EVIL PLAN.

A HYPOTHESIS...

DOES THE ROOT OF ALL THIS TROUBLE LIE IN...SPACE?!

THE SOURCE OF THE ORBS, STONES AND METEORITE IS ULTIMATELY LINKED TO OUTER SPACE. THERE ARE EVEN POKÉMON WHO ARE THOUGHT TO HAVE COME FROM THERE. MORE RESEARCH ON THEM IS CLEARLY CALLED FOR.

Pokémon Info
№141 Starmie
Mysterious Pokémon
Height: 3' 07"
Weight: 176.4 lbs.
Starmie's center section - the core - glows brightly in seven colors. Because of its luminous nature, this Pokémon has been given the nickname "the gem of the sea."
№125 Lunatone
Meteorite Pokémon
Height: 3'03"
Weight: 370.4lbs.
Lunatone was discovered at a location where a meteorite fell. As a result, some people theorize that this Pokémon came from space. However, no one has been able to prove this theory so far.
AREA
CRY
SIZE
№126 Solrock
Meteorite Pokémon
Height: 3'11"
Weight: 339.5lbs.
Solrock is a new species of Pokémon that is said to have fallen from space. It floats in the air and moves silently. In battle, this Pokémon releases intensely bright light.

▲ THREE POKÉMON THAT COULD BE CALLED SPACE POKÉMON. ARE THERE MORE OF THEM OUT THERE...?

MOSSDEEP CITY...
MOSSDEEP SPACE CENTER!!

▲HOENN IS FAMOUS FOR ITS DEVELOPMENT OF SPACE TECHNOLOGY. WILL THE ROCKET AT MOSSDEEP BE USED FOR FURTHER RESEARCH ON EXTRATERRESTRIAL LIFE FORMS?

Message from
Hidenori Kusaka

The two main characters in this story arc, Ruby and Sapphire, change their clothes a couple of times during the story. Their change of outfit before they head for the Seafloor Cavern is part of a particularly memorable episode for me, especially because Ruby's change of heart coincides symbolically with his change of clothes. Even *I* am touched when I read over that episode! Most of this volume consists of the fight against the bosses of the two evil organizations. It's such a heated final battle! I hope your blood boils when you read it...!

Message from
Satoshi Yamamoto

The father-son battle between Ruby and Norman, Ruby's maturing and new resolve... There are all sorts of core episodes in each volume. But vol. 20 is a parade of battle after battle!! Battles occur up high in the air at the Sky Pillar as well as down low under the sea in the Seafloor Cavern. I hope you enjoy these battles in which sometimes you can barely tell friend from foe.

More Adventures Coming Soon...

While battling formidable opponents Legendary Pokémon Kyogre and Groudon, Ruby and Sapphire recall childhood experiences that shaped their dreams—and pushed them away from others. What is the mysterious connection between their two memories?

And what is the clue to awakening three Pokémon who just might be able to save the day...?

AVAILABLE NOW!

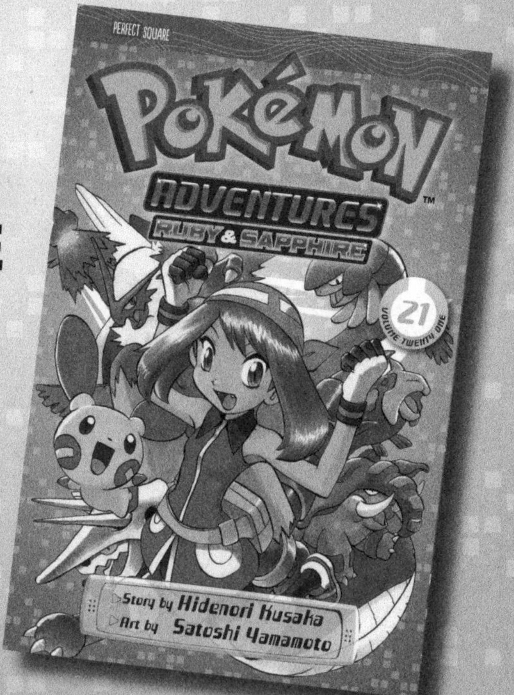
PERFECT SQUARE
POKéMON
ADVENTURES
RUBY & SAPPHIRE
TM
21
VOLUME TWENTY ONE
Story by Hidenori Kusaka
Art by Satoshi Yamamoto

The adventure continues in the Johto region!

POKÉMON ADVENTURES
GOLD & SILVER BOX SET

Includes POKÉMON ADVENTURES Vols. 8-14 and a collectible poster!

Story by
HIDENORI KUSAKA

Art by
MATO,

SATOSHI YAMAMOTO

More exciting Pokémon adventures starring Gold and his rival Silver! First someone steals Gold's backpack full of Poké Balls (and Pokémon!). Then someone steals Prof. Elm's Totodile. Can Gold catch the thief—or thieves?!

Keep an eye on Team Rocket, Gold... Could they be behind this crime wave?

www.viz.com

PERFECT SQUARE

ALL AGES
ratings.viz.com

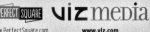

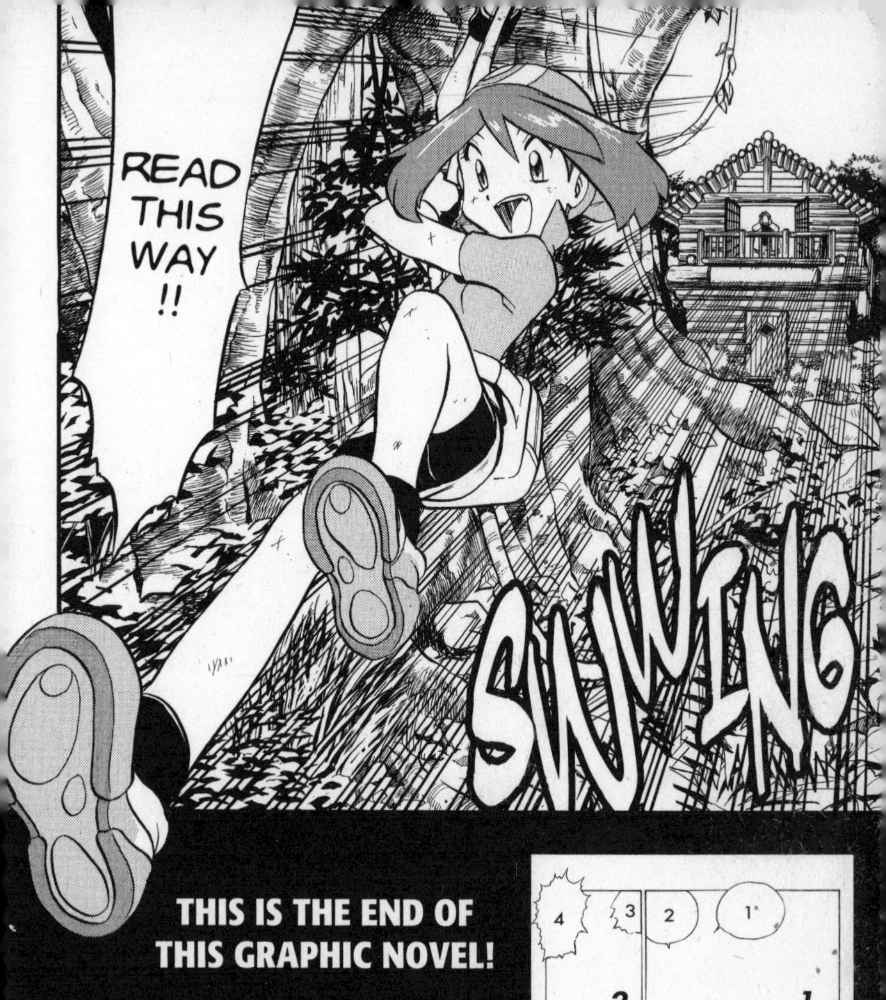
READ THIS WAY !!
SWWING

THIS IS THE END OF THIS GRAPHIC NOVEL!

To properly enjoy this VIZ Media graphic novel, please turn it around and begin reading from right to left.

This book has been printed in the original Japanese format in order to preserve the orientation of the original artwork.

Have fun with it!

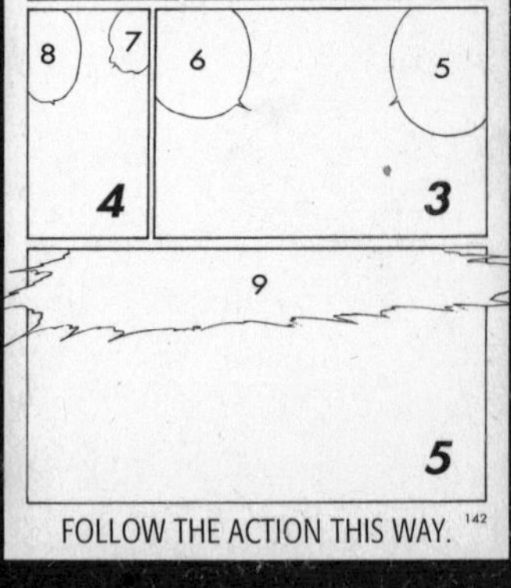
1
2
3
4
5
6
7
8
9
FOLLOW THE ACTION THIS WAY.